Darkness swept before me
Spread like snowmelt on the grass
I trembled, reached out blindly
Afraid you'd fade away

The ice surrounded me instead.

It sliced me like a blade
And I could not feel you in it
I reached into the swirling current
But I was frozen by the waves

I sank to my knees
And softly wept as I let myself admit
I allowed myself to lose you
Watched you slip into the tide

And now I see so clearly
Me.

Alone before I knew you
Desolate before I held you
Adrift before I found you
Ruined before I loved you

Me, alone again.

Me, a willing widow
Laid to waste before we wed.

JENNA BROOKS

EDITED BY: VICTORIA L. HOBSON

An Early Frost

October Snow, Part Two

❋ ❋ ❋

This is a work of fiction.
Names, characters, businesses, organizations, places, events, and incidents are either products of the author's imagination, or are used fictitiously.
Any resemblance to actual events, locales, organizations,
or persons (living or dead) is entirely coincidental.

❋ ❋ ❋

©2014 Jenna Brooks
All rights reserved.

"Frozen"
©2014 Melodie Ramone
Used with permission

Passages from
"Echo"
©2002 J.L. Brooks

ISBN: 1499503350
ISBN-13: 9781499503357

The author gratefully acknowledges the generous contributions of:

Melodie Ramone
Janie Brooks McQueen
Brad Bailey
Stephanie Neighbour
Patrick Hills
John Tanner
and
Belle Brooks

**Special thanks to
Janice Ridgeway-Dickenson**
(Dropping the rope, ma'am)

Husbands, love your wives, even as Christ also loved the church, and gave himself for it

　　　　　　　　　　　　　　　　　　　Ephesians 5:25

DEDICATION

✽ ✽ ✽

"Loving a woman means that you look beyond her rage. You look for her pain, and then you confront it - head on.
So you can keep fighting me, but there is no amount of ugly you can throw at me that's stronger than the way I love you.
And I want that to be my legacy: you were always safe with me."

P.J.
June, 2006

✽ ✽ ✽

This story is dedicated to battered women who believe themselves to be ugly.

Seven days.

He tapped his fist against the bars that covered the etched, cloudy glass of the tiny window in his cell. A jolting pain shot up into his forehead, and he relaxed his jaw, absently rubbing the side of his neck.

He took the three steps that spanned the distance to his cot, laying down with his arm over his eyes. The folder which held his homework for the Batterer Intervention Program jabbed into his side like a reminder, and he fished it out from underneath him, glaring at the cover.

Simon Reynolds C2-145: BIP

"Yeah," he growled, clenching his jaw again as he resisted the impulse to rip it in half. He hurled it across the cell.

She probably thinks it'll be okay now.

He smirked as he rolled onto his side, remembering the feel of the gun in his hand, the perfect balance of the span from the muzzle to the trigger. He clenched his right fist and closed his eyes again, vaguely aware of his heartbeat speeding up as he thought of the surprised look on her face - the way that her mouth had hung open, gaping at the blood that spread down the sleeve of her blouse.

She didn't scream, though.

Simon squirmed uncomfortably as he remembered the sound of his daughter's screams.

She did the screaming. That's all she cared about. Her mother. Not me.

He rubbed the side of his neck again, considering the fact that with all the time he had been locked up, he'd have no chance with his daughter: she was, most likely, fully brainwashed by her mother by now.

She's just a mini-mommy at this point.

He sat up quickly and returned to the window. It struck him as yet another injustice, that another spring was passing him by.

A large, brown spider was resting in the web it had made in the corner of the frame. He grinned, reaching for the clear plastic cup on the sink. With a few short puffs of his breath, he lured the spider onto the sill, and covered it with the cup.

He played with it for a while, bumping its legs with the rim of the cup and watching it dart from side to side, frantically looking for escape.

"Nope. You're gonna die today."

After a few minutes, he knocked it to the floor and crushed it under his heel.

He sauntered over to the wall to retrieve his homework. This was important, completing the program - everything, all of his plans depended on getting a good recommendation.

He paused to draw the "X" across May 21st, and smiled again as he thought about his plans.

Six days.

❋ ❋ ❋

chapter I

WILL SIGNALED THE server for the check. He knew that he wouldn't get a direct response, but he mentioned it anyway:

"You just aren't yourself lately."

Maxine raised an eyebrow, taking a sip of wine as she kicked him lightly under the table. "I never did know what that means, 'not yourself.'"

"You're dodging me again."

"I *am* 'myself'. I'm just in a quiet mood."

"For a few weeks now," he insisted.

"I know." She reached for his hand, intertwining her fingers with his. "It was a tough year. I'm tired."

"Nothing more than that?"

"No, nothing. And thanks for dinner." Amused, she added, "You know, you can stop staring at me any time now."

He laughed, then kissed the palm of her hand. "Caught. But I'm not the only one - guys have been checking you out all night."

"You notice stuff like that?"

"Sure. Being with a beautiful woman means vigilance."

"Mmm. I'll start dressing down."

Will noticed how she turned distant then. She pulled her hand away, seeming to find something interesting beyond his right shoulder.

He thought again about the days when they were together - not simply standing in the same room, or seated at the same table, but connected. Best friends. Will had no idea what had gone wrong between them, and Max wouldn't even acknowledge that they were losing each other.

"So," he offered, "I was thinking... It's coming up on a year since..."

She shook her head, still staring past him. "Not now, okay?"

They were quiet while he signed for the check, and then he decided to try again. "I'm taking a few days for Memorial Day. Let's go someplace. Get away for a while."

It seemed to get her attention, and she smiled at him. "I can do that."

Her voice took on the smoky, raspy tone she had when she spoke softly, and Will was caught off guard by the impulse to tell her that he loved her.

He recovered quickly. "Great. Where do you want to go?"

"You haven't planned anything? Really?"

"Nope. If you want, we can get in my truck and just drive until we run out of gas."

She laughed, and he was struck by how long it had been since he heard her do that.

"What's funny?" he asked.

"You plan out *everything*, Will. I like this spontaneous side of you."

He grinned wryly. "I'll keep that in mind."

Max took his hand as they walked to her car. Aware of his sudden feeling of grateful relief, Will let the thought fully occur to him.

I'm losing you.

"Hey, Remmond," she said, "you're squeezing my hand pretty hard there."

He loosened his grip. "Sorry."

She pulled her hand away, dramatically stretching her fingers before she unlocked the car door. "That's okay. But I'll never play the violin again."

He opened the door for her. As she slid into the driver's seat, she looked up at him and smiled again, and he let himself hope that he was wrong.

As he got into her car, he thought about the fact that it had been a difficult year for her. She'd had a life made up of far too many difficult years. At least, that's what he gathered from the little he knew about her; but in the months since her best friend was murdered, Max had moved from New Hampshire to Boston to be with her friends, then finished college. Her father had died at the end of December, and Will had trouble believing that she was as indifferent to his passing as she seemed to be. Now, she was planning to move back to New Hampshire for law school. And she had allowed Will into her life. As he thought about it, he decided that perhaps he was being a bit demanding. Maybe a lot demanding; certainly, he wasn't being as understanding as he could be.

But Max was the first woman in far too many years whom he had allowed into his life. Will had been a determined bachelor, and he liked it that way. His existence had revolved around his career, and the countless brief relationships he enjoyed were no more than a diversion - until he met Max. He had jumped the gun with her several weeks earlier, when he told her that he loved her, blurted it out after one too many glasses of champagne as they sat on the rocks at Rye Beach on his birthday. He knew that it was a massive blunder as she looked away, stammering something about what a huge step that was. They hadn't discussed it since.

"Will?"

He startled. "Yeah?"

"I was asking if you want to stop by and see Dave and Sammy."

She pushed her shaggy blonde hair behind her ears as she glanced at him, and the diamond teardrop earrings - a gift from Jo, just before she was killed - sparkled in the dim light from the dashboard.

"Sure." With his hand in his pocket, he fingered the small velvet bag which held the engagement ring he had carried with him since his birthday.

She took another quick look at him. "You okay?"

"Fine. Just thinking."

"About the Brandi Reynolds case?"

"Yeah," he lied. He felt a rush of guilt as he realized how distracted he was from his work. Brandi Reynolds was his newest client, a woman whose estranged husband, eighteen months earlier, had shot her in the shoulder at a visitation exchange. Simon Reynolds was scheduled to be released from jail in a week, and his ex-wife was frightened. As he was being arrested, Simon had threatened that next time he would "take out the kid, too."

Max touched his leg. "You met with her today, right?"

"For two hours." He stared out the window for a moment, then turned to look at her. "I wish you had your J.D. already. If you were an associate at the firm, I could discuss it with you."

"Yeah, well... I should tell you what I've been thinking about lately."

She maneuvered her car into a small space in front of the townhome where Dave and Sammy lived, then sat quietly as she gathered her thoughts.

Will watched her, taking a deep breath as he waited, caught inside the dread of needing to hear a truth that he knew would take him apart.

After a full minute had passed, he reached out to massage the back of her neck. "Tell me," he murmured.

She nodded. "Okay. I've been going over it for weeks now..."

They jumped as Dave opened Will's door.

"Hey, you guys coming in?"

Will dropped his head to his chest, then stared up at him, annoyed. "Timing, man."

"No. That's okay." Max was visibly relieved as she got out of the car. "We can talk about it later."

She hurried up the steps to where Sam waited at the front door, while Will slowly exited the car, leaning against it as he watched her.

"Way to go, moron," he mumbled.

"What's going on?"

Will rubbed the back of his neck. "She was about to tell me something important."

"Any idea what?"

"Yeah." He was still looking toward the house as he said, "I think she's leaving me."

Sam poured the coffee as Max rummaged around in the refrigerator. "Sammy, no brownies or anything?"

"Sorry. Ty ate everything in sight tonight." She nodded toward the center island. "But..." She winked. "Check that top drawer."

Max grinned as she pulled out a small white bakery box. "You *angel*," she sighed happily. "Ooh, cheesecake cookies. I need a fix."

"That usually means trouble. Come sit down," Sam said, pulling a chair out for her. She noticed again that Max was losing weight, which didn't look good on her - she was already naturally slender.

Max sat at the table with a cookie in each hand and one protruding from her lips, her voice garbled as she tried to talk around it.

Sam laughed. "Chew, will ya?"

She nodded, reaching for her coffee. After several sips, she cupped her hands around the mug and stared into it as she spoke. "I've been thinking about a few things."

"You have been kind of distracted."

"I know."

"And...?"

"Sammy," she was still examining her coffee, "how are you doing lately?"

Sam waited for her to look up before she answered. "I'm not all there myself these days."

"I can tell."

"Maybe 'cause it's almost at the one-year point."

"Maybe." Max leaned back in her chair, reaching behind her to retrieve the box of cookies from the counter. "Among other things."

"Hand me one of those," Sam said. "What other things?"

Max took another cookie for herself, then slid the box across the table. "Will wants to take off for the holiday weekend. I told him I'd go."

"Good. I think that would be good for you."

"I suppose," she said listlessly.

"Max, what's up with you?"

She rose quickly, grabbing their mugs to top them off. "I'm restless, I guess."

Sam watched her for a moment, then said, "I don't know about you, but I could use a week or two away from everything."

Max returned with their coffee. "I wish," she mumbled.

"Jo would hate this, how... I don't know, you and I are just..."

"Boring," Max muttered.

"Yeah."

"A year ago, we were planning your wedding." Max laughed softly, remembering. "Did I ever apologize for inviting the entire town of Strafford behind your back?"

Sam waved it off. "It was great. I still get emails from some of those people. You know," she added, "I've been thinking that we should head back up there sometime over the summer. Dave still talks about buying a camp near Bow Lake."

Max secretly wished that all of their good memories weren't wrapped around Jo's murder. Or suicide. Or whatever would best describe what had happened to her, because it seemed to Max that recalling their years together was just an invitation to mourn again. She felt like she and Sammy had been cheated somehow, because it wasn't bad enough that Jo was gone: they'd lost their own history when Jo died, because their memories were wrapped around her - and remembering always led to pain.

"I don't know, Sammy. Don't you think it's a little soon to be thinking about that?"

"I guess so."

They sat quietly, thinking it over.

Sam broke the silence. "Dave wants to go stay at his parents' house over the holiday weekend. They haven't seen the kids since Christmas."

"Really?" Max chuckled. "You'll be staying with his *parents* for your anniversary?"

"Nope. We're leaving the kids with them for an overnight, and heading into Boston. Just the two of us." She picked wearily at the cookie. "I wish we could have a week together. I miss my husband lately."

"Maybe you can find a way to extend the weekend."

"Doubtful. Geez, I'm getting claustrophobia these days. I'm not cut out to be a housewife."

"Oh, please. You're a lot more than a housewife, Sammy."

She shrugged. "Not really. I spend a few evenings a week running that DV support group, and the rest of my life is all about Dave and the kids. I'm out of the house by myself maybe ten hours a week. Seriously, it's just not all that fulfilling." She grabbed one of Max's cookies, breaking off a piece and popping it into her mouth. "And you know how many hours the guys are putting in, wrapping things up here. Then I think about how once we move to New Hampshire, I'll have to start all over again..."

Max sighed sympathetically. "I know. But you'll be working with Will, and that's gonna be interesting. Did you finish your certification up there?"

"Yup. Last week." Sam brightened a little then. "I can start at the center as soon as we're settled in."

"And you still want to move, right?"

"Sure I do. I've never liked Boston all that much. But once we get up there, life will be the same - just in a different place. I want to do *more*. Dave and Will are gonna be out-straight, setting up the practice, and you'll be in law school..." She touched Max's cheek. "You'll be even busier than you've been this past year. I'll never get to see you."

Max looked away. "We'll see." She folded her arms, bowing her head toward her chest and closing her eyes. "I'm tired," she mumbled.

Sam stroked her hair. "C'mon, sweetie. Tell me."

"I just don't sleep well anymore."

"You've been under a lot of stress, you know."

She seemed to change her mind about her response. "I know. That's probably it."

"Is it?"

"I think so."

Sam had never seen her so withdrawn. "Max, what is it? Is it Will?"

She looked up then, exasperated with herself. "I don't *know*. I feel like I'm conjuring up my own problems."

"Things are so good that you're miserable, huh?"

Max nodded, but Sam knew that there was more to the answer.

"You think it can't last," she offered.

"It never does."

"Max, listen to me."

"I am." She got up and walked to the window. Catching her reflection, she said, "Hey, I look darn good for someone my age."

"You look good for someone *my* age, and don't try to change the subject."

Max was arranging her hair. "I've been thinking, I should go brunette, like you."

"You'd look silly. Your eyebrows are too light. And enough about that - are you listening to me?"

"I'm listening." She returned to the table, standing beside her chair with her hand on her hip.

"Max, it can happen. Happily-ever-after *can* happen. Look at Dave and me."

She shrugged. "That's you guys. Not me."

As Sam started to respond, she heard Dave and Will coming into the house. "Talk later?" she asked regretfully.

"Sure."

Watching how Will and Max interacted, Sam couldn't see any problems between them - none that were obvious, anyway. Will did seem a bit distracted a few times, but he and Max were affectionate, laughing together, talking about the move to New Hampshire.

They were sitting on the loveseat, holding hands. "*Nice*, guys. Clever way to get rid of me," Max teased. "Tell me that we're all finally going over the wall, and then I get an apartment up there and none of you come with me."

"Yup. It was my idea," Will said. "You've been getting on my nerves lately."

Max kissed his hand. "Oh, right. You can't live without me and you know it."

That was when a shadow seemed to pass over Will's mood. He stood quickly, reaching for her cup. "Let me refill that."

"Thanks. Just half a cup. We need to get going."

Max pulled into the parking area at her apartment building, scanning the lot for Will's car. "Where did you park?"

He pointed ahead. "Over there."

She pulled in next to his car, then leaned over and kissed his cheek. "There are boxes everywhere, but how's about coming in for a nightcap?"

"Huh?"

"I have a chardonnay chilling in the fridge."

"Yeah, sure. Sounds good."

He slowly exited the car, moaning as he stretched his arms over his head, and Max gave him a playful wolf-whistle.

She loved the shyness in his smile as he said, "Well, thanks, doll. Same to you."

He took her hand, glancing around the parking lot as they walked to her door. "I'll feel better when you finally live in small-town New Hampshire."

"Ditto. How's the hunt for the new offices going?"

"Looks like we'll be going to Nashua." He took her keys and opened the door, waiting for her to go in ahead of him.

"Yikes. That's as bad as Manchester, you know."

"That's where the real estate is."

"What happened to that place in Londonderry?"

"Gone," he said. "It lasted less than a week on the market." He turned the heavy lock on the door and added, "I suggested to Dave that we buy one of those old houses in the commercial district. In the long run, we'll spend a lot less doing that than renting office space. He likes the idea."

Will looked around the tiny studio apartment, struck again by how plain it was - cold, even, and barely furnished. She had just the sofabed, with a couple of occasional tables, and a small dining room set that she bought from Goodwill. She kept her clothes in boxes and her books stacked on the windowsills. The walls were stark white, and she had left them empty for the entire time that she lived there. The only picture in the place was a small, framed photo of herself with Jo and Sam in front of a Christmas tree. He'd asked her about the picture once, and she quickly said, "Christmas. The one before Jo died." Then she changed the subject.

Max called out from the kitchen, "You could move closer to where I'll be, couldn't you?" She came back into the room with the wine and two glasses, looking at him hopefully.

He looked away as he took off his jacket, surprised by his own composure, and still wondering if he should raise the question at all. While she seemed more amiable at the moment, her mood had been constantly shifting and changing in recent weeks. If she was thinking about ending their relationship, then at least he would finally know - and he needed to know.

He took a deep breath. "Do you want that?"

She stopped. "Huh?"

"You heard me." He faced her then, standing with his hands in his pockets, and his fingers brushed the ring again. He felt his composure starting to dissolve.

Flustered, she set the wine on the small coffee table. "I did, I just - I don't know why you would ask me that."

"I'm worried. You have something to tell me, remember?"

"And you think... What? That I... Will, are you thinking I want to end things?"

"I'm wondering." His voice was low, and a bit gruff, but Max saw the emotion in his eyes. "At least, I've been thinking that you might be on that road. And if that's the case, then you need to tell me."

"I'm..."

He held his hand up to interrupt her. "But," he said, his tone softening, "if I got this wrong, then after you tell me what's really on your mind, I want to talk about us."

She nodded reluctantly as she handed him the wine bottle, and they were quiet as he filled their glasses.

She took a sip, then another, longer drink, and he waited.

"Let's sit down." She inclined her head toward the small table in the dining area.

Will pretended not to notice the gesture. He sat on the sofa, holding his hand out for her to sit beside him. He thought she seemed reluctant, but she perched on the edge of the couch.

"Okay," she sighed. "Here it is."

He took another deep breath to ease the sudden pain in his gut.

She was speaking rapidly. "I've been unhappy lately. Thinking about things, trying to decide what I really want."

He nodded, lifting his glass to his lips and drawing in half of the wine.

"The thing is..." She tapped her nails against her glass, thinking. "Okay. It's just that... I don't want to go to law school." Her eyes widened. She seemed surprised that she had said it, and she waited for him to respond.

After a few seconds, Will asked, "And...?"

"And... What? That's what I've been thinking about."

He opened and closed his mouth a couple of times before he answered. "Well... Okay. I don't get it. Why have you been so secretive about it?"

"Because everyone is so high on me being a lawyer. It's hard to walk away from."

He was trying to make eye contact with her, but she was looking straight ahead. "Is that all?"

She brushed something invisible off of the coffee table. "If I said 'yes,' would you believe me?"

Will didn't answer.

She set her glass on the table and ran her hands through her hair. The light caught her diamond earrings again, and he wondered if she was thinking about Jo.

He caught her hand. "So, what else?"

She sank back into the plush cushions, pulling Will's arm around her shoulders as she settled in. "Truth is, I feel like I owe it to Jo somehow. Like she left me all her money so I could go be a lawyer - I told her once how I wanted to do that."

"That's a lot of guilt to carry around." He rested his chin on top of her head. "I didn't know her all that well, but I get the impression that she wouldn't have wanted you to live any life other than what *you* want."

"True."

"Have you decided what you want to do instead?"

She shook her head as she retrieved her glass. "Not yet."

"Need any help figuring it out?"

"Maybe. I'll let you know." She pulled back to look up at him. "You aren't disappointed?"

Will frowned. "No. Of course not." Her expression turned doubtful, and he said, "Max, it's not my place to be disappointed in a choice you make for yourself." He took her glass from her then, carefully setting it with his on the long table behind the sofa. "You'd be a gifted attorney, no doubt. You have an incredible talent, an instinct for it."

She smiled softly. "Thanks."

"But that doesn't mean you have to make it your career. Do what you want to do." He moved back from her, putting some space between them. "Ready to talk about us?"

"Sure." She tucked her legs under her as she shifted to face him.

He gently pushed her hair out of her eyes. Her eyes shone with intelligence; and that, more than her looks, was what drew him to her. He had always felt something magnetic about her, some kind of a deep wisdom, a knowledge of life and of people that he wanted to understand - because no matter what else happened, she was already a permanent, ever-present part of his existence. It made him uneasy sometimes, that he was no longer the sole arbiter of the direction of his life.

She was waiting, nodding her encouragement.

"Max...Why do we never talk about what's going on with us?"

"*What?*" She was immediately impatient. "Oh, please. We do."

"No, actually, we don't. We aren't the same anymore. Not since..."

"I need a refill."

He wasn't going to be dismissed. Not this time. "Not since I told you I love you."

"You were drunk." She stood, grabbing the bottle and refilling her glass.

He was surprised by her sudden terse, almost accusatory tone, and he noted that her hands were shaking a little. "Max..."

She shook her head. "This is a bad time to talk about this. I shouldn't have said I would."

"Why is it a bad time?"

Her head snapped up, and where he expected to see anger, he saw no emotion at all.

"Okay." He tried to take on a more gentle tone, but he couldn't hide his annoyance. "Clue me in, then. When is a *good* time?"

"Will, look - it's been a long day. For both of us. We need to go to bed." She looked away, flustered, rolling her eyes to add levity to the moment. "I mean, I want to go to sleep. I'm tired."

"Believe me - I know exactly what you mean."

He stood then, and the smile left Max's face as they stared each other down. Will thought they were like two boxers in the ring.

"Sounds like a covert message in there," Max mumbled.

"Yeah, well, we do that a lot, don't we?" He folded his arms.

She felt her face turning red. "Maybe you have something to tell *me?*"

"You mean you'll stand still long enough for me to say it?"

"Not with *that* attitude, I won't. I think we should say goodnight."

"No. Not yet." He sighed deeply, forcing himself to calm down. "It's been a year, Maxine..."

"That we've *known* each other. We've only been together for a few months, and you're all pissed off because - what? Because I won't sleep with you?"

"I didn't say that." Will knew that his frustration was getting the best of him, but he was quickly moving past any concern over his behavior. "Seriously, is that what you think of me?"

"Isn't that what it *always* is with guys?"

He clenched his jaw, deciding it was best for both of them that he ignore the question.

"Well, go bark up another tree." She was finally looking directly at him; yet Will had the vivid impression, one he had felt before, that she was talking to someone else. "If you wanted a slut, then you *so* picked the wrong woman. I mean, if what we have now isn't enough for you, then..." Her voice trailed off. She wasn't sure she wanted to finish the thought.

Will was pacing the length of the room, struggling to keep his temper in check.

"'*Slut?*'" He laughed in cynical disbelief. "So, what we have here - at least, through *your* eyes - is that I'm a dog for wanting to make love to you, and you'd be a slut if it happened."

"This is an awe-inspiring closing, Counselor."

She was watching him guardedly, and Will became aware of how much he felt like an intruder.

"Why is this such an issue for you?" she was asking, her face hardened with sarcasm. "No other prospects at the moment?"

"No. Because I'm not looking around. Are you?"

She gasped. "Don't you *dare* talk to me in that tone."

"Although I wonder why I'm hanging in sometimes, because you seem to have this need to tear me down. And for some reason, I'm putting up with it. And why? Because..." He stopped, confused and horrified that he was about to say, "Because I made the mistake of loving you." Something inside him knew that she wanted him to say it - or perhaps, she simply expected him to.

He turned away, struggling to cover it up. "What are we *doing?* It's like we get together every night so we can rip this *apart.*"

Still pacing, he laced his fingers on top of his head, and Max thought he looked like he was under arrest.

"I don't get this. I can't..." He stopped, staring at the ceiling. "Okay, you're right. You are. I'm one of those typical guys. A despicable stalker-type who just wants to chase you down, bed you down, and then carve a notch in my belt." He turned to face her then, and froze in disbelief as she quickly backed away from him, her eyes wide with something that made him cringe inside.

He put his hands out to the side, showing her he was backing off. "I'm not a threat to you, Maxine."

She couldn't look at him. She felt exposed, like Will was seeing more than she wanted to reveal, and she sipped at her wine to avoid him.

A few seconds went by before Will continued. "Look, something's gone very wrong. You won't let me any closer to you than a kiss, or holding you - and so I'm thinking, you want a commitment."

He took a cautious step toward her. "I want to commit. But I can't *reach* you. I don't get what's going on with you. I can't even tell you that I love you, let alone ask you to marry me..."

She gasped, and it caused her to choke on the wine. "*Marry you?*" she sputtered, wiping at her mouth. "Get *married?*"

He felt breathless for a moment, like someone had knocked the wind out of him. He took her glass from her hand, chugging the rest of her wine. "Hey, I didn't mean to be disgusting there, darlin'." He resisted an impulse to throw the glass against the wall, and strode across the room to set it on the dining table instead. "I'll let you get some rest."

She was still coughing as she held up her hand. "Will, wait..."

"No, I'm out."

Her eyes widened again. "*Out?*" she managed.

"Going home." He grabbed his jacket as he went out the door, being careful to close it quietly behind him. The anger he had felt moments before was unsettling to him.

Max looked through the small window beside the front door, watching him as he stood beside his car. He ran his hands through his hair, then rested his forearms on the roof of the car and leaned his head into his hands.

Don't go.

She tried to stem the tears that blurred her view of him.

*I didn't mean it. I didn't **mean** it.*

As she watched him drive away, she kicked the door - once, then again, and then she pounded on her front door until the pain made her stop.

※ ※ ※

Sam sat at her vanity, watching Dave walk the baby back and forth at the foot of the bed.

"Is she getting there?"

"Yeah." He hummed softly for another minute, then said, "If she's still sick tomorrow, though, I think we should take her in to be seen."

"She's teething, Dave. She'll be fine in a few days."

He nodded toward the bedroom door. "Let's put her back to bed."

He lowered the baby carefully into the crib, still humming. "There you go, Hope," he murmured, pulling the quilt over her back.

Sam leaned against his shoulder, and they watched her sleep. "She'll be fine," Sam said again, rubbing his back.

"Ty didn't have this much trouble with teething."

"I know. He was an easy baby." She stood on her tiptoes to kiss him. "You're such a worrier."

They left the nursery door open as they returned to their bedroom. As they slid into bed, Dave asked, "So what's up with Max?" He opened his arms for Sam to curl up against him, as he did every night.

She laid her head on his bare chest, listening to his heart. She smiled, feeling reassured as she heard it speed up, like it always did when she laid against him.

"Not sure." She kissed his neck. "I think she needs to get away for a while."

"Yeah. It's been almost a year now. How's she doing with it?"

"She's okay. With that, anyway. I think it's the other things that are really bothering her." She drew lazy circles on his chest with her fingers, listening as his heart beat even faster. As he kissed her, his cell phone started ringing.

"Ignore it," she groaned.

It stopped, then started ringing again immediately.

Dave sighed. "That's Will's ringtone, babe. I should answer it." She rolled away.

*You have **got** to be kidding me.*

"Tell him I hate him," she joked.

"I will." He turned on the light as he grabbed the phone. "Hey. Talk about timing…" He sat up then, frowning. "What? Where are you?"

"What is it?" Sam asked.

He held up his hand to silence her, listening intently. "I'll be right there. Put the desk on for me." He paused, then said, "Yes. This is David Delaney. You're…?"

Sam was watching him, alarmed.

Dave was pulling his jeans on, balancing the phone against his shoulder. "I appreciate that, Jimmy. I'll be there in fifteen minutes… Yes, absolutely. Thanks." He stuffed the phone into his pocket and reached for a T-shirt.

"What's going on?"

"Will's at the police station."

She reached for her robe. "What happened?"

"D and D. Bar fight."

"*Will?*"

He leaned across the bed to kiss her. "Be back as soon as I can."

chapter 2

THEY WERE SILENT during the drive back to Will's house.

As he pulled into the driveway, Dave glanced over to where Will sat in the passenger's seat, his head against the headrest and his eyes closed.

Pulling the keys from the ignition, Dave muttered, "Let's get you inside."

Will shook his head, reaching to open the door. "I'm fine. Thanks for getting me out."

"Wait. What happened?"

Will stopped, then settled back into the passenger's seat, staring straight ahead. "I screwed up. Bad night."

"No kidding. I'm asking why."

He didn't answer.

"C'mon. Talk to me. You and Max had another fight?"

He nodded slowly. "It's not gonna work out."

"It can't be that bad."

"Sure." Will laughed bitterly. "Okay. If you say so."

"The drinking... How much did you have tonight?"

"I'll just keep plugging away at it. Wait for her to come around again." He was still slurring his words, and Dave was having a hard time understanding him. "Thanks, D. That'll work."

"That's not what I'm saying." He wasn't used to this attitude, not from Will. "Hell, I'm not sure *what* I'm saying. I don't know what's going on with you and Max lately. You two used to be so tight..."

He jumped as Will's fist connected with the dashboard.

"I need to be alone, Dave." He shoved the car door open with his foot.

Dave started to protest, then thought better of it. "See you at the office."

He watched, concerned, as Will made his way unsteadily to the house. His gut felt tight. He wondered if Will's demons were rising up again.

Inside his house, Will tossed his keys to the side, and then noticed the packet that his realtor had slipped under the door. He remembered that he was accepting the offer on his house.

He wandered over to the staircase and looked up toward his bedroom.

"Nah," he muttered, knowing that he wouldn't sleep, and wondering if he had anything to drink in the fridge.

He fumbled for the lights in the kitchen, disoriented for a moment as they came on. His eyes went straight to the small photo on the sill over the sink. In it, Max looked out over the ocean at Rye Beach, with the wind lifting her hair back from her face and her lips curved in a tentative smile. She had that removed look in her eyes, the expression he so often saw on her: guarded, but with something more than that. Like a longing, Will thought.

He remembered teaching his little brother to swim, decades earlier, during one of the summers they spent at their grandparents' home on Lake Winnipesaukee. Nicky had stood on that dock every day, watching Will enjoy the water, begging him to teach him to swim. And when Will had finally relented, encouraging Nicky to jump in - promising repeatedly that he would catch him - Nicky wore that same expression: guarded, even fearful, but tempered with the desire to jump.

I'm scared, Will. You can't miss. You have to catch me.

Jump. I'll catch you. I promise.

He picked up the picture of Max.

He was fascinated by her eyes, partially because they were the purest shade of blue that he'd ever seen, but also because she rarely seemed to look directly at him. Or at anyone, actually, except for Sammy. She was relaxed with Sammy, natural - and that happened nowhere else, with no one else. Not anymore, because he had somehow managed to lose his connection to her. It seemed to him that lately, Max's eyes always focused just a little bit beyond whatever - whoever - she was looking at.

His throat felt tight, and he thought he should have another drink, just to help him relax. He glanced at his watch, shocked to see that it was almost three o'clock, and remembering that he had to be at the courthouse by nine.

He realized that he still hadn't reviewed the file on Brandi Reynolds, and the sudden grip of guilt jolted him almost sober. Then he remembered that his briefcase was in the trunk of his car, and that his car was still in the lot at the tavern, and he groaned.

Enough. I can't do this again.

He opened the drawer next to the sink and dropped Max's picture inside. An hour later - after he had jotted down some notes on Brandi Reynolds, and listed what he needed to do at the courthouse in the morning - he retrieved the picture and placed it back on the sill.

※ ※ ※

There were no open spaces on Salem Street, so Max parked her car in the back of the building, in Dave's reserved spot. Church bells rang out, and the distant, hollow echoing reminded her of the Sunday mornings and the Wednesday evenings, and the Friday and Saturday afternoons that she'd spent at her father's church when she was young.

Her hand went to the cross she wore around her neck, the one Jo had left for her.

You wanted me to wear it. Why didn't ***you*** *wear it? Maybe you would still be here.*

She let go of the cross and shook her head quickly to clear the thought away. Jo's death had saved Sammy and the baby, and that was where Max preferred to leave the past. But for some reason, on this morning, her mind - normally so able to deftly sidestep unpleasant thoughts - wouldn't let her escape the fact that it was almost the first anniversary of the night that Jack Seever killed her best friend.

Max recalled what she said to Dave that night: "She wanted to leave anyway." It was the truth, and Jo arranged her escape from life by goading Seever into a murderous rage - one that she made sure was directed at her. Max couldn't stem the spiteful pleasure she took from the fact that if Jo - ever the master manipulator - was determined to somehow maneuver her way out of life, she did so while putting Sammy's abuser away for good.

She understood what Jo did. But at the same time, Max agonized over the fact that Jo had lied to her, at least technically, because Jo had promised that she wouldn't commit suicide. And Max wondered how her friend got to that point of despair, how she sank to the depths of an all-consuming rage which drove her to chase down her own death. Max wondered sometimes if she, herself, could get there. In her rational mind, she knew that she never would; but it was the one facet of Jo's death that she wanted - for some reason, needed - to comprehend, and she couldn't.

If I wanted to check out, suicide-by-psycho wouldn't be my preferred method, that's for sure.

That thought, she managed to sidestep.

She pulled the rearview mirror down, checked her makeup, and wondered again if she would hear from Will. She remembered turning her cell phone off the night before, and that she had forgotten to turn it back on, so she rummaged through her purse until she found it. She didn't want it to matter so much, whether or not he had called. But it did. She started chewing on her lip as she realized that it mattered a lot.

The screen came to life with an image of the two of them, a picture that Will had recruited a total stranger to take during an autumn getaway in Maine, just a couple of weeks before Hope was born. Will appeared at Max's door on a Friday morning, right after she got home from class, wearing his weathered, brown leather jacket and ripped jeans. Max remembered how her breath caught in her throat when she saw him, how handsome he was, how she had never used the word "beautiful" to describe a man before.

He handed her the keys to his truck and said, "You pick it, doll. Let's go. You could use a break."

And I've been telling him he's predictable?

She gazed lovingly at their picture. Will stood behind her, bending to wrap his arms all the way around her waist. The sun glinted off of his face, making his hazel eyes look golden. His brown hair - too long for a professional man, she thought, but she loved long hair on a man - looked blonde in the sunlight. He had a mischievous grin on his face. Max's mouth was open wide with laughter, because Will had been tickling her ribs under her jacket.

She smiled softly, lightly touching her lips as she remembered their first kiss: it was that very night, on their way back from a day of wandering around in Portland, a day of exploring the art galleries and antique shops, and sitting on a bench by the ocean talking about whatever occurred to them. She told him that she wouldn't have made it without him after Jo died, and there was a sudden, deep emotion in his eyes. He put his arm around her, and she curled up against him, and he said, "That's what I'm here for, darlin'."

They had their arms around each other as they made their way back to his truck. They were often affectionate with each other, because they were friends. Best friends, they agreed on that; but this time, the feel of his arm around her made Max uneasy in a way that she hadn't been in years.

On the way home, they managed somehow to head in the wrong direction, and wound up heading north on Route 9. By 6:30, Max was complaining that she was starving, so they doubled back and found an intimate little café in Old Orchard Beach.

After they shared a massive lobster bake, and as Max finished her third glass of wine, Will slid a small gold box across the table.

"Here," he said, then he sat back and smiled expectantly.

Inside the box were the emerald cascade earrings that Max had admired in one of the antique shops. She gasped, and with her guard down from the wine, came around the table to plop down on his lap and throw her arms around his neck.

*I knew exactly what I wanted to do. What I wanted **him** to do.*

She closed her eyes as she remembered the scent of the ocean on him, mixing with the leather of his jacket and his aftershave. She remembered the look in his eyes as she drew back: the warmth there, the delight that he took in her joy. And she recalled thinking again that he was simply a beautiful man, and she kissed him quickly - just a glancing touch of her lips against his - and then she wondered if the surprised expression on his face meant that she shouldn't have done that. After all, until then, they had been just good friends.

And as she shifted, ready to stand up, he ran his hands through her hair and around to the back of her neck. He pulled her close, looking into her eyes and then at her lips, then back to her eyes again.

"Stay here," he murmured, brushing his lips against her cheek, and then her mouth - once, then twice, and she remembered how she wanted him to kiss her more than she had ever wanted anything. And when he finally did, she thought it was something beyond a simple kiss: it felt more like he caressed her lips with his, and she returned his kiss with a passion that surprised her. Until that moment of letting herself go, she had believed that she couldn't - shouldn't, actually - feel that way. It was a memory that she loved and dreaded every time she brought it back, but she couldn't stay away from it.

She glanced at the mirror again, tucking her hair behind her ears, fingering the earrings that Jo had given her. She felt a painful shot of adrenaline go through her as she realized that she had no idea where the emerald earrings were.

"Oh no," she whispered, thinking about all of the boxes at her apartment. She hoped they were there. She decided that they had to be inside one of them.

She hurried from the car, taking the steps to Sam's door two at a time.

"Sammy?" she called out. The radio was blaring at the far end of the house.

As she entered the kitchen, she said, "Mornin', love."

Sam hadn't heard her come into the house, and she jumped, spilling some of the cream she was carefully pouring into a small crystal decanter.

"Sorry." Max was hanging her jacket over the back of her usual chair.

"No problem." As she reached for a sponge, Sam gave her an appreciative once-over, saying, "Yikes, look at *you*, all fixed up. You look gorgeous."

"Thanks."

"Coffee?"

"'Course. Silly girl."

As she poured, Sam asked, "So, what happened last night?" She turned to study her for a moment. "You okay?"

Max nodded, then stopped. "Actually, no. I think I'm really messed up, Sammy."

"Did you talk to Will yet?"

Max shook her head. "We had a fight. A bad one. I said some things... The last thing he said was that he's out." She took the mug Sam was handing to her.

"'Out'? Meaning what?"

Max shrugged.

"So... You haven't spoken since he left last night?"

"He hasn't called." She stared at the wall, surprised at the impact the words had on her. "I was thinking, maybe I'll stop by his office today."

Sam braced herself with a deep breath as she sat across from her. She took Max's hand and said, "Okay, listen. Something happened late last night." Seeing Max's stricken expression, she hurried to explain: "He's fine. He's okay. But he got hauled in by the cops."

It took her a moment, then she asked quietly, "What happened? Where is he?"

Sam thought she was strangely composed about it.

"Drunk and Disorderly. He lucked out - the cop who grabbed him is a friend. They called Dave."

Max mumbled something unintelligible, then gulped some of the coffee as she stood up.

"Max?"

"I have a terrific effect on people, don't I?" She took another sip and reached for her jacket. "Gotta go."

"No. Don't."

Max stopped, confused by the Sam's sudden edginess.

"Sit down, Max. Will's in court up in New Hampshire. So you can't see him 'til later anyway, and we need to talk."

She took her seat. "About...?"

"I'm tired of this."

"Of what?"

"I want you to tell me what's going on with you."

Max looked away, trying to think of a way out. She thought that if she had any idea what was going on in her own head, she'd be more than happy to tell Sammy about it.

"Please." Sam took her hand again. "You've been weird lately..."

"More than usual, huh?" She grinned, hoping to distract her.

Sam was insistent. "No jokes. You're worrying us."

"'*Us*'?" Max bristled then, thinking about being a topic of discussion among her friends. "Who's included in 'us'?"

"Dave and me. And yes, Will, too. Look, even Ty has asked if you're okay. You're too tired, you're way too thin, and we can't chalk it up to finals and getting into law school anymore."

Max withdrew her hand and started picking at her nails. "What did Will say?"

"He's worried that you're leaving him."

She rolled her eyes. "I wasn't planning on it."

"You sure about that?"

"Why is he talking to you guys? It's between him and me."

"Max, he says he's tried to talk to you. You deflect with him like you just did with me."

Where she was annoyed a few moments before, Max suddenly felt deflated. "I can't, Sammy," she mumbled. "I don't know why, I just can't be what he wants. No," she hurried to explain, "that's not fair. I mean, what he needs. I just can't do the male-female thing. I don't have it in me."

"What are you *talking* about?"

"I don't know how to explain it... Look, he's younger than me."

"Not much," Sam countered.

"He could still find a woman he could build a better life with. Someone who at least has her head on straight..."

"Who isn't so 'messed up'?"

Max rolled her eyes again, then nodded.

Sam wasn't convinced. "Well, if that's how you feel, then why were you about to go find him?"

She opened her mouth to answer, then seemed to rethink it. "Know what, Sammy? That's a really good question. I don't know. I guess it's a good thing you stopped me."

That wasn't the answer Sam was looking for. "You love him."

Max averted her eyes, casting about for something else to look at.

"You love him," she repeated softly, ducking her head so Max would have to look at her.

She finally nodded, resigned. "Yeah."

"At least you admit it."

"Good for me. The first step is admitting you have a problem." She looked down, picking at her nails again. "With the way I love him, look how he's winding up."

Sam was turning impatient again. "That's a dodge, and you know it."

"Fine. Then look how *I'm* winding up." Max stood, reaching again for her jacket. "I'm a mess. I don't even know myself anymore. And on that note, I'm outta here, because I have packing to do."

Sam watched silently as she hurried from the kitchen, becoming aware of the thumping overhead. Hope was done napping, and she liked to announce her awakening by grabbing the side rail of her crib, and then bouncing happily until someone showed up.

She squealed as Sam walked into the nursery. She held her arms out, waiting to be picked up - and in doing so, plopped backwards, sitting with wide-eyed surprise. Then she broke into giggles, bouncing and waving her arms up and down.

Sam laughed with her. "Well, my goodness, Hope, did you fall down?" She gathered her daughter into her arms, kissing the top of her head and tamping down the usual rush of guilt that she felt. She'd become so practiced at pushing it away that she barely noticed it as she maneuvered her mind in another direction, thinking about what Max had said - and deciding that her excuses and rationalizations were ridiculous.

It is a dodge. She's just afraid. But Will won't make his move, either. He spends more time talking with us about it than with Maxine.

She wondered how she could bring them together. Dave had warned her against interfering, but with all of the time that Will and Maxine spent bending their ears, she felt completely comfortable with doing a little meddling.

At least it'll keep my mind occupied.

✸ ✸ ✸

As he came down the hall from the clerk's office, Will saw Dave waiting for him in the open lobby of the Rockingham County Courthouse.

"Got time to eat?" Dave asked.

"You're a hell of a guy, Delaney. You drove all the way to New Hampshire to buy me breakfast?"

"Nope. It's on you." He appeared jovial, but he was assessing Will's demeanor. "How's it going?"

"You mean, am I hungover? No. If you're asking about the Reynolds case, we have another hearing on the thirty-first."

Here it comes, Dave thought. He had seen it before. "What happened?"

"His side requested it. Reynolds wants visitation with Alexa."

"Of course he does." Dave sighed, both aggravated and a little alarmed. "How tough will this one be?"

"Depends on the judge. New Hampshire isn't like Massachusetts - there are still some people in the system up here with connected brain cells."

"There's a diner a few doors down. Fill me in over breakfast."

They were settled into a booth a few minutes later, and after the waitress poured coffee, Dave said, "Tell me about it."

"Reynolds found himself a new lawyah, Counselah," Will quipped in a Boston accent. He became serious then. "He'll go for custody, at least at some point, but he doesn't really want that. He just figures that in going for everything, he'll get something. He hooked up with Jefferson Marshall."

"Never heard of him."

"He's new to the game. Fathers Rights guy. Used his daddy's money to hang out his own shingle up here."

Dave frowned. "No. You mean *Emerson* Marshall?"

"Yup. That's Dad." With a sarcastic grin, Will added, "And Jeff's following in his pop's footsteps - even notching it up a bit."

"Translate that for me."

"Jeff is becoming known as the go-to guy for dads who want the upper hand in a divorce. Especially if there's going to be a custody battle."

"Do I need to know about this?"

"Probably not, but I'll tell you anyway."

"Naturally," Dave sighed, settling in to listen.

"It's something of a new trend. 'Divorce Games' is the working title. It goes way beyond the usual stuff, like cleaning out the bank accounts and refusing to move out of the house." He smirked as he thought about Reynolds' demand to see Alexa. "Or going to a judge for immediate visitation with the kids he never had an interest in, not until the woman goes for a divorce." He chugged the rest of his coffee, then slid the cup to the edge of the table. "Wow. I could take this stuff intravenously today. Anyway..."

Dave smiled to himself. This was Will at his best.

Will nodded his thanks to the waitress who was refilling his cup. "Here's how he works it. Jeff advises his client to pick a fight with the woman he wants to divorce. Get her upset enough, frightened enough, whatever it takes to provoke her to attack - or more often, fight back. From what I've heard, he tells them that stealing her keys or her cell is especially effective. And he should hold it over his head, get her to claw him up a bit, then..."

Dave groaned.

Will nodded in response. "That's right. As soon as he gets a mark on him, he calls 911. Gets her arrested on a Domestic. And then suddenly, he's in the driver's seat."

Dave was slowly shaking his head as he listened. "It never ends."

"It doesn't. It's like a game of Whack-a-Mole. You remember Janie Givans?"

He tried to place the name. Will represented clients who were caught up in the Family Court, and almost all of them were women. "I think so. You had a good resolution with her case, right?"

"Not what I wanted, but the best we could get. Got what we did only because her ex wanted her to forgive the back child support. That was almost a year ago, before I knew about Divorce Games, but something about her case always bothered me."

The waitress took their order, and Will continued:

"Anyway, that's exactly what happened to Janie. Right down to the cell phone bait, and then he used it as leverage. I've been advising every client about it ever since I found out."

"I don't know how you keep your sanity, man."

"Me neither. Mini-Marshall isn't even hiding what he is. His website blares it out, that he's strictly Daddy's Rights - they're even running a two-day *workshop* next month for dads who want to stick it to the mothers of their kids." He stifled a yawn, reaching for his coffee again. "For the low, low price of only two thousand dollars, Jeff's gonna teach the guys how to screw the mothers of their children. To the *wall*. Seriously, D - the only lifeline I have left is the thought of getting out of Massachusetts."

Dave wanted to change the topic. It was difficult to listen to the reality of what Will did for a living, and he did wonder at times how Will managed to do the work that he did.

"By the way," he said, "on that topic, there's a house in Hudson. Just a few minutes from the main drag in Nashua."

Will leaned forward. "Commercial?"

"Yeah. And the owner is an attorney, so it's set up already. And it's vacant."

Will whistled softly. "How much?"

"Six-seventy. It's huge - over six thousand square feet, including the offices. Great parking, quiet area. Sammy was worried about Ty going to Nashua schools, but if we live there, he'll go to Hudson."

"So wait - we're changing the plan? You guys are gonna live where we work?"

He nodded. "If you agree to set up the firm there. Sammy and I will buy the place, and since I'll be deducting a good amount, we'll count that as your contribution to running the place."

"Hmm. Not charging me rent? Makes me feel like a poor relation." But Will was thinking that he liked the idea. The arrangement that Dave was describing would open doors for him, as well.

"This is business, Will. It's only fair that if Sammy and I get the benefits of owning it, that you be compensated somehow. More than that, it saves us a fortune - combining work and home, instead of buying a house and then renting office space."

Will glanced at his phone, distracted by the fact that the call coming in wasn't from Max. "Let's go take a look before we head back," he said.

"I have the realtor meeting me there for a second showing..." he glanced at his watch, "in forty minutes. By the way, it's not even ten minutes out of Londonderry. That'll make Max happy."

He waited for Will's response. When Will started busying himself with his cell phone, Dave asked, "Is that her texting you?"

"Nope." He was reading something on his phone.

After a few moments, Dave said, "Hey."

Will looked up.

"What happened last night?"

"C'mon, D," he moaned, "let it go. I have enough to contend with right now. Besides, this is between Maxine and me."

"That hasn't stopped you before." As Will gave him an exasperated look, Dave said, "Okay, then let me ask you this: is the drinking becoming a problem again?"

His expression turned hard. "Watch it."

"Will, I have to know."

He opened his mouth to protest, then seemed to relent. "Yeah," he mumbled. "I guess you do."

"You can't do this again, man."

"Dave..."

"The last time... If I thought there was an issue here, I wouldn't have let my guard down."

"That was years ago." He stopped, realizing that he was being defensive when he had no right to be. "No, you've got the right to ask. You do." He pushed his cell to the side, leaning forward. "It's actually your responsibility to know."

Dave relaxed a little. "And?"

"I caught it when I got home last night. I saw what I've been doing, and I'm not falling into it again." He paused, then a grin spread across his face.

"Something funny?"

"Thinking about your version of an intervention. Back in the day, remember? You nearly broke my arm, dragging me out of that bar that night."

"Yeah, and I'd hate to have to do it again, Remmond."

"You and me both. People were calling me 'Lefty' for two weeks." They laughed, then Will said, "I know I got some favors last night, Dave. I won't waste them. If I can't handle being with Maxine, then I have to make a decision."

Their meals arrived then, and when the waitress walked away, Will continued. "Although I think she's already decided anyway, so it's moot."

Dave decided to busy himself eating so Will would keep talking.

"On the other hand, if she does want to be with me, then I'd better learn how to handle it, because I don't think I can let her go." He pushed his plate to the side, leaning forward again, looking down at his clasped hands. "I just don't know how to reach her, Dave. I think she wants to be in this. I *know* she does. But then she says or does something that..." He recalled her reaction to his comment about marriage, and fell silent for a moment.

"It really is getting that bad, huh?"

"Yeah." Will looked up then. "I actually decided last night that I was done with her."

Dave resisted a smile that he knew was inappropriate. "How long did that last?" he asked.

"About an hour."

"Thought so. I know the feeling."

Will considered it briefly. "That's right - you do."

"I waited three years for Sammy to give me another chance."

After a moment, Will asked, "Remember calling me the day after she finally said she'd marry you?"

"Actually, I don't."

"Not surprised - you were in an alternate universe. That was the second time I ever heard you get choked up." He leaned back, smiling at the memory. "The first time was when Ty was born."

"Remember that day I came home and found out that Sammy had moved out?"

The smile left Will's face, and he nodded.

"Come to think of it," Dave said, "you dragged *me* out of a couple of bars back then."

"You were in bad shape."

"Yeah. And I had no chance with her until I got real with *myself*. I messed it up pretty bad."

Will's eyes narrowed as he asked, "You trying to tell me something?"

"I *am* telling you something. When it's off in the ditch like you're describing, you may want to take a look at yourself."

"C'mon, Delaney," he scoffed. "I don't even know what I'm dealing with when it comes to Maxine."

With a level stare, Dave said, "Then for some reason, she doesn't trust you."

Will was silent as he allowed it to sink in.

Dave's phone vibrated, and he picked it up from the table. "Look, if I could hold out, so can you. The moment is gonna show up, so be there for it. But only if you're there for the right reasons." He checked the text that had come in. "Sammy says I have to bring you home for dinner tonight."

Will was staring absently out the wall of windows behind Dave. "Well, whatever Sammy says, goes," he mumbled. He picked up a piece of toast, taking a couple of bites before he said, "You may be right. You *are* right. She doesn't trust me." He focused on

Dave again. "Just so I'm prepared, Sammy's inviting her for tonight too, right?"

"Probably. But we aren't supposed to know that."

"We're all supposed to pretend that you and Sammy don't know what's going on?"

"Pretty much." He pointed to Will's plate. "You gonna eat?"

Will shook his head, then pulled out his wallet and tossed some bills on the table.

"Besides," Dave said, "I don't know what's going on. You haven't really told me anything."

"I know." He slid out of the booth. "Let's get going. I have the truck today - let's take that. Give the realtor the impression that you're kinda broke."

"That'll do it."

"Don't diss a man's truck, Delaney."

Dave exaggerated a surprised expression as they approached Will's pickup. "Hey, you washed it."

He shot him an irritated look. "It rained a couple days ago."

Dave slid in, then repositioned himself as a tear on the leather seat snagged his pants. "You need to get a new truck, man." He checked the console. "Still just a CD player. Even Ty knows how to hook up his phone to play music."

Will grunted something unintelligible as he started the truck, then scrambled to turn down the stereo as the music started.

The song came up loud, an old hard rock ballad about the girl who got away. Dave stared briefly at the CD player, then out the window for a moment, trying not to laugh as he turned to Will.

"Really?"

Will busied himself with examining the side mirror, waiting to pull out into the traffic.

"I think my ears are bleeding," Dave chuckled.

"You want to bleed? Keep talkin'." Will merged into the line of cars, then took a hard right. "Which way to 102?"

Dave pointed ahead. "Take a right up there. So what happened last night?"

"Told you. We had a fight." He settled in as he pulled onto the main road. "I said something stupid."

"What stupid?"

He rubbed at the stubble on his chin. "I said the 'M' word."

"Aw, no."

"Yep." He glanced at him regretfully. "And she actually, literally choked. She reacted like I suggested group sex or something."

Dave breathed out with an exasperated whoosh. "You know better. She's nowhere near ready to even think about marriage."

Will leaned his head back against the rest, stretching his legs. "I don't need to hear it again. I'm tired of it." He drummed his fingers on the steering wheel, tapping harder as he became more animated. "Maybe if I had a clue, knew something about what's up with her... All I know is, she has secrets." He took another quick look at Dave, who was suddenly, intently studying the scenery. "I have to tell you, I think you know what those secrets are." When Dave didn't respond, Will added, "At least, some of them."

Dave nodded. "Some."

They traveled in silence for several minutes, and Dave said, "Thanks for not asking."

"I don't appreciate you knowing her secrets, and I don't," Will muttered. "I know maybe one of them. The baby she gave up for adoption, and she only spilled that one by mistake because she was drunk."

"I don't like it, either." Will was his oldest friend, going all the way back to their college days, and Dave hated having to keep anything from him.

"There has to be something you can clue me in on. There's something scaring her, and whatever it is, it's bad."

Dave thought about it briefly, then said, "She has been withdrawn lately."

"Is it because of Jo?"

"That's what I thought for a while, but I don't anymore. When we talk about what happened, she seems pretty centered."

Will thought about Max's expression as she backed away from him the night before. "Dave, I need to know. Last night..." He stopped, not wanting to say it.

He looked up. Something in Will's tone alarmed him. "What happened?"

"Last night, it seemed like she was afraid of *me*."

Dave decided that was the dividing line. Will was right: he needed information. "She had it pretty tough growing up. Her dad was a pastor..."

"Yeah, she told me that."

"... and he was one brutal son of a bitch." He watched Will's face turn hard.

After a few seconds, Will asked, "How bad?"

"About as bad as it gets." Dave turned to look out the window again.

Will nodded, wincing at the sudden, searing pain in his gut. "He went after Maxine?"

"Her mother. Not Max - not that I know of. But I have to tell you, I think there's something there." He paused briefly, struggling with the decision of whether or not to continue.

"C'mon, Dave. I need to have more to go on."

He was tapping his foot, staring straight ahead. "Sammy thinks she was sexually abused. So do I."

The rage that rose in Will was unlike anything he had ever felt. The truck drifted to the shoulder of the road as his mind fragmented into a hundred horrifying images.

"Steady," Dave said.

"That explains a few things," he mumbled. As he recalled the things he had said the night before, he wanted to turn the truck around and go find her. He decided to view the house as quickly as possible, and then get back to Boston.

They passed the *Welcome to Hudson* sign, and Will looked around impatiently, nodding his approval.

"This is nice out here," he said. Hudson seemed to be much more wide-open than most of the other towns in New Hampshire, with expansive fields and rolling hills, and lakes bordered by tall pines.

"Take a right at the stop sign." Dave pulled the listing packet for the property from his briefcase. "House is right there after the turn."

Will pulled to the curb in front of a sprawling, white, antique Colonial, with black shutters and a barn-red front door. He whistled softly. "Wow. How old?"

"Eighteen-forty," Dave said. "You know how Sammy loves these old houses. She lost her mind when she saw this. I promised her I'd nail it down." He was smiling proudly, and Will thought he was acting like he already owned it.

Will glanced at his watch as he said, "I think Delaney-Remmond has a new home."

❊ ❊ ❊

Max looked around her tiny apartment, surprised to realize that she was done packing. She was ready to go. The only item not boxed up was the four-by-six photo of the girls and her, the one that was taken the Christmas before Jo was killed.

Her cell alerted her to a text coming in. She muted it, picking up the picture and gazing at it wistfully, recalling how simple life seemed back then. They had been three friends, best friends, sharing their lives and loving each other.

She was suddenly, acutely aware of the passage of time, of the changes that she had made in the year since Jo died. And she realized that she was glad for those changes. It was something like an inside-out sensation of déjà vu, because she would never be in that place again, and she didn't want to be.

Life was kind of meaningless, in a lot of ways. Just sad.

She thought about her daily routine back then: she got up every morning - as late as possible - then went down to Jo's apartment for coffee. Worked at the restaurant, headed to the bar, then home to pass out. It was safe, and it was easy, and she never had to think about her rudderless life. Or her past.

Knowing Jo changed all that. Jo had challenged her. She tried - with some success - to make her confront the reality of her abusive father and her battered mother, and the painful legacy of that kind of a childhood. She encouraged Max to move beyond the walls that she had constructed around herself.

Max felt her stomach clench with the guilt of acknowledging that now, she had moved beyond Jo.

*She **wanted** me to move on. I just don't know where I'm supposed to go now. I hid myself away for years.*

But I'm not ready for Will. I can't go forward, and I can't go back.

"I'm nowhere," she whispered.

She took faint notice of the fact that she was approaching a decision, and she told herself that the decision wouldn't be terribly painful - if anything, it would be a relief. She slid the photo into her purse, then pulled it out, wrapping it in tissue. Her cell was beeping again.

The text was from Sam, inviting her over for dinner. Max bounced the phone lightly in her hand, thinking about it as she surveyed the apartment.

"Not tonight, Sammy," she said as she typed the response.

No thx. Moving today.

A few seconds later, Sam was calling. Max sighed, anticipating the argument that was coming.

"Hey, Sammy."

"You're kidding, right?"

"No. I'm going to load up my car, make a couple trips if I need to, leave the bigger pieces of furniture here."

"Just like that?"

"My lease started May fifteenth. The apartment's been mine for a week. I want to get going."

"Geez - were you going to at least say goodbye?"

"For pity's sake, Sammy, I'm not heading overseas. I'm moving an hour north. You guys will be there soon enough."

"At least come for dinner. What's the hurry?"

"I have everything ready to go. I won't even have a coffeemaker for the morning. And besides," she scanned the apartment again, and her stomach turned over, "I really want to get out of here."

"Then come for dinner, and just stay here tonight."

"I don't think so."

"C'mon, Max. Please?"

Max knew what she was doing. "So...What time is Will showing up?" When Sam didn't respond, she added, "Tell you what. I'll run the first load of stuff up to my apartment, and if it's not too late, I'll stop by when I get back."

"In other words, I can go pound sand."

"Basically."

"Fine." Disappointed, she muttered, "Go ahead. Be an old maid."

Max burst into laughter. "'Old maid'? Look, I need to get going. I'll call you tonight."

"Wait - what about you and Will?"

"Don't know."

Sam could tell that she wasn't going to get any useful information from her. "Okay. Careful driving. I'll try to come see you before we head down to see Dave's folks."

"That's right," Max said. "When are you going?"

"Friday afternoon. We have to be back here by Monday night." She paused, debating whether or not to remind her about the holiday weekend and Will's plans with her.

"I know. It's not much of a break," Max answered.

"Well, Will's taking some time over the holiday, remember? Dave's pulling extra duty for now."

Max knew what she was trying to point out, and she ignored it. "I know," she said again as she reached for her purse. "Talk to you tonight."

She noticed a missed call and an unread message on her phone. The call was from Phoenix, from her mother - she had moved to Arizona to live with her sister after Max's father died. Max made a mental note to call her back when her mood was improved, because her mom couldn't handle stress anymore. Not even a little. Her blood pressure was bad.

Max brought the text up, assuming it was from Sam, and she started chewing on her lower lip when she saw it was from Will.

Be there at 1:00. We need to talk.

"No. I can't." She started to type out a response, then deleted it, shaking her head as she turned her phone off and slipped it into her purse.

By noon, she had managed to fit everything that she was taking with her into her car. She stood in the entry of the apartment and wondered if she should take some kind of sentimental last look around, because so much had happened while she lived there.

Like falling in love with Will.

She moaned softly. "That's not me," she whispered. "It just isn't." She thought that the time they had together had been something of mirage.

Not a dream, because dreams aren't cruel like that - it was just a fantasy.

An image flickered in her mind's eye, subliminal in its effect; then, she remembered her father again, and rage flared in her stomach. When she closed her eyes, she could feel again the crushing shame of his mockery, the crippling pity she had felt for her mother - and the militant resolve she developed early in her life, the determination that she would never allow herself to be some helpless, gullible little woman, cowering under the fist of an idiot husband.

She grasped the doorknob, and her eyes drifted down to the marks at the bottom of the door, the smudges that she made when she kicked it the night before. She moaned again, wanting to see Will - moved by a need so strong, her hands were shaking.

"I have to *go*," she snapped, refusing to acknowledge her hope that he would come after her.

She dropped the keys to the apartment beside the front door, slamming it behind her as she left.

chapter 3

"Six days to go, Simon. How are you feeling about your progress?"

Simon Reynolds smiled warmly, hoping he appeared appropriately docile. "Good, I think." He nervously tapped the arms of his chair. "Isn't the important thing how *you* feel about my progress?"

Dr. Beaumann chuckled. "Sure. But I'd like your perspective."

"Well," Simon shifted in his chair, leaning his forearms on the desk, "to be real with you, Doc, I'm nervous. I'm actually thinking, maybe I'm not ready to leave, you know? I'm scared that I'll blow it somehow." One of the inmates who had completed the Batterer Intervention course had told Simon to say that, clueing him in on the buzz phrases that the therapists and the courts liked to hear.

Dr. Beaumann nodded approvingly. "That's actually a good sign, Simon. It means that you've developed a sensitivity to your behaviors, and the impact you have on others." He scrawled something on his notepad, and Simon resisted the impulse to try to see what it was.

"I never looked at it that way." He lowered his head for a moment, then sighed heavily as he sat back in his chair. He regarded the doctor with an expression that was engaged, but uncertain. "I'll never go down that road again, that's for sure."

Intrigued, Beaumann said, "Explain that for me."

Simon knew that this was a pivotal moment, the one which he had rehearsed for weeks. "I'll never assume that I have some kind of an automatic claim on anyone. Not Brandi, not Alexa - and certainly, I won't be going near them unless I'm allowed to." His face was starting to feel wooden, and he bowed his head again to hide it, mumbling, "I can't believe what I did."

There was silence in the room as Simon steeled himself. The rage he was suppressing threatened to disintegrate his calm, sorrowful demeanor, and he knew that he still needed to deliver what was called the "money line." He couldn't use excuses like the drugs he was on that day, or how Brandi had used the courts to persecute him - the issues Simon's lawyer had raised to sway the judge to leniency.

He could hear a clock ticking somewhere behind him. He searched his memory, and brought back the shock on her face that day, the way she tried - even as she went down to her knees - to cover herself. Mock heroics. Protecting the kid from seeing the blood, and making him look like a monster.

As his stomach lurched with the outrage of it, he felt nauseated. The pain shot up his neck again, and he looked up then, running a trembling hand through his hair. "It makes me sick to my stomach, Doc."

Beaumann was watching him carefully. "I can see that." He jotted down another comment, then took a form from the drawer of his desk. "You've done an amazing amount of work here, Simon."

He nodded. "Thanks."

"And I'm very happy to say, we can close this out."

Simon was careful not to show the elation that replaced the rage. "I'm grateful for the confidence you have in me, Doc." He couldn't wait to be able to stop groveling.

"You earned it." He signed the form, and said, "I'll be taking this upstairs this afternoon, and you should be preparing yourself to head back out there." He smiled as he stood and offered his hand. "Congratulations, Simon."

Simon clasped the doctor's hand. In a quiet voice, deciding it was the last time he would ever utter the words, he said, "Thanks for everything, Doc."

※ ※ ※

Will pulled into the lot at Max's apartment building with his phone to his ear, trying to reassure Brandi Reynolds about the impending visitation hearing.

"Brandi, you need to calm down."

"Calm down? That demonic prick *shot* me. And that judge let him plea down to being reckless, so that means he hasn't done anything bad enough to lose his rights to Alexa? Do you know what he said when they arrested him?"

"I know. I read the file." He was surprised by his own level of impatience, something he never experienced when dealing with his understandably distraught clients. He rubbed his forehead, willing himself to focus. "But your attitude is going to cost you. You need to get ahold of yourself."

Will wasn't surprised anymore by the vulgar language that traumatized women could use. He let her vent for a minute, and when she started to cry, he berated himself for his attitude. He glanced toward Max's apartment, then deliberately turned away so he could concentrate on his client.

"Brandi, listen to me."

"I am. I'm trying, Will. I just can't believe that there's even a chance that he would get visitation with Alexa. He said he would *get* her."

"I know. The courts aren't big on denying rights to a father." He thought again, like he did almost every day of his life, how much he hated his work. How disgusted he was by the blind, unthinking procedures and rituals of the Family Court. "He took a batterer's course in prison…"

"So he can perfect his craft?" she snapped.

A jolt of adrenaline went through him as he thought about how right she was, but he didn't address it. "So the courts will be satisfied that he's less of a threat. But he won't get unsupervised visitation. He'll be monitored."

"By who? His mom? She hates me. His dad is a drunk…"

"No. They were complicit in what happened. Look," he consciously relaxed his body, rubbing at his brow again, "I'm not going to let up. I promise you that. We can't keep him from Alexa, because he's jumped through all of their hoops. But we can make sure he's never alone with her."

"I should just grab her and run."

Will secretly agreed, but he quickly responded with, "No, Brandi. You can't. And I didn't hear you say that."

"Fine." She was starting to cry again, but she kept her voice level. "What's next?"

"The hearing is on the thirty-first. We need to meet before then." He thought about Sam. "We just hired an advocate at the firm. I'm going to hook you up with her."

Brandi laughed bitterly. "I had one of those when all this went down. They're window dressing."

"Not this one. She'll coach you on how to act while you're in the courtroom, and she'll be with you for the entire process."

"You know her?"

"I do. And she's the best there is."

"Okay. Whatever. Give her my number."

She sounded completely indifferent, and Will knew that he should say more, but he needed to see Max. He wrapped the call up quickly, setting a time for them to meet after the holiday weekend and before the hearing. "Call me with anything you need, okay?"

"Sure."

He tossed his phone into his briefcase, loosening his tie as he scanned the lot for Max's car. When he didn't see it in its usual spot, he hurriedly exited his truck and looked around.

There was no one around, so he went to her door and peered through the small window beside it, cupping his hand over the glass to block the glare. Then he slowly turned away, leaning his back against her door and looking heavenward.

"Great," he mumbled. "Okay, where'd you go now?"

He sprinted back to his truck, retrieving the phone from his briefcase and pulling Max's number up; then he changed his mind, deciding to call Sam first.

She picked up immediately. "Will. Hold on a minute."

He could hear Hope crying in the distance, and Sam asking Dave to go get her.

"I was just about to call you," Sam said. "Dave just got home..."

"What's going on? Did she head north?"

"Yeah. I called her earlier today, and she said she wanted to take off."

"Thanks for the headsup there, Sammy."

"Hey, back off. Hope's been a handful today. Besides, I didn't know what you were doing up there. I wasn't going to start calling you in the middle of a hearing or something."

He wondered why he was taking it out on her. "I'm sorry, honey. I didn't mean that." He started the truck, wondering what to do next.

She sighed. "I know. Come on over. We'll feed you while we figure something out."

"Be there in a few."

The traffic was heavy, giving him time to reflect on the past few months and the deepening unease he felt around Max. He knew he was right about her, that she was drifting away from him; and now, with the glimpse of her history that Dave had provided, he was able to put a few pieces of the puzzle together.

As he sat at a crowded intersection, he struggled to pinpoint a moment when everything changed, and decided that there likely wasn't one. That perhaps with her history - and his - they'd never really had a chance.

Don't think that way. There's a key to this somewhere.

He started with the night before, at the restaurant, and he recalled the short, ivory dress that she wore. She had a thing for short skirts, which Will didn't mind one bit, because she had legs that he would catch himself daydreaming about in the middle of a deposition.

Will caught how his mind was tracking, and he rubbed the back of his neck, fully exasperated with himself.

Maybe she's right about men after all.

It seemed to Will that something went wrong between them after New Year's Eve, when they went to the firm's black-tie party at Wellington Place. In spite of the way he'd just admonished himself, he lingered over the memory of the way she looked that night. She wore her hair long and loose, and a strapless, silver, glittery thing that he teased her as being barely a dress. He had never seen her like that, and she was stunning.

Max overdid the champagne a bit, but she was what Will had called a "happy drunk" - animated, charming, chatting with everyone Will introduced her to; yet, not one of the men who tried to get her attention had even the slightest success with her. He spent that evening reveling in how she made him feel, enjoying how obvious it was that she was with him.

And now, Will could almost feel her there again, curled up on his lap with her arms draped around his neck. She had whispered things to him that he quickly lost the ability to process. The weight of her body pressed into him, and with her lips brushing against his ear, his only surviving sense was touch - and even that was consumed by the way she was wrapping herself around him.

Midnight arrived, but they didn't join in the countdown with everyone else. Instead, Max was lightly touching her lips to his closed eyes, then his cheek, and then leaned into him just as the crowd shouted "*Three!*" And she kissed him in a way that he knew he would never forget, a kiss that lasted well into the New Year.

The traffic was still crawling along. It wasn't a warm day, but he was suddenly sweating, and he jabbed impatiently at the air conditioning a few times before he remembered that it wasn't working.

He took a long, deep breath to clear his head, and it caught in his throat as he realized that they had been in a downward spiral ever since the night of the party.

It went too far.

He knew he was right. About that part of it, anyway. She started distancing herself well before he told her that he loved her.

They had bolted from the New Year's party and gone back to Will's house shortly after midnight, and their bodies were locked together before he closed the front door. Max was in his arms, unbuttoning his shirt, running her hands all over his body and kissing his chest - and then, she seemed to freeze.

He remembered how she backed away, her hands over her mouth as if she was in some kind of pain. Her eyes were closed, and she was breathing in short gasps, shaking her head.

Then she said something that he didn't understand, something his instinct for her told him not to ask about:

"No. You're *wrong*." It came out slurred, but he heard it clearly.

He followed her as she walked unsteadily up the stairs and wandered into his bedroom. She laid on his bed, curling up on her side with her eyes wide open. Will had pushed the memory away after that night, but he recalled now that her expression was chilling, a mixture of fear and contempt.

She looked like she hated me.

A minute later, she was asleep. Will wasn't sure how long he watched her from the doorway of his room, wondering what had happened to her, what she was thinking about in that moment before she froze.

Eventually, he took off his tux and changed into his jeans, then carefully slipped Max's shoes from her feet and laid beside her, gathering her into his arms.

At some point during the night, he felt her press tight against him, wrapping her arms around him. He stroked her hair, then realized that she was awake and she was quietly watching him.

"I'm sorry," she whispered.

He tightened his arms around her. "Don't. It's okay."

She started to say something, but stopped. Will was sure, at that moment and ever since, that she wanted to say, "I love you." And that one moment was the most confusing thing of all about that night.

The other thing he was sure of - one of the few things that he knew, even within the enigmatic, tangled-up mess they were calling a "relationship" - was that somewhere in the middle of that night, she became much more to him than what she had been for the three months since they became a couple. During that night, he crossed over from enjoying her, wanting her, and caring about her, and it seemed to him that he started loving her. At least, that was the night that he admitted it to himself.

And that's where it began to unravel.

Will knew there was something important inside that thought, but he didn't know how to find it. Something to do with her father, of course; however, he suspected that she had other secrets, and he had no idea how to contend with problems he couldn't see. More than that, he had no concept of how to deal with an adult woman who had been abused as a child.

He thought about his clients, mostly battered mothers who were disjointed, confused, wanting only a safe place and for someone to protect them. Those women, he could understand, and he was effective with them. But his expertise was in dealing with abused mothers, not their children. Not the girls, anyway. In the scope of his practice, he frequently had the opportunity to counsel the sons of those women, and he was able to help to some degree - but the girls were normally so withdrawn and mistrusting that they were impossible to reach.

Then he thought about Sam. She would have at least some insight, because her work occasionally involved kids who lived in abusive homes.

Another obstacle, Will thought, was that he didn't know what else might be affecting Max. He often wondered why she never mentioned Jo, why she stopped talking about her within a few weeks of her death. Jo was like a sister to her. Max was there as Jo died; certainly, that had to be at play.

*Maybe not. The people she **does** confide in don't think so.*

Will knew that he needed to know what her secrets were, and - maybe more important, he decided - the reasons she wouldn't tell him. He recalled Dave's comment:

For some reason, she doesn't trust you.

"*Why* don't you trust me?" he muttered.

He caught the peculiar feeling of guilt that rose up inside him, like it always did when he had even the smallest critical thought about her. He decided that this time, he was going to think it through.

His low-level hum of guilt started after the holiday party, because it seemed to him that he had crossed a line that night.

How? By responding to a beautiful woman who's undressing me?

And it *was* a response, and that was a pivotal point to him, because he never knew where the lines were. He had sensed Max's skittish nature right from the start, from the day he first met her at Dave's wedding. He never pushed too hard, or took her for granted, or assumed anything at all. Afraid of scaring her off, he was cautious with her to the point of paralysis.

That's part of the problem. I was never so intimidated by anyone. Not until her.

He made sure she knew that she was completely free to be what she was, and do whatever she wanted to do; yet somehow, in spite of the care he took to accommodate her, he was feeling like some kind of a predator. When he compared the way he felt at the holiday party to the way he felt at that moment, it came clear to him how being with Max was affecting his own confidence, and how destructive the situation was becoming.

I'm tired of trying to prove that I'm not whatever it is she's afraid of.
*And I'm **really** tired of being careful.*

He thought about the ambivalence she showed toward anything that might require a commitment. Will knew that she loved him; yet, she would tear him down with backhanded accusations and innuendo if he got too close. And she was escalating lately. Hostile. Sometimes, she even seemed unstable. She was in his face with her mistrust, as she had been the night before - and while he was certain that many of her problems could be traced back her father, he suspected that there were other issues, as well.

*You're **hoping** it has nothing to do with Daddy.*
He massaged the back of his neck again.
I wouldn't have a clue how to deal with that.

He decided it was way past time to get the details out of her, because the woman had an inherent aversion to the things she wanted most.

As he pulled up in front of the townhouse, his hand started to cramp, and he became aware of the force with which he was gripping the steering wheel. He stretched his fingers, thinking about Max's habit of stroking her own lips with her fingertips when she wanted to be kissed. It was one of her unconscious gestures, an unintended show of the passion that Will knew she had for him. She had told him, just once - with her head down, almost in a whisper - that no man had ever affected her the way that he did, and she wasn't used to that kind of intense emotion. Before him, she said, she had tucked away that part of herself, found a safe place inside her own head, and it wasn't there anymore.

He bristled as he suddenly understood where his guilt emanated from.

"There isn't a damn thing wrong with it, lady," he muttered, wondering how her carefully constructed emotional sanctuary had failed to lock *him* out.

Maybe that safe place is me. You'd rather I didn't love you? Left you buried alive?

He got out of the truck, wondering if maybe that was exactly what she wanted, at least on some level - and what that meant to them.

You won't even allow the idea of a future. It's like you can't see one. You won't even look.

He shoved the door shut with his foot.

I need to stop having an argument with a woman who isn't even here.

He caught his reflection in the window, and quickly composed himself.

"Hey, you," Sam called from the front window of the house. "Get in here."

Will looked up, managing a smile. "Yes'm. I'll be right there."

He dug his phone from his pocket, deciding that whatever else was going to happen, Maxine Allen was not going to win this round.

As he knew it would, her phone went directly to her voicemail, and he was prepared to leave a message that gave no indication of anything wrong between them.

"Hey, doll. Sammy told me. We need to talk. I'm tied up here for the evening, so if it's not okay for me to stop by around eight o'clock, call me back and let me know. I'll call when I'm on the road."

He studied his reflection in the window again as he slid the phone into his pocket, recalling something he said to Dave, back in the days when his friend was dying inside after losing Samantha:

She can escape lots of things - but she can't outrun the way you love her.

He nodded, resolved. "That's damn right," he mumbled.

chapter 4

"Mama?"

Brandi turned from the bathroom vanity mirror, hurriedly arranging her T-shirt to cover the scar on her shoulder.

"What is it, baby?"

"Gamsy's here. She says to hurry *up* already."

She bent down to place a quick kiss on Alexa's nose. "Go tell her I'll be out in a minute."

Alexa took off running. "Lexi - don't run in the house, okay?" she called after her. She turned back to the mirror, coaxing her auburn hair into a barrette, then skimming her lips with a red lipstick.

Her eyes drifted back to her shoulder, and she took one more look at the scar that the bullet had left there. That Simon had left there. She vaguely recalled being on morphine in the hospital, laughing hysterically, telling the nurses - who seemed horrified by her words - that Simon took the concept of "parting shot" to a whole new level.

I told them. I tried to tell everyone that he was going to kill me. Then he shoots me, and they buy his story that he didn't know what he was doing? Idiots.

"Brandi?" Her mother appeared in the doorway.

"Hi, Mom. I'm ready."

"What were you thinking about?"

"You know."

Her mother nodded. "You went redhead again. I love it."

"Me too. Simon hated it." She made a face in the mirror. "Screw you, Simon."

"Let's forget about him for a while. We need to get Lexi some clothes." She stroked her daughter's hair. "Life has to go on, baby."

"Life goes on," she mimicked her. "Yes, it does." She was tidying up the vanity, angrily stuffing hair bands and barrettes into a small wooden case. "Okay. Know what I'm thinking about? I'm wondering how I'm supposed to 'go on' in a world where some *psychopath* can sit in the middle of my life by virtue of the fact that he could *shoot sperm*."

Her mother busied herself by helping Brandi clean the vanity. "Did you talk to your lawyer?"

"Yeah. He'll do what he can, but Simon's gonna get visitation." She noticed that her mom was looking much older lately, somewhat pale and a little too thin, and she made herself calm down. "I'm sorry, Mom."

"It's okay, honey." She gave her a lingering kiss on the forehead. "Have you thought any more about moving home with us?"

"Yeah. I think I need to do that."

"So do Dad and I." She drew in a shaky breath, but her smile was genuine. "I have to say, I'm relieved."

"I keep thinking, I'm thirty years old, and I'll be living with my mommy and daddy." She shoved the box of her hair accessories into the cabinet with too much force, and it broke open, the contents spilling onto the counter.

"Oh..." Brandi picked up a small barrette that was decorated with ceramic daisies and roses. Two of the flowers had broken off, and her hands shook as she examined it. "Oh, no... Lexi's favorite..." She slowly looked to her mother, her eyes filling. "Mom, I broke Lexi's favorite barrette."

She leaned on the sink, pressing it to her heart while her mother held her.

"Mom," she gasped, "he's going to hurt her. *Don't let him hurt her.*"

She kissed her head, whispering, "We won't, baby. It's going to be okay."

But Brandi knew, like she knew in the weeks before Simon tried to kill her, that he was going to play the drama out to the end - and like before, no one was going to stop him.

※ ※ ※

Sam playfully ruffled Will's hair as he sat at the kitchen table. "You *so* need a haircut."

He tucked his hands behind his ears, comically fluffing his hair. "I've been told I look sexy this way."

"Dave, stop telling him he looks sexy."

Dave sat across from her, bouncing Hope on his lap. "Okay."

Tyler was giggling. "Good one, Mom." He glanced at his sister, chewing on her fingers while she stared at his plate. "Can I give her some of the sauce?"

"Just a little."

He scooped up a fingerful, rising halfway out of his chair to put it to her lips. She sucked it in eagerly, then Tyler shouted as her baby tooth came down on his finger.

"Bit you again?" Dave asked, amused.

"Yeah." He dunked his hand into his water glass, and the men erupted into laughter at the expression on Sam's face.

Tyler smiled at her hopefully. "Oops. Sorry, Mom."

"Finish your dinner. Is Brad still coming over?"

He nodded. "We're gonna try to learn his new guitar." He glanced at his father. "Brad's dad got him a brand new *guitar* for his birthday. Nice, huh?"

"Sure is," Dave said.

Tyler was hurriedly finishing his meal. "Brad's dad is really great."

"Sounds that way."

He sighed heavily, giving his father a look of resigned aggravation. "Mom's right." He chugged the rest of his water, and Sam groaned.

"Your *hand* was just in that glass, Ty. And what am I right about?"

"That Dad can't take a hint."

"Sure I can," Dave said. "You want a guitar. Next time, ask."

"Wow - really? You'll get me one?"

"We'll negotiate." The doorbell rang, and Dave said, "There's Brad. You all done?"

"Yeah."

"I'll get your plate. Go let him in. And keep the guitar in your room, okay? Hope has to go to bed soon."

Tyler gave his mother a quick kiss, then went around the table and hugged his father before he sprinted from the room.

Dave watched him run toward the front door. "Love that kid," he murmured.

"You're a lucky man, Delaney," Will said.

"Don't I know it."

"But you do realize that you're going into negotiations with an exceptionally intelligent nine-year-old, right?"

Dave laughed. "I'll call you in if I need you." He felt Hope relaxing in his arms. "She's falling asleep. I'll be back as soon as she's settled in."

"I'll have the coffee ready," Sam said. She tapped Will's hand as she got up. "You having any?"

He checked his watch. "Nope. It's almost six. I need to take off."

"You talked to Max?"

He shook his head. "Left her a message."

"So she'll be expecting you around seven?"

"Eight."

"Eight? Why are you leaving now...?" A smile spread across her face as she caught on. "Not making it easy for her."

"That's right. I want to see what she's going to do."

She turned serious then. "Will…"

"I know, Sammy. I'm playing the game only because at the moment, I have to." He rose from his chair. "She's kind of holding all the cards, you know?"

She turned on the coffeemaker, then pulled a travel mug from the cupboard. "What's going on with her?"

"You know her better than I do, kiddo. Any ideas?" He gathered several plates from the table, setting them on the counter behind him. "I've got only an outline."

"Outline?"

"Just a little bit about her father."

"Oh."

Will took note of her closed expression, and decided to let the awkward silence hang between them so she would keep talking.

Finally, Sam said, "She's had it bad."

He nodded, waiting.

Another minute went by, as Sam watched the coffee brew and Will watched her.

"Okay. Uncle." She looked up then. "What do you need?"

He sat at the counter. "Whatever you can tell me."

"I don't have as much as you might think, hon. Jo knew the details a lot better - they were older than me, closer in age, and I was more like the baby sister of the group."

She was wistful for a moment as she thought about the days of the three of them; then, she felt the rush of the guilty hatred that rose in her every time she thought about her ex. Jack had killed Jo almost a year earlier. He got sentenced to thirty years, but Sam often played with the thought that if he ever got out, she would kill him with her bare hands. Slowly. Like he did to Jo.

"Hey." Will was watching her, concerned. "You okay?"

"Yeah. Fine. Anyway, I just have snippets that I've managed to get out of Max, just here and there. And Dave, he doesn't talk much about her, but I think he knows more than I do." Her adrenaline started pumping as she thought about Jo again, then she shook it off.

"Her father was abusive, and I think it was a lot more than physical. For her *and* her mom." She took note of Will's hands balling into fists, and she covered them with her own, waiting for him to calm himself a bit before she continued.

"Any details?" His voice was raspy.

"The physical abuse, that's a fact. So-called 'spankings' that were actually beatings." She felt his hands tensing again. "You want to know more?"

He nodded.

"She's told me a few things that raise all the red flags about sexual abuse." She paused then, watching his face turn ashen.

He'd been hoping that Dave was wrong. "Give me some time here, Sammy," he said quietly.

A minute later, she asked, "Ready?"

"Yeah."

"She told me once that the good pastor made comments about her body. She was already chesty by the time she was fourteen, and he'd ridicule her for that - things like, she would come home from school and he'd ask, 'What did you and the twins do today, Maxeene?'"

She continued in spite of Will's groaning. "That's how he said her name, like he was mocking her. And he confided in her like you would a wife, back when she was a little girl. Lots of slandering her mother. And in high school, he chased away every boy who showed even the slightest interest in her. So what do *you* think the chances are that he didn't go after her?"

They stared at each other. Will could hear the faint sound of the music coming from Tyler's room, and the grandfather clock in the entry chiming six times, and he wanted to stay distracted so he wouldn't have to respond.

Finally, he said, "Zero."

"That's my feeling about it, too." She rubbed his hands briskly. "And that means you've got your work cut out for you, because she probably has a lot of triggers."

"Triggers." He nodded, recognizing it. "I know that term. It's…"

"Events, circumstances - things that remind her of him."

"What I don't know is how to avoid those."

"It's hard to do - it can happen at any time. Besides, if she's going to overcome them, she has to confront them, if you know what I mean." She sighed, apprehensive. "This won't be easy."

"Especially since I can't get her to hold still for a minute. The closer I get to her, the faster she withdraws."

"That's how she is with everyone."

He regarded her thoughtfully. "Not really. Not everyone. And she seems to push me away harder than anyone else."

"After she draws you in."

"So you see it too." He glanced at his watch, then toward the front door.

Sam nodded. She had never known Will to be so unsure of himself, and it was troubling her. He was the extrovert of the group, the confident, charismatic one - and he was changing.

"It's getting tough to handle, Sammy."

She asked hesitantly, "You're thinking of giving up on her?"

"No." He shook his head for emphasis. "I have bad moments, but no, I'm not."

"I do know this, Will." She filled the travel mug with coffee. "She loves you."

"I know it, too," he said. "And it's scaring her to death. So tell me this: do you do much work with women who were abused as kids?"

"When I can, which isn't often. There's no funding for after-abuse problems, for women *or* for children." She was tapping the cup on the counter, distracted as she added, "There isn't even much interest in the issue. Certainly, there's nothing out there for someone like Maxine."

"What can you tell me about it? About what happens to women like her?"

She was quiet while she considered it. "I think in a way, she hates being a woman." Then after a pause, she said, "No, that's not quite it. She hates how it *feels*, being a woman."

"That's something of a distinction without a difference."

"Not really. Think it over. She likes being female, but hates what it brings into her life. And the flip side," she added, looking at him pointedly, "is that men are not to be trusted. Period. And that church she grew up in, they were heavy into 'Jezebel' theology, so she didn't come out with a great perspective on women, either."

A thought occurred to him then. "So she's pretty much locked away from everyone. Trusts no one." His face went slack with the realization: "Even... Including *herself*."

"If there's such a thing as a 'typical' characteristic among the women I work for, that's it. No trust. I wonder sometimes if Max thinks that men are basically evil. In her case, if she had to do that old psych exercise - you know, the 'fall and I'll catch you' thing - she'd stand there and starve to death before she would trust anyone to catch her." Sam sat across from him at the counter with her chin in her hand, a look of longing on her face. "Jo was the first person she trusted in a very long time. And when she died, Max lost more than I think any of us realized."

"Is that a part of what's going on? Do you think being around me reminds her of that time?"

"I think it reminds her that you were there for her." She regarded him lovingly. "You were wonderful. So I really don't think that's what you need to focus on. It's the other things."

Will was thinking about Max's sarcasm, her hostility when she was stressed, especially because of him - and those episodes could occur suddenly, over anything. Or nothing at all. And the impression he had at those times, that she was dealing with someone else, was happening more and more often. "Sometimes, she reminds me of... I mean, my clients can be... Let's just say, they can get pretty ugly."

"Sure," Sam answered. "Think about their lives. How betrayed they are. They walk in to see you, and they're already primed for you to do the same thing."

"So, a kid growing up in that kind of hell is going to be, as an adult... What?"

"I don't know, Will. When it comes to Maxine, I'm not the expert I'd like to be." She handed him the travel mug. "And overall - generally, I mean - you probably know more about the issues than I do, because of your work. But that's what you need to figure out about Max. We don't have the details." She retained her grip on the cup as he grasped it, and their eyes met.

"Then I guess I'd better get busy," he said.

"Yeah. Just be careful, okay?" She let go of the cup, leaning forward to kiss his cheek. "With *both* of you, I mean. Because you matter, too."

Will thought about the many years that had passed since his fiancée died. Two hours after Michelle had accepted his proposal, a drunk driver ran a red light and hit Will's car - on Michelle's side - with enough force to knock her into Will's seat. Her head broke his collarbone, her elbow shattered his ribs, and she stared mutely into his eyes as he watched her die. He'd never been able to bring himself to tell anyone that he buried Michelle with their unborn child.

As his shock eventually gave way to grief, and Will felt his life go cold, he made a deliberate decision to stay that way. He'd had many relationships throughout the years, all shallow and just for the diversion, and none that he allowed for more than a few weeks. Most of them were unknown even to Dave, who was his only real friend until Dave and Sammy got married - and since then, Will had begun to open up more. But Maxine was the biggest surprise of his life, someone he never expected.

Sam was watching him, waiting for a response.

"Not this time," he said quietly. "I've spent half my life being careful with myself. No more."

She was uneasy as she said, "This may be way over your head, you know."

"Oh, it is." He took a sip of the coffee, thinking it over. "It absolutely is. But if I walk away from her, we both lose. If I hang in there... Well, look at what happens if I win." He looked out the window behind her, watching the new leaves stirring on the birch tree just outside the window, thinking about the miracle of spring and of things coming back to life. "She's lost, Sammy. But she's tearing me down, and I need to understand how to handle her."

"I've noticed it lately. You don't have the strut you used to have." She smiled apologetically at his bemused expression. "Seriously, Will - she's getting to you in some pretty unhealthy ways."

"So you miss my strut, huh?" he grinned.

"Yeah, I do." She touched his cheek. "You need to take it back. You *both* need for you to take it back."

His smile faded quickly. "You know, you're right. I'm not going to help her by letting her lead."

"I agree, as long as you keep some balance there."

He thought it an odd comment for her to make. "Of course," he said.

"I mean it, Will. You tend to be... Let's just say, you take charge pretty quickly."

"You're saying I'm..."

"Dominant."

He frowned. "I thought I was just assertive."

Sam was shaking her head as he spoke. "Dominant," she insisted. "Annoyingly Alpha-male. And if you want her to bolt, that's the quickest way to get her to the door."

"Seems I'm just getting my head handed to me today."

She tapped his nose. "Stop being a knuckle-dragging ape, and I'll be nicer."

They laughed together for a moment, then Sam turned solemn again as she said, "She needs you, Will. She's not doing well these days."

"I know. Sometimes, I think... It's like she lives in her own private hell, and comes out every now and then to take a look at what might have been."

Sam was nodding. "That's her. Exactly."

"If I let her call all the shots here, she'll stay right where she is."

"Hell's a pretty tough place to visit, though," Sam said. He was deep in thought, and she waited until he returned his attention to her. "Can be pretty hard to escape. Trust me."

"I know. But... I can't leave her where she is. I just can't."

She gazed at him gratefully. "You know I adore you, Will. And I don't want you hurt." Her voice trembled as she added, "But I love *her*, too, and I was really hoping you felt that way."

"Yeah, well, the way I see it," he slipped into his leather jacket, "the only thing worse than being in Hell is being abandoned there."

Dave came in then. "She's asleep," he said, reaching for the coffee. He turned to Will. "You outta here, Remmond?"

"Yeah. Listen, I'm all wrapped up at the office, and the Reynolds case is on coast. I'm gone 'til Tuesday."

Dave nodded. "Check in once or twice, okay? I'm extending the offer on the house in Hudson tonight."

"You bet." He bent to kiss Sam's cheek, thinking that he couldn't care less about the firm or where they were going to move it to. Not at that moment. "Thanks, kiddo. See you next week."

She grabbed him for a hug. "Go get her," she whispered.

"I will." He clapped Dave on the shoulder as he hurried past him. "Later."

※ ※ ※

Max finished storing her plates in the cupboard of her new kitchen, then turned to study the remaining boxes she had stacked in the living room, wondering which one held her coffeemaker.

"Should've marked all of 'em," she grumbled, scanning them for which one might contain her earrings, and thinking it was a good time to take a break. Instead, she reached for the one box that was labeled, the smallest one, which held the things she valued most. Several sheets of wadded newspaper filled the emptiness of it, and she thought about the year that had passed since she'd added anything to it.

She pulled out her ancient jewelry box. The lid had been stuck closed for as long as she could recall; now, it had a large crack in the wood. Mildly annoyed, she took it into the bedroom, staring at the emptiness there and reminding herself that she needed to find the box with the air mattress, if she wanted to avoid sleeping on the floor.

She returned to the living room and began rifling through the old photos and letters in the box. She came upon a poem she started when she was in high school - one she had added to with each loss she'd suffered throughout her life.

And now I see so clearly,
Me:
Alone before I knew you,
Desolate before I held you.
Adrift before I found you,

She thought it interesting - prophetic, she decided - that the final line ended in a comma.

As she reached into her purse for a pen, her hand closed around the Christmas picture, and she put it on the floor beside her as she sat with the poem in her lap.

Ruined before I loved you.

She began to cry as she added:

Me, alone again.
Me, a willing widow,

Her need to see him was growing, and she felt trapped by it, out of control. The pain on his face the night before was like a pounding in her head.

*I'm ruining **him**. This whole thing is impossible.*

"It doesn't have to *be* that way," she whispered. "Does it?"

She tossed the poem to the side and buried her face in her hands.

Drawing in a trembling breath, she grabbed it and put it back into the box; then, on an impulse, she placed the picture on top of it. There was a remnant of her that wasn't done, not yet, and she was clinging to it.

*That's the life I left behind. Maybe this entire **box** is just that - the life I left behind.*

As she hurriedly stuffed the newspaper back into the box, she thought, *Not much of a life in there.*

A quick check of her cell told her it was after seven o'clock already. She wondered if Will was on his way, hating the ambivalence of trying to decide whether or not to dodge him, and confused by the amiable tone of the message he left earlier that day. As she sat there contemplating it, a call from him came in, and she hit *Ignore* before she realized that he would know she had done so.

She ran her fingers across the screen, caressing the picture of the two of them while she waited for the message indicator to light up.

"Wow. That was one quick 'ignore' there." Will waited for Max's voicemail greeting to end, then kept his tone light as he said, "On my way, darlin'. See you in a bit."

He was pulling into the parking lot of her apartment complex as he left the message, searching for a spot where he could see her car, but where she would be unlikely to notice his. He found a place just beyond a cluster of forsythias at the corner of her building, and backed into the spot so he was mostly hidden but still had an unobstructed view.

Fifteen minutes ticked slowly by before she emerged from the building and walked quickly to her car. Will was caught off guard by a rush of disappointment; after all, she was doing exactly what he expected she would do - yet as he watched her, he willed her to turn back. He regretted deceiving her, and he didn't want to confront her in that way.

She suddenly stepped back and kicked the door shut, resolutely turning her back to it and leaning against her car. She was typing something into her cell. He watched her walk quickly back into the building as his phone started buzzing.

Buy me dinner?

His chest was tight, and he realized that he needed to take a few breaths, which he did before he answered:

You bet.

The wallpaper on his phone was his favorite picture of the two of them, the one he had gotten the old man to take on that perfect autumn day in Portland. He smiled softly, remembering how he tickled her just before the man snapped the picture. He loved the laughter on her face. And he recalled how he was different then, stronger, someone she could lean on. She trusted him then, and she didn't anymore - and Dave was right. Much of it was his own fault.

He mocked himself for a moment, thinking of how he had messed things up, and longing for who they once were.

Stop it. That isn't what she needs. One of us has got to be okay here, or she'll pull us both under.

He waited for another ten minutes, making several decisions in that time - the first being that he would never again play detective with her; then he started the truck and pulled it into the space next to her car. His heart was racing. He needed to see her, had been waiting for it all day, and now he was too nervous and distracted to think clearly.

Her engagement ring was still in his pocket, and he put his hand over it. He knew, of course, that he wouldn't be doing anything with it. Not yet. But he was keeping it with him like an amulet, like a talismanic piece of a dying hope that he couldn't let go of. And the abrupt, vivid mental image he got of himself shocked him.

He remembered taking her to an orchard in early October, a week before their day in Portland, and not far from where he was at that very moment. They spent the afternoon picking apples, wandering through the fields hand in hand, talking about their relationship.

Max had spread their blanket under a Paula Red tree, sitting with her legs tucked under her, holding her hand out for Will to join her.

"When Jo died," she said, "I thought I'd never be that close to anyone again. She was my best friend, really the only one I ever had, and I thought she would be the last."

Will remembered the way the sun lit up her hair, and the look in her eyes as she offered him one of the apples. Her shyness as she held it out to him, smiling as she said, "You're my best friend, Remmond. You really are." It was the first time that he had ever seen her truly content.

I let you down, Maxine. I've been in this for all the wrong reasons.

He pulled the ring from his pocket and placed it carefully in the glove compartment, making one final decision: he would remove from the equation the one dominant power that she had over him - because she needed her best friend back, for however long it took for her to confront the things that were destroying her.

Max's name wasn't on the directory of the secured building. He cast about in his mind, trying to remember her apartment number, and he laughed quietly as it came to him: Max had called him right after she signed the lease, saying, "Apartment 208. If you need a memory prompt, that's the same as my I.Q."

He pushed *208*, ignoring the thought that she wouldn't respond, and opened the door when the buzzer sounded. He took brief notice of the fact that he had lost the urge to sprint up the stairs to the second floor.

There you go, Sammy. Working on the "strut."

The door swung open immediately when he knocked. Her expression was pleasantly noncommittal, and she sounded fully detached as she said, "Hi, Will."

He leaned against the door frame, holding his keys out to her. "You pick it, doll."

Her façade began to crumble. Her eyes filled up as she shook her head in disbelief.

Quietly, he said, "Let's go."

chapter 5

It seemed to Will that they bolted from New Hampshire like they were shot from a cannon.

"Seventy-five." He was leaning close to her, checking the speedometer. "When did you grow a lead foot?" Stroking her hand where it rested on the wheel, he said, "Hey, you're white-knuckling pretty good there, darlin'. Relax."

She nodded, rolling her shoulders and then her head. "I really needed to get out of Boston today."

"I know."

She glanced at him. "You always do."

They crossed the Piscataqua Bridge into Maine just after sunset. "So we're safely out of New Hampshire now," Will joked. He pointed ahead. "So let's get you some dinner."

Max made a quick assessment of her faded jeans and frayed sweatshirt. "We'll go casual," she said. She whipped into the parking lot of a small bar and grill, pointing to the sign that said *Two Dollar Drafts*. "Want to be the designated driver?"

"No problem." He came around to the driver's side, opening the door for her and offering her his hand.

It had become his habit to give her a quick kiss as he pulled her from the high cab of his truck. She was puzzled when this time, he set her on her feet without an embrace of any kind.

The restaurant was almost empty, and they found a booth with a view of the harbor.

"It's spooky-beautiful at night, isn't it?" she asked, gazing at the lights that danced across the water.

"Sure is." They ordered their drinks, then Will asked, "Any idea where we're going tonight?"

"Nope. Well... Why?"

"I'm assuming that at some point, you may want to sleep. Thought I'd call a hotel."

She was silent for a minute, busying herself by looking for something in her purse. When she answered, Will had to lean close to hear her.

"I want to go to Portland," she said softly, and Will heard the longing in her tone.

Their drinks arrived then. She slid from the booth without looking at him, mumbling, "Order for me. I'll be right back."

She wound her way around the tables in the cramped dining room, stopping to ask a server where the rest rooms were. Will watched her, mildly amused.

No worries, Maxine.

He ordered their meals, then pulled his phone from his pocket. Max overheard what he was saying as she returned to the table.

"... two side-by-side rooms?" He paused. "How's about across from each other?"

She slid into the booth and waited while he finished making the reservations.

"Done," he said as he set the phone on the table. Taking in the confusion on her face, he asked, "What's up?"

"So... You got us each a room, right?"

"Of course." He watched her down half of her drink.

"Okay. I just... Never mind." She chugged the rest of it, setting the mug on the table with a thud. "That was too good." As she tucked her legs under her, settling in, she said, "I guess we should talk."

Will signaled the bartender for a refill for her. "We will. When you're ready."

That wasn't the response she expected, and she puffed her cheeks out as she exhaled loudly. "Okay, Will. What's going on?"

He shrugged. "Whatever you decide is going on." He gently pushed her bangs out of her eyes, then briefly caressed her cheek as he added, "Nothing more, nothing less."

"Don't be cryptic. We unraveled last night because I didn't want to talk."

He noticed that she was watching him intently, instead of looking just beyond him, and he knew he was on to something. "I've done some thinking today, that's all."

"Oh, wait..." She smirked knowingly. "Is this reverse psych?"

"No." He frowned, wondering if they were actually about to argue over why they weren't talking. "It isn't. I don't do that."

"You sure? Like, I wouldn't talk last night, so now we just aren't going to talk at all?"

She was becoming frustrated, and Will wasn't sure if that was what he wanted, or if it was even a good thing for her. It certainly wasn't helping him out, not in any way.

"Max, it's fine. If you want to talk, then let's do it."

"Oh, please. Don't you *dare* patronize me." Her refill arrived then, and she drained almost half of it again before she spoke, regarding him with a wariness that had him questioning his own motives. "Well played, sir," she said, lifting the mug to salute him.

He felt a flash of anger; then, a realization hit him, one so vivid that it rendered him speechless for a moment:

Oh no you don't. That's not who I am.

Will had no idea where the thought came from, but he was glad for it. Guilt was trying to rise in him again; and this time, he wasn't going to allow it. He had done nothing wrong.

He sat back in the booth, rolling and unrolling the edge of a napkin for a few seconds before he responded.

He looked directly into her eyes, his voice so soft that she strained to hear him. "Don't do that, Maxine. Don't accuse me of being someone I'm not." Her eyes shifted to the side then, and he said, "Look at me, please."

She seemed a bit shaken as she did so, and he consciously made his voice and his expression as gentle as possible. "Sometimes I get the feeling that you're talking to someone else."

Her eyes remained fixed on his, but her expression became a cold, practiced indifference. "Well, I'm sorry you feel that way."

Let her off the hook.

"That's very generous of you, Ms. Allen," he said, copying her formal tone as he took her hand, "because it does kind of suck."

It lightened the moment as he hoped it would, and she burst into surprised laughter.

"So," he continued, "you let me know when you're ready to talk. In the meantime, let's disappear from life as we've known it."

Her senses were on alert. Something in his attitude was making her nervous. "Sounds good," she said.

They settled in to a more comfortable mood of enjoying the evening, talking about what the plan was for their vacation, and deciding in the end not to make any plans. They shared their meals with each other, and were getting up to leave when the tavern started filling again for the band that was setting up at the far end of the room.

"Want to hang around for one more?" Will asked, pointing to her empty mug.

"Getting me drunk, huh?"

"Getting you to unwind."

"I'm doing both," she laughed, watching the people filing in. "But I think I'd rather hit the road."

He took her jacket from the back of her chair, holding it for her as she slipped into it. "You're sure you wouldn't rather stay? We haven't danced in a while."

"I'm sure." She flicked her hair to the outside of the jacket, smiling up at him. "I'm beat."

"Okay." He took her hand to lead her through the crowd. "We're Portland-bound, then."

They rode in silence for a few miles, then Max asked, "So what happened to you last night?"

He grinned. "I figured you knew. Sammy told you?"

She nodded, reflecting again on the course of his life since he met her.

"It was just a brawl," he said, extending his body in a cat-stretch from the legs up as he settled in to tell her.

Max was distracted by her reaction to watching him extend his body that way. He was tall, and athletic, and she thought that he knew exactly how handsome he was. And sometimes, like now, she wondered if he did things like that just to get to her.

She crossed and uncrossed her legs, nervous because he was different somehow. More in control than he had been recently, and that made her feel less in control. And she didn't like it.

"Parts of the night are kind of hazy," he was saying, "but I drove around after I left your place. Decided to stop in at Rowdy's Pitstop..."

"Rowdy's?" she gasped. "That dive over on Bennet?"

"Yeah. I think I was uniquely self-destructive last night." He caught the distress on her face, and quickly added, "I was having a hard time believing I talked to you the way I did."

Her mouth fell open. "The way *you* talked to *me*?"

"Yeah. Anyway, I'm at the bar - probably on my seventh or eighth bourbon, so I'm gettin' there - minding my own business, and this skinny, twenty-something redhead parks herself on the stool beside me. Within a few minutes, she's trying to work her way onto my lap."

He was chuckling, while Max felt a grip of jealousy that was unlike anything she had experienced before. "Charming," she muttered.

"No, not really," Will said. "Turns out she was mad at her boyfriend, and wanted to see what he'd do if she hung herself on another guy."

"So of course, she picked *you*." At this point, Max was chewing on her bottom lip. She wondered how he could be so completely clueless, talking about a lap-riding little redhead as if it was all a big joke.

"And here comes Junior..."

"The boyfriend?"

"Yup. Comes over just after the girl takes her jacket off and starts hanging all over me. He's giving me crap, and I'm trying to ignore him and get out from under his girlfriend, and then she tells him she's going home with *me*." He rubbed the stubble on his chin, smiling broadly.

"*Really*, now?"

Will nodded, caught up in telling the story, oblivious to her reaction. "I said, 'No, little girl, you're not. But thanks anyway,' and she gets the offended thing going and throws her drink in my face. If I remember correctly, that's when Junior got really upset. He started mouthing off about how I 'dissed' his woman - and worse, that she wasted a seven-dollar drink." He was laughing aloud now; and Max, in spite of herself, was starting to find it humorous, as well.

"So Junior takes a swing at me - and this guy's a peanut, maybe one-twenty, soaking wet - so I ducked it and put him in a headlock while I finished my drink."

Max burst into uncontrollable laughter as Will said, "He's squealing and swearing, wriggling like a bunny rabbit trying to get away, and two of his buddies jumped me. They were no bigger than he was, so *that* was a one-two layout. Then I remember looking around for Junior, yelling something about wanting 'Bunny' to come back."

She was wiping at her eyes, catching her breath. "Where was he?"

"No idea. Disappeared into the night." He sighed dramatically. "Bittersweet, it was. Never got to give him the goodbye I wanted to."

"Tragic."

"Yeah. And the next thing I knew, Jimmy O'Sullivan was putting the cuffs on me."

"Sammy said he's a friend, huh?"

"He owed me a couple of favors. I took care of his brother on a few minor issues, pro-bono."

"So, what happened to the skinny little redhead?"

He shrugged. "Don't know." He glanced in her direction, hearing the edge in her voice. "I assume she left with Junior."

"Mmm." She laid her head against the headrest, closing her eyes. "I'm sleepy. Thanks for the bedtime story."

"You relax. We'll be there in half an hour."

"Will?"

"Yeah?"

She opened her eyes, staring straight up as she said, "I just got jealous."

"I wondered. Sorry..."

She shook her head. "Don't. You didn't do anything wrong."

Her words went through him with a jolt. She had never before said anything like that. Usually, she seemed to want him to feel guilty.

"Okay," he said, nodding once.

"I'm trying to recall a time, any time, that I was ever jealous over a *man*." She turned her head to face him then.

He was skeptical. "You're telling me you never felt that way before?"

"I never allowed it. The last thing I was *ever* going to do was fight for a man."

It occurred to him that she was, at that moment, more open than he had ever known her to be, and he restrained himself from trying to get too much from her too quickly.

"You think that's weird, huh?" she asked.

"I don't know. Maybe you just know your worth." He knew that wasn't the case, but he didn't know what else to say to her. And it would keep her talking.

She lifted her head from the rest, sitting forward with her forearms on her thighs. "No, I just hated the whole idea. I remember in high school, I thought the girls who got into catfights were morons. Like, what guy is *worth* that?"

"What were you like then?"

"Huh? In high school?"

"High school, college..."

"Oh, I was the quintessential good girl until..." she stopped, seeming confused. "In high school..." She laughed nervously. "Whatever. I was... It's boring."

She was stammering, and he decided to stop there.

"I need a drink," she sighed.

He didn't agree, but he said, "There's a bar at the hotel." Glancing at the dashboard clock, he added, "Should still be open for a while."

She laid her head back again and closed her eyes. "Wake me up when we get there."

A good girl until, she had said. Will thought that could mean a lot of things.

They made the rest of the trip in silence. As he turned into a long, winding driveway, Will reached to the side and rubbed Max's leg gently.

"Hey, doll. Wake up. We're here."

She opened her eyes slowly, then sat up to look around. Seeing the building, she broke out laughing. "Holy cow," she swung her head to stare at him. "Are you *kidding* me?"

Will was parking the truck on the circular drive that led to a massive private estate - an antique Federalist, perched on a rise that looked out over the ocean. Max took in the lights, and the manicured grounds, and craned her neck to see the ocean view at the back of the main building.

"Yeah, sorry. The Dew-Drop Inn was booked solid." He came around to open the door for her, but she was already climbing out, reaching for him to lift her to the ground.

She was laughing with delight, and she threw her arms around his neck as he set her on her feet. "You *beautiful man*," she squealed. "I can't *believe* you did this."

He let himself hold her close. It was something he'd never been called before, and suddenly, he felt ten feet tall.

She pulled back, her eyes wide with her excitement; then, her expression became like a caress, as she looked from his eyes to his mouth. Standing there with his arms filled with her - the woman who held a life for him that he never saw coming, whom he never expected he would love so completely - he felt his resolve melting away.

Not yet.

He took her face in his hands and kissed her forehead. "Let's check in," he said softly, taking her by the shoulders and putting her firmly away from him.

He scolded himself for the momentary amusement he felt as she touched her lips, because the confusion on her face was painful to him. But he knew he was doing what she needed - what they both needed, although he hadn't yet figured out how it would work. His intuition was telling him that his passion for her, and her ambivalence - even hostility - toward it was masking the truth. That same instinct told him that Max's passion for *him* might be an even bigger issue.

Still, the sudden tension in his body was difficult to endure, so he distracted himself by hurriedly retrieving their overnight bags from the back of the truck's cab. He threw them over his shoulder, then extended his hand to her. "Come on."

She nodded, reluctantly taking his hand. She was watching him with that same look of uncertainty, and he thought again that he was on to something. She was looking directly at him a lot more than she normally did.

A pleasant, elderly woman with a thick Mainer accent was at the front desk. Max stared at Will, astonished, when she heard the woman say, "Five nights, Mr. Remmond, is that right?"

On their way up the stairs to the second floor, she said, "We're staying here 'til Monday?"

"If that's what we want to do. No plans, remember?"

"You're spending a fortune on this."

"It's not so bad." They were at her door, and he added, "It'll be worth it."

"Oh, *really?*"

She was looking at him with suspicion again, and Will knew what she was thinking. He tamped down the exasperation he felt, then realized that his exasperation was probably a healthy response: the woman was giving him whiplash, with the way her mood could do an instantaneous one-eighty. A few minutes before, she wanted to be kissed; now, she was making insinuations. But she was failing in satisfying her need to make him feel like a predator, and he was glad he had made that much progress within himself.

Deciding it best to ignore the accusation he heard in her comments, he responded with a simple, "Absolutely."

Will took the suite that looked out over the grounds, giving Max the one that faced the ocean. He dropped her bag by the door as she gaped at the beauty of the room: it was twice the size of her apartment, with high ceilings, and windows that were almost as tall as Will. It had gleaming hardwood floors, and was decorated in a seacoast theme, with varying shades of blue and beige. A king-size bed, with the pale blue bedding already turned down, was positioned in such a way that the first thing Max would see in the morning was the ocean.

Will watched her blissfully take it all in, his enjoyment of the moment tempered only by the fact that she could be so completely awed by it. He thought that he should have done this much sooner.

She gasped as she peered through the sliding doors which opened to an expansive balcony.

"Oh, Will..." She waved him over. "Come look." She slid the door open, stepping out into the stiff breeze that was blowing in off of the ocean. Wrapping her arms around herself, she moaned, "Ooh, it's chilly out here."

He stood behind her, vigorously rubbing his hands up and down her arms to warm her. "Told you it would be worth it," he said, smiling down at her as she turned her head to look up at him. He bent to rest his head on her shoulder, against her neck, wrapping his arms around her as she reached up to cup his cheek.

They stayed that way for a long moment, gazing out over the water, before Max whispered, "You were right."

After a few more minutes, she started to shiver. Will said, "Let's get settled in."

Max sighed regretfully, then shook her head.

"It'll all be here in the morning, Max. Let's get you warmed up."

"One more minute. You can keep me warm." She turned to face him, curling up against his chest, laying her head against him as she sighed again. "It's like Heaven here."

He tightened his arms around her and rested his chin on top of her head. The sound of the ocean, the rhythmic lapping of the waves on the rocks, was having a hypnotic effect on him. He struggled to keep his eyes open, remembering that he hadn't slept at all the night before - and then, he felt Max going limp in his arms.

He tensed his arms, catching her as her legs gave way.

"Wow," she said, pulling back to look up at him, "I guess I'm tired."

"Damn. I thought I had the power to make your knees buckle."

He thought she would laugh. Instead, she clasped her hands behind his neck, her eyes on his, and she said nothing.

"Just a joke," he grinned.

She raised her eyebrows, smiling faintly. "Maybe to *you*."

It occurred to him that her cryptic, witty comebacks were yet another of her escape hatches. He stopped himself from asking what she meant, asking instead, "Ready to go inside?"

Her mouth dropped open, just a little, like she was about to say something but thought better of it.

"Sure." She turned abruptly, and Will thought she actually stomped her feet as she went back into her room.

Guess she's doing another one-eighty here.

He closed the glass door carefully, turning around to see Max standing in the middle of the room with her hands on her hips, openly glaring at him.

Here we go.

He regarded her quietly, thinking again about two boxers in the ring.

She folded her arms. "I want to know what's wrong with you."

Will stayed silent, waiting for her to vent it out.

"I mean, you're being wonderful, and affectionate and charming and funny, and doing all these sweet, sexy things that you know will get to me. And yet, I feel like you're sidestepping everything I say. Like you're sidestepping *me*."

Will was struck by the fact that she was, unknowingly, describing exactly how he had felt for so long - and that what he had unintentionally done was to give her a look at his side of their relationship.

He opened his mouth to say so, then decided to let her figure it out for herself. "I know," was all he said.

"I mean, you act like you want me, but it's like you're *playing* with me. 'Come here, go away, no thanks.' You're just running hot and cold - like you won't..." Her voice trailed off then, and Will saw the light go on.

She looked at her feet, uncrossing her arms and jamming her hands into the pockets of her jeans. "So, it isn't reverse psychology."

"No."

She glanced at him then, quickly averting her eyes. "It's payback."

"*No*," he snapped, and that brought her attention back to him immediately.

Will knew it was not the right time to have a discussion, because they were both exhausted and not thinking clearly; but that comment, he decided, was one that they couldn't sleep on.

He gestured toward the bed. "Have a seat."

She perched on the edge of the bed, her head down, so dejected that his stomach turned over. He crouched on the floor in front of her.

"Look at me." His voice was almost a whisper.

She did, and he took her hands in his. "What you just said - the way you're feeling, how it's a lot like what I've been going through - that was all an unintended consequence of those decisions I mentioned."

"Okay," she mumbled listlessly.

"Want to know what I've been thinking about?"

"Sure."

"I'm not going to agree with what you think of me, Max. More than that, though - I'm not going to agree with what you think of *yourself*."

She was listening, he could see that. He thought she would ask what he meant, but her response surprised him:

"Good." She laid back on the bed, covering her eyes with her arm. "Good for you."

"Is that sarcasm?"

She shook her head. "No, I mean it. I know I'm a mess."

"Maxine..."

She propped herself up on her elbows then, studying him suspiciously. "Tell me the truth. Are you still attracted to me?"

He erupted into laughter. "Is that a serious question?"

"*Yes*," she snapped, offended. "I want to know. You seem to have an awful lot of self-control going on here."

"I'm sorry, darlin'. I shouldn't laugh." He pulled her up to a sitting position, holding her hands as he answered, "Yes. Of course I am."

She seemed unconvinced. "Well, that's nice to know."

Will wondered how long she would remain appreciative of the fact that he wanted to sleep with her, because it certainly was an issue at other times.

He saw that she was still doubtful, and he said, "And you don't believe me."

She shrugged.

He drew a deep, frustrated breath, thinking of several things to respond with and knowing that none of them would work. Finally, he said, "Lady, you go through me like a *laser*."

That got her attention, and he hurried to continue. "But there's a problem here, and we can't pretend nothing's wrong. You use how I feel about you as proof that you're right about me, and we need to back up. Figure things out. Because I want you long-term."

She was searching his eyes. He ran his hands through her hair to the back of her neck, remembering how he had done that the first time he kissed her.

He added, "As in, forever."

He thought she would bolt, and he waited for it, but she appeared to be thinking it over.

"So... We back up? What's the plan here?" she asked.

Will sat beside her on the bed. "Don't have one. Not really, because I don't know what we're up against. And I want you to trust me enough to tell me, however we get there."

"So until I... What?"

"Until we figure out what's wrong," he took her hand again, looking at her regretfully, "I guess we're back to being best friends."

"I don't think I can do that. Can you?"

"Doubt it." He put his arm around her shoulders, pulling her to him, and they were quiet for a while.

"Will?"

"Hmm?"

"I've really been bad for you, haven't I?"

"What? *No.* Maxine..." He stood, bowing his head, worn out but knowing he needed to resolve it. "If anything, I haven't been what you needed. Look," he crouched before her again, "a long time ago, I lost the ability to feel for anyone the way I feel about you. That part of me was dead. And you know, the truth is, I didn't want it resurrected. I was perfectly happy to leave myself just as I was. Safe."

He paused, waiting until she looked at him.

"And you know how that is, right?" he asked.

Her eyes widened as she understood what he was saying.

"Yeah," he nodded, "we *are* a lot alike, aren't we?"

"I... Guess we are. Wow."

"So then I meet you, and suddenly I'm not so content anymore with what I've been." He paused, smiling nostalgically. "The day we met, that first dance... Women like hearing the 'what were you thinking when' stuff, right?"

She smiled. "Yup."

"It was like I was flat on my back. You were looking up at me, talking about Dave and Sammy and the wedding, and I kept losing track because I never saw *eyes* like yours before. And I was actually thinking, where the hell have you been all my life?"

She rolled her eyes. "Oh my gosh, Will, that's bad."

"I know. And I've had that same thought every day since."

Max pushed the wind-blown hair from his forehead.

Me too.

"Don't tell Delaney," Will was saying. "He'll beat me senseless with it."

"Deal."

"So, now I'm not safe anymore, and yeah - that makes me nervous." He rose, pulling her to her feet.

"I just wonder what I've done to your life."

"I didn't have a life, darlin'. And that makes you a miracle."

The expression on his face, mixed with the guilt she felt, brought tears to her eyes.

He ran his thumb across her cheek, wiping a tear away. "I'm not walking away from this," he whispered.

She took his hand from her face, turning it over to kiss his palm, then intertwined her fingers with his. Their eyes met, and it seemed to him that she wanted to say, "I love you," but he knew that she wouldn't - and he decided that it was something he could live with.

"Thanks for coming to get me tonight."

"Thanks for running away with me." He kissed her cheek. "Let's get some sleep."

She reached for him then, wrapping her arms around his neck and burying her face against him. "I'm sorry," she whispered. "It's all such a mess. I don't want to hurt you."

"I know." He held her close, relieved that it was settled for now. "I know that."

"I don't know how to do this. Loving you should be easy."

Will closed his eyes, leaving her words suspended between them for a moment before he said, "I love you, too."

chapter 6

I LOVE YOU, too. It echoed in her head. She'd thought he would never say it again.

Max was still mostly asleep as she reached for him, opening her eyes slowly and wondering why he wasn't there; then, she came more fully awake.

Why would he be here? We've never woken up together.
Yes, we did.

Until that moment, she had managed to bury her memories of New Year's Eve, preferring to assign her behavior that night to too little sleep and too much champagne.

And a drop-dead gorgeous man in a tux.

She rolled onto her back and closed her eyes again, hoping she could go back to sleep before the thoughts came, but knowing they would surface anyway.

He'll never understand. I don't even understand. I just can't be normal.

She cringed inside as she thought about how aggressive she was that night, the way she was hanging on Will at the party, deliberately arousing him just because she could.

No. I couldn't do that. Not to him.

But she knew she had done exactly that. She hadn't behaved that way in years, the way she was with Will that evening. She recalled getting ready for the party, slipping into the dress she bought for it - it was short, and tight, and it hid nothing. But it was perfect for going to an elegant holiday party, which was another thing she hadn't done in years. She remembered her excitement as she twirled in front of the mirror, watching it sparkle, admiring herself - and the way Will looked at her when she opened the front door.

It took him a moment; then he said, in that lazy drawl he had sometimes, "Darlin', you really are the most beautiful woman I've ever seen."

I felt alive.

Then he teased her about the dress, asking where the rest of it was, and something tilted inside her. Laying there now, she clearly remembered the feeling: it was like a contemptuous defiance, the same passive-aggressive animosity that she had so often felt throughout her life.

Her father's face superimposed itself on the memory, and she recalled how he spat out words like "wanton" and "whorish" when he saw a woman who was dressed in a way that he deemed immoral.

*Yeah? Well watch **this**, you prick.*

Her eyes flew open, and she threw the covers back, sitting up quickly. She stared at the empty place beside her.

"Leave me *alone*," she hissed, unsure which man she was saying it to.

She felt the need for something normal, something to bring her outside of her own head. She opened the drawer of the nightstand, fumbling for the remote control, thinking she might find a weather report on the TV.

It came on with a commercial for a lingerie company, some kind of a prime-time "fashion" show, and Max couldn't suppress a groan as she was confronted with the images of the mostly-nude women.

*What the hell are you **doing** in here?*

She gasped, frozen, as she remembered the magazines in her father's office. The naked women, with their legs spread open and their hands caressing their own bodies. Their eyes were half-closed, and Max remembered that even as a seven-year-old, she knew she was looking at something evil.

She recalled how she had no idea, not then, what it was they were doing - but there were so *many* pictures. Men with women, women with women, three and four people in all sorts of positions. And the women all had their mouths hanging open. Some had their tongues out like they were waiting for Communion.

*I asked you a **question**, Max-eene. What are you doing in my office?*

But she had been shocked by the images, and she was terrified of her father, and she couldn't respond.
Her mother had come in then.

Come with me, Maxine.

Max recalled studying her mother intently, repelled by her, wondering if she looked like the women in the pictures - and then wondering if she, herself, would also look so disgusting one day.
He was going to kill me.
Vestiges of her deadened memories were dodging in and out of her conscious mind: her bedroom door flying open, her mother screaming. The wind blowing the curtains inward, and the rain coming in, landing on her bare feet.
On his back.
She cried out, not realizing she had done so.
The phone on the nightstand was ringing. Her hands trembled as she pushed the hair from her face and reached to answer it.
"Morning, doll," Will was saying. "Get some good sleep?"
She cleared her throat, still shaken. "I sure did."
"You just woke up?"
"Yeah. You?"

"Heck, no. I've been up for two hours. Went for a run, cleaned up, I'm ready to go."

Max scanned the room. "There's no clock in here. What time is it?"

"Almost ten."

"Wow. Sorry."

"You needed the sleep. Hit the shower, and we'll go get breakfast."

She set the phone down, realizing that she was desperate to see Will.

An hour later, she knocked softly on his door.

"It's unlocked," he called out.

She peeked inside. Will was on his cell, and he held up a finger, then pointed to the phone. "You bet, Em... Yeah, I'll talk to her right now, but I think you can go ahead and count on us... I will. 'Bye."

"What's up?"

"C'mon in. That was Dave's mom." He gave her an admiring once-over as she stepped into his room. "Damn, you're beautiful."

Max looked down at her faded jeans and red tank top, deciding against making a joke about his standards. "Thanks," she smiled.

But she loved it when he talked like that. He had a way about him, a good ol' boy attitude, one made all the more enticing by the fact that he certainly didn't live like a good ol' boy. He carried a briefcase and wore tailored suits to work, and Max had been in the courtroom many times as he did battle for his clients. One of the many arrogant, hostile judges - one whom Will often wound up in front of - had a habit of mocking him, commenting that Will was "truly, *truly* a passionate advocate." He was, and Max thought he was brilliant. And she admired Will's restraint, because he never let it get to him. He was one of only a very few lawyers who specialized in defending mothers, and as a result, he was hated by most of the players in the system. But he seemed to never even notice the barbs that got thrown at him.

Then at the end of the day, Will parked his black sedan - his "status crate," he called it - in the garage. He tossed aside his suit and his briefcase, put on jeans and a flannel shirt, and became the guy who drove an old pickup truck, with nothing on his mind more pressing than scoring good seats at a Red Sox game.

He opened his arms to her, and she snuggled against him for a lengthy hug. "What did Emily want?" she asked.

"I think you and I forgot what this Saturday is."

Max pulled back, puzzled. "What?"

"Dave and Sammy's..."

She moaned. "That's right. Their first anniversary."

"Sean and Em are throwing them a surprise party Sunday evening, after they get back from Boston. We're invited."

"Oh." She smiled regretfully. "Guess we'll be cutting this a day short."

He cocked his head, tightening his arms around her as he looked down at her. "You're liking it here, huh?"

She took a deep breath, and Will had the impression that she was gearing up to say something that was difficult for her.

"I like being here with you," she murmured.

He didn't respond, but Max saw something playful in his eyes.

She bumped her body against his, feigning offense. "Look, Remmond, you're supposed to say something like, 'Me too.'"

"I don't know, Maxine," he drawled. "Not much action here. This platonic routine is tough to take."

"That's *your* choice, buddy. Not mine."

His eyes drifted to her lips. "Yeah. I think I must be crazy," he said softly.

"No, you're just really smart."

"And getting really frustrated." He kissed her forehead, then pulled her close again.

"And I think..." She paused, unsure, and then decided to say it. "I think maybe you do love me."

She felt his reaction. His body tensed for just a second, and she drew back to see the emotion on his face.

"Yeah," he whispered. "I do." He blinked a few times, running his thumb along her bottom lip. "You know, I woke up this morning, and it felt wrong - unnatural - that you weren't next to me."

"I know what you mean."

"You do?"

She nodded, then stood on tiptoe to kiss his cheek. "I did some thinking this morning. I'm starting to get what you're doing. And I get why you're doing it..."

"Sounds like there's a 'but' there."

"I don't think I'll ever be normal."

Will shrugged. He didn't want her to say it was hopeless. "What's 'normal', anyway?"

"You're gonna get hurt, Will. More than you already have."

"Not your problem." He let her go then, turning to grab his wallet and keys from the dresser. "And you need to do better than that, if you want to talk me out of this."

He expected her to deflect it, to respond with a witty comment, but she didn't.

Max said, "That's the last thing I want."

"Is that right?" He put his arm around her shoulders as they left the room, thinking that things were going much better than he had hoped for. "Let me buy you breakfast, and we'll talk it over."

By noon, they were walking hand-in-hand back to the hotel, continuing the debate they started over breakfast.

"All I'm saying is, if you don't have a norm someplace - a fixed point of reference - then you have no standard with which to assess *any* behavior," Max insisted.

"Bit of a fallacy there, Maxine, since it's the culture itself that defines 'normal'."

"That's just it. You're mud-stuck on trying to define the concept. I'm trying to explore its application."

His head was spinning. She had been debating him for the better part of an hour, and efficiently taking him apart. "Okay, wait. Let's say there is such a thing as 'normal'." He ran a hand through his hair, trying to fashion a comment that would stump her, and knowing he couldn't. "Actually, you know what? You win. Uncle."

"*Score.*" She moved in front of him, walking backwards and using both hands to point at him, chanting, "You. Tapped. *Out.*"

He laughed, regarding her with a mixture of admiration and pride. "Honors in Philosophy. I should know when I'm in over my head."

"Darn right, Remmond."

At the hotel, they strolled around to the back, climbing over several of the boulders that fronted the water's edge. They found a large, flat rock, warmed by the sun, to relax on.

Max looked up to see Will staring at her. "What's on your mind?" she asked.

The ocean breeze was blowing her hair around, and he smoothed a few strands from her face. "You're brilliant. I've never known anyone like you."

She rolled her eyes. "Then you need to get out more."

"No, you are. You've got a mind that doesn't quit. It's fascinating."

Max squirmed uncomfortably. "Now I need to figure out what I'm doing with my massive intellect."

"Any ideas there?"

She shook her head.

"Definitely not going into law?"

"Definitely not." She watched a sailboat drift along the horizon. "I think." She looked at him cross-eyed, and they laughed together.

"You have lots of time to figure it out," Will said, watching the boat drift along.

"For the summer, I want to be like that sailboat out there."

"Not a bad idea."

"Join me, Remmond. We'll be beach bums."

Will nodded, pensive, watching a seagull circling the water. "I could handle that."

"Yeah? Really?"

He stretched his legs out, leaning back on his hands. "Sometimes, I wonder if I'm burning out."

She was surprised by the sudden fatigue on his face. "Why?"

"I don't have the drive I had before. I don't know... I don't feel like I make a difference anymore."

Max had moved behind him, and was massaging his neck.

He groaned. "Thanks, doll. That feels good."

"You were saying..."

"I got a call from an old friend. Professor at the law school. He asked me if I ever thought about a career change."

"Teaching?"

"Yeah." Will thought about his restlessness, the feeling of futility he so often came away with after a case reached its always-tentative resolution. "I was thinking the other day, I spend my life javelin-catching for women whose lives are going to be owned by the court system. I'm there for the mop-up, and I make no impact at all."

"That's not true, Will."

He took her hand from his neck and kissed it. "Yeah, maybe that was a little overdone."

She pulled her hand away and began rubbing his shoulders.

"But so many of my cases involve domestic violence. And I listen to these bastards who claim the name of 'husband' like it means a woman transferred title on her life. I see them in court, or in a divorce depo, reaming the woman they once said they *loved*. The mothers of their children." He shook his head, and a brief, bitter laugh escaped him. "And the abusers, the yahoos who start screaming about alienation as soon as they find out that the kids they terrorized don't want to be alone with them… So I've been thinking, going into education… Maybe that would make more of a difference. Attack the issues on the front end, you know?"

"Do you think you could give up practicing law?"

"Probably not. Not completely. But I'd scale it back, and I think I'd feel a lot more effective."

Max wrapped her arms around his neck from behind. "I had no idea you were so unhappy."

"Hey, I'm happy right now," he quipped, grasping her hands.

"Jo got accused of being an alienator." She was close to his ear, but so quiet that he barely heard it.

Sensing an opportunity, he pushed her hands over his head and turned to face her.

"Tell me more about her. You don't talk about her much."

"I know. It's hard." She wanted to tell him, but there was a secret to protect, one that only she and Dave knew - and Max was worried that she'd reveal it if she ever started talking.

But Will was there, and he was her best friend, and she wondered if maybe she could risk it.

"That's why she stayed married to Keith for as long as she did, but he was really the alienator - that's how she lost her boys." She swallowed hard. "Matt and Johnny turned on her for a while. It was the end of her." Catching herself, she added, "I mean, she had a lot of trouble coping with it, you know?"

"I'm sure. I've seen a lot more alienating fathers than I have mothers." Max had fallen silent, and he prompted her with, "Jo was a real piece of work, from what I've heard."

Max laughed, but it was hollow. "She was something. You didn't want to wind up in her crosshairs, that's for sure. She could take people apart."

Will could sense the conversation heading into banalities, and decided to take a chance. He took her hand. "You were with her when she died."

"Yeah," she whispered. closing her eyes, remembering the frantic search for her friend that night. "Jack had her at his house. We didn't get there in time."

"I remember." Gently, he added, "But I always thought there was more to what happened."

"There was." She opened her eyes then, and decided to tell him. "But only Dave and I know. Sammy can never find out. It's a secret."

"It'll stay that way."

She reminded Will of what he already knew: that Jack was going to use Sam's baby as a weapon. She talked about Jo's love for Dave and Sammy, and Tyler, and how she was determined that Jack was not going to hurt them - and then, she told Will about watching Jo turn suicidal.

Will was forming the picture in his head.

"Oh no," he muttered. "Not that." He felt sick inside, thinking about Max carrying that truth inside herself for a year. She had watched her best friend commit an unstoppable, violent, slow-motion suicide.

Max was saying, "... so she found a way to check out, and take Seever with her, so to speak."

"She manipulated him into..."

"It was suicide by abuser. She rigged it so that she gets to leave, Seever goes to jail, and Sammy and Dave live happily ever after."

Will thought it odd, that she was so composed; then, he understood why.

"But what about you?" he asked quietly.

Max's expression turned hard then. "Yeah. What *about* me, huh?" She rose abruptly to her feet, kicking at a rock. "It took a lot out of me to forgive her."

"But you have forgiven her?"

She nodded. "I have my moments. Hell, I'm having one right now." She stretched her arms over her head, sighing deeply. "And I do have trouble understanding why she wound up the way she did. I think about that a lot. But yeah, my perspective's pretty good, ninety percent of the time." She looked down at him and winked. "The other ten percent of the time, I just drink too much."

"I have to ask - I mean, I wonder how *I* would feel - did you ever feel any resentment toward Sammy?"

Her face fell. "Honestly, yes. But I got over that as soon as I decided that Sammy made some mistakes, but Jo made the decision - and she did *that* because of a lifetime of guys like Seever. He'll rot in jail, so at least that makes some sense." A small smile formed on her lips as she added, "Besides, every time I look at that baby... Well, you know."

Will nodded. "I do."

He seemed withdrawn then, and Max asked, "What?"

"You're coping pretty well with what happened to Jo."

"I think so. Like I said, I have my moments, but it gets easier as time goes by."

"So that's not part of the problems between us." He drew his legs up and wrapped his arms around his knees. "I was pretty sure it was an issue."

Max looked away, scanning the horizon for the sailboat. "I don't think it is. Not between us, anyway."

"Because I was thinking before, maybe being with me reminds you of the worst time of your life."

"Geez, Will - you weren't even *around* during the worst time of my life."

Her mouth dropped open as she realized what she had said, and she turned to see Will staring up at her, his expression unreadable.

Stunned, she sat beside him again. "Did I really just say that?"

"You sure did." He was glad that she tripped herself up. There was no way for her to deny it now, that there were more secrets to tell.

"I don't know how to explain it." Her voice was weak, and Will could see her trying to duck inside herself for cover. "I'm not sure what I meant by that."

When he didn't respond, she got to her feet again, pacing nervously for a minute while he watched her.

She isn't ready.

He held his hand out to her and she stopped pacing, seeming reluctant at first and then grasping it like a rescue line.

"Want to go into the city?" he asked.

She nodded. The relief on her face was palpable. "That would be nice."

They spent the afternoon wandering through Portland's business district. Max managed to keep them away from the antique shops, hoping that Will wouldn't remember the emerald earrings he bought for her in October. Her stomach sank every time she thought about it. Losing the earrings tarnished the memory of one of the best days of her life, and she wondered how she could have been so careless with something she should have cherished.

Will steered her into a coffee shop, and they took a table that looked out at the street. Max cringed when she saw, almost directly across from them, the store where Will bought the emerald earrings. She glanced around for a different table while Will got their coffees, but the café was filled.

"Here." He slid a large styrofoam cup across to her as he sat down. "Dark roast, double cream and sugar."

Smiling gratefully, she took a sip and said, "We should go walk around some more with these."

"You have too much stamina for me, doll. I need a break."

Max took another furtive glance at the antique shop. "You know, I'm actually getting kind of tired, too."

"Want to head back?"

"I think so."

He handed her a lid for her cup. "There's a heated pool at the hotel. We should go lay in the sun and ignore it."

"I'd love to."

"Bring your swimsuit?"

"Uh, no. I didn't think of that. Closest thing I've got to a bathing suit is a lace teddy." She burst into laughter at his expression. "Remmond, you just went *totally* blank."

"You're killing me, darlin'." He leaned in closer. "You need to be careful. A man can take only so much."

She moved toward him, holding his eyes on hers. In the sultry voice that she knew he couldn't resist, she murmured, "By the way, it's black."

With his mind wandering, it took a moment for him to react. Then he moaned softly. "This is getting painful."

She sat back, tossing a sugar packet at his chest. "C'mon. You were wondering, and you know it."

"Yeah. I was. This whole situation is leaving way too much to the imagination."

"Okay, I'll change the subject." She patted his hand. "No more about the black teddy."

"Good."

Smiling sedately, she whispered, "I also have a *pink* teddy with me."

He leaned back in his chair, gazing at the ceiling for a moment, and then returned to her with a level stare. "You're a cruel, cruel woman, Maxine."

"I know." She rose from her seat and leaned across the table to plant a kiss on his cheek. "Now *this* is payback."

"Like you have no idea."

"Stop looking down my shirt, Remmond. You'll feel better."

"Talk about a logical fallacy," he grinned. "Don't lean over, then."

"Let's go dancing tonight."

The shift in topic caught him off guard, and it took him a moment to adjust. "Dancing? Okay. Sure. The lounge at the hotel has music pretty much every night."

"It looks like a dressy place. And I did bring something I can wear."

He smiled at the excitement on her face. "I keep a spare suit in my truck."

"Really?" she laughed. "Like, as a rule?"

He nodded. "For when I wind up pulling an all-nighter at the office." He picked up their cups. "Let's go. We'll get dinner, and then I'll take you dancing." He inclined his head toward the window as he handed her the coffee. "How's about we stop across the street, and I'll get you something nice to wear tonight?"

She tried to keep the smile on her face, but Will saw the change in her mood.

"Something wrong?"

She glanced nervously at the window. "Nah, let's just head back."

"Okay. You sure nothing's wrong?"

"Yeah. I just really want to go out tonight."

She was obviously distracted as they made their way back to Will's truck, and he had no idea what had happened. He searched the moments just before her mood shifted, but couldn't find anything that should have upset her.

As he unlocked her door, after several minutes of stilted conversation, he decided to ask - and this time, to get an answer.

He took her hand as she climbed in, and she gave him a watery smile.

"Thanks." Puzzled when he didn't let go, she pointed to her hand and said, "I need that back when you're done with it."

He leaned against the open door. "Tell me."

She quickly averted her eyes, and he said, "No, don't look over there." He gently took her by the chin, turning her to face him. "Look here."

The tears started the moment she met his eyes, and she whispered, "I don't know where my earrings are."

Will shook his head, not understanding, wondering how a missing pair of earrings had turned into this. After he opened and closed his mouth a couple of times, he simply asked, "*What?*"

"I don't know where I put them. I haven't seen them in weeks."

"The ones Jo gave you? Darlin', they're in your *ears*."

"Not these." She hastily removed them, tucking them into her purse. Drawing in a shaky breath, she said, "The ones *you* gave me. My emerald ones," her chin was trembling as she finished weakly, "that you gave me that day last October."

He started to laugh, and it offended her enough that she stopped crying.

"What on earth are you *laughing* at?"

"You left them with me. Remember? You were wearing them the night after finals, when we went to the show, and you were worried that the clasps were weak."

"Oh..." She recalled it then, slipping them off of her ears, wrapping them in a napkin and handing them to him. "That's right..."

"I got them fixed for you." He was wiping at her cheeks. "You were exhausted that night. Two brandies after dinner, and you were completely zoned out. No wonder you didn't remember."

"You have them."

He grunted with surprise as she leaped from the truck, throwing her arms around his neck.

"*You* have them," she squealed. "Where are they?"

"They just came back a couple days ago." He hugged her and set her back on the seat as he nodded toward the glove box. "In there. I forgot to give them to you."

It didn't occur to him until after he shut her door and walked around to the back of the truck. He hurried to climb in, and was greeted by her look of absolute confusion.

Well, she knows now. May as well play it out.

She looked from the ring laying in her hand to Will, then back at the ring.

"What is this?"

Will rubbed at his chin for a moment, considering the options for an answer, and concluding that the truth was the only viable response.

"Will?"

He sighed. "Not exactly how I wanted to ask you to marry me."

chapter 7

"Have you heard from either one of them?"

"Nope," Sam answered. She handed Dave a towel as he emerged from the shower. "Their phones are off."

"Guess we'll tell them when they get back." He smiled down at her. "You love that house."

She nodded hard, spreading her arms wide. "Only about this much. You're sure he's accepting the offer?" she asked again.

"Yup. I talked to him personally. We'll have the contracts back in the morning. And by the way, he agreed to rent it to us in the meantime, if you still want to hustle up there."

"*Yes.*" She was beaming. "Tell him we want that. As soon as possible."

"I will." He smiled as he thought about Tyler, running full-tilt through the field behind the house. "Ty lost his mind over that yard."

"'Yard'? It's two acres, Dave. You call that 'land.'" She wrapped her arms around his waist. "Room to grow. I can't wait to plant peonies." She looked up then to see him staring off into space. "What?"

"We're going to be back and forth between two states for a while, closing things out here, settling in up there - I'm a little worried about it. That's an awful lot that falls on you."

She wished that they could simply enjoy the moment. "I can deal with it."

"What about your work? You know, we really should have discussed this more."

"I'm all set. One more meeting, then on hiatus until we go over the wall. And *you* worry *way* too much."

He kissed the top of her head. "If you say so."

"But I'll need lots of TLC." She poked him in the stomach. "And that anniversary present you keep hinting at."

"Which you get on Saturday," he said.

She pretended to pout. "You probably haven't even gotten my present yet." When he didn't answer, she said, "Come on, have you?"

"This is a no-win for me, babe. If I say I have your present, you'll be after me to tell you what it is. If I say I don't, I'll be sleeping on the couch."

"Darn right," she muttered.

"Saturday," he said again, draping the towel over her head.

She pulled it off, winding it up and flicking it at him. "And then," she sighed happily, "we can start the process of actually moving out of Boston." As she went into their bedroom, she said, "By the way, I checked into gun laws up there. You were right. As soon as we have an address, I can just go get one."

Dave followed her into the room. "Nine millimeter's the best one for you."

"Probably."

He slipped into his jeans, then sat on the bed and pulled her onto his lap. "Damn shame it has to come to that," he mumbled. "You carrying. Makes me nervous."

She rolled her eyes. "Don't start again. I always stay safe. And if I ever did need to draw, I'm a hell of a shot, remember?"

"So I've heard." Sam's gun hobby had developed after a friend invited her to take a class. One of the instructors at the firearms school had told him that Sam had the best "eye" he'd ever seen.

"That wife of yours," he'd told Dave, the admiration evident in his voice, "she could nick a mosquito's ass at fifty yards."

Dave rocked her back and forth for a few moments, wishing she had chosen something safer for her work, something that didn't involve the volatile, dangerous extremes of rage and vengeance. He didn't like the idea of having a gun in the house; but still, he wanted her to have one on her when she worked nights at the DV centers.

"*Dave*," she said sharply, and he came out of his reverie.

"Huh?"

"You promised us pizza. Let's go."

※ ※ ※

Max slipped into her pale green dress, her eyes on the ring, guarded - watching it like it was an unexpected stranger in her room. It rested on the antique oak dresser, on top of the black velvet bag she had taken it from.

She approached it slowly and picked it up again. She thought it was actually breathtaking. It was an ornate, heirloom design done in white gold, with emerald-embedded scrolls surrounding the diamond.

Not exactly how I wanted to ask you to marry me.

She looked into the tri-fold mirror that rested on the dresser, oblivious to her reflection as she tried to remember her reaction to finding the ring. She knew she handled it badly.

Will had said, "I've had it for a while now."

Max was glad she was sitting in the truck when she found it. She had felt lightheaded, sick to her stomach.

Gazing blankly at the ring, she had asked him, "Are you *crazy?*"

He didn't answer, and she was surprised when she looked up at him and found him with a wide smile on his face.

"No," was all he said.

"Oh, yeah. You are." She was turning it over in her hands, thinking about how she simply couldn't. Not that. Not being someone's wife. She glanced at him again; and for an instant, the sight of him was oddly confusing to her, like she didn't know him.

"What should I do with it?" she asked, sullen. She could tell that Will was trying not to laugh.

"It's not *funny*," she snapped.

"I know." He took a long, deep breath. "Whatever you want to do with it, doll. It's your ring."

She had slipped it back into the velvet bag, then pulled it out again. "It's beautiful," she mumbled. She felt cloyingly self-conscious, claustrophobic - like he was waiting for her to perform, to do something she was wholly incapable of doing.

But she slid across the seat, pressed up against him on the drive back to the hotel, quietly studying the ring like it was a fascinating artifact. As he turned into the driveway, she said again, "This is beautiful."

"Hang on to it." He put his arm around her shoulders, giving her a quick squeeze. "It's up to you. Wear it on your right hand, if you want. Just let me know if it makes it to your left," he smiled down at her, "so I can rent a blimp."

After he parked the truck, he pulled her close and kissed her on the forehead, and she thought, *I have an engagement ring. From my best friend. This is getting bizarre.*

A knock at the door startled her, and Max wondered how long she had been standing there in front of the mirror. She checked her reflection, grabbing a peach-colored lipstick and quickly running it over her lips. Fluffing her hair out, she smiled as her emerald earrings caught the light, and she thought again about how the things she loved were always safe with Will.

She extended her left hand, holding the ring above it; then she switched hands, slipping it onto her right.

Will audibly gasped as she opened the door to him.

"I'm not going to make it easy for you, Remmond." She leaned against him as she pretended to straighten his tie for him.

He said nothing as he took in her hair, flowing over her shoulders to the top of the pale green, strapless dress, and slowly scanned her body all the way down to the silver high heels she was wearing.

"Waiting for comment," she said. "And be impressive. I'm becoming high-maintenance."

He took a step back, still gaping, and said, "Know what I'm thinking?"

"Besides the obvious?"

"Yeah, besides that. I'm thinking you have got to be God's finest work, darlin'."

She pulled on his tie, bringing his face close to hers and kissing him on the cheek. "I suppose that'll do." She let go of him, and turned back to the room. "Let me grab my bag."

Will enjoyed watching her as she walked away. "Take your time," he said.

The evening was unusually warm, with a light breeze coming in off of the ocean, and they strolled slowly along the brick path to the hotel's restaurant.

"Beautiful night," he said.

Max pointed to the sky. "It's a full moon." There was a light, dreamy tone to her voice, so alluring that he felt himself react physically to it.

His hand went to the back of his neck. "Mmm. Seems like all things are conspiring for romance here."

"Losing your resolve?"

He swung the door open, taking her arm as she went through it. "Like you said, you aren't making it easy on me."

He was keeping his guard up, though. She was becoming more difficult to resist - and the more overtly seductive she was, the more he sensed something disturbing. A darker motive was driving her, and he knew now that it had to be about her father. But Will was also aware that he himself was a catalyst, one that brought out the battle she was waging with a guy who had been dead for five months. Pastor Allen had died just before the New Year.

He felt like he'd been hit in the chest by a two-by-four.

Just before the New Year.

He recalled his confusion the winter before, over the fact that she'd had virtually no reaction to her father's death. She never discussed it, never even brought it up again.

At least, not to anyone else.

He didn't have enough of the details, not yet; but with what he did know about her history, he realized that Allen's death would have been a huge emotional event for her.

She was walking ahead of him, and when she turned to smile at him, Will felt pulled in too many different directions. He was fragmented among her needs and his desires, and her desires and his own survival instinct, and the fact that he had brought her to Maine to figure things out. That wouldn't happen if he gave in now.

They were seated at a table at the far end of the room, in front of the wall of windows that looked out over the ocean. The sun was just below the horizon, and the sky was streaked with mingling shades of rose, coral, and gold.

Max glanced around the crowded restaurant, then gave Will a knowing look. "So, whoever reserved this spot for us is a little richer tonight, huh?"

He didn't look up from the wine list he was studying, but a smile played around his lips as he said, "Such cynicism." He closed the folder, pushing it to the edge of the table. "Champagne? This feels like a big night."

A sudden sense of foreboding came over him as he said it, and he decided to pay attention to it.

The server was a small, older woman in a starched white shirt and black trousers.

"I love your dress," she said, smiling hesitantly at Max. "It's just beautiful."

After she hurried off for the champagne, Max recalled her days of waitressing - only a year ago, she mused with some surprise - and she turned her attention back to Will.

"Was this really my life?"

"Hard to believe, isn't it?" He reached across the table, pushing a lock of her hair aside. "You're wearing your earrings."

"I am." She touched her ear lightly, and the diamond ring sparkled in the dim light.

Will felt a thrill go through him, a far more intense reaction than he thought he would have. He grasped her hand, turning it to look at the ring, and she smiled shyly as their eyes met.

"Step two," he murmured.

"Two?"

"Step one was you believing that I love you."

She stared at him quietly for a moment, then nodded.

The champagne arrived a minute later, and after the server poured, Max raised her flute. She took on a Valley Girl cadence as she said, "It's, like, *man*datory to do, like, a *toast* with this stuff, *right?*"

Will picked up his glass, grinning. "Pretty much. I never know what to say."

"Me neither."

"And you're a little too convincing with the accent there."

She made a face at him, then said, "Okay, wait. I've got it. To best friends."

"You know it." He touched his glass to hers. "Best friends."

They had a relaxing meal, keeping the conversation light and pleasant. Will was careful to limit himself to one glass of champagne, but Max had downed three glasses before he took notice.

Soft, slow music wafted in from the lounge, and Will gently lifted the flute from her hand. "Come dance with me," he said.

She walked ahead of him, and he thought she seemed steady enough. He hoped he had caught it in time. The last thing he needed on his hands was a fully uninhibited Maxine.

Several people had ventured into the lounge, but just one couple was on the small dance floor. Will took Max's hand, twirling her once and then pulling her into his arms, enjoying her delighted laugh.

She rested her head on his chest, just below his neck. Her hair had a musky scent to it, her body was tight against his, and his mind was tracking in a way he didn't want it to. He knew he needed to distract himself quickly.

He pulled away slightly, and she looked up at him.

"Having a good time?" he asked.

She draped her arms around his neck and played with his hair. "I don't know, Counselor," she mimicked his drawl. "Not much action here."

He laughed as he recognized his own words.

"This platonic stuff is hard to take, you know? I may have to look around a bit."

The ominous feeling returned. Sensing that he was being baited, he responded by drawing her close again.

The song ended then, and they moved to a small table in the back of the room.

"Buy me a drink, Remmond?" She smiled up at him.

Will recalled Sammy's warning about taking control too quickly. He didn't want to make decisions for her; certainly, he didn't want to treat her like a child. But he knew that she shouldn't have any more, and this was going to be a problem.

He thought it over for a moment. "You bet. Be right back," he said.

At the bar, he pulled his wallet from his pocket, laying a twenty-dollar bill on the ledge.

The bartender hurried over. "What can I get ya?" The tall, heavy-set young man, with *Brucie* on his nametag, set a napkin in front of him.

Will mumbled, "See the blonde over there?"

He chuckled. "Uh, *yeah*. She's been the topic around the restaurant tonight." He gave Will an admiring look. "Good for you, man."

Max looked up at them, and her eyes narrowed. She sat back in her chair and crossed her legs.

"Thanks so much, Brucie." Will stared at him dully. "And keep it down, okay?"

"Sure."

"Anyway, she's had a little too much to drink already. So I don't want anything more than half a shot in her drinks. Lots of ice. And if you have to, cut her off after three."

Brucie's mouth dropped open. "You want her sober?" he muttered. He looked in Max's direction again. "Really? You, like, shy or something?"

"You gonna do it?"

"Okay, man, you got it. I guess." He gazed longingly at her again. "But you must have some big problem with the shy thing. I *nevah* saw legs like that."

"Just get me an amaretto sour."

"Anything for you?"

"Plain tonic. Highball glass."

He frowned, still staring at Max. "She can't be your sistah. You two was way too chummy dancing."

"Want to move it there, Brucie?" Will turned around to look at her then, thinking he couldn't blame the guy.

"Okay, but... Wow."

He continued muttering to himself as he poured the drinks, then regarded Will with sympathy as he set them on the bar.

Will was grinning as he took the drinks back to the table.

"What's so funny?" Max asked.

"The bartender. He's a moron."

She took a sip. "What'd he do?"

"Nothing he needs to be punched out for." He responded to the confused expression on her face with, "Maxine, you tend to command a lot of attention, especially with the way you look tonight."

"Oh. *Golly.*" She glared in the direction of the bartender. "I'll have to be more careful next time." She looked around the lounge. Several of the men were staring at her, and the resentment grew inside her as she wondered why she couldn't simply wear a pretty dress for an evening out with Will. She wanted to impress him, not these strangers who appeared to be fixated on a few parts of her body.

She felt embarrassed, on display - and then she felt rage. It lasted only for a moment before she heard her father in her head again, in a subconscious whisper that she barely noticed.

Whorish.

Then she felt nothing at all.

Will followed her eyes, watching as they turned cold, and a word played around the edges of his mind - something he had discussed with Sammy, and he struggled to retrieve it.

Max downed most of her drink then, glancing at the dance floor. "I'm getting bored," she said. She emptied the glass and set it down with a thud. "Let's get this refilled while we dance."

It came to him then.

Trigger.

Will noticed how she distanced herself from him, physically and otherwise, and that her comments became increasingly caustic as the evening went by. Three dances and two drinks later, he looked pointedly at the bartender, who gave him a thumbs-up. Will wondered if the guy had actually just winked at him.

"Want to take off?" Will asked.

Max nodded, rising from her chair. "This was fun, though. Thanks."

He was relieved, because he didn't want to have her cut off. She was too obviously tipsy, starting to slur a bit, and he thought it a good thing that she'd had only half the alcohol she intended to have. She had slammed her drinks down too quickly.

He was also mindful of her tone: she sounded like she barely knew him.

Max stifled a yawn, stretching her arms over her head, and Will noticed that most of the men in the lounge were riveted as the length of her short dress traveled to the tops of her thighs.

She did that deliberately.

Will had no idea how he was going to handle the rest of the evening, but he knew something was coming.

"What time is it?" she sighed.

"Almost midnight."

She seemed surprised. "Still early. Oh, well..." She extended her hand to him. "Care to walk me home, Mr. Remmond?"

He took her hand, then brought it to his lips for a lingering kiss. "Thank you for a wonderful evening, Ms. Allen."

They were almost to the hotel when Max said, "Let's go around back. I love the ocean at night."

"You aren't tired?"

"A little. But I'm not ready to sleep yet." She slipped her shoes off as they reached the path that led to the boulders.

They found the place where they sat earlier that day. Max smiled down at her feet as she stepped onto the large, flat rock, wiggling her toes. "It's still warm," she said, sitting with her legs stretched out in front of her.

Will sat beside her, taking off his suit jacket and putting it around her shoulders.

"Thanks." She wrapped it around herself and glanced in the direction of the lounge.

He nodded, watching the surf crash into the rocks below them, trying to mentally prepare for whatever was going to happen. He acknowledged to himself that it was fully a matter of when, not if, and he tensed as it came clear to him that he was likely ill equipped to handle it.

A few minutes later, she commented, "You're quiet. You okay?"

"Yeah. I'm fine." He took note of the fact that she sounded drunk - and she was still looking behind his back toward the bar.

"I think I had a little too much," she giggled, taking another fleeting look over his shoulder.

He handed her shoes to her. "Maybe we should get you back to your room."

Her demeanor changed instantly, and she shot him a look that sent a chill through him.

"Okay, Daddy."

She was unsteady as she got to her feet - and too eager to leave, Will thought - and he caught her around the waist as she lost her balance.

"Mmmm... Finally." She dropped her shoes and leaned hard against him, running her hands along his chest, then down his sides to his hips, pulling him against her. There was nothing loving or even gentle in her touch: she was being rough with him, aggressive - and the hatred in her eyes gave him the surreal feeling that she was a sudden, total stranger.

He took a step back. "Don't do that," he muttered.

"Right." She caught him by his belt, yanking him toward her body again and then deftly undoing the buckle. "You're telling me you don't want it?"

Will pulled her hands off of his belt, and she stood unsteadily on her tiptoes, kissing and then biting his neck. He let go of her hands to grasp her shoulders, trying to gently push her away, and she had his shirt almost completely unbuttoned before he could stop her.

"*Hey*," he snapped. "What are you *doing?*"

"What you wanted." Her hands were inside his shirt, caressing him, and she was slurring as she mocked him. "Isn't this what you've been after?"

He grabbed her hands, wrenching them away. "I don't want this."

"C'mon." She laughed bitterly. "You all say that. You say 'no' when you really mean 'yes.'"

She was nibbling on his bare chest, moving down his stomach, and Will was both confused and repelled by the fact that his body was responding to her.

He grasped her head firmly, lifting her face to his, forcing her to look at him.

"Stop it. *Now*."

She raised an eyebrow, laughing at him again. The loathing in her eyes was devastating.

He had never before been in a situation where a woman was touching him against his will, not with that kind of intensity and hostility, and his reaction stunned him: he felt a repulsed contempt for her that was completely foreign to him, and a straining, suffocating sensation that was something like catching a lungful of water. As he confronted the fact that it was Maxine who was drowning him, the betrayal of it sickened him.

He stepped back again, watching the wind whip her hair over her face, thinking he could actually hate her. Her narrowed eyes were fixed somewhere just beyond him. She had a feral look to her, and he wondered how someone so incredibly beautiful could be so ugly inside.

The hell with her.

As he moved further away from her, he hesitated as his own words returned to him:

It's like she lives in her own private hell.

Sammy had warned him, but he had thought himself invincible and gone after her anyway. He mocked himself for believing he could win, for his naïve determination that loving her could save her.

Just walk away.

He continued to back away slowly as he considered it. He thought he would do it - or at least, that he should. His pride demanded it. She was becoming abusive, luring him in and then tearing him down, treating him like he was no more than a means to some sick end that she was determined to reach.

She turned her back to him, standing a few feet away with her head in her hands, telling him to go away, leave her alone - that if he had any brains, he would get out of her life.

I think maybe you do love me.

A quiet moan escaped him as he finally, fully understood what loving her would cost him.

Max had warned him, too. She tried to tell him. But he couldn't let go of the woman he had known - the woman she was before the poison inside her had metastasized, and created the stranger who stood before him now.

He remembered her eyes, watching him in the middle of the night, and the feeling of having her safe in his arms. And his picture of the two of them, her laughter, and his arms around her. Sitting by the ocean with her the October before, when she told him that she wouldn't have made it through Jo's death without him, and how everything between them shifted to something deeper in that moment - and the look on her face later that day, just before he kissed her for the first time.

You're my best friend, Remmond. You really are.

His chest was painfully tight as he remembered it.

Then he asked himself if he would have chased her down anyway, had he known in advance what would happen, and his reaction was immediate:

Yes.

With that, he knew that he had just chosen the course of his life.

Max was facing him again, watching him suspiciously, demanding to know what he was thinking.

But Will wasn't listening: he was searching her face, looking for some show of the beauty that he knew was someplace inside her. He needed to know what had happened to her, and he decided that was going to find out. Tonight. But she was drunk, and raging, and he prepared himself for the fact that this was going to be bad.

And it could end even worse.

He picked up her shoes.

At least she won't be alone.

He took her arm. "Let's go."

She struggled briefly, losing her balance as she jerked her arm away. The alcohol was taking full effect, and she stumbled, swaying back and forth too close to the edge of the rock.

Shaken, Will grabbed the back of her dress and pulled her into his arms. With his lips against her ear, he yelled, "*Enough.*"

Max froze. "Wow," she mumbled, her hand to her forehead. "How much did I have?"

He scooped her into his arms. "Way more than you should've." He was sure that Brucie had gone heavy-handed with the liquor anyway, to help him out with his "shy thing".

If I see him again, I'll break his neck.

The desk clerk grinned as they came in, then hid his amusement with a short coughing fit. "G'night, folks," he called out as Will carried her up the stairs.

He set her on her feet at the door to her room, holding her up with one arm as he unlocked it. "Okay, c'mon," he muttered as he walked her in. "Let's get you to bed."

"Ooh... 'Bout time." She wandered unsteadily to the dresser, fumbling to remove her earrings. She tossed them in the top drawer, then turned to face him.

"I'm ready for *any*thing, stud."

She started to giggle again, and Will recalled the sound of her laughter, how infectious it was.

"Whoops. Losing the sour puss there, Remmond. Be careful, or your face might crack."

She's drunk. Let it go.

"I'll be watching out for that, Maxine."

"Such a clever boy."

He thought about the day they met, dancing with her, looking into the eyes that now regarded him with utter contempt. He felt like he'd been sucker-punched.

She can't outrun the way you love her.

Will wasn't a praying man, but it seemed to him like the thought came from God Himself.

He said, "Takes two to have a fight, Max. You're on your own."

"Ah, so he's going *patronizing* now." Her eyes narrowed. "Aren't you a smart boy," she hissed. "*So* together. Never a crack in the armor."

Will turned the covers down on her bed. He knew better than to answer, but she was starting to wear him down.

He heard her mumbling something, and looked up to find her staring blankly into the mirror, running a comb through her hair. He thought she said, "I don't need *you* to fix me, *stud.*"

"I can't hear you, Maxine." He didn't intend for it to come out sounding so combative.

She threw the comb at him, and he caught it with one hand, placing it gently on the desk.

She exhaled loudly through her gritted teeth. "I'm not your pet project, you know? There's nothing. At *all*. Nothing at all that's wrong with *me*." She was tripping over her words, and Will thought it was just as much from the dam bursting as it was from the alcohol.

She's not done. Not even close.

He ran a hand through his hair, then stood with his hands on his hips, staring down at the floor.

"So what's the script here? I'm supposed to play Eliza to your Higgins? *Forget it.* I'm not your daughter, big shot." Tilting precariously as she lost her balance again, she grabbed the edge of the dresser to steady herself. "Know what? I think *you're* the one with the problem. Maybe... I think there's something wrong with *you*, with a guy who has no interest in a real *woman.*"

He looked up sharply. "What are you *talking* about?" he asked quietly.

"Where do you get off? All alone with some dirty pictures?"

"*What?* Maxine..."

"Can you *stop saying my name like that?*"

Will struggled to keep his voice level as he asked, "How am I saying your name?"

Her voice built to a furious crescendo as she responded, "Like it's *some kind of a cuss*."

He shook his head, confused. "I don't..."

"I'm bored to death. I'm so outta here..." She tore off his jacket, and threw it at him as she snatched her purse from the dresser and headed for the door. "Go to hell, Will. And don't wait up."

Will made it across the room in a few quick strides, just as Max grabbed her shoes from where he had dropped them beside the door.

He stood in front of it, his arms folded. "Where are you going?"

"None of your damn business, buddy. You're just my friend, remember? Now *get out of my way*." She tried to push him aside, but she couldn't budge him.

"Going to pick up a guy, huh?"

"Why not? I bet I can find one who's man enough to sleep with me." She looked him up and down. "Probably more than one, *stud*."

Will stepped to the side so she could go if she wanted to. He knew that what he was about to say was going to level her, and he didn't care. It was time.

"Hey, if you're going to be a slut tonight, then just stay here with me."

She gasped, and the flash of raging pain in her eyes made him hate himself in a way he never had before.

It seemed to Will that everything turned slow-motion then.

She swung her silver shoes hard, directly at his head. He stopped her easily, catching her wrist; then her other hand came toward his face, and he caught that as well, pushing her hands down to her sides and holding them there.

"No," he said softly, his voice gravelly with pain. "You're not going to do that."

Neither of them moved for a full minute. They stared at each other, with Max seeming paralyzed, and Will trying desperately to figure out how they could find their way back from all of the lines they'd crossed that night.

Max dropped her shoes, then her purse, and then she started to tremble. She had her hands over her mouth as she backed away from him, and he recalled how she did the same thing on New Year's Eve. Then he thought about how she touched her mouth when she wanted to be kissed, and the contrast made him dizzy with the regret of it.

She was shaking her head in horrified disbelief, still backing away, until the bed caught the back of her legs and she sat down, her hands still over her mouth.

Watching her rapidly coming apart, Will started to panic, thinking he should have kept his mouth shut. He wondered what he had been thinking, saying that to her.

I can't do this. I don't know what you need.

His thoughts were running frantic, because he knew that she was retreating someplace inside herself - and if she went too far, she'd find plenty of good reasons to stay there.

"Maxine..." He knelt in front of her, trying to pry her hands from her face. "Please..." He sat beside her then, pulling her into his arms and rocking her slowly.

She was making quiet sounds, a muted shrieking with every breath. He tried again to move her hands, with no success; then, she fell suddenly, jarringly silent as she looked over his shoulder. He turned, following her eyes, and saw that she was staring transfixed at their reflection in the glass doors to the balcony.

"What is it?" he murmured, wrapping her in his arms again. "What is it?"

Her voice was muffled behind her hands, but he heard her: "Ugly. It's all so ugly."

"What's ugly?"

"*Look* at us. Look at *me*."

He quickly turned her away from their reflection then, reclining on the bed and bringing her down with him. She curled up against him, and he stroked her hair and talked softly to her until she was calm again; then, he gently pulled her hands away from her face.

He couldn't leave it like that, because the memory of her hands over her mouth would eat him alive. He knew that. It was already killing him.

She was staring at him, motionless. "Will..." she whispered. "This is hopeless. It is. You don't know..."

He pushed her hair from her face, then ran his hand down her cheek, stopping at her lips. He gently kissed her.

She laid very still, and when he pulled away and looked into her eyes, she said, "This will never work."

"You're wrong."

"You don't *know*," she said, louder this time, and he could hear her despair.

"And I want to." He held her as he said, "It's time for you to tell me."

chapter 8

It was almost dawn. Will watched her sleep, knowing that he wouldn't be able to rest, knowing that sleep was the last thing he wanted. He couldn't leave her unprotected from her own mind that night as she slept.

At the end of the night, she had pleaded with him to stay.

"Don't leave, Will. I need you here. *Please* don't leave."

He'd had no intention of going across the hall to his room, and when he told her that, she had dissolved into tears again - crying in his arms with the anguished relief of finding a safe place to collapse. She had fallen asleep from the exhaustion, and moaned softly several times as she drifted off.

In the silence afterwards, Will couldn't escape the impact of learning the hellish secrets she had carried for most of her life. He was shocky, his thoughts scattered and disoriented - alternating between a love for her that was now the center of his existence, and the mortal rage he felt toward the monster who took her apart.

That son of a bitch is lucky he's dead.

She had been sleeping with her arm around him, her face against his chest; now, she moaned again, turning over and facing away from him. He curled up against her back, wrapping her in his arms, and kissed her hair as he whispered, "I love you."

A moment later, she pressed closer to him, and he knew that she had heard him.

"I love you," he said again, wanting her to hear it in her sleep. He wanted to obliterate her memories of her father - to erase his legacy, and replace it with the one she deserved.

Every muscle in his body tensed as he thought of her as a little girl, terrified, bloody, and marked by his belt. It was worse than he suspected, every bit as horrifying as the cases he dealt with every day. And even more so because it was *her*.

They had talked for hours that night. At the end, Will asked her one final question - but he knew the answer from what she had already said. It was Max who wasn't aware of it.

"Did he sexually abuse you?"

"*No.*" She shook her head forcefully. "Not that."

But she seemed conflicted, and Will asked, "You're sure?"

"He did some weird things, like making nasty comments about my body." She folded her arms across her chest. "And he had this habit of walking right into my room - no knocking, just waltzing right in - like, right after I got out of the shower. But I always made sure I stayed covered."

"Oh." He knew this story, as well. He heard it a lot. "No lock on your door, huh?"

She had paused then. "No. He wouldn't let me have a lock on my door."

They were sitting on the bed, with Will stretched out on his back and Max sitting beside him, her legs tucked underneath her. At that point, she moved closer, grabbing his hand.

Decades later, and her hands were like ice.

"And the belt, when did that stop?"

"Nine or ten. I think. It's hard to remember." She laid down next to him then, her head on his chest.

He took a deep breath, then asked, "Did he use the belt with you fully dressed?"

She raised her head to look at him, confused again. "I don't know... You mean..."

"Did he make you take your pants off?"

The color drained from her face as she nodded. "I have scars," she whispered, looking away.

He had stayed calm for her sake. But laying there with her now, a tortured sound escaped him, and she stirred.

She has scars.

He realized then that he was holding her too tightly, and he forced himself to relax. She was mumbling something about being alone.

"Shhh," he kissed her cheek, pulling the quilt over her shoulders. "I'm right here. Go back to sleep."

Will thought he should try to occupy his mind with something, anything other than the truths Max had told him that night, because he wasn't coping well. At the same time, he knew that trying to escape it would be an exercise in futility - and more than that, he needed to be stable when she awakened. If he didn't find a way to deal with what she had told him, didn't resolve it somehow, he would be useless to her.

He had known, before she confirmed it, that her father had to be heavily into pornography. All the symptoms were there, the exact same behaviors that were recounted to him over and over again by his clients and their children.

"I found some of his porn magazines when I was a little girl." Her voice trembled, but she had pressed on. "I thought he would kill me, he was so out of control. He said he'd leave if I told anyone, and Mom wouldn't be able to take care of me, so I'd wind up in a stranger's house. And you know, I thought that would actually be good, except I couldn't leave my mother. I had to take care of her."

"A preacher with a porn hobby," Will replied, disgusted.

Max's face was wooden, and he had a flash of an image in his mind, of someone sinking into quicksand.

"He was bizarre," she said. "It was like he was never really *there*. Mentally, I mean - he was always someplace else. And you could never 'disturb' him. He'd fly into a rage. But we always had to look like the perfect family. It was like living inside a picture."

Something had occurred to her then, and she sat up, studying him thoughtfully. When Will asked her about it, she said, "I've never seen you even *look* at anything smutty."

"I never cared for it much, but it didn't bother me when I was younger." He was quiet for a moment before he said, "Now though, in my work, I see too much of what it does. Way too much. It's poison."

She became visibly distraught then, speaking so rapidly that Will had to concentrate to understand her. "You know, he would trash my room on a regular basis. And Mom's things - he would break them, throw them around, go into the bedroom or her bathroom and just rip it apart." With a distant, helpless look in her eyes, she added, "He never trashed his *own* things. Just ours. But he'd say he 'lost it' because he lived with 'contentious women' - and he'd pick fights with Mom over nothing, and then disappear for hours. It felt like he was constantly setting her up to be his excuse for whatever he wanted to do."

The breath she drew in had a wheezing, grating tone to it. "And there was this one night, a couple of men from the church came over - I think I was twelve then - and I was eavesdropping, sitting at the top of the steps while they talked to him."

"Do you remember what they said?"

She nodded. "Someone had seen him at one of those places that guys go to. The ones with the booths, where you pay to go in and watch..." She started picking at her nails, then tugging at strands of her hair.

Will took her hand in his own, holding it steady as she continued: "But he said it was all a lie..."

Her voice had an odd, lyrical cadence to it. She was slowing down, and Will wondered what that meant.

"And he said that the man who saw him had been trying to get him booted from the church ever since he got there..."

Then he noticed that her voice was repeatedly trailing off at the end of a thought, and he knew that something was surfacing.

She was pulling at strands of her hair with her other hand, and he gently grasped it.

"They believed him?" he asked.

"Yeah. But he was furious after they left. Just completely out of control..." She swallowed hard, and went silent.

"What is it?"

She pulled her hand away and pressed it to her stomach, looking just over Will's shoulder.

"Max?"

She rose quickly, still somewhat unsteady. "I need some air," she mumbled.

Will took the quilt from the bed and joined her on the balcony. He wrapped it around her from behind, knowing that it would be easier for her to speak if she didn't have to look at him.

Bending to her ear, he asked quietly, "What did he do, Maxine?"

It came out in a rush of anguished whispers, and he stayed close so he could hear her.

"He saw me on the steps. I ran into my room, and I slammed my door shut but there was no lock on my door and he kicked it open. So I kind of curled up in the corner by my bed and covered my ears. He screamed at me and *screamed* at me, and I couldn't *take* it anymore."

She was pulling the quilt around herself like a cocoon, and Will held her tighter.

"And I picked up my shoes from the floor and I threw them at him, and I started screaming back at him, and I said he was a liar and a bastard and I *hated* him. I said I wished he would *die*. And I meant it. I did."

"I know."

"Then he charged at me, and he grabbed my hair, and he threw me on my bed and he started slapping me in the mouth. And... Will, he tore my shirt. He was...I could feel him. It was turning into something *else*."

His mouth went dry. He closed his eyes, sickened by it.

"My mother finally got there, and she hit him with something, and she was beating on his back and screaming that she would kill him. And then he punched me. In the mouth. Hard." She paused to catch her breath, and her hand went to her chin as she said, "I was bleeding. I had blood all over myself. And he dragged my mother to their room, but there was no *noise* then. I wondered if he had killed her, and I was afraid to come out of my room so I didn't know until the next morning. They acted like nothing had happened."

He steadied her as she swayed forward.

"I'm dizzy... I'm going to fall." She seemed to be struggling to breathe, and she clutched at his hands.

"I've got you."

"I don't feel well..."

Will thought about giving her the option to stop talking, but it was finally coming out and he wanted it done. He waited until she seemed settled again, then said, "There's more."

Max was nodding slowly, still hanging on to his hands, but her voice grew stronger as she said, "When I got older, he let up on the physical stuff. But then he started calling me names. Like 'whore' and 'Jezebel'. And 'wicked'. He was especially fond of the word 'slut'."

She pried his hands from around her waist and stepped away, her back still turned to him.

"So I decided to be one." Defiant now, she added, "And I *was* a slut, until just a few years ago. I don't even know how many..."

She hesitated, and Will resisted the impulse to reach for her.

"I hated them, Will. It was easy, sleeping with a guy I hated."

She turned to face him then, ready to confront him, ready to see his disgust. "Did you hear me? What I said?"

"I heard you."

"I thought you'd have some kind of a reaction to that."

He cleared his throat. "I do."

She waited, searching his eyes, not seeing his need to brace himself before he spoke.

His throat was closing, making a suffocated, clicking sound - and he was thinking, *I haven't cried in years, and this sure as hell isn't the time for it.*

Distraught, she whimpered, "Say something, Will. Please say *something*."

Instead, he wrapped his arms around her waist, lifting her off of her feet and burying his face in her neck. It took him another minute to compose himself, and then he said, "I'm so sorry, baby. I'm so damned *sorry*."

She was clinging to him, breathing too fast. When he whispered, "You're safe now," he felt her body shudder violently against him as she wept. He had the vivid sensation that her sobbing went straight through him. And that with each labored breath she drew in, and with every release, another demon was gone.

"I feel like I'm ruined," she gasped. "I've always felt ruined."

"*No.*" He didn't know how to respond to that. But he knew he couldn't leave it unanswered, and his anxiety overwhelmed him. His voice broke as he said, "No. You're not."

She pulled away, needing to see his face, incredulous at the tears in his eyes.

"You're not ruined, baby. You're just starting out."

She shook her head, and he was desperate to find the words that would work.

"You're a miracle. You're *my* miracle. Finding you was the most incredible thing that ever happened to me."

"I can't do this," she sobbed. "I can't see myself that way."

"Then let me do it *for* you."

And in the moments that followed, he saw something open up in her. He watched as the constant veil of cautious self-preservation lifted from her eyes, and she was completely there, with him, for the first time.

She whispered, "I love you, Will..."

He thought his heart would stop.

"*So* much."

He closed his eyes, holding her tighter as she hid her face against him.

As he finally exhaled, he said, "I love you too, darlin'."

The morning sunlight was spreading across the bed, and Will watched it turn her hair golden. She moved tightly against him, her head turned just enough that he could see her face. He had always thought that she had the most beautiful lips he'd ever seen.

He left them bloody.

Picturing her mouth gushing blood, he felt rage surging inside him again. His heart was beating so hard that he thought it might wake her, as he realized how easy it would be to stop seeing her as Maxine, and to start seeing only what her father had done to her.

Then it occurred to him: that was all she could see when she looked at herself.

Get the hell out of my head, Pastor. I'm not going to let you suck me in.

And he decided that no one would hurt her, not from that moment on, not while he had breath left in his body.

Never again. That's it. It's done.

Her breathing was slow and steady, and he laid his head against hers, careful not to disturb her.

Just after eight o'clock, she rolled onto her back, stretching her arms over her head. With her eyes still closed, she mumbled, "Will?"

He was propped on his elbow, smiling down at her. "Good morning."

She opened her eyes slowly, staring quietly at him, and Will could tell that she was remembering the night.

"Are you okay?" she asked.

"Yeah." He took her chin in his hand, lifting her face to gently kiss her.

She touched his eyes, taking in the dark circles underneath them. "You didn't sleep."

"I'll sleep tonight."

She sat up, worried. "Why were you up all night?"

He pulled her back down and kissed her again, lingering this time, and it seemed to her that something was decided. *Sealed*, she thought, and she drew back to look at him, curious.

He said, "I'm a little hypervigilant, I guess. You were having a rough night."

Max pictured him watching over her as she slept, standing guard. She took his face in her hands and kissed his eyes, then held his head against her neck.

"You beautiful man." His arms came around her, and she whispered, "I love you."

chapter 9

"CALL FROM YOUR lawyer, Reynolds."

He sat bolt upright, tossing aside the magazine he was reading. "Thanks."

In his hurry to get to the phone, Simon moved too far ahead of the guard.

"Three steps ahead," he warned. "Slow down."

Simon nodded, wondering briefly if he could kill the guy and get away with it. "Sorry."

He reached eagerly for the phone, glancing up at the guard. "Line...?"

"Six." He backed away, and Simon thought that the five extra feet of space didn't do much to afford him any extra privacy.

He punched 6. "Simon Reynolds," he said.

"It's Jeff Marshall. How are you holding up?"

"I'm about ready to..." He remembered the guard standing behind him. "... get on with my life," he finished weakly.

"I know. Hang in there. Four days to go."

"Yeah, I'm marking the days."

"Anyway," Jeff said, "I got your paperwork on the Batterer's Intervention. Excellent job."

"Thanks," he mumbled.

"And we have a hearing on the thirty-first for visitation."

That brought a small smile to Simon's face. "Fan-damn-tastic, Jeff. What are my chances?"

"I think they're good. It depends on the judge we get, and how hard opposing counsel fights it. She managed to get Will Remmond, and he's got a reputation..."

"Of what?"

"Full-on mother's rights."

He guarded himself against the cussing that threatened to escape him. "Is he good?"

"Yeah, he is." He paused, and Simon heard the smugness in Marshall's attitude as he added, "But I'm better."

"Okay."

"He'll try to force you into supervised visitation, but we'll beat him back on that. Are you set with a place to live after you get out?"

"I'll be going to my brother's house. He has an in-law that he uses for guests."

"That works. Stay away from your parents, at least until we have you established, got it?"

I 'got it' the other ten times you told me, jackass.

"Absolutely, Jeff - don't worry. I want my daughter more than anything else."

"I know you do. We'll make it happen."

They agreed on a time to meet at Marshall's office before the hearing, and Simon clenched his free hand into a white-knuckled fist as he thanked him again.

As he hung up, the guard asked, "You okay, Reynolds?"

He turned, taking on a surprised expression. "Yeah. Why?"

"That." He nodded toward Simon's hand.

Simon stretched his fingers, staring at his hand until he could look up with an appropriately melancholy affect. "It's been too long since I saw my mom," he explained, "and my lawyer says I need to avoid her for a while when I get out."

"She sick?"

He shook his head. "She's alone with my dad, and he's a mean drunk."

The guard seemed to accept that. "Let's head back."

In his cell, Simon stared blindly out the window, going over the phone call, thinking about the people who interfered in his life. Got in the way of his family. The ones who helped his wife get away, and then helped her turn his daughter against him.

He bit the inside of his cheek until he drew blood. He moved to the sink and spat into it, watching the blood slide toward the drain.

She managed to get Will Remmond, Jeff had said, like this Remmond guy was some kind of a superhero.

*So they have a hero now. Like they need someone to save them from **me**.*

His head throbbed with the rage of it, and he stared himself down in the small mirror over the sink. He spat into the sink again, and the blood pooled at the drain.

*Who the **hell** is Will Remmond?*

❋ ❋ ❋

"C'mon. We'll head north."

"Will, I think you should get some sleep." Max handed the server her coffee cup for a refill.

"Won't happen, darlin'," he said, leaning across the table to kiss her cheek. "I'm just not tired."

She smiled weakly at him, then looked down to where she was playing with his fingers. "Now you know everything. And you're still here." She shook her head slowly. "Wow."

"Why wouldn't I be?"

"I don't know... I put you through an awful lot."

He intertwined his fingers with hers, waiting for her to look up. "Nothing I couldn't handle."

She looked doubtful, then her expression became agonized. "You think I don't remember what I did last night?"

"I know you do." He saw that her struggle was deepening. He tapped their joined hands on the table and said, "Okay. Talk to me."

"Yeah. I need to." She scanned the crowded restaurant. "Can we head out of here?"

"You bet."

They were on the road ten minutes later. Will reached across the seat, pulling her over to sit close to him, and waited until she was ready.

Max wasn't sure where to start. Several minutes went by before she decided on what to bring up first. She said, hesitantly, "I've been with a lot of men, Will."

"I know."

"Have you thought about that?"

"Speak up a little, Max."

"Okay." She opened her mouth to continue, then sighed, discouraged, and looked at the floor. She'd never been adept at discussions that involved the truth about how she felt. She was much better at - and far more comfortable with - talking about what she thought.

"Hey," he rubbed her leg, "just say it. You're gonna want to talk about it sooner or later."

"You mean you don't?"

"The only talking I want to do is with the guys who hurt you." He rested his arm behind her, across the top of the seat, and she moved closer to him.

"You're kidding."

He shook his head, and she saw the muscles working in his jaw. "No," he said quietly, a menacing tone to his voice, one she had never heard before. "I'm not kidding."

"I made choices, you know."

"If that's what you want to call them." He glanced at the road signs. "Want to take Route One?"

"Yeah."

Will didn't seem inclined to elaborate, and she didn't know if she wanted him to, but she nudged him anyway. "I don't understand what you're saying."

"The choices you made... They weren't honest choices."

"Sure they were."

He glanced at the sign they were passing. "Hold on," he said.

He pulled into a rest stop, over to the far end, where he parked the truck under a group of shade trees. After collecting his thoughts, he turned to her and asked, "Before last night, how much of your past factored into your decisions?"

She thought he sounded strangely clinical, and that she was seeing a different side of him.

"You mean, how much did I remember? Not all of it, not even a lot of it. But enough to be smarter."

He shook his head. "No, not 'remember' - how much of it were you *conscious* of?"

"I don't get what you're asking."

"Look, you were a kid who came flying out of an insane asylum with no money, no plan, and no one to trust. And a bellyful of rage that came from a couple of decades of being violated by the guy who was *supposed* to be the safest place in the world for you."

He realized he was getting too loud when she gently put her finger to his lips, and he stopped to take a calming breath before he went on.

"I see it all the time in my practice, Max. A boy will come out of one of these violent homes, run wild, and he gets compassion. And he should, don't get me wrong - but the girls get condemned. The boys are called 'troubled' while the girls are called... Other things. The entire system tends to hold women more accountable than men, and it drives me nuts. Because the needs... The emotional makeup is different."

She was fascinated. He'd never talked that way before. "That's not exactly politically correct, Counselor."

"Yeah, well, that's not my thing."

"Different how?"

Will was tapping the back of the seat, looking beyond her through the window, thinking deeply. "The boys, believe it or not - they're the ones who try to understand, try to find the reality of what happened to their mothers. They process it, you know? I honestly believe that when they do the legwork, they have a real chance to turn out okay. They make their way in the world."

It was an unexpected glimpse of his philosophical side, and she listened intently.

"I never bought that conventional wisdom that they're somehow destined to become abusers themselves, and when I get the chance to talk with them, that's what I tell them." His voice took on a softer tone as he added, "A lot of them kept in touch with me over the years, and they're centered, productive men now."

He shifted his gaze to her face, suddenly at a loss for words as he thought about her past. "But the girls..."

Max waited a moment, then prompted him. "Safety," she said.

He nodded. "Yeah. And for some reason, one that I don't fully get, they base that feeling of safety on being *accepted*. They go out there damaged, and scared, and they look for somewhere safe. The problem is, they have no idea what 'safe' looks like, because they've never seen it - and they sure as hell aren't going to learn about it in this culture."

"Jo and I used to debate whether or not this is the most misogynistic culture in human history. She said it is." Max was relaxed now, deep into the conversation - eager to learn more about his thoughts.

"I'd probably side with her."

"In the end, I did."

Will seemed preoccupied again, and she lightly touched his cheek. "What?"

"I'm thinking about my cases, how the men are so quick to claim 'victim' status, and then everybody comes running to make it all better. The women have to bottle it all up until they explode, and then they pay for that, too. Because if they do start talking, they're judged even more harshly."

Max was slowly coming to understand why it was that Will seemed to elicit such hatred from other men.

She recalled Ray Bailey, one of the only decent men she had known growing up. Max's father had managed to get Ray "defellowshipped" from the church. Ray was always coming to the defense of the women there, speaking his mind and admonishing the men in the church about the things he thought were wrong, and Max's father absolutely hated him. She remembered him saying, "He gets the women thinking they're being mistreated, and then they hold their husbands to impossible standards." When Ray suggested assembling a church panel on addressing the pornography problem in their small congregation, Pastor Allen decided that was the last straw. He made the case for the Deacons - way too easily, Max thought - that Ray was a troublemaker, causing conflict, and he drummed Ray out of the church. Only one of the other men in the church protested, and they got rid of him three months later.

Max was sixteen then, and she had mocked her father for it, asking him more than once, "So, exactly how is it that respecting women raised the standards too high, Daddy?"

She couldn't recall for sure, but she thought that the last time she asked it was the last time he ever slapped her.

Will was saying, "We got off track here. We're talking about you."

"I like these discussions," she protested. "You've got some unusual ideas."

"That's why Sammy thinks I'm some kind of a knuckle-dragging simian."

A smile passed quickly across her face. "I'm fine with it."

"The thing is..." He hesitated, then said, "If you would've gone out and slept with someone else last night..."

Max looked down at her hands, and he kissed the top of her head. "Don't do that. Look at me."

She did, but she was anxious. "I wish I hadn't *said* that. I can't believe... I wish I hadn't done what I did."

"Then after this, how's about we decide that none of it ever happened."

"We can't do that, Will."

"We can do whatever we want. And then maybe you can extend me the same deal for what I did."

She opened her mouth to argue it, but he spoke first. "Anyway, if you had done that last night, it wouldn't have been the same as if you were to do it tonight. Or after tonight. Because now, you're making choices out of a different mindset. An awareness that you didn't have until now."

"So you want me to believe it honestly doesn't bother you?"

"It bothers me. Sure it does. But like I said, what I'm bothered by are the guys who hurt you before you cleared your head."

"Seems like you're reaching a bit. Like you're trying to excuse me so you can feel better about being with me."

"And you seem determined to regard yourself as some kind of a marked woman." He hurried on, ignoring his reaction to her comment - thinking maybe she had a point, but not wanting to examine it. Not at that moment. "Look, I'm not putting you on a pedestal. I'm being realistic. Because I'm not as invested in your sense of pride as you are."

"Pride?"

"Yeah. Like you weren't taken in. Couldn't be manipulated by guys who wanted to use you."

It hit a nerve, and she briefly considered it.

"Maybe," she mumbled.

"Besides, what you did before me is none of my business. And Max," he took her hand, "there's something else you aren't thinking about."

"What?"

"I'm not a virgin anymore." He grinned wryly.

She burst into relieved laughter. "Then just forget it, Remmond. The engagement's off."

"We aren't engaged until that ring makes it to your left hand." He brought his arm off the back of the seat, pulling her to him. With their faces close together, he said, "Know what really floors me about you?"

She shook her head.

"I think about what you've gone through, things that would have completely destroyed a lesser woman, and yet you still have this incredible capacity to love. Like the secret you've kept to protect Sammy. The way you love her kids. And look at what you care about here - how I feel, what you think you put me through, worrying about everything but yourself."

She ducked her head, embarrassed, and Will smiled as he saw her fingers move to her lips.

He cupped his hand under her chin, lifting her head. "Feeling better?"

"Much."

He brushed his lips against her cheek. "Okay." He whispered in her ear, "I was going to kiss you and make it all better." He pushed her hair away, talking softly against her neck. "But if you're all set..."

"I'm actually..." She lost track of the thought as he pulled the strap of her camisole aside and kissed her bare shoulder.

"You're actually...?"

"Very needy right now," she sighed, lifting her head as he left a trail of kisses along her throat.

"What do you need?" he murmured.

She closed her eyes. "A man who really loves me."

"Right here, darlin'." As his lips found hers, he said it again. "Right here."

chapter 10

"Brandi."

A chill ran through her as she turned from the candy rack at the checkout, and faced the woman behind her. Brandi knew the voice, because even when Simon's mother spoke quietly, she had an malevolent shrill to her tone.

"Mrs. Reynolds," she bit out. She resisted the impulse to add, "Are *you* stalking me now?"

"Where's Alexa?"

Don't borrow trouble, Brandi, Will had said. *For the duration, you're competing for Miss Congeniality.*

"She's at home."

"By herself?"

Brandi thought that Katrina Reynolds actually seemed hopeful that Alexa was home alone.

If you run into them, 'yes' and 'no' answers. Anything more than that, you'll start chatting. And after a minute, excuse yourself. Politely.

"No." She returned the pack of gum to the rack. "Excuse me, Mrs. Reynolds. Have a nice day."

Brandi was almost to her car when she heard Katrina shouting from somewhere behind her:

"Four days, Brandi! Then he comes home!"

She dove into her car and grabbed her phone from the dash. "Be there, be there," she chanted softly.

"Law offices of Delaney-Remmond," a woman's voice answered.

"Is Will Remmond there?"

"Attorney Remmond is on vacation until Tuesday. Are you a client?"

She ran a trembling hand through her hair. "Yes."

"Name?"

"Brandi Reynolds. Can you reach him?"

"This is the answering service, ma'am. He'll check in for his messages. Would you like to leave one?"

She squeezed the bridge of her nose to keep herself from crying. "Tell him to call me. As soon as he can. He has my number."

The woman was typing rapidly. "Is there anything else?"

"No. That's it. 'Bye." Brandi tossed her phone onto the passenger's seat. She picked it up again to call her father, then decided that she should get out of there.

Before the crazy old bitch keys my car or something.

She scanned the lot, didn't see Katrina anywhere, and hurriedly took off for home.

I guess I didn't really have anything to tell him, just wanted to hear his voice.

She decided there was nothing wrong with that: it was kind of like falling in love with the doctor who was trying to save her life. That was the analogy her best friend had used the day before.

"I know, I *know*," Brandi had answered. "But Jules, you should *see* the guy."

"Hot?"

"Mmm. Six-two or so, hazel eyes, great smile. Definitely works out, *no* doubt."

"Ow. You got it bad, Branders."

"And long hair, the kind you want to just grab handfuls of. Almost to his shoulders..."

Julie laughed. "We need to go out tonight. You're going crazy."

"I probably am. I need to pack more, though. I'm still in the process of moving in with Mom and Dad."

"Yeah. Sorry 'bout that, by the way."

It's not fair.

She turned onto the street where her parents lived, deciding that all in all, things could be worse - at least, within this part of her life. She had a great family, all standing behind her, and Alexa was safe there.

For now.

She sat staring through the windshield with Katrina's words echoing in her head:

Four days.

✸ ✸ ✸

Will turned the radio down. "You've never been this far north?"

"No, the farthest I ever went into Maine was last October, when we got lost." She grinned at him, poking him in the ribs. "Told you we were heading in the wrong direction." She laid her head on his shoulder, thinking that her life needed to stand still, right there. It was perfect.

"Yeah, well, that turned out okay."

"I remember." She reached for her purse, and pulled her cell out. "I've had this picture here ever since." She turned her phone on to show him, and the screen came up with *11 Missed Calls*. "Ugh. Never mind," she said as she turned it off again.

"I guess I should check my messages soon," Will grumbled.

Catching his tone, Max asked, "You really are burning out, aren't you?"

"Maybe. Could be that I'm just so glad to be on the lam with you that I can't picture going back to Boston." He gave her a quick kiss on the head, keeping his eyes on the winding road.

"Where are we going?"

"Beats me. We'll know it when we see it."

Max moved away from him far enough that she could lay on her back with her head on his leg, dangling her bare feet out the window.

"That's illegal, Ms. Allen."

"I haven't seen a cop since we left New Hampshire." She smiled up at him. "Besides, I have a great lawyer."

"Wrapped around your finger." He nodded toward a sign as they passed it. "State park up here. Let's check it out."

He pulled in to a small, graveled parking area. "Look at this," he said, as the vista of the lake appeared in front of them.

Max sat up quickly and looked around.

"Oh my gosh..." she breathed.

The water was deep blue and perfectly still, surrounded by tall pines and towering oaks and maples. A dock extended fifty feet out. They walked to the end of it, and sat together quietly, taking it in.

After a few minutes, Will extended his hand. "Give me the ring."

"What? Why?"

He waited. His expression told her that he was serious, so she slipped it from her finger and put it in his hand.

He closed his eyes for a few seconds, then turned to her.

Max was looking at the ring in his hand, and he lightly touched her chin, lifting her head toward him.

"Right here," he said, catching her eyes. "I want to do this right."

"Will..."

"I know. You don't want to. But just in case you change your mind, I want this to be the memory - and not you finding your ring in my truck." He took her right hand, and slid the ring back onto her finger. "I want to be your husband, Maxine. If you ever decide that you want that, too..." He kissed her hand. "Just don't say it'll never happen. Okay?"

She was struck by how he phrased it; and for the first time, she allowed the thought to linger, that she might one day call a man her husband. It had never before occurred to her that there could be more to it than just being someone's wife.

She smiled into his eyes. "Okay."

"Yeah?" He seemed stunned. "Okay?"

She nodded, mimicking his shocked expression.

"Option's open?"

"Option's open." She thought she had never seen him smile that way, like he was in some kind of disbelieving awe. She shifted onto his lap, straddling him as she pushed him onto his back, her hands on his chest.

"Whoa," he laughed. "I'm being ravaged."

"Yup." She laid on top of him, sprinkling him with kisses on his face and neck. "I'm kinda desperately in love with you, Remmond."

He sat up and wrapped his arms around her waist, holding her on his lap. With their faces close together, he said softly, "The platonic thing didn't last long."

"It didn't. But it lasted long enough."

"Hope so."

"You wanted me to trust you." She saw the question in his eyes, and she said, "And I do."

He pulled her close, his head resting against her neck. "You're an incredible woman, Maxine Allen," he sighed.

They sat that way for another minute, then Max rolled off of his lap and stood up. She held her hand out to him and said, "C'mon. Let's go back."

"Already?" He took her hand and got to his feet.

She slipped her sandals on. "We have to head back to New Hampshire tomorrow. And I want a re-do."

"Of what?"

She glanced away, then caught herself and looked directly at him again.

"Last night," she said.

Will nodded. "Yeah. Absolutely." He picked her up to hug her, and she was momentarily breathless from how tightly he held her. "Anything you want."

"Ooh, I *like* that," she purred. She pulled back, studying his face, playing with the hair at the back of his neck. She took on her low, sultry tone, and she said, "I *like* being in charge." Then she ran her tongue around her lips, pressing them against his ear and breathing softly.

Will was mesmerized. He moaned as she planted several delicate kisses on his throat.

She stopped suddenly, smiling mischievously as she gave him a quick peck on his cheek.

"Okay, let's go," she said cheerfully as she squirmed from his arms.

His head fell back, and he looked up to the sky for a moment, then grinned down at her. "Payback, huh?"

"Yup." She winked at him. "That platonic stuff was hard to take. You'll be paying for that for a long time, Remmond."

He broke into laughter, then changed to a dramatic, solemn expression as he clutched at his chest.

"You're just killin' me, doll," he said, and he deliberately tipped sideways, off of the dock and into the lake.

Max shrieked in disbelief. "*Will!*" she shouted, falling to her knees on the dock and reaching for him as he surfaced, whipping his hair from his face and smiling broadly. "What are you *doing?* Isn't it freezing?"

"That's the idea. No shower available." He reached for her hand. "It's not too bad - come on."

She scrambled to her feet, backing away. "What? No. I can't swim."

"You went swimming at Bow Lake last summer."

"No I didn't. I never go in over my waist." She watched him treading water, and she shook her head. "I can't swim," she said again.

"I'll catch you. C'mon. I'll let you dunk me."

"It's so *deep*."

"Good thing, too. You can't feel all the wildlife on the bottom."

"That doesn't help, Will."

"Sorry." He floated on his back for a few seconds. "You look like you really want to jump in, Max."

"I... Nah. Come on out of there."

He faced her again, treading water with one hand while he pointed at her with the other. "You. Tapped. *Out*."

"Not yet, I haven't." She folded her arms and stared at him. "We don't have any dry clothes."

"Towels in the truck," he insisted, and then he disappeared under the surface.

He went deep, and Max lost sight of him after a moment; then, she felt something poke her foot from behind.

She shrieked again, turning to see Will with his arms resting on the dock, grinning up at her. She crouched, grabbed the top of his head, and dunked him.

He resurfaced quickly. "You sure you don't want to jump in? It's a hot day. Feels *great* in here."

She appeared to be thinking it over, and he said again, "I'll catch you."

Max slipped her sandals off. "You promise?" she asked hesitantly.

Will took in her wide-eyed expression, and the way she was nervously tapping her hands on her thighs, and he found it difficult to talk around the sudden lump in his throat.

"I promise," he said.

She balled her hands into fists, closed her eyes, and jumped.

He caught her immediately, going under for a moment as he held her head above the surface. Then he kicked his way up again, quickly, before she could panic.

She was bewildered by his expression.

"Will?"

"I can't believe you did that." With an incredulous shake of his head, he said, "You amazing..."

"Oh, c'mon," she smiled, pleased with herself. He maneuvered them toward the dock, and she grabbed the side of it as she said, "I knew you'd catch me."

"I know." He kissed her gently. "That's exactly what I mean."

He had a way of making her believe that he admired her - that maybe there were things about her that were admirable. That maybe, there was more to her than what she saw in herself. No one had ever done that for her.

With her hand on the back of his neck, she pulled him close.

"Kiss me again, Remmond," she whispered. "You need some serious payback."

chapter II

"Listen, Will - I'm glad you're having a good time, but give us a call soon, okay?"

Dave tossed his phone on the table, taking a box of dishes from the kitchen counter.

"Leave them be, Dave." Sam was sitting cross-legged on the counter, making a list of the day's errands.

"He has messages he needs to return."

"How many messages can he have? He's wrapped up his cases here, and we aren't in New Hampshire yet." She set the list aside. "You're the one who said, 'Remmond, take a vacation already.'"

"I know. I also told him to check in a few times. He has the Brandi Reynolds case up there, and she's been trying to reach him. Gina's already taking calls for him, and she left *me* a message to have him call her." He put the box on the counter again to reattach the tape. "I'm going to have to tell her to just go ahead and schedule him out of the new offices for Tuesday. I have no idea what he wants."

"By the way, I never asked him - how did that happen, that he got Brandi Reynolds?"

"Her lawyer called him before she went on maternity leave, asked him to step in." He set the box by the kitchen door. "He's a sucker for those cases."

"I think you miss him." She grinned at him, dangling her legs from the counter.

"C'mon."

"Never thought you'd get caught up in a bromance, honey," she teased.

Dave stood in front of her, pulling her forward so she straddled his waist. "I'm just a little overloaded, I guess. We really needed this weekend off."

Sam rested her arms on his shoulders, leaning forward so their foreheads touched. Looking up into his eyes, she said, "Something else is bothering you."

"Yeah."

"What?"

"Not sure." He lifted his head and kissed her on the nose. "I wonder... I get the feeling sometimes that he's on his way out."

She frowned. "From the firm?"

"From practicing law. Period."

"Wow. Really?"

He nodded. "Maybe he's just exhausted. But he's nowhere near as involved as he used to be."

"Maybe this time off will help. In the meantime, why don't *you* call his client back, and leave the young lovers alone?"

"That's the other thing I'm worried about."

"What?"

"Us. We have no time together." He pulled her closer, and she wrapped her legs around his waist. "Real life set in at some point," he said, "and suddenly the old guy is off someplace being young, and I'm here being a stodgy old man."

Not again.

"You are not." She hoped her laugh sounded genuine. "'Old guy'?"

"Well, yeah - he *is* older than me."

"What's up with you lately? We're fine." She noted the lines that were forming around his eyes and the creases on his forehead. "You know what *I* think of you?"

"I wonder sometimes."

"You stop that." She clipped his shoulder. "I think you have no idea how fantastic you really are. You never did see yourself realistically." She was massaging the sides of his neck. "You're a lot more than you think."

He looked skeptical, and she sighed, frustrated by the way he was always second-guessing himself.

"Dave, all these things you worry about - did it ever occur to you that they're the things I never have to concern myself with? Because you take care of it all?"

"You have plenty of things to do," he said.

"Yes, I do. And I'm able to do those things because of *you*. And more than that, old man..."

He grinned at her. "Maybe I was a bit dramatic."

"You were. More than that, you're absolutely brilliant, a great lover..."

"Just great?"

She sighed again. "Earthquake-inducing."

"That'll work."

"And you're seriously hot." She played with a lock of his dark, curly hair. "Ya'll got this body that just don't quit," she added in a playful southern accent, and then she smacked his shoulder again. "So lighten up."

He put his hand up to stop her. "Okay, that's enough," he said. "I'm already tired of myself."

She snuggled up against him. "You're the only one."

He held her, reluctant to interrupt the moment, but he had put it off for long enough.

"Sammy, there's something else we need to talk about."

Of course there is.

"Mmm. And what would that be?"

He pulled away from her and said, "The other night, when I picked you up after your group at the center..."

The expression on her face told him that she knew what was coming.

"I heard about what you said, about that guy who came in right at the end."

"That fat-ass yahoo who thought he could intimidate me?" She rolled her eyes. "What an incredible twit."

"Baby, they said he was furious."

"Yeah? Well, I had just spent two hours with his ex-girlfriend. So was I."

"You called him an amoral, misogynistic bastard?"

"No, I called him an amoral, misogynistic *prick*."

"Sammy..." he groaned.

"I'm not an idiot, Dave. I wouldn't put a battered woman in danger - he didn't hear me. He had already stomped out."

"But the others heard you."

She faked a sorrowful expression. "I was hormonal. I think I had an estrogen rush or something." She said it with a sarcastically plaintive tone, and Dave was irritated that she wasn't taking him seriously.

"Sammy, what you do - it has plenty of hazards already built in. You don't want to be pouring gasoline on a fire, you know? What if he had heard you?"

She was nodding impatiently as he spoke. "I know, I know. I get it. I'll tone it down." She smiled hopefully, holding her arms out to him. "Lift me off of here. I need to check on Hope."

Dave watched her hurry out of the kitchen. His stomach was in knots. Sam was changing in ways that left him feeling like he didn't know her at times, and she was becoming increasingly reckless in recent months. When she had the opportunity, she was openly combative with some of the men who happened to show up at the center. And she seemed to actually enjoy confronting them, which was what concerned him the most.

He knew that she still hurt over Jo, and he wondered at times if she was still grieving the murders that had happened shortly after she started at the center. A little boy was shot by his father; then four days later, a young mother was stabbed to death, and

Sam had worked with both of the victims. She said she was fine, but Dave had his doubts. She tended to feel guilty over things that she had no control over - continually trying to prove that she wasn't some kind of a bad seed.

He was relieved that at least she was done at the center, and that she and the kids were heading to the house in New Hampshire in a couple of days. They had cancelled their plans for the weekend, and were going to spend their first anniversary getting ready for them to move.

It certainly wasn't Dave's first choice for an anniversary celebration, but it was what she wanted, and she was too excited for him to protest; besides, he was happy to get her out of Boston. Away from the city's DV center, and off to somewhere safer.

But in the back of his mind, he knew he was kidding himself. No place was really safe, not for someone doing the work that she did, and he made a mental note to get a security system installed at the house.

And to watch carefully, and figure out what was really going on with Samantha.

❊ ❊ ❊

Will was sleeping, so deeply that it was difficult to hear him breathing.

Max pulled his arm from underneath the pillow, checking his watch and laughing softly as she saw that it was only nine o'clock.

"So much for our night out," she whispered. She kissed him gently on the cheek as she returned his hand to where it was before.

He would be upset that he fell asleep, she knew that. But he'd been awake for thirty-six hours straight, with most of that time spent dealing with her, and she wasn't about to wake him.

She looked toward the door, thinking she should probably head back to her room and knowing that she wouldn't, because she wanted to wake up with him. As she turned the light off, it occurred to her that she wanted to wake up with him every morning.

Will was still laying on his stomach with his arms under the pillows, in the same position he was in when she started giving him a backrub two hours earlier. She nudged him gently until he moved onto his side; then, she curled up with her back against him. His arm came over her, and she hugged it tight against her body as she reflected on their time in Maine.

Closing her eyes, she thought of the night before, and the way he held her. *You're safe now*, he'd said, and her eyes filled as she felt again the relief of it.

Fool.

She squeezed her eyes tightly shut.
Miracle. **His** *miracle.*
She thought about Will's arms coming around her as she hit the water that afternoon. She had wanted to jump into that water because she *knew* he would catch her, and she wanted to know that feeling.

You're a fool, Max-eene.

She drew her legs up, remembering how she wanted that kiss, the one they shared in the lake, to last forever. She told Will that on the way home. And they laughed, and he said that was as bad as, "Where have you been all my life?"

Wait until after he screws you and dumps you on your ass.

Turning her face into the pillow, she thought again about the way Will had fought for her.

Hard to believe, because he knows exactly what you are.

Which was something she couldn't comprehend, because he knew exactly what she was. Probably even better than she did, because he had endured the brunt of her anger.

She tightened her hold on his arm, hugging it to herself just beneath her breasts.

Looks like the girls are happy in that sweater, Max-eene.

Cringing, she moved carefully out from under Will's arm and sat up.
This can't work.
When she looked down at him, her heart began beating erratically as she thought, only for a second, that he was her father. She realized that she must have been a little bit asleep, because Will looked absolutely nothing like him. And she understood that her father had gotten into her head again.
Into my bed again.
The hair stood on the back of her neck.
She looked anxiously around the room, wondering where the thought came from. Her father had been on her bed only that once, when he chased her into her room and was on top of her, slapping her, ripping at her shirt.

Maybe I'll tell the deacons that you were in my bed again, Dad-dy.

She glanced at Will, still sleeping beside her, and quickly slid off of the bed. Standing at the window on the far side of his room, she looked out over the hotel's grounds, trying to capture the memories of those final days of being terrorized by her father.

Bet you don't know which one of them is great in the sack. Look around the room at the next meeting, why don't you?

Max was seventeen then, and she hadn't slept with any of the church elders. She was already promiscuous, what she called "a proud Jezebel," and mocking her father with it every chance she got - but she wanted only to provoke him with the comment about the deacons. Make him wonder. Show him who had the power now.

She remembered it clearly now, the day that she finally took over - standing in the doorway to his office, slowly smoothing gloss onto her lips and regarding him with humored contempt. She threatened him with the fact that she could expose the truth about him any time she wanted.

Either that, or maybe I'll just screw every nice boy at your church, **Dad-dy**.

He had come instantly out of his chair, his legs hitting the bottom of his desk so hard that it tipped precariously, and he charged across the room.

Max didn't turn to run, didn't move at all. "*Do it*," she hissed, and he stopped dead, staring at her in bewildered, shaken disbelief.

Her smile was one she had practiced for years, waiting for that moment.

"C'mon, *Daddy*. Leave a mark on me. Because the next time you do, I'm calling the cops. And no, I don't give a rat's *ass* what happens after."

She stayed with her friend Annie for a while after that. When she eventually went home, they pretended it had never happened - except for the fact that Pastor Allen was careful to avoid her. She was perfectly content with the arrangement, biding her time until she left for college.

Max recalled what Will said earlier that day, about going out into the world with the way she was at that age. Hating men. Hating most people, and not caring at all about the rest. She didn't know if she agreed with him, that she bore so little responsibility for the things she did back then; but she understood his perspective, and it was worth thinking about. She thought that his comment about her pride had been a direct hit.

She turned from the window and watched him sleep, wondering how he could possibly be in love with her. It seemed wrong somehow - degrading, toward *him* - that she wanted to drop her clothes on the floor and crawl back into his bed. As she imagined the ways in which she could wake him, her feelings for him went suddenly, completely flat at the same time that pain flared in her stomach.

Twisting the ring around her finger, she thought, *I can't. That's not what I am.*

She swiped at her eyes, wanting to wake him up and tell him that he was wasting his life on a woman with a reverse Madonna-whore complex. And she wanted him to hold her while she cried over it.

Eventually, she felt calm enough to return to his bed, and she curled up facing away from him again.

His arms came around her. "Love you," he mumbled, but she could tell that he was still dead to the world.

She bit her lip to keep from crying again. In the moment before she fell asleep, she thought again, *He fought for this.*

And she whispered, "I love you, too."

The next thing she knew, sunlight was coming in the picture window, and she opened her eyes, becoming aware of Will nuzzling her neck.

"Good morning," he murmured, close to her ear. "I have something to make up to you."

Max recalled her thoughts from the night before. She rolled over to face him, running her hand along the stubble on his cheek. "You're starting to look like a beach bum. I like it."

"So do I. And I'm sorry I fell asleep."

"Don't be. I'm glad you did. You were worn out."

"You know," he lifted her to lay on top of him, "I want to wake up with you every morning for the rest of my life."

"Mmm. We'll talk." She settled in, playing with his hair. "You really mean it, don't you? You're done with the bachelor thing?"

"Oh, yeah. I've been done for a while now."

She was tracing the contours of his face as if she was memorizing him. "I really do love you, Will Remmond." She kissed him then, desperately longing for it to be different - for it to be an uncomplicated moment of two people who loved each other, waking up together to a beautiful day.

"You have *no* idea what it does to me when you say that." He smoothed her hair from her eyes, and she could tell where his mind was going to as his hands traveled down her back.

Her body tensed immediately.

"Will..." She started to push away from him, and he tightened his arms around her.

"Wait."

"I can't even think about that."

"I know," he said reassuringly. "I know. Don't worry about it. I'm not looking at this like we ran away for a few days, and now everything's fine."

She propped herself up with her elbows on his chest, her eyes wide with anxiety . "I don't know if I can ever... I really don't know what's going to happen."

"Neither of us does. So why are you worrying about it now? It's not like there's a time limit or anything." He gently rubbed her back. "I know you aren't ready. I don't see how you could be."

"Really?" she asked. "You're okay with that? Then why are you..."

"Running my hands all over you?" He laughed softly. "There's a beautiful woman in my bed. I have a pulse. It's one of those typical-guy things."

She didn't seem amused; if anything, she became more troubled. "This can't be easy for you."

"Is it easy for *you*?"

She ducked her head, recalling her thoughts the night before. "No."

"I mean, sure - I could spend a few hours here making you go crazy." His hands were inside her shirt, on her bare back, and he ran his fingers slowly down her spine until she shivered. "But you're cleaning out a lot of baggage. So trust me, I'm not expecting anything."

She looked up then. "But what if I never get there?"

"Don't underestimate us. Besides," he grinned, "we aren't even officially engaged. I'm just *not* that kind of a boy, Ms. Allen."

She punched his shoulder. "Yes you are."

"Okay, I am. And so, until you decide that you want those hours of unbridled passion..."

"Geez, you're arrogant."

"I know. For good reason, too. So, until then," he ran his hands down her ribs, encircling her waist as he left a gentle kiss on her neck, "what's wrong with being held and touched by a man who loves you more than anything in the world?"

Will had never seen her eyes turn dreamy before, and he savored the moment, thinking he wanted to make that happen more often. "No pressure, darlin'. It'll happen someday. When you say so."

"Wow," she mumbled, suddenly confused.

"Wow, what? You still think I really am one of those typical guys?"

She shook her head. "I've been going Jekyll-Hyde with you for how long now, and in the end, *you're* the one who says 'no'?"

"I'm not saying 'no'. I'm saying we have time. Later." He nuzzled her neck again, breathing softly against her ear as he said, "When I can have *every part* of you."

She closed her eyes. "I really love how you talk," she whispered.

"On the other hand," he teased, bringing her face close to his again, "I may just use sex as leverage to get you to marry me. Make *you* suffer for a change."

She bit his bottom lip, hanging on to it as she mumbled, "That could work."

"I'll keep it in mind," he mumbled in response.

She rolled off of him. "I'm hungry, Remmond. Feed me." She got off the bed as Will stretched, groaning.

"I didn't even buy you dinner last night."

"I know." She bent over him, kissing him quickly. "I'm going to shower. Be ready when I get back."

"Yes, ma'am."

Max hurried from his room, thinking about what he had said, and wondering if she should tell him her thoughts during the night. She decided there was no reason to ruin their last hours in Maine with yet another difficult conversation.

As she closed her door, she caught her reflection in the mirror at the far end of the room. She studied her reflection, how small she appeared to herself. She thought that she looked frightened.

Of what?

It was a moment she'd experienced only a handful of times throughout her life, a feeling of arriving at a fork in the road. Almost every other time, she had gone on the path of least resistance; this time, though, was different. She couldn't imagine her life without Will.

I'm sick of this. I'm letting a dead guy control me.

All at once she realized that by her choice to play proxy - and she knew that it was her own choice, no matter what Will said - her father was now also controlling *him*. It was as if her father was reaching out from his grave, wrapping his cold, dead fingers around Will's neck, and she herself was facilitating it.

"Not him." She leaned her back against the door, shaking her head. "Not Will."

He's paid enough.

She knew that she had to choose a side. And then, she had to stay put.

Max made a silent promise to herself - and to Will - that she was going to do just that. Stay put. Because for the first time in her life, that was exactly what she wanted to do.

Three hours later, they stood hand in hand on their rock, the one where they had talked, and dreamed, and planned - and done battle. They watched the thick, gray clouds circling in over the ocean.

"We'll come back," Will said.

Max wrapped her arms around his waist. "When?"

"Soon, darlin'." He planted a kiss on her head.

They made their way back to the truck, and Max turned to take one more look. A couple of seagulls landed on the spot where they had just been, and she tugged on his hand.

"Look." She pointed to them, and Will smiled.

"Yeah," he said, his expression wistful. "Let's leave them right there."

As they drove away, Max slid across the seat and laid her head on his shoulder. "Soon, right?" she asked.

They were at the end of the hotel's long driveway, waiting to turn onto the main road, and he put his arm around her to pull her closer. Smiling down at her, he said, "Promise."

"Okay."

Max lifted her eyes to his.

She said, "That's good enough for me."

An Early Frost
Part Two

*And that's where love is revealed: in abandoning the outcome, casting
the self aside, inviting the consequences that will come.
Even if the love we offer to others is not received -
which may be the definition of loneliness -
that doesn't mean it ceases to exist, because real love
ignores the cost, braves the darkness, lights the way.*

*The measure of love within the human heart is revealed by
the price we are willing to pay to express it.*

chapter 12

SAM GLANCED AT her phone.

"*Yes.*" She snatched it from the corner of her desk. "Finally."

"Sammy? You there?"

"About time, Maxine," she said. "Where have you two been?"

"Maine. At the Dew-Drop Inn." She smiled up at Will. "Will thinks I'm a cheap date."

He chuckled, giving her hand a quick squeeze as he merged onto the highway.

Sam was asking, "Are you ever coming home?"

"Regrettably, yeah. We just crossed the bridge into New Hampshire. Happy anniversary, by the way."

"Thanks." She propped her legs on the desk, reaching for her coffee as she settled in. "How is everything?"

"Hmm. What's 'everything'?"

"C'mon, Max. Dish."

She turned to Will. "Sammy wants me to dish."

"Up to you." Then he whispered, "Tell her we eloped."

"Nah. She'd faint, and I don't know if she's holding the baby."

"Hey, guys - what are you talking about?" Sam was anxiously tapping her fingers. "What happened?"

"Will wants me to tell you we eloped."

She brought her legs off the desk with a thud. "*What?*"

"We didn't. He's just being bratty."

"Geez..." She sat back again. "Smack him for me. You guys had a nice time?"

"Wound up like that, yeah." Max quickly kissed Will on the cheek.

He looked surprised. "What's that for?"

"Sammy said to smack you," she whispered, and kissed him again.

Sam was waiting. "So...?" Several seconds later, she growled, "Maxine..."

"Hmm?"

"Okay, fine," Sam sighed. "Put Will on."

Still amused, Max handed him her phone. "She wants to talk to you. Being nosy."

"She's like that." He grinned as he put the phone to his ear. "Hey, kiddo. Happy anniversary."

"Sounds like it went well."

"It did." He winked at Max, trying not to laugh.

Sam waited again. When he didn't elaborate, she snapped, "You two had better be stopping *here*," and she was loud enough that Will held the phone away from his ear.

"Whoa," he said. "Settle, Sammy. We'll be there in a couple hours. I'm stopping by my house first."

She checked her watch. "Staying for dinner, right?"

He tapped Max's hand. "She wants us to stay for dinner."

"She's making dinner *today?* Dave's a bum."

Sam heard her, and said, "We're ordering in. We have a ton of stuff to do."

"It's a date, Sammy. See you soon."

"Wait," Sam hurried to stop him from disconnecting. "Have you checked your messages?"

"Yup. Tell Dave thanks for taking care of Brandi Reynolds." He remembered their new home then, and quickly added, "And the house - congratulations."

"Thanks. The kids and I are moving in on Monday. You helping out?"

"Yes, ma'am. Absolutely." He tapped the brakes as they approached heavy traffic. "Gotta drive, Sammy. Be there soon."

As he handed Max her phone, she asked, "Absolutely what?"

"Helping Sammy and Dave move on Monday."

"Move…?"

"Yeah. They're renting the house in Hudson until the closing. Dave left me a message. So did Em, by the way - with Dave and Sammy moving this weekend, they had to redo the party."

"What's the plan?"

"They reserved one of the dining rooms at the Plaza for tomorrow night. Talked them into meeting them for dinner, got them a sitter and everything."

Max rolled her eyes. "The Plaza. I need to unpack. I have no idea where my dressy clothes are."

He squinted, trying to see ahead to what was slowing them down. "This is strange. Memorial Day weekend, the traffic should be heading out of Mass, not towards it."

Max shrugged. "I don't mind. It gives us a little more time alone." She reached to turn on the air conditioning.

"Doesn't work," Will said. He glanced at her sweatshirt. "You have anything on under that?"

"Huh? Under my shirt?"

"It's getting hot in here already. Thought you'd want to take it off."

"Stop smiling like that." She started to pull it over her head. "And yes, I *do* have something on…"

"Damn," he mumbled.

"So stop staring." She looked at him archly. "Actually, on second thought, feel free."

Will tensed, thinking again about her triggers and hoping he didn't hit one.

Her hair fell over her face as she pulled the sweatshirt off. She stuck her bottom lip out, blowing upwards, and he couldn't help laughing.

Max reached for her sweatshirt again. "Maybe I should put it back on. I know I'm distracting you."

"You are. And don't put it back on." He moved the truck a few feet forward. A breeze blew through then, and he said, "That felt good."

Running her hand up his leg, she asked, "What felt good? I didn't do anything yet."

"Yet?" He turned to look at her, still cautious but intrigued. "You're not helping to lower the temperature in here, Maxine."

"You're right. Here," she started unbuttoning his shirt. "This'll help."

Will grabbed her hand, and she stopped, giving him a questioning look.

"I don't trigger you anymore," he said.

She was quiet for a moment. "No, you don't."

"So you know what I'm talking about?"

She nodded, then finished unbuttoning his shirt and pulled it open for him. "It's actually been a while since that happened. With you, anyway." She sat back, thinking it over. "Other men do, I'll admit that. But not you. I feel safe with you." She sighed then, annoyed that there was anything left to resolve. "Still, there are those other things I'm dealing with."

"I know." He glanced at the road, then returned to her. "There's more to figure out."

It still seemed jumbled in her mind, but she decided to tell him about her thoughts the night before.

"I was thinking about it this morning. See," she shifted to face him, "last night, I was laying there with you, and every time I thought about us - the good things, the way you love me..." Her voice trailed off.

"And what happened?"

"I kept hearing things in my head."

He frowned. "What things?"

"Him. My father. Things he said. It was like he was arguing with me, kind of... He was getting in the way. I thought about you."

She faltered, and tried again. "Us, I mean... Oh, *damn* it," she muttered, frustrated with her seeming inability to get the words out.

"Hey. What's that about?"

It seemed to Max that the closer she got to Will, the more difficult it became to talk with him freely. She was starting to think that rage was the only emotion she could express honestly.

His eyes were on her, concerned, and she followed the impulse to bring her fist down on the seat.

"I am *going* to *say* this."

Will covered her fist with his hand. "Okay," he said, and he waited.

It came out in a rush. "I watched you sleeping, and I felt like I couldn't love anyone as much as I loved you at that moment. And you know what I wanted? I wanted to get naked and wake you up." She paused to check his reaction, hoping he wouldn't respond with one of his witty comebacks.

He was somber, watching her quietly, and he nodded for her to continue.

"And I thought of several creative ways I could do that, too. And all of a sudden..." She couldn't say it. He wouldn't understand, she was sure of it; more than that, he had already been hurt enough.

"Tell me."

She looked out the window at the beautiful spring day, and the regret she'd felt so many times before was there again - the sadness that no day would ever be normal. Just simple, and happy, and not grayed out from the shadows cast by others. Max often envied people who were free to enjoy life, because she always saw herself as being on the outside looking in. And she didn't want Will to be out there with her.

That, she realized, was the best reason of all to tell him the truth. At the same time, she wished he would stop bringing it out of her - because a few minutes earlier, she had been having fun.

"I felt nothing for you. It was like a door slammed shut."

She faced him then, confused by his lack of a reaction. He seemed to be waiting for her to say more.

"That doesn't bother you?" she demanded.

"Well, I'm not happy about it, but I think there's more to it. And even if there isn't, don't you think it would be kind of *expected* at this point?"

Something occurred to her then, and she put her hand to her forehead as she said, "No, wait - that's not right. Know what I felt?"

He shook his head.

"I felt... like I wasn't good enough for you. And then this weird, defiant kind of hostility. Towards *you*. For no reason. And I waited until it passed, but it's scaring me. It's like I can either stay away from you, or I can hurt you. No middle ground."

"That's what you were trying to say this morning."

"Yeah. And I don't know how to deal with it." She caught his expression. "You're right. I am dealing with it."

"You are. But why didn't you wake me up?" He tucked her hair behind her ear and kissed her forehead. "You shouldn't have been alone with that."

She was shaking her head as he spoke. "No, you're wrong. I needed to be alone with it."

"Why?"

"Because you can't fix everything, Will. I need to be able to stand on my own." She touched his cheek apologetically, but she continued. "It's all interrelated, all these destructive things I do. Because I tend to latch on to people, like I'm collecting them. I turn them into a place for me to hide. Jo, Sammy..." She rested her hand on his leg. "You. I'm always looking for a hero, you know? I set people up to act like my savior. Then when they fail..." She paused, trying to find the words to explain. "What you said about safety, how girls look for safety..." She noticed the traffic moving, and she pointed to the road.

He pulled the truck forward a few feet, then turned to her again. "You were saying."

"I think it's one of the things that abused kids suffer with. It's hard to be close to people, because they become nothing more than a means to an end."

"A place to be safe."

"Or a place to dump the poison, or distract me, or to use to feel nothing." She briefly considered it. "All of which could be the same thing, I guess, when you think about it."

"Could be." He felt his usual appreciation for her intellect, and held back a smile that he knew would be inappropriate for the moment. "Probably is."

"So I was thinking about it this morning, and I just... I finally got mad. I've let what my father did go past me - through me - and I've been punishing you, because you *are* that safe place." She put her hand up as he started to speak. "No, Will. This time, *you* need to listen."

"Okay." He nodded once, surprised. "Go ahead."

"I'm sorry, and you need to let me say that - because when you won't let me, I feel helpless. And I don't want to feel helpless anymore. I mean, I can agree, that there are things I've done that were less my fault than my father's - but there have been times that I knew I was hurting you, and I didn't care. I was just so *angry*. And after he died, I had no way of resolving things. So I started in on you." She started tugging on strands of her hair. "I took a lot of sick satisfaction in that, in the power I had over you."

Will opened his mouth to respond, and she gave him a look that stopped him. He gently pulled her hand away from her head.

"Then you took it away. I didn't know what to do." Her expression changed briefly to one of reluctant admiration. "You completely outsmarted me, you know." She inclined her head toward the highway. "Road's opening up a little."

They moved for a slow quarter-mile before they had to stop again.

After he returned his attention to her, she said, "You know, I make these... They're like secret agreements with people, like a contract. One that they know nothing about, because it's in my own head, that they'll never expect too much of me. Or anything at all, really. Never hurt me, make me uncomfortable, criticize me..."

Will was caught off guard by the sudden tightness in his throat. He had needed - badly - to hear what she was saying, and he hadn't realized it until that moment.

"And when they break my secret contract, I attack. I know how to hit people where they live, especially men. Especially *you*. And I'm sorry."

"Maxine..."

"I don't want you stuck inside my past. I don't want to be stuck there, either. I love you." Her voice broke. "I did awful things to you. I need you to forgive me."

He nodded, clenching his jaw and hoping he could hold himself together.

"Done." He reached for her, and she curled up against him. "You don't sound at all like you feel nothing, you know."

"I was just thinking that. Thanks for listening." She laughed softly as she added, "And you can talk now."

Will stroked her hair. "You won't like what I have to say."

"That's okay."

"Okay then. Marry me."

She laughed again with the relief of it. "Geez, Remmond." She poked him in the ribs. "Option's open on that, remember?"

"Just wanted to make sure."

"And you need to move this truck."

He glanced ahead. The traffic was moving again.

"Finally opening up," he said. He kissed the top of her head. "We'll be there in no time."

The realtor's sign in Will's front yard said *Under Contract*.

"You signed off on it, huh?" Max whistled softly. "That was fast."

"Yeah. Got full price."

"When did that happen?"

"Sent her the P and S on..." Will was frowning, trying to recall it. "Wednesday." He pulled into the driveway. "I think I need more coffee."

He retrieved his duffel bag from the cab of the truck as Max stood on the walkway, studying the house. "You did a nice job with it. You've had it for eleven years?"

"Almost twelve." He threw the bag over his shoulder, coming alongside her and scanning the large front porch. "Never did get around to replacing those windows, though."

"You don't seem too attached to the place." She took his hand as they climbed the front steps. "Twelve years is a long time."

"I bought it as an investment more than anything else. It was the ultimate handyman's special, and I got it for almost nothing."

"You did the work on it yourself?"

He nodded. "Grab my mail for me?"

She pulled a bundle of letters and circulars from the mailbox beside the front door. "You're just one surprise after another, Remmond."

"I like building things." He unlocked the front door, waiting for her to enter. "This is only the second time you've been here."

"I know. And I don't even remember much about that night."

"You took off fast the next morning." He put his arm around her, giving her a quick hug. "Long time ago," he said, wanting to dismiss the topic.

Max looked around the entry, taking in the tall ceilings, the mahogany staircase, and the formal dining room beyond an arched doorway to her right. On her left was a library.

"This is beautiful," she said. "Did you build those bookshelves?"

"Yeah." He pointed straight ahead. "C'mon. Kitchen's this way."

"Perfect," she sighed as she entered. It was a massive room, open and airy, with stone accents and an island that could seat six people. "I love the Mediterranean design. But this is definitely a cook's kitchen..."

Will tossed the duffel bag into the laundry room just off the kitchen. "And I don't cook," he said, finishing the thought for her.

She smiled, looking around. "Just seems odd."

"Like I said, it was an investment. I had planned on fixing it up and selling it within five years." He pulled two water bottles from the refrigerator, handing one of them to her. "But life got busy." Leaning against the counter, he opened the water and said, "I'm actually looking forward to signing off on it. It's a nice house, but it's been just a place to sleep and shower."

"It sold pretty quickly. You haven't gotten an apartment yet."

He shook his head. "Nope. And I'd better move on that, or I'll be homeless on June thirtieth."

"Getting just another place to sleep and shower?" she asked, watching him take a long drink.

"Pretty much. That's the life - all work." Noticing her expression, he said, "You're thinking about something."

"I'm kind of sad."

"Why?"

"You deserve more than that."

Max thought he would somehow minimize it, but he said, "I want more than that." He opened his arms to her, and as she laid her head against his chest, he added, "It all depends on what you decide."

She was uncertain, but she asked it anyway: "Have you thought about moving in with me?"

"What?" Will was shocked by the question, and it took him a moment to continue. "No, I haven't. I'm... surprised by that."

She took his water from him, setting it with hers on the counter behind him. Grasping both of his hands, she leaned against him, smiling up at him hopefully. "You said you want to wake up with me every morning."

He nodded slowly, thinking it over.

"I want that, too," she said.

"It's a big step, Maxine."

Her eyebrows went up, and she said, "This, from the guy who wants to get *married?*"

"Yeah," he mumbled. "Tough to argue that one. I guess just living together... It's not the step I want to take."

"Think about it?"

"I will." He paused. "I am. I just don't want it to become a substitute for marrying you. I don't want something temporary, you know?"

"Love isn't what's temporary, Will. Marriage is."

"We'll talk about it." He was unsettled, wondering if living together would become her firewall against marriage.

She lifted his hand to check his watch. "We should head out soon. They're expecting us for dinner." Noting his troubled expression, she said, "I'm not dumping the idea of getting married. I just want to be together while we work it out."

"So do I. You're staying here tonight, right?"

"Either here or at Sammy's. I mean, I don't want to *impose* or anything," she teased as she wrapped her arms around his waist.

Will didn't answer, appearing instead to be considering it.

"*Hey,*" she laughed, swatting him on the back.

"I don't know, Maxine," he drawled. He grabbed her around the waist and lifted her to sit on the counter, standing before her. "You *are* kind of inconvenient - pretty annoying, actually - but as long as we aren't strictly platonic anymore..."

"Watch this," she said, wrapping her legs around him. She grasped the back of his neck, pulling him in for a kiss that he thought rivaled New Year's Eve.

※ ※ ※

"Hey Sam-*mee*, we're here," Max called out from the entry of the townhouse.

"*Hey!* Hold on..." She came sprinting from the dining room. "Come here, you." She wrapped Max in a lingering hug, then reached for Will. "I should yell at you guys, disappearing like that..."

Will handed her the champagne they'd brought with them. "Time to celebrate. Where's Dave?"

"He took Ty over to Brad's house for the night. He'll be right back."

"Where's my goddaughter?" Max asked, handing Will her jacket.

"With Dave. He's keeping her busy while I pack." She gave Will a quick kiss on the cheek and returned the champagne to him. "Go put this in the fridge for me. I need to tape up one more box." She took Max's arm, turning for the dining room. "C'mon."

"We just got here, for pity's sake." She pulled her arm away. "You already want to dump Will?"

"That's right. I've been waiting days for this."

"It's gonna take him all of thirty seconds to put that in the fridge, Sammy. You won't get much information in that time."

"You'd be surprised."

Amused, Will said, "I'll take my time."

Sam closed the door as soon as they were in the dining room. "Okay, give me the condensed version," she demanded. "I'm *dyin'* here. What happened?"

"Seriously, there *is* no condensed version." She seemed to be at a loss as she added, "I have no idea where to begin."

"Start with Wednesday night. He left here, and all I knew was that he was off to find you."

"Well, he found me."

"I swear, Maxine - if you go mysterious on me, I can't guarantee your safety tonight."

She exaggerated a wide-eyed expression of terror. "Ooh, I'm shakin'."

"*Please....?*"

Max tested a box for its sturdiness before she sat on it. "Okay. As condensed as I can make it..."

She gave Sam an outline of the days they spent in Maine, omitting the more dramatic incidents and focusing on the pleasant times. As she wrapped it up, she held out her right hand.

"Oh..." Sam took her hand and admired the ring. "That is absolutely *gorgeous*." She hesitated, not sure that she wanted the answer to the next question.

"Yeah, it hasn't made it to my left hand yet," Max smiled. "I just haven't decided what I want to do yet, so I'm wearing it on my right hand instead."

Sam was disappointed. "You don't want to marry him? Really?"

"Yes and no." She looked at her feet. "I asked him to move in with me, though."

"Nice. Is he going to?"

"We're figuring that out."

Sam took her hand again to examine the ring. "It's *so* beautiful. He loves you, Max."

"Yeah, I know he does. No doubt." She went silent, thinking again about the lengths Will had gone to in order to win her over.

"You should see the look on your face right now." Sam touched her cheek. "You're over the moon for him."

"He's an incredible man, Sammy."

They heard Dave coming in the front door, and Will greeting him.

"Let's go celebrate," Max said. "Will and I want to get out of here early - let you and Dave have at least some kind of an anniversary."

"This, my friend, is a truly great anniversary," Sam countered. "We have a home. A real one. And Dave rigged it so I get to go there on *Monday*." She sighed happily.

"You look like you could burst into song."

"I may. Wait until you see our house. It's perfect."

"Home," Max corrected her.

"Yup." She pulled Max to her feet. "Our home."

They spent a couple of hours over dinner, managing it around the boxes and the clutter from the impending move. Will noticed that every time the subject of their escape to Maine came up, Max brought the topic back to the new house in Hudson, which the Delaneys were more than happy to discuss.

He asked her about it as they drove back to his house.

"You were keeping it pretty close to the vest," he said.

She reached for his hand. "I'm not ready to talk about it too much. It feels really private, like it belongs only to us, you know? It's just... Ours."

"I like that." He kissed her hand as he turned onto his street.

"And I *don't* like riding in this status crate." She stared glumly out the window. "I can't sit close to you."

"Almost home," he said. "I thought we should go classy for their anniversary."

"I still want my kiss when I get out of the car," she pouted.

He glanced at her as he pulled into his driveway, thinking she was being adorable, and deciding not to mention that to her.

She opened her door as soon as he parked the car, climbing out of the sedan and leaning against the side of it, waiting for him.

Will was enjoying her petulant expression as he came around the car to her. "You really do hate this thing, huh?"

"It's not us."

"You're right." In one fluid motion, he gathered her into his arms, laying her back against the hood of the car and kissing her deeply.

"This is us," she murmured against his lips.

After another minute, she said, "We really should take this inside."

"We really should."

"The neighbors are probably watching."

"Bet they're learning a few things, too."

She laughed softly. "You're killing me, darlin'," she said.

"Want me to stop?"

"No."

He whispered in her ear for a moment.

"You do have the power to make my knees buckle, Remmond."

"I know."

"*So* arrogant," she sighed. She could feel his smile against her lips.

"With good reason."

"Yeah?" She nibbled on his bottom lip, mumbling, "I don't know, Counselor. There's not quite enough action going on out here..."

"You're right." He pulled away reluctantly, taking her hands and walking backwards, bending to kiss her as he led her to the house. "Let's take it inside."

chapter 13

FINALLY. THE LAST weekend I'll be locked up.

Simon opened the tattered Bible that the prison's pastor had given him, resisting the impulse to start ripping the pages from it and jamming them down the preacher's throat.

And the last Sunday I need to be put through one of these asinine services.

He took on a benign demeanor, acting like he was listening intently to the message while he tried to figure out exactly how many minutes were left until Tuesday morning at ten o'clock. The powers-that-be liked the fact that he had found religion. They actually believed that he had done so, and that it somehow made him a safer person for his kid to be around.

The preacher was talking about men loving their wives. Maybe the good Reverend had a woman who knew how to treat a man, but Simon thought it unlikely, and he wanted to stand up and give the guy a five-knuckle message of his own. Women were all about their Feminist theology. He had read some message boards during his allotted time on the Internet, and articles from Fathers Rights groups - which was how he found Jeff Marshall - and he decided that those guys knew exactly what was going on: women had been deceived, turned mean by Feminists. They thought they were specially entitled somehow; and even more galling, they believed that they deserved special treatment, especially after they were someone's mother. He had met several guys in jail who wore crosses, and who felt the same way he did. And that was the one thing the religious guys believed that Simon could agree with: the women were way out of control.

Hey preacher, want to talk about the women who demand that you kiss their asses or they walk away? And you lose your kid?

"It's not your place to discipline your wife..." the pastor was saying.

No one else is doing it.

"... and it's not your right to teach her a lesson."

Wrong.

But for only an instant, something hurt, deep inside him. In the recesses of his memory, Simon briefly recalled it being different somehow: years ago, he had felt love for her. And she had loved him, he knew that.

At least, I thought she did. Like Dad says, you can tell when a woman's lying because her mouth will be moving.

He knew back then that he and Brandi were going places. He had always wanted to own his own gym, and she sat with him planning it, and they had dreamed together. The idea got his father involved in his life again - for the first time, really - and that had been the best part of it all. The steroids had been his father's idea, and he was right: Simon needed to be his own best ad for what he wanted to do. Being locked up, he'd actually put on another twenty pounds of muscle, because steroids were easy to get and he had more time than ever before to hit the gym.

Worked my ass off, and all she did was bitch.

The memory of her was faint now, fragile - maybe she was on to something, he mused, that the drugs had changed him, and the continuing pain he felt in his gut was something that felt strange to him.

Yeah, well back then I also thought Dad was a prick. Mom made way too much out of a few fights that turned bad.

Like he said - marry a bitch, you wind up here.

The preacher was explaining how a woman might drift away, find a new man - one who would protect her in the way that God designed.

Simon thought about it again, how Brandi had found herself a hero, and the familiar pain coursed up the side of his neck.

She managed to get Will Remmond.

In just a few days, Brandi was going to get the lesson of a lifetime. If all that mattered to her was using his kid to humiliate him - cloning her into a miniature Brandi - then she had no right to her anyway.

Then, he would go find the hero. It wasn't even revenge: it was justice. Putting things back to their natural state. It had been a long time coming, and he moaned with the anticipation of it.

The preacher was looking at him curiously, and Simon nodded and said, "Amen."

❋ ❋ ❋

"Feed me, Remmond."

Will rolled onto his back, sleepy, smiling with his eyes still closed as Max crawled on top of him and gave him a lingering kiss.

He opened his eyes when she pulled away.

"Wow," he said. "Look at you."

"I got up early." She bent over him, letting her hair fall across his face, dragging it back and forth. "Decided to get all fixed up today."

He slowly stretched his arms over his head. "Lady, you're giving me *no* incentive to get out of this bed." He pounced then, grabbing her suddenly and rolling on top of her, peppering her with light kisses on her face and neck while she shrieked with laughter.

"I love you, Maxine. Marry me."

"Hmm. Careful what you ask for." She poked at his ribs. "You never miss an opportunity to say that, do you?"

"Never. Besides, I've heard that ninety percent of closing a sale is repetition."

"Sale?" she asked, raising an eyebrow and poking him again.

"I'm getting to the point of bribes." He propped himself up on his elbows. "So what's your price, doll?"

"My price...?" Tracing her fingers along his chest, she said, "Maine."

"Done. It's yours."

He turned serious then as he took in her expression.

"You really weren't ready to leave Portland, were you?" he asked.

"No. I needed more time with you, away from everyone." She pushed on his shoulders, and he rolled away to sit up.

He agreed with her. They needed more time. "Okay, wait a minute. Let me think," he said.

She ticked it off like a litany. "Party tonight, then tomorrow we help them move. And Tuesday, you're back to work. Then you and Dave have to get the relocation done. And court on Friday, right?"

"Yeah." Will watched her mouth forming a pout. "I'll figure something out," he said, running a finger across her lower lip. "No worries."

"There's no way, Will."

"Sure there is. I'll check on a few things, and we'll get at least a day to ourselves."

"In Maine?"

He nodded, smiling as she brightened a little. "This weekend."

"Really?" She crawled onto his lap, delighted, straddling him with her hands on his chest. "This weekend?"

"Promise. Can you hold out 'til then?"

"*Yes.*"

She fell on top of him and hugged him, and he held her, thinking again about his career - wondering if what he hated more was his work, or the amount of time it took away from her.

"I just adore you, Remmond." She was planting kisses all over his face. "I can't wait."

He gave her a quick squeeze. "We need to revisit that idea of being beach bums," he sighed.

Maybe Brandi Reynolds should be my last client.

Will was stunned by the level of relief he felt from that thought.

"Okay." He sat up again with Max still wrapped around him. "Let's go get breakfast."

❋ ❋ ❋

Dave wandered into the kitchen to find Sam sitting at the counter, gazing lovingly at the small pink box that held her gift.

She looked up as he came in. "I'm gonna cry again," she said.

He pulled her to her feet, smiling down at her, remembering her reaction the night before. "I don't think I've ever seen you that excited over a present."

"You are, seriously, the most incredible man in the world." She lifted her head for his kiss.

"We'll take them to the house with us tomorrow," he said.

She carefully took one of the peony plants from the box. "Pink. All four of them, pink - how did you know? I never said what color I like, just that I love peonies."

"I was watching you at the nursery last week. You kept going back to the pink ones." He reached for the coffee.

"*Careful,*" she snapped, as his arm came too close to the box.

"Sorry." He refilled her mug, then took one from the cupboard for himself. Sitting across the counter from her, he asked, "What would you like to do today? Nothing going on until tonight."

"Did your folks invite Will and Maxine?"

"I don't think so. I think it's just the four of us."

"Darn." Returning the peony to its box, she asked, "Do you think they'd want to join us?"

He grinned, recalling how he walked in on them the night before. "I have a feeling they've got plans."

"You never told me what you almost interrupted last night."

Dave inclined his head toward the screened porch off of the kitchen. "Will had her in a liplock out there that needed an 'R' rating."

"Excellent." She smiled at him over the rim of her mug. "God bless him. He said he'd go get her, and he did."

"Yeah, but did you notice how burned out he looked? They really went through something in the past few days."

"Max was pretty secretive about it."

"So was Will. But yeah, they're tight again. Finally."

"And now," she patted Dave's hand, "we need to get them married."

"Sammy..." he groaned.

"What? You suddenly have something against marriage?"

"Quoting a vastly intelligent woman," he kissed her cheek, "let them be." He stood, taking his mug from the counter. "We have to pick Ty up. Any more packing to do?"

"A little. Let's do some shopping and take the kids for ice cream."

Kids.

She thought about Jo, and felt her mood starting to disintegrate. "We can get to the packing later," she added, and her voice sounded weak to her.

"Sounds good. Let's get dressed."

She put her hand on his arm as he turned away.

"Dave?"

He noted the change in her tone and her expression, and that when she smiled up at him, it didn't quite make it to her eyes.

"I just love you," she said softly. "And I love my family."

"I know you do."

She reached for him, and he gathered her into his arms.

"You show us that every day of your life, babe," he said, but his thoughts were unsettled. Thursday would be exactly a year since Jo's murder, and he was certain it was bothering her. He considered whether or not to bring it up.

Instead, he asked, "You okay?"

"Yeah." Behind his back, she dug her nails into her palm; then, she gave him her best smile. "Sometimes, I just can't believe how lucky I am."

❋ ❋ ❋

"Where's my shirt?"

Max shrugged. "Beats me."

Will climbed into the truck. He tried to sound stern as he said, "Give me my shirt, Maxine."

She closed her eyes, her face scrunched up in a wide grin, rapidly shaking her head.

"You lech," he laughed. "C'mon. I'm not driving all the way to New Hampshire half-naked."

"I think you are." She looked him up and down. "You gave that shirt to me, after all."

"No, I asked you to hold it for me while I loaded the truck."

"Inconsistencies and misunderstandings in contractual arrangements are construed against the initiator, Counselor."

"Lord have mercy..." he sighed. He glanced around the cab of the truck. "Where did you put it?"

She shrugged again.

"Okay, I'll be right back."

"Going into the house to get another shirt?"

"Yup."

She patted the pocket of her shorts. "Oh, dear. Look what I've got..." She was watching him carefully, the laughter bubbling out of her as she waited for him to pounce. "I dare you, Remmond. Try to get your keys back."

"This is sexual harassment, you know."

"You're welcome."

He erupted into laughter.

"Hey," she pointed at him, "*you're* the one showing off your pecs. Getting all sweaty. And when you poured that bottle of water down your back, and it came over your chest..." She smacked her lips, admiring him again. "You need to be careful, darlin'," she purred. "A woman can take only so much."

"Is that right?" He grabbed her hand and pulled her closer. "Bottom-line me. What's the ransom on the shirt?"

"Marry me."

He went instantly motionless. He stared at her, astonished.

Max was nodding, her expression a mixture of amusement and apprehension.

"What did you just say?" he managed.

"All I need from you is a little time to get used to the idea. Time to work through things."

He searched her eyes. "You wouldn't joke around about this."

"No."

"Am I awake?"

She pinched his side. "Yup."

"No, really - am I?" He looked around the truck and then back to her. "Did you just say you'll marry me?"

She held up her left hand. The ring sparkled in the sunlight, and he felt again like he couldn't speak.

"Come here," she said, "before you pass out." She could feel his heart pounding as she held him. "You okay?" she asked.

"She's asking if I'm okay." He took her hand from his shoulder and gazed at the ring. "'Okay' isn't even... Maxine..."

She thought that his struggle to find the words was the sweetest thing she had even seen.

He looked up. "Tell me what happened here."

"You mean, what was I thinking when?" she teased.

"Yeah."

Max pulled his keys from her pocket. "Let's go. I'll tell you on the way. Oh," she reached behind the seat, "and here's your shirt."

He tossed it aside and reclined against the door, lifting her on top of him, thinking that she had just handed him the world and not comprehending how that could be.

Then he decided that it didn't matter, because she was there, and the world she'd just given to him was filled with possibilities. Ones that he had never before allowed himself to consider. His former life of straight lines, of minimal upset and even fewer risks, was over.

"In a minute," he said. "I want to kiss my fiancée."

They had just crossed into New Hampshire when his cell started vibrating, and Will took it from his pocket and handed it to her.

"Turn it off for me. You were saying..."

Max turned the phone off and tossed it to the side. "Last night."

He covered a smile, briefly turning his head to look out the window.

She rolled her eyes. "I saw that, Remmond."

"What about last night?"

She rested her head on his shoulder. "I woke up around five, and I was already thinking about it as I woke up, about being married to you. I think I was dreaming about it. And about something Jo said once, that she wanted to die of a broken heart."

"Now that's interesting." He took her hand. "She was... What's a word that would describe her?"

"They haven't invented it yet. I wish you could have known her better."

"So do I."

"She wanted to be so much in love, that when her husband was gone it would be the end of her. She thought that would be the most beautiful life that anyone could live."

They were quiet for a moment, then Will said, "That's an incredible thought."

"And I realized that's what would happen to me. I mean, I'd never get over you. That's part of what scared me so much, being with you."

He pressed her hand to his chest, still thinking about the wisdom of her friend.

"Promise me you'll never go away." She looked up at him expectantly.

Will knew it was no more than a wishful reassurance, but she seemed to honestly want to hear it.

He kissed her hand. "Promise."

Max nodded, satisfied. "Anyway, I was half asleep - and when I looked at you, I thought for a second..." Her voice became strained then. "I thought that you were my husband."

He glanced at her, not understanding the change in her tone. "And?"

"When I realized I was only dreaming, I was so *disappointed*. And then I couldn't get back to sleep," she said. She turned to face him, tucking her leg underneath her as she settled in. Studying his expression, she asked, "What are you thinking?"

It took him a few seconds, then he said, "I'm sort of flat on my back again. That's how you decided?"

"Yeah. So I got up and took a shower, and I was thinking about the past year..." Her voice faltered.

He put his arm around her. "What?"

It came out in a stream of raw emotion. "You fought for me, Will. I left, you came after me. I attacked, and you stood there and took it. I was getting more and more ugly..."

He thought about her staring at their reflection in the glass door, and his thoughts earlier that same night about leaving her, and he tightened his arm around her.

"... and you loved me anyway, you know? Enough that you went to the pits of Hell and back with me."

Will knew he would take to his grave the memory of his thoughts about her that night. He hoped it would soon feel like the distant past, because he wasn't going to live well with it.

She was saying, "It's like... We're like one person in a lot of ways. Or, more like two people who are so right together, it's hard to find the place where one of us ends and the other begins, you know?"

He nodded.

"And the thing is, I've felt like that for a long time. I just didn't want to feel that way. On top of everything else, I've been mad at you for *that*. Really resentful, like you tricked me into coming outside of myself or something." After a pause, she added, "And I was hopeless. But you know all about that."

"Distant past," he said softly.

"Hmm?"

"Nothing. When did the ring switch hands?"

"Just before I woke you up. I was sitting on the bed for a long time, just looking at it and thinking about the past few days, trying to work through this aversion I have to actually being married."

"It's been a lot of changes in a short time," he said. "We'll figure it out."

"I just want time. Room for us to figure it out. I'm not sure what that means, except that I want to lose that feeling I get when I think about being a wife."

"What's the feeling?"

"Like I'm suffocating. Seriously. I start to panic."

He nodded, wishing he could understand it better, because it troubled him as well. He was finding it difficult not to take it like a rejection.

"And in the meantime," she stroked his cheek, "you're still thinking about living together?"

"Yeah."

"Good thing, because a bunch of your furniture is in the back of this truck, and you aren't getting it back."

He laughed. "If you leave me, I get custody of my bed."

"No way, Remmond. Possession is nine-tenths of the law, remember." As she laid her head on his shoulder again, she murmured, "And I'm not going anywhere."

chapter 14

"Delaney, the look on your face was priceless."

"I'm sure."

The bartender was waiting. Will was still laughing as he said, "Two bourbons. Neat."

"We had no clue," Dave said. "Sammy almost called Mom and Dad to cancel at the last minute." He looked around the elegant, dimly-lit room, where thirty people milled about, enjoying the after-dinner music and drinks. "They would've disowned me if we'd done that."

Will handed him his drink. "One year, Dave. Congratulations." He raised his glass, and they downed the drinks in unison.

"Having another?" Dave asked, sliding his glass across the bar.

"Later. I'm pacing myself." He scanned the room. "Can't find Maxine."

"Sammy said something about fresh lipstick. She's probably with her." He motioned the bartender for a refill. "Looks like things are going well with you two."

Distracted, Will said, "C'mon. We've known each other too long for you to hedge it. Just ask."

"No problem. So the engagement's official, huh?"

Will stopped searching the crowd. He lowered his head for a second, then looked up, a knowing smile on his face. "Sammy saw the ring."

"First thing she checked was Max's hand."

"Of course she did. She doesn't miss a trick."

"Way to go." Dave clapped him on the shoulder. "Glad you took my advice."

Will ordered a tonic, then asked, "What advice?"

"How to reel her in, like I did with Sammy."

"Get real, Delaney. The woman married you out of pity. She's *so* far out of your league."

"You're right," he grinned. "And I could say the same to you, friend."

"No argument there."

"So why the secrecy?" Dave asked, taking his drink from the bar.

"There's no secrecy. It just happened this morning." He returned to looking for Max. "This is your night, D. Yours and Sammy's." He nodded toward where the band was beginning its next set. "There they are."

Max found him in the crowd immediately, glancing over to him, smiling as she excused herself from an elderly man who had stopped her for a brief chat. It seemed to Will that he and Max could sense each other's presence, and he loved the feeling of it.

"That's Dad's old Army buddy," Dave nudged him. "Henry's a real ladies' man. Better go get her."

Will leaned against the bar. "Nah. I want to watch her walk over here." She was wearing white again, a flowing jumpsuit with a plunging neckline, and Will thought she radiated a classiness that was unlike anything he had ever seen before.

Dave watched him watching her, a wide smile on his face as he mumbled, "You're gone, Remmond." He drained his glass, spotting Sam as he set it on the bar. "See ya."

He and Max met in the middle of the room, and Dave stopped her to whisper something in her ear.

A brief look of surprise passed over her face, then she nodded and extended her hand to let Dave see the ring. She laughed at something he said as he bent to kiss her cheek; and as she glanced at Will again, he had a momentary vision of celebrating their first anniversary. He thought about living with her, growing old with her, and he imagined the first time she would call him her husband. And spending a lifetime being able to call her his wife. It was astonishing, he thought, that he had managed to wind up where he was at that moment - that he was anticipating the future, reveling in it. It was a new experience to him, because he'd never had quite so much to live for.

"There you are," he said as she finally made her way over to him.

"Sorry." She took his hand, lifting her head for a quick kiss. "Sammy was grilling me about wedding dates and stuff."

"What'd you tell her?"

"That we weren't official until about twelve hours ago, and we've barely had time to talk about anything."

"Which she didn't accept."

"Nope." The bartender appeared then, and she ordered a bottled water.

"You don't want something stronger?" Will asked.

Max perched on the stool he was leaning on. "Have you noticed what happens when I drink?"

Will hesitated, then decided not to respond.

"I'm not going there again." She touched his cheek. "You know what I mean."

He wanted to lighten the moment. "You quit smoking, now drinking... You aren't giving up sex, are you?"

She arched her eyebrows, smiling playfully. "I don't know, Remmond..."

He clutched at his chest, moaning.

"I mean," she tossed her hair, taking on a comical Brooklyn accent, "here I-*yam*, dressed to the ni-yuns, *tryin'* to get your attention, and you haven't even *danced* with me yet."

"Too good with that accent again, Maxine."

She leaned against him with her forearms on his chest, looking up at him adoringly. "Ya *know*, doll-face," she batted her eyelashes, "it'll be easiah lookin' down my shirt if we're *dancin'*."

The man in the seat next to her sputtered, choking on his drink.

"You're right." Will grabbed her hand. "C'mon."

On their third dance, Dave tapped him on the shoulder, then put his arm around her, pulling her away. "It's okay now, Maxine. The A-Team's here," he grinned. "Besides, you owe my wife a dance, Remmond."

"You learned how to lead yet, D?" Will winked at her. "He tends to be awkward with the girls."

"Which explains why I'm married and you aren't."

"Geez, guys," Max sighed. "I'm about to go dance with Sammy."

"Come here, gorgeous." Dave pulled her into his arms. "Remmond, stay off of Sammy's feet."

"I'll do my best." He planted a quick kiss on Max's cheek. "Next dance is mine."

Will opened his arms wide as he approached Sam, and she hugged him hard.

"You did it. Congratulations."

"Thanks, kiddo. You played a big part, you know."

"I'm so relieved, Will. And she looks so happy." She smiled lovingly at him. "So do you."

"She was worth the wait." As he led he to the dance floor, he looked over his shoulder to where Dave and Max were dancing.

Sam recalled how exhausted he seemed the night before. "But I have a feeling it wasn't easy."

"It wasn't. There were some bad moments."

"And apparently some pretty good ones."

He nodded. "A lot more than I hoped for." Max was watching him, blowing him a kiss.

They were quiet for a while as they danced, then Sam said, "All these years, I really thought you were determined to stay a bachelor for the rest of your life."

"Know what?" He smiled down at her. "I was."
"Will?"
She spoke softly, and he bent his head closer to hear her.
"Thanks for bringing her home."
Will pulled back to respond; then, seeing the tears in her eyes, he held her close for a moment first.
"It's okay, Sammy," he said. "It's all going to be okay now."

❋ ❋ ❋

Simon hung up the phone, and the guard said, "Let's go."
As they made the short walk back to his cell, Simon was again mentally computing the number of minutes left until Tuesday morning at ten o'clock.
He stood just inside the cell, staring at the small window across the room, lost in thought. The call from his brother had been a disappointment: Chuck wasn't at all supportive, telling him that he needed to accept the reality of the divorce, let Brandi get on with her life, and focus on rebuilding his own life and being a good father to Alexa.
Resentful, he reflected on Chuck's situation. He had been married to Cassie for a decade - and she was a good woman, the kind who appreciated a good man; therefore, Chuck had the luxury of living with his three kids going to sleep in the same house with him every night.
Chuck knew nothing about women like Brandi. She had ferreted out Simon's weak spots early on, and became an accomplished button-pusher within a couple of years - something that the prison shrink had said was just an excuse.

No one can push your buttons unless you allow them to do so.

He snorted, deciding that Beaumann was an idiot - that all of the merciful, meddling "professionals" were totally clueless, thinking themselves saviors when they were really puppets. The shrinks, the preachers, the lawyers - they all had Messiah fantasies about themselves, and Simon thought that his own lawyer was no different.

Simon, the one phrase the judge will zero in on is, "She pushes my buttons." **Do not** *let that come out of your mouth.*

Jeff Marshall was just another idiot. Simon suspected that he probably wasn't even married.
Chuck told him that Brandi was living with her parents again, and Simon could only imagine what they were saying about him. Marshall thought it was a problem, as well, and planned on going for custody after a few months of visitation.

He'll try to force you into supervised visitation, but we'll beat him back on that.

"Will Remmond isn't forcing a *damn* thing," he hissed. He had done a search on him earlier that day. He wasn't just some hack lawyer: he was head of his own firm in Boston, with some guy named Delaney.

She managed to get Will Remmond.

"Wonder how she 'managed' *that.*"
Wonder if she's screwing him yet.
He grabbed the flat, musty pillow from his cot, throwing it against the wall and holding it there as he punched it repeatedly.

✳ ✳ ✳

Tyler came running full-tilt through the back door of their new house.
"Mom - look at *this.*" He skidded to a stop, just short of bumping into a box of china plates.

"Hey, careful there, Ty." Will reached down to pry his hands open. "Whatcha got?"

"A *frog*." He held it up for Will to admire.

He grinned. "Nice." He opened a can of beer, then took the frog from Tyler, calling over his shoulder, "Hey Samantha, come look at this."

"You like our house?" Tyler asked. "Did you see all the land we have?"

"I did. It's amazing. Time to start asking your dad for a horse, Ty-guy."

"Wow. A horse...?"

"What about a horse?" Sam wandered in, preoccupied by something on her phone. "What's up, guys?"

"Just suggesting to Ty that he start the discussion," Will grinned.

Irritated, she said, "Thanks so much for that, Will. What are you holding there?"

He held the frog up to her face, and she shrieked.

"Will, I should *smack* you." She clipped his arm and muttered, "That is *so* first grade."

He chugged his beer, winking at her. "You're such a girl, Sammy."

"And you're still a knuckle-dragging ape."

"It's just a frog, Mom," Tyler sighed.

"Take it back outside, honey. I hate frogs."

Max wandered in from the living room, wiping her hands on her jeans as she announced, "I'm starving, and I want pizza."

"Ordering it right now," Sam said, looking at her phone again. "What's left to do?"

"Not much. Beds are made, living room's set up - I even got your curtains hung for you."

"I love you, Maxine."

"Then order one with onions and mushrooms. And sausage."

"I did." She set her phone on the counter and took a beer from the refrigerator. "Want one?"

"No thanks. Got a soda?"

"Sure. Orange?"

Max nodded.

Sam handed it to her. "So, tell me how beautiful my antique house is."

Will jumped up to sit on the counter, and Max stood between his knees, taking a long drink before she said, "It really is beautiful, Sammy. Love the detail." She turned her head to ask Will, "Did you see that library?"

"Yeah. The wallpaper's going to be a project, and those shelves need a little work." He tossed his empty can into the sink.

"Having another?" Sam asked.

"Thanks. Seriously, I'd replace the shelves at some point with a sturdier wood."

Sam handed him another beer. "Dave's been wondering if we should have had a more thorough inspection done."

"The man's going gray with all the worrying he does," Will said. "The house is fine, Sammy. I gave it a good look. The things that need done wouldn't have stopped you from buying it."

"That's what I told him." She took a few sips of her beer, then decided that she wasn't in the mood for it and handed it to Will. "Here. You can have this one, too." As she took a soda from the refrigerator, she said, "We need to get him to loosen up."

"Where is he?" Max asked.

"He went to run some errands and get us some supplies."

"And Hope's with him, right?"

Sam smiled. "Of course."

"He needs to start sharing her sometimes. He's always wearing that baby."

"I know. He doesn't want her to think she's less important than her brother." She sighed, troubled. "He works at least sixty hours a week, then divides the rest of his time among the three of us. Plus he keeps tabs on Matt and Johnny, and his parents... He needs to cut loose a bit." She sat at the table, reaching to tap Will's hand. "You two should go have a guys' night out."

"You mean you want to send your domesticated husband out with a knuckle-dragging ape? He'll come home at four a.m. smelling like booze and cigars."

"And scratching himself in indelicate places," Sam added.

Max had taken a sip of her soda just before Sam's comment, and she choked on it as she gasped with laughter. She stood over the sink, coughing.

"Sorry, hon," Sam said.

Max waved her hand, motioning that she was fine.

"You'd think I asked you to marry me," Will mumbled, and she started coughing again.

Laughing helplessly, she gave him a high-five. "Good one," she sputtered.

Tyler ran in then, banging the screen door behind him. "Dad's home," he announced, grabbing his mother's soda from her hand and chugging it.

"Boys are just so noisy." Sam rubbed her temples. "Go wash up for dinner, baby."

Dave was coming into the kitchen with Hope balanced on one arm and several grocery bags hanging off of the other. He looked around, impressed. "You all got a lot done here."

"Give me my goddaughter." Max took the baby from him, holding her up in the air and cooing to her. Hope chewed on her fingers, giggling, and Max asked, "She's still teething pretty heavy, huh?"

Sam nodded. "She has another one coming in."

"Here, D. Catch." Will tossed his unopened beer to Dave. "Sammy says we need a night of debauchery soon."

"Yeah? Great." He popped it open and took a long drink. "I'm in."

Sam rolled her eyes. "I didn't suggest all-out hedonism, guys - but I do think you could use a night out."

"Maybe this weekend," Dave said.

Will shook his head. "Next weekend." He smiled as Max looked up from the baby. "We have plans for Friday night and Saturday."

Her mouth fell open slightly. "We're all set?"

He nodded. "All set."

She handed the baby to Sam. "Can I see you outside please, Will?"

"Sure." Eyebrows raised, he got off the counter and followed her out the back door to the patio. He closed the door quietly, then turned to her. "Okay, so what's..."

Max jumped into his arms, wrapping her legs around his waist.

"That's a relief," he laughed. "I thought I was in trouble."

"Oh, you are." She traced his mouth with her fingertip. "You're in *so* much trouble."

"I am?"

She kissed him gently, then whispered in his ear.

Will walked her over to the patio table, sitting with her straddled across his lap.

"Knees buckling, Remmond?" She was nibbling at the hollow in his neck.

"You know it. You call me 'arrogant' for a lot less than that, doll."

She whispered again, and he closed his eyes.

"Oh, yeah," he sighed. "I'm in big trouble."

chapter 15

WILL SAT IN his car in the parking area of the new offices, double-checking his schedule. He had four consults, plus the meeting at the end of the day with Brandi Reynolds.

My office isn't even set up yet. I should've told Gina not to book me for a while.

He sighed heavily and got out of the car, locking it before he remembered his briefcase. Annoyed, he went around to the passenger's side to retrieve it; then he smiled as he opened the door, remembering Saturday night, standing in his driveway with his hands full of Maxine.

Bet the neighbors did learn a few things.

He pulled his phone from his pocket. Max was busy setting up the apartment that day, but he wasn't waiting until five o'clock to talk to her.

"Hey," she said. "I miss you already."

"I'm running all day. Let me take you out tonight."

"*Definitely.* I'm up to the best part of my body in laundry."

"Too many possibilities there, darlin'." He leaned against the car. "Don't wear yourself out, though."

"You neither. Why so busy today?"

"Gina scheduled a few consultations." He considered his options for delegating them to the three associates who had relocated to New Hampshire with them. "I can't see myself taking any new clients right now."

"Good grief. Already? Dave and Sammy are still moving in."

Will was thinking about the situation he would leave Dave in if he bailed out at that point. They'd lost half of their associates with the move, and Dave had the new house to contend with at the same time that he was closing out in Boston and setting up the practice in New Hampshire. Will realized, with a fair amount of resentment, that he was staying on for a while longer.

"Thanks for taking care of everything there," he said.

"This is a one-time thing, Remmond. I don't do housework."

"I know." He took a quick glance at a text that came in from Dave. "I'm not real happy about it either."

"I keep picturing myself devolving into a mumu-wearing, chain-smoking old lady with twenty-five cats." She sighed heavily. "Sorry. This situation makes me grumpy."

Will was uncomfortable with it as well, and he said, "Do whatever you feel like doing. Whatever's left over, we'll just deal with it later." A call was coming in from the courthouse, and he decided to ignore it. "I'll be home around five, and I'll get you out of there. We'll go someplace nice."

She didn't answer.

"Max?"

He could hear the smile in her voice as she said, "I like the sound of that. 'Home around five.'"

"So do I." Another call was waiting, from Dave this time, and he was becoming annoyed from the intrusions. "We just need to hold out until Friday night."

"Not promising anything. By tomorrow, I may have to kidnap you."

"Please."

"You're on. See you tonight."

Will checked his messages: Dave called from Boston to let him know that their systems would be up and running at the new offices by four o'clock, and the court clerk had a question about the hearing on Friday.

"I'm sure you'll figure it out," he mumbled.

Friday, Maxine.

He took a few moments to look at the picture of the two of them on his cell, and it seemed to him that he was in the wrong place at that moment. It wasn't only that he didn't want to be there: it seemed to Will that he was supposed to be someplace else - because this wasn't what his life was about anymore. And Max's life wasn't about doing laundry and hanging curtains, and waiting for him to return from another endless day of windmill-tilting.

I am burned out.

He recalled a lengthy conversation with one of his associates, several weeks earlier. Melissa had wandered into his office after a hearing, shut the door, and burst into tears. The judge had awarded her client's daughter to the child's father, agreeing with him that the mother was guilty of Parental Alienation, and giving her two hours of supervised visitation per week until she got "reeducated."

"Will, we had four doctors *testify* to the abuse," she sobbed. "We had her pediatrician - Lisa's doctor for *five friggin' years* - telling the court that this kid was molested. And the reason they took her away from Robin was because Lisa was afraid of the guy who did it?"

Will let her cry it out, and when she was calm, they talked about whether or not Family Law was her calling.

"What does it say about me if I walk away?" she demanded. "That they beat me down? I can't live with that."

"Melissa, it's not a..." He was about to say that it wasn't a game, but he stopped. He knew that it was a game.

She was standing by the window, looking out at the street. "Yes it is," she said. "And you know it. It's all about egos. Lawyers one-upping each other. Politics. And lots and lots of money." She returned to the chair across from him, tapping her fingers on his desk, regarding him with a cynical smirk. "Know what we do for a living, Will?"

He did, but he didn't respond.

"We stand there and hold their hands while some pissed-off, spiteful judge gets even with them."

She was right.

Will was surprised that Melissa chose to relocate with them. He was sure she would walk away; and when she didn't, it drew him back in - because he decided that if she could hang in there, so could he.

I don't want to anymore.

He looked at the entry to the offices, where the sign on the door announced their practice with the unpretentious phrase *Delaney-Remmond*, and he was nostalgic for the days of building their firm. He smiled as he recalled that their first offices were just a few doors down from Rowdy's, the Bennet Street dive where he and Dave drank cheap beer and argued about which name would come first.

"'Remmond-Delaney' is awkward," Dave insisted. "Face it, friend. You have a clumsy last name. 'Delaney-Remmond' rolls right off the tongue."

In the end, Will had bargained for permanent dibs on offices in exchange for putting Dave's name first.

"Hey Will, *wake up.*"

He was startled by Sam calling to him from the front door of the main house.

"That's the third time I yelled it," she laughed. "What were you thinking about?"

He scanned the front of the house, wondering if Max would want to settle down in a home of their own. He decided he wouldn't mind that at all - maybe another fixer-upper.

"Coffee," he answered. "Lots of it." His phone was vibrating again, and he checked it quickly, grimacing as he slipped it into his pocket. The last thing he wanted to do was to have a morning chat with Jeff Marshall.

"Come on in." She went back inside, and he trudged up the walkway, thinking he was spending way too much time around the Delaneys lately. He paused at the door.
I need to talk to Dave soon.

✳ ✳ ✳

Max pulled a creased, yellowing photo from her old jewelry box. She broke the lid in half prying it open, but it didn't matter - she hated the thing anyway.

Her expression turned grim as she studied the picture of herself, looking into the camera with wide, anxious eyes, the candles on her birthday cake creating a soft glow under her face. She counted six of them, because she had no memory of that day, no idea how old she was in the photo.

Probably a good thing.

She set the picture on the dresser that Will had brought from his house, then opened the drawer where she had carefully arranged his jeans and T-shirts, grinning mischievously as she quickly rearranged the jeans so that her favorite pair was on top. The jeans with the rips in the knees, the ones that he said were a little too tight on him.

She had unpacked Will's things first because they smelled like him, and she was feeling somewhat lost after being with him every minute for a week. It wasn't enough for her, and she still wondered if her clinging was becoming annoying. Will had laughed when she asked him about it the night before. She touched her lips, smiling faintly as she remembered how he answered her.

He'd made a copy of their picture, the one they both had on their phones, and it was perched on the corner of the dresser. She pulled it forward a little, then turned it so she could see it from anywhere in the room.

"Love you, Remmond," she whispered.

Remembering that he wanted to go someplace nice for dinner, she surveyed the remaining boxes - most of which contained her clothes - and picked up the one that she hoped had her nicer things inside.

"Nope," she sighed, closing it and moving it against the foot of the bed.

Four boxes later, she was pulling badly wrinkled dresses out, wondering what she had been thinking in packing shoes on top of them. She realized that she didn't own an iron, and she wouldn't know how to use it even if she did have one.

"Okay, a choice between buying an iron and buying something new to wear." She grabbed her purse from the bed and found her phone.

Like that's a conundrum.

There was a mall only a few miles away. She tossed the phone on the bed, heading for the shower.

"A little black dress," she said quietly, stopping to check her reflection in the mirror.

No. **Red***. It'll drive him crazy.*

She checked the clock on the bathroom wall, surprised to see that it was already well after ten o'clock.

✳ ✳ ✳

Simon dropped his bag beside the front door of the in-law apartment.

"Looks good, bro. Thanks," he muttered.

"Yeah." Chuck shifted uncomfortably. "You know that Cassie isn't happy with this, right?"

"I'll be a good boy," he said. "Tell her not to worry. I won't be here long."

"The fridge is stocked." Chuck was on his way out the door. "And I have to get to work. Call me if you need anything."

As Simon watched him drive away, he felt a freedom that he hadn't experienced in years.

He reveled in the quiet relief of being alone. Truly alone. Not like the solitude within the prison, where the guards could - and did - walk by the cells any time they wanted, staring inside at the inmates like patrons at the zoo. Real solitude. No one breathing down his neck.

Looking around for an outlet to charge his phone, his eyes rested on a picture on the mantle of the brick fireplace, a portrait of Chuck and Cassie and the kids. They were huddled together on the bleachers of a grade school gymnasium, gathered around Charlie, the oldest, apparently celebrating some kind of basketball championship. Britt, the elder daughter, was kissing Charlie's cheek, and five-year-old Sara hugged her father's leg. She was gazing up at him like she adored him.

Feeling a momentary sense of generosity, he told himself that Chuck deserved the family he had. Chuck had a life ahead of him. He was strong enough to hold it together, and smart enough to have picked a good woman.

Not a castrating, controlling, loud-mouthed bitch.

There was an outlet by the fireplace. He plugged the cell into it, and then called his father's number.

"I'm here," he said. "Yeah, it's all good. Bring it over in about an hour... I do need it, Dad. Trust me, they're after me."

After a moment, he said, "They're going to get rid of me, one way or the other."

That, he believed.

His daughter wasn't even two years old the first time Brandi threatened to divorce him - which made him insane, because *she* was the controlling one. Not him. She nagged him incessantly about how sloppy he was, complaining about cleaning up after him even after he put in an eight hour day at the gym, lecturing him about the "dangers" of steroids when she knew that his physique was part of his job.

She whined that he spent no time with the kid - as if he had the energy to deal with a whiny kid after a hellish day of listening to customers bitch and moan about the equipment and the staff, the hours and the supplies. Then, she would get all pissed off over the way *he* talked to *her*, too stupid to understand the simple fact that respect was something she had to earn. Simon thought it incomprehensible, that a woman could abuse a man the way his wife did - controlling his every move, pushing every button until she pushed him over the edge - and then whine about the consequences.

And when she called the cops on him after that last fight, that was it for him. Or he thought it was, until she decided that he would have no place in his daughter's life.

If I'd been a better shot, it would have been settled once and for all.

His father was asking him something.

"Missed that. What... Come around back. Make sure no one sees you."

He took one more look at the picture of Chuck and his family as he ended the call; then, he slammed the picture face down on the mantle.

❋ ❋ ❋

Will was on the phone, but he waved Brandi into his office, smiling at the little girl who was clinging to her hand.

"I'll be there at noon anyway. We'll try for it then."

He hung up and motioned to the chair across from him as he rose from his seat. "Sit down," he said, coming around his desk and crouching in front of Brandi's daughter.

"This is Alexa," she said. "Lexi, this is Mr. Remmond. He's a friend of Mama's."

"Hi, Alexa," Will said. He was careful to keep a few feet between them, unsure of how skittish the child might be after all that had happened.

Alexa stared at him impassively, then buried her face in her mother's shirt, mumbling something they couldn't hear.

"What did you say, honey?" Brandi pulled away a little, and Alexa moved to rebury her face. She lifted her arms for Brandi to pick her up, then whispered something in her mother's ear.

Brandi looked apologetically at Will. "She said you're calling her 'Alexa', and you should be calling her 'Lexi.'"

"My mistake." As Alexa settled in on her mother's lap, he stood and said, "It's really nice to meet you, Lexi."

He thought that she almost smiled at him. "Beautiful child," he said softly. Alexa was tall for a five-year-old, with straight, waist-long pale blond hair and bright blue eyes.

"I know she is. So does she." Brandi laughed nervously.

The girl was still staring at him, but with some interest now. "Are you the nice man Mama told me about?"

Will looked to Brandi, amused.

She stroked her hair. "He is, baby. He's going to help us."

Alexa nodded once, turning to face Will and appearing to soften slightly. "Okay. You won't let Daddy shoot me?"

Brandi gasped. She'd had no idea that her daughter was thinking that way.

Will's stomach gripped, but he gave no indication of it. "That's right, Lexi. I won't let him do that."

There was a soft rapping on the door, then Gina poked her head into the room. "Samantha Delaney is here, Mr. Remmond."

"Good. Send her in." He returned to his chair as Sam entered the office.

Will noticed that she seemed distracted as he said, "Brandi Reynolds, this is Sam Delaney. She's the advocate I told you about." He motioned to Alexa. "And this is Lexi."

"Hi." Sam pulled a chair over to sit beside them. "Gina's not busy out there right now," she said, glancing from Will to Alexa and then back again.

"Lexi, would you like to help the lady out there do some of her work?" Will asked gently.

She looked up at her mother.

"She could probably use the help, baby."

Will got up and opened the door. "Gina, you needed an assistant today?"

"I sure could use one." She came to the doorway and gave Alexa her best grandmotherly smile. "I pay in lollipops, if that's good with you."

Intrigued, Alexa looked to Brandi again. "Can I, Mama?"

She nodded, and Alexa scrambled off of her lap. Gina offered her hand, and they disappeared into the outer office.

Sam watched them leave, smiling faintly. "She's so pretty," she murmured.

Will took his seat again. "Okay, Brandi, here's what we have."

He explained the process of the hearing that would happen on Friday, and cautiously reminded her of the fact that since Simon had met every requirement the court had ordered, he would likely be awarded visitation with Alexa.

Brandi became visibly upset, and Will hurried to add, "But we have Janice Franklin for the judge, and she has a reputation for being careful. Simon made an overt threat against Alexa. Believe me, I'll be pounding on that like a drum."

"He won't have her alone, right?"

"I can't guarantee it," Will shook his head, "but not if I have anything to say about it."

"What you need to remember," Sam interrupted, "is to act like you're anxious for Alexa to have a relationship with her father."

Brandi was aghast. "*What?*" She turned to Will. "That's *insane*."

"She's right, Brandi. And that's why she's here - to coach you through the process."

"That's the *last* thing I want," she sputtered. "I can't pretend..."

"You'd better learn quick, or you risk giving him what he wants," Sam said, and Will thought she was being a little insensitive.

He cut her off. "What we're aiming for," he explained, "is for you to have as much control over Alexa as is possible. The standard the court relies on is 'best interest of the child' - and their definition of the theory is that it's best for children to have a stable, ongoing relationship with both parents."

"He tried to *kill* me. He shot me in right in front of *Lexi*."

"Doesn't matter," Sam said. "They let him plea it down."

Will was tapping his pen on the desk, impatient now, but Sam wouldn't look at him.

He cleared his throat and continued. "The only charges the court can consider are the charges he was convicted on, and those won't keep him from Alexa. The goal is reunification, and the court can go to extremes in trying to make that happen."

"But the more reasonable they think you are, the better they'll like you, and the more they'll listen to your concerns." Sam's tone was sarcastic, and cynical to the point of rudeness.

Will shot her another cautionary look, but she avoided it.

"It's been about twenty minutes, Brandi," he said, glancing at Sam again. "Might be a good idea for you to spend a couple of minutes with Alexa."

She nodded, shaken. "I'll get some water while I'm at it."

After she left the office, Will leaned back in his chair and asked, "What's going on with you?"

"Me? Nothing." Looking over her shoulder toward the outer office, she asked, "Can we bring this in for a landing? I need to run an errand."

"You're okay?"

"Sure." Under her breath, she added, "Always. Charmed life."

"What was that?"

She shook her head. "Nothing."

"Talk to me, Sammy." He couldn't read her. She seemed fine earlier that day, and the change in her mood was both worrying and frustrating him. "Are you up for this today?"

"Lay off, Will." She folded her arms, glaring out the window.

"No problem." His voice was stern as he added, "But the priority here is the client. Whatever's bugging you, dial it back. And if you can't, then excuse yourself."

They stared each other down for a few seconds, then Sam muttered, "*Fine*. So sorry, boss."

Brandi was at the door, and Will decided to ignore Sam's sarcasm.

"Let's finish this up," he said.

Sam took on a pleasant, detached expression as she unfolded her arms.

"Fine," she said again.

chapter 16

Will unlocked the door to Max's apartment. It occurred to him that it would be the first time in his adult life that he said the words.

As he opened the door, he called out, "I'm home." He tossed his briefcase on the floor.

I could seriously love this life.

"Hey." Max was coming out from the bedroom. "I'm supposed to throw myself into your big, strong arms and say, 'Welcome home, dahling,' right?"

She appeared in the entry to the living room then, wearing a clinging, silky, deep red dress. It was longer than what she normally wore; but when she turned around to show it off, Will's eyes were fixed on the way it was hugging every part of her body.

Strolling slowly over to him, she twirled around again to show him the dress, and said, "That's no way to treat a lady, Counselor. No comment at all?"

With his hands in his pockets, he bent to give her a gentle kiss.

"Hmm. Not what I expected," Max said. "I thought you'd grab me and plant one on me."

He gave her another quick kiss. "If I touch you in that dress, we may not make it out of this apartment tonight."

"It *is* nice, isn't it?" She took his hand and ran it along her waist. "It's silk."

"I know." He slowly moved his hand down her side. "Very nice."

She took his other hand and wrapped his arms around her waist. "You don't want a welcome-home kiss?"

"Depends. You want dinner?" Will saw the laughter in her eyes, and he said, "You're doing this to me on purpose."

"Oh, yeah." She was playing with his hair, running her fingers down the back of his neck.

He shivered. "Last chance, Maxine."

"C'mon, Remmond. You're a big ol' boy. You can control yourself..." She squealed as he lifted her from her feet, cutting her off with a long kiss.

"Welcome home, darlin'," she whispered.

Will carried her to the sofa, reclining with her on top of him. He decided that there was only one more thing that was needed to make life perfect, and that was being married to her - but in the meantime, he didn't want to spend another night without her, and he made his decision.

Talking softly against her neck, he said, "I need this to be my life."

She rested her forearms on his chest, looking at him hopefully as she asked, "What are you saying?"

"I'll get the rest of my stuff up here. We'll put whatever doesn't fit into storage."

She gasped. "You're officially moving in?"

"Yeah." He thought that her expression was a lot like his must have been when she said she would marry him.

"Oh my gosh, Will..."

"Might be just temporary, though."

Her face fell. "Why?"

"Because I'm hoping you'll think about buying a house with me."

She opened her mouth to respond, but she couldn't think of anything to say. She stared at him silently.

"I want to have a home with you," he said. "So think it over."

"A house?" She pulled away from him and perched at the end of the sofa. "Us? Seriously?"

Will nodded. "Seriously. Just something to consider."

"Wow." With her hand to her forehead, she said, "We're taking a lot of big steps here lately."

"No hurry, darlin'. But it's something I'd like us to keep on the back burner for now."

"Why?"

"Like I said, I want us to have a home." He sat up and took her hand. "And you look suspicious."

She studied him for a moment, tapping her free hand on her thigh.

"Tell me," he said.

"Well, it isn't a good idea - financially, I mean - to buy a house with someone you aren't married to, you know?"

He laughed. "I get it. You think I'm pushing for the wedding."

"I have to wonder."

"Actually, you don't. Come here." He pulled her into his arms, and she laid her head on his shoulder. "We're together. We're working it out. And nothing's going to happen unless you want it to." He leaned back to look down at her. "Okay?"

"Okay. I'll think about it."

"Good."

She kissed him quickly. "Dinner?"

"Let's go." He stood and offered her his hand.

"Know what, Remmond?"

"What?"

"It is kind of a nice idea. I'll give you that."

"Thanks."

"Maybe someday," she mused, "we could get a house that we fix up together. Maybe one of those old farmhouses. I like those."

"So do I." His phone was vibrating, and he pulled it from his pocket and turned it off. "Let's talk about it over dinner."

❋ ❋ ❋

Sam had some difficulty believing how easy it was to buy a gun in New Hampshire, and how many places there were to go shooting.

In her bedroom, she locked her door before she pulled the 9MM handgun from her purse, enjoying the weight and the balance of it as she aimed it at the window. It had a sleek look to it, all black, and carrying it in a back holster was more comfortable than she thought it would be.

"You don't want it hidden in your purse if you need it," the woman at the gun shop had said. "You want to be able to reach back here," she guided Sam's hand behind her back, "and draw."

Sam knew that Dave was concerned about having a gun in the house, but something about the kick as a gun went off in her hand - the explosion of it all around her, and the force of it - had a calming effect on her. A calm that she knew he wouldn't understand. It gave her the feeling of power that she'd needed so desperately after the murders that happened, one on top of the other, right after she started at the center.

She still thought about them every day, Jeremy and Joanie. Jeremy was only ten years old when his father shot him to death at a visitation the boy was ordered into - even after the father said he was going to kill either Jeremy or his mother. Or both. Jeremy's mom begged for someone to listen, to get involved, to do something. It was one of Sam's first cases, and she found out quickly that judges didn't appreciate anyone questioning their decisions, and that state legislators were useless - and that the judge in Jeremy's case had been through his own acrimonious divorce five years earlier. As she discreetly researched other judges, she discovered that to be the case more times than not, and she understood early on the futility of raising concerns.

And then four days after Jeremy was murdered, Joanie Millerton was stabbed to death by her husband, right in front of her daughter. The guy had been allowed to simply walk away from his arraignment for breaking Joanie's arm the day before. No bail, no mention of keeping him locked up for a while - which they could have done easily under Massachusetts law - and they didn't even hold a Dangerousness Hearing, even though Sam was screaming for it. Millerton simply went home, picked up a knife, and stabbed Joanie to death.

Then everyone was duly horrified, and it was all over the news, and the D.A. ordered an investigation on herself. That was it. Millerton didn't even have a trial date yet.

When Sam sarcastically mentioned to some of the other advocates at the center that the knife gave him enough of an advantage - that he didn't need to break her arm to keep her from fighting back - she started to get the reputation of being "difficult". Some mistook her grief for insensitivity. And their reactions served only to enhance her contempt for much of what went on there, because she thought that the marches and awareness campaigns and slogans were fine for getting some press and decorating T-shirts, but did nothing to save the lives of Jeremy and Joanie - both of whom Sam had known, and worked with, and cared about.

In the aftermath of the killings, Dave asked her dozens of times how she was doing, especially since they happened so close to Jo's murder. But Sam didn't know how to tell him that she was suffering; besides, he had turned so strange, so rigid after Jo died, that she couldn't bring herself to dump more on him. Thinking it meant that she was getting stronger, she held it inside.

Max had asked her about it too, and when she said she was doing fine, Max said, "No you aren't. Let me know when you want to talk. And in the meantime, do some thinking about something."

When Sam asked what she meant, Max answered, "You tend to think you're responsible for things that aren't your fault."

Sam felt impotent way too often, constrained by the state laws and regulations that prevented her from being as effective as she knew she could be.

But more than that, the entire system was now a kangaroo court - a place where embittered, vengeful judges used terrified children to get even with mothers, and "Collaborative Law" attorneys got rich from throwing battered women and children into the line of fire. Literally.

More than anything else, though, she believed that she had let Joanie and Jeremy down, and set Jo up, and there was just no way to find redemption for that.

Sometimes, she thought that she needed to walk away from what she was doing and find a way to make a real impact. Go to college, maybe law school - find a more direct way to infiltrate the court system. Do something that mattered. Not only in memory of Jo and the others, although that was a factor; but because she felt a real passion for the issues that she was so unable to affect. She'd lost too many years of her own life to being abused and violated, and then she lost Jo. Then she lost two clients to abusers. The body count, thanks to the Family Court, stood at three in less than a year.

Dave was trying to open the door, and she jumped.

"Hey Sammy - am I in trouble or something?" he laughed.

"Hold on." She checked again that the gun was unloaded, then placed it carefully on top of the highboy before she unlocked the door.

"Hey," she said, wrapping her arms around him and lifting her head for a kiss. "I really missed you today."

"Won't be much longer. We're almost done down there." Dave rested his chin on her head. "Ty wants to know what's for dinner, by the way. Hope's napping?"

"Yeah. She was fussy today. She didn't like the sitter, either."

"How'd the meeting with Will go?"

She pulled away, taking his hand and leading him into the room. "Brandi Reynolds has the most adorable little girl," she sighed. "Alexa. Just beautiful."

"It went well?"

"It was hard to deal with, thinking about what they've been through." As she sat on the bed, she looked up at him with miserable eyes and added, "And what they still have to go through. How is it even a question, that her father may get her alone?"

Dave grabbed a pair of jeans from the dresser, tossing his suit onto the bed as he answered, "Will's as good as it gets at this stuff. He won't let it happen."

"He's lost before."

"Not that many," Dave countered. "And he's pretty confident about this one. You're going to be in the courtroom for the hearing, right?"

She nodded. "Hope's going to have to tolerate that sitter again."

"She'll be fine."

"And I'll have to do better than I did today."

"Why?" He crouched in front of her. "What happened?"

Sam stared at the floor, wondering if she would ever again have a day in her life where she wasn't pumping adrenaline. It seemed to her that Brandi and Alexa were about to fall through cracks that should have swallowed her up, as well - but other people paid the price for her safety. Others had paid for her bad choices, and there was no way to repay them. No way to ever make it right, and she knew that she was approaching the point where she couldn't deal with it anymore.

Dave watched her mood go dark, and the emotions passing across her face.

"Sammy." He took her hands in his. "Talk to me."

She smiled weakly. "This move has been hard," she lied. "Harder than I thought it would be. So I was kind of terse at the meeting today, and Will and I got into it a little."

He didn't believe her. "It's more than that."

"No, it's not." She was becoming defensive, and she pulled her hands away.

"You know, I think it's time you get honest with me," Dave insisted. "You're wearing pretty thin on something. Especially in the past few weeks."

Her mouth dropped open. "You're kidding, right?"

"No." Confused, he asked, "And what did that mean?"

She didn't answer.

Dave sat beside her. "Is it about Jo? Thursday's one year..."

"Let's drop this."

He watched her staring at the floor again. "I want the truth, Sammy."

She rose quickly, turning her back to him, wondering if he had any idea what an unimaginable hypocrite he was being. As she headed for the door, she heard him behind her.

"Hey." He grabbed her arm, shocked when she jerked away violently, glaring at him.

"*Don't*," she hissed. "Don't *do* that. Just... Get off me, will you? I can't even *breathe* around you anymore."

"Okay, that's it," he said quietly. "I want to know. What's wrong with you?"

"With me? Really?" She mimicked the way he was standing, crossing her arms high on her chest and scowling hard. "Okay. Here's what's wrong with me: I'm not sure anymore who or what it is you're married to."

"*What?*"

"And you can stop standing there all self-righteous, demanding honesty, when you've been lying to me for a year now."

He felt his pulse pounding in his head.

She knows.

Sam pointed into his face. "You're after me for... What did you call it? 'Wearing thin'? While you're so damned *guilty* over what Jo did that you created this life of utter perfection in her memory."

She paused, so distraught that she was unable to catch her breath. "No, actually, you act like *Jo* created our lives here. You stand guard like this family is a painting that hangs in your own private museum, and we spend our lives tiptoeing around this... This sacred *shrine* of yours that we can't touch. You're always perfect, all's well, you don't need anything," she mocked, then her voice broke as it fell to a whimper. "So what, exactly, do you need *me* for?"

Dave was horrified. She was tearing it all down, and he felt a paralyzing mix of shock and regret - and a relief that he didn't understand.

Sam's eyes were filled with tears, her voice straining as she said, "You're working yourself to death, and all I can do is watch - because there's this secret that you keep, one that you decided I was too stupid to figure out."

He was shaking his head. "No, Sammy... That's not how it was."

She ignored it. "Do you ever let down anymore? You rarely even smile at us. Your life is like a *marathon*." The tears streamed down her cheeks, and she backed away from him as he reached for her, putting her hands out to ward him off.

"Don't touch me," she hissed.

She had never said that before. Dave stopped, shaken - not only by her words, but by the fact that somewhere inside himself, he'd known that she was coming apart and he had avoided it.

"I've tried, Dave. I've tried to see the good side of it, tried to reassure you, tried to build you up. But all you ever see are the things you think you fail at. And of course, then you need to be better. Do better. Work harder. I know you love us, but that's not the reason you do what you do. You do it all because you're trying to repay a *debt*."

Dave sank onto the bed again, then dropped his head into his hands.

She's right.

"You're spending your life repaying her, and you use me, and Ty - and Hope..."

She was openly sobbing now. Dave wanted to comfort her, to tell her how sorry he was and that it would change, but he knew she wouldn't let him. Not yet. She had the right to vent it out, and he had the obligation to listen while she did so.

"You're raising her like she's your own. You honestly seem to think that she is, and how do you *do* that? Do you have any idea how small I feel around you?"

Dave couldn't look at her. He'd known that she felt that way as well, and he had allowed it.

"The truth is," her voice turned bitter as she said, "at the end of the day, all we are is the package you deliver to Jo's altar."

His head snapped up.

"Know what else? She would *hate* what we've become. You think we're honoring her? That she would've wanted us to wind up like this?"

Stunned, he managed a brief shake of his head. "No."

"And do you really think that if you perform well enough, I'll forget the fact that she's dead, that he carved her up on the front lawn of his house because of *me?*"

"Oh no..." He leaped to his feet, reaching for her. "That's not true, Sammy."

She made it through the door before he could stop her.

She was standing motionless in the hallway as he ran from their bedroom, listening to Hope crying from the nursery.

"I can't, Dave. I can't go get her," Sam said. "I need to calm down first. You go."

Ambivalent, unsure that he should leave her alone, he said, "Wait in the bedroom. We need to resolve this."

She went back in, closing the door quietly.

Several minutes later, Dave heard Tyler calling for him from the bottom of the stairs.

"What's up, Ty?" He descended the steps with Hope in his arms.

"Mom said to tell you she'll be back later."

Dave threw the front door open just in time to watch Sam drive away.

"Take your sister." Dave handed him the baby. "Put her on her blanket in the living room. I'll get you a sandwich."

"You and Mom fighting?"

The stress was all over his face, and Dave's initial instinct was to smooth it over. To lie to him - but Tyler already knew there was an issue, and lying about that wouldn't help him feel better.

... always perfect, all's well, don't need anything...

Dave decided he'd been running the marathon for long enough.

"Yeah," he said, "we're having a fight."

"Wow. What about?"

"That's none of your business." Dave grinned at him, and Tyler's face brightened considerably.

"But it'll be okay, right?" he asked.

"Absolutely. Don't worry about it. Mom just needs some time to herself." He motioned toward the living room. "Go on."

"Can we order pizza again? I don't want a sandwich."

"Sure." Dave reached into his pocket for his phone, then remembered it was upstairs, still in the pocket of his suit.

In the bedroom, he retrieved his phone, then wandered over to the picture window and looked out at the land.

It's perfect.

He became conscious of the fact that somewhere in the back of his mind, he had added one word:

Jo.

He suddenly realized that he did that all the time, with every milestone, every point of happiness, with every moment that he knew he came shining through - because she had died to protect the life he had. His entire life was wrapped around her, measured by the enormity of what she did, and he would never be able to repay her. He would never be able to live up to it.

He felt a grip of guilt as he admitted to himself that sometimes, he was angry at her for that.

It had to count for something, Jo. I wanted to take good care of what you gave us. I do owe it to you.

It occurred to him that he was doing just the opposite. Sam was right about that. She was right about everything she'd said.

He took his wallet from the nightstand and pulled a picture from it, the one he kept behind their wedding portrait. Jo sat on the picnic table by the lake, at the house she had rented the summer before, with her bare feet on the bench and her arms resting on her thighs. Her blonde hair blew across her face, and her smile gave no indication of the despair she felt then.

You had us fooled, love. Completely.

His eyes welled, and he blinked a few times. He missed his friend.

You were the master manipulator, after all.

Dave frowned as he thought, *And now I'm one, too.*

A picture of Hope was nestled in the sleeve beside it. In it, she was reaching up for him like she so often did, her eyes wide and needy.

He decided that a good thing, a miraculous thing came from his determination to preserve Jo's memory: the fact that he did regard Hope as his own. She was an innocent little girl who had been left to him to raise and protect, and he loved her, and she was his now - even if it did begin with a sense of obligation to the child Jo had entrusted to him. For whatever reason, Dave never thought of Hope as being Seever's child; but instead, he regarded her as Jo's legacy. And it had grown into something beautiful. That much, he'd gotten right.

It occurred to him that he'd never told Sammy any of that, and she needed to know.

He returned the pictures to his wallet; but this time, he placed Jo's inside a sleeve with the other photos he carried.

Then he gazed sorrowfully at the wedding portrait. They were looking out over the calm and deep blue lake, with seagulls circling around them. Dave remembered that moment, standing behind Sam with his arms around her and her head leaning back against his chest, and he recalled how he believed that everything was finally right.

She looks so content.

Jo was murdered five days later. And Sam had known, had lived alone with it for all this time, while he chased down redemption for a sin he had never committed. Staring out the window at his perfect plot of land again, the vista grew blurry, and he swiped at his eyes.

I'm sorry, Sammy.

A sudden sense of urgency struck him, and he headed for the stairs.

❈ ❈ ❈

Max yawned, groaning loudly as she stretched out on the bed. "Thanks for dinner."

Will watched her extend her body, enjoying the way the silk dress moved with her.

"Can't resist." He wrapped his hands around her waist and pulled her to him.

She laid on her side, facing him. "So, what do we domesticated types do now?"

He raised his eyebrows.

"Huh-uh. You promised me dessert." She loosened his tie and opened several of the buttons on his shirt.

Will propped his head on his hand. "It was bait and switch."

"Well then, I guess *you're* gonna have to be dessert." She slid her hands inside his shirt and around to his back, lightly stroking it.

"Well, to be honest... If I'm going to be an inanimate object, I'd rather be this." He was running his hand down the skirt of her dress, grabbing a handful of it at her thigh and slowly moving it up her leg.

Max laughed softly. "You want to be a dress?"

"Anything that's all over you..."

She was nibbling on his neck. He tried to finish the thought, but then she took his hand and was kissing his fingertips slowly, one by one.

"You lost your train of thought there, Remmond."

"Yeah."

"Too bad. It sounded so clever."

She gasped then, startled, as the door buzzer went off in the living room. She sat up and looked toward the door. "What? Who's that?"

Will groaned. "So close," he muttered. "You expecting anyone?"

"No." She slid off the bed, adjusting her dress and then grinning at him. "When, exactly, did you unzip my dress?"

"Told you - arrogant for good reason." He sat up and reached his hand out to her. "Here. I'll fix that."

"I've got it. I'm gonna be careful around you, Remmond."

He looked down at his shirt. "I think I'm more undressed than you are, doll."

The buzzer went off again.

"I'll go see who it is," she said.

"No chance you'd ignore it?" he asked wearily, but she was already out of the room.

Will rolled off of the bed, pulling his tie the rest of the way off and tossing it on the dresser.

"What's this?"

He picked up the picture of Max at age six. Taking in the long, straight, pale blonde hair and the deep blue eyes, he was confused for a moment as he wondered why she had a photo of Alexa.

Max poked her head through the door. "Dave's here." Noticing that he held the picture in his hand, she said, "Oh, that's an old birthday pic." She came to stand beside him. "I found it today while I was unpacking."

He was fascinated. "You and Alexa Reynolds look almost exactly alike."

"Really?" She took the photo from him, studying it.

"Yeah. Same hair, same eyes..."

Same expression.

Max dropped it back on the dresser. "Gotta open the door for Dave. C'mon."

Will nodded, turning to follow her; then, he went back to the dresser and picked up the picture. He thought again about what Max's father had done to her.

I thought he would kill me.

He reflected on how she had survived him, and silently railed against the fact that she grew up needing to survive her own father.

You won't let Daddy shoot me?

His heart was pounding as he remembered the simple horror of her question.

"No, sweetheart," he mumbled. "I won't." As he tucked the photo into his wallet, he said again, "I won't."

chapter 17

"I CAN'T BELIEVE she went all this time knowing, and she never said anything." Max was making a mental list of all the places Sam might have taken off for. "And I can't believe I had no clue."

"I *live* with her, Max. I didn't know." Dave was still standing by the front door with his hand on the knob, looking like he wanted only to get out of there and search for her. He turned to Will. "How long have you known?"

Will leaned against the doorway to the kitchen, and nodded toward Max. "She told me last week." He rubbed the back of his neck and said, "So she isn't at her mother's house."

"No. I even called Barley's, and a few other places in Manchester - some of the friends she had there. No one's seen her."

"And she's been gone how long?" Max asked.

"Over four hours."

"No answer on her cell?"

Dave pulled Sam's phone from his pocket, holding it up for them to see. "I don't think she left it behind on purpose. She tends to forget it anyway, and she was pretty upset."

Will sighed. "Okay. What next?"

"Beach house?" Max suggested. "She may be trying to connect somehow with the past, so I'm thinking she's visiting places where we were together."

"Maybe," Dave mumbled. He considered it, then said, "I'll take a drive up there."

"Will and I can head into Manchester. She may have gone back to the old apartment."

"Thanks. Let's go."

Will was slipping into his jacket. "You okay, D?"

He was looking at his feet as he nodded. "I will be. As soon as I find her."

"Dave," Will said quietly.

He looked up.

"You did what you thought was right."

"Yeah. And now, she's out there tonight thinking that Jo is dead because of her." He pulled his keys from his pocket as he turned to open the door. "She's been alone with it for a year."

"We'll find her." Max grabbed her purse from the desk. "Let's go, guys."

As they headed for Manchester, she sat silently beside Will, lost in her own thoughts.

After several minutes, he gently rubbed her leg. "She's okay. Just working through it."

"I know."

"You're thinking about how you blamed her for a while."

"I wonder if she knew." The days that followed Jo's death had passed in a blur of confusion, rage, and misery, and Max was sure she didn't always hide the brief resentment she felt toward Sam.

"I'm not sure it made a difference anyway," Will said. "I mean, as soon as she figured out what happened, she probably decided that you blamed her - and she would have thought that whether or not it was true."

"Maybe."

They were quiet again for a while, then Max said, "I used to blame myself for what my mother went through."

"That happens a lot."

"I remember looking out my window the morning after my father…"

She stopped, and Will reached for her hand.

Max held on to him as she continued. "The morning after he assaulted me. It was only September, and there was already frost on the grass, and I thought it was something like my life. Like a frost settled over it. It was over before it ever started." She moved a little closer to him. "At twelve years old."

"That's when you gave up?"

"Yeah."

"And look at you now." He pulled his hand away and wrapped his arm around her.

"Look at both of us." Max was watching his expression. "You gave up after Michelle died."

"That was it for me." He glanced at her. "Or so I thought. And it's interesting, what you just said," he continued, "because the day after her funeral, I went to her grave. Just to be with her for a while." He paused, remembering the grayness of the day, and the visceral reaction he had to the aura of coldness that surrounded her. "I was still on crutches from the accident, and it was hard to get to her. It was like I was moving in slow motion. And I remember approaching the gravesite, thinking it seemed like she was locked inside a black-and-white photo."

Imagining it, Max had to look away.

"We'd had a hard frost the night before, and Michelle - her grave - was surrounded by hundreds of dead roses. I mean, they looked perfect, but they were frozen solid. They looked like they were in suspended animation or something. I was doped up on painkillers, and I remember panicking - thinking that if those roses ever thawed out again, they'd fall to pieces."

She lowered her head so he wouldn't see her wiping her eyes.

"So I get what you mean - that feeling of life being over before it started," he said.

They were at the end of the exit that would take them to the apartment. As Will waited to turn onto the main road, he said, "You brought me back to life, darlin'. I'll never be able to match what you've done."

Max said, "It must hurt, that I'm so reluctant about the marriage thing." Mumbling, she added, "About lots of things."

"You're doing the best you can." But it troubled him more and more, the feeling of being punished for sins he'd never committed, something that he couldn't affect or resolve because he'd done nothing to cause it. It seemed to him that he was an innocent man doing someone else's time - and that if she would just take the chance, she would see that it was safe. That it was the right thing for both of them.

They pulled up in front of the apartment building, and Will lifted her out through the driver's side door, holding on to her for a moment before he set her on her feet.

"Love you," she said hopefully.

"Love you too. Don't worry about it."

The old Victorian was completely dark. A very large realtor's sign was perched at an angle on the front lawn.

Will watched her carefully: Max appeared to have no reaction at all to being there.

"I lived here," she said, "and I barely remember it." She stepped into the yard, looking around the side of the house for lights. "It's empty."

Will reached for her hand, and as they returned to the truck, he wondered if she wanted to talk about that night. He remembered Dave's voice on the phone, devoid of emotion as he said, "The bastard killed her, Will. He killed Jo. She's dead on his front lawn." And Will made it to Manchester in a pressurized, eighty-miles-an-hour straight line from his house.

"I remember your eyes when you told me she was dead," he said softly. He deposited her on the driver's seat of the truck, and she sat facing him.

"She lied to me, Will."

He nodded. "I know."

"Jo said she could never kill herself." She smirked. "Which technically, she didn't, and Jo was all about the technicalities. Makes me mad, even now. She tricked me." She looked down at her hands. "I'll never understand how she got to that point. I mean, I can understand dropping the rope. Giving up." She glanced up at him sheepishly. "That's a big no-kidding, huh?"

Will noticed that she was picking at her nails, and he took her hand.

She slid across the seat, pulling him into the truck. "But what I can't comprehend is the *finality* of what she did. Even at my lowest, I found something to care about."

"You sure you forgive her?"

She nodded. "In my heart of hearts, yeah, I do. But I can't let go of this one thing that I don't get. I wonder sometimes… How fragile *is* life? You know, could anyone get there?"

"I don't think so. I don't think it's true, that everyone has a breaking point."

"I just need to understand it."

"You're like that." He started the truck, smiling at her affectionately. "Okay, so we need to figure out where we're looking next. Where else would she connect?" All at once, it occurred to him, and he stared straight ahead for a moment before he turned to Max.

"Oh my gosh…" she gasped. "That's where she is."

"Wait. I'm not sure it's a good idea for you to…"

"*Go*," she insisted. "Hurry."

Ten minutes later, they pulled to the curb that fronted Jack Seever's darkened house. Sam's car was across the street.

Will pulled his phone from his pocket.

"Dave, her car's here at Seever's place."

Max was already out of the truck, and Will said, "We'll go find where she is. You head back to the house, and we'll make sure she gets home okay."

He followed Max to the back of the house, where Sam stood glaring through the patio doors into the kitchen.

Max touched her arm. "Hey."

She remained very still, not looking at Max as she said, "That's where it started. They said he chased her out the front door."

"That's right."

Sam folded her arms then, turning to confront Max directly as she asked, "So how'd she get him to do it?"

Will watched them, thinking he didn't want Max to be in the position she was in at that moment. He thought Dave should be the one dealing with Sammy, and he started to say so; then, something about the scene in front of him stopped him, and he took a step back. This didn't involve him. It didn't even involve Dave. This was between Sammy and Maxine.

Max didn't flinch. "She stole your cell phone. Manufactured a text conversation between you and her that she knew would drive him over the edge, and then she just let it all take its course."

She nodded thoughtfully. "What was the texting about?"

Will thought it was the only moment that Max hesitated.

"She made it out to be that you got an abortion."

Sam had no discernable reaction. "Really?"

"Yes."

"So..."

Max knew this was going to be the money question, and she braced herself for it.

Sam asked, "Why did he kill *Jo* for that?"

"Because she tricked him into believing she talked you into it, and that she then facilitated it."

Sam's eyes shifted to the side as she recalled a conversation they'd had the summer before. "When I asked you if she was suicidal, did you tell me everything you knew?"

"Yes."

"What was it like for you that night?"

Will wanted to intervene then; instead, he jammed his hands into his pockets and examined the overgrown grass in the back yard.

Max said, "What I remember the most is how badly I wanted to kill him."

He looked up. She had never told him that.

"I wanted to grab the knife and give him what he gave her."

Sam nodded again. "I know what you mean." She looked over to Will. "Did you know?"

"No." He slowly approached them. "Not until a few days ago."

"She died because of me." She was staring through the patio door again, wondering what had happened in that room.

Max shook her head. "That's not true, Sammy."

She turned away from the door, staring at the ground near Will's feet. "Yeah it is."

It had been four years of being Sam's friend, and four years of watching her tear herself down for things that weren't her fault.

Throughout those years, Max had sometimes wondered if the reason Sammy kept blowing up her own life was because of the weight of the misplaced guilt she carried, guilt that her mother had infected her with before Sammy was old enough to understand. Max had come to believe that her friend would arrive at a point of such mental fatigue that she then created a situation to justify her guilt. And throughout Sam's life, people had coddled her, comforted her - and Max understood that lately, she was trying to break free from that.

Max resisted the urge to hug her, to offer soothing banalities, and her tone was harsh.

"*Samantha.*"

Her head snapped up. "What?"

"Jo was *done*. She was checking out. One way or the other, and there was no way to stop her."

"Max..." Will put his hand on her arm.

"No." She pulled her arm away, keeping her eyes on Sam's as she said, "She's coming apart because she's been coddled for way too long, and she doesn't need it and she doesn't want it. Right?"

Sam seemed defiant, as if she wanted Max to challenge her. "I was sitting safe at home while he killed her."

"Exactly. While *he* killed her."

"But she was here that night because he was after *me*."

"She was here because she found her way out, Sammy."

"I set it in motion."

"You did *not*. You didn't set a damned *thing* in motion. You aren't the catalyst of doom, like you think. A whole lot of people got there before you did, and you aren't going to make sense of it by claiming responsibility."

Sam began to turn away, and Max grabbed her arm, roughly pulling her back around to face her.

"Do you want the truth or not?" She didn't wait for an answer. "You didn't give her the way out. Jack did that. *He* was the one she used. And if he hadn't come along, she would have found something or someone else." Max's voice betrayed the pain she felt as she said, "I was there, for every moment of the end of her life. Her physical death was a pure formality."

Sam gasped. "Maxine..." She reached for her, but Max moved away, avoiding her.

"No. We don't need that, Sammy. We need you to finally get real."

Will turned his back to them again, rolling his head and then his shoulders to ease the stress of it.

Max let go of her arm, and they stared intently at each other. Another minute went by as she watched her struggle with it; then, Sam bowed her head, sighing deeply. A sadness came over her that made Max want to comfort her, but she knew that her friend had to decide, on her own, to accept it.

"You know that?" Sam asked softly. "You know that for sure?"

"Yes. She was our best friend. Do you really think I could lie about it?"

"No." After a few seconds, Sam whispered, "She really did want to die, Max." She lifted her head then, looking for her response.

"That's right, honey. She did. And it had nothing to do with us."

"You still ever feel like killing him?"

Max shook her head. "I don't think about him too much anymore."

"I need to get better at that. It's been hard."

"Dave needs to move on, too," Will said. "He knows that now."

"He does his best." Sam thought about the things she had said to him, and she realized that she had no idea how to make amends.

Max took her hand, then turned to Will.

"Ready to go, Sammy?" he asked.

"In a minute." She looked into the house one last time, brooding about the things that had killed Jo, the insanity of others that finally took her down. As she thought about the misery that Dave had lived through for a year, she decided that she needed to finally let her go, and start helping him to do the same. They had both messed up - but Sam knew that Dave's mistakes were made out of love. Her own mistakes came from something else.

"I need to go home," she said. "Let's get out of here."

Sam stood in the driveway of her house, needing to see Dave every bit as much as she dreaded doing so.

When Max had asked her whether or not she wanted the truth about Jo, her initial reaction - in her own mind - was that she didn't want to know. Now, she realized that she had again built a comfortable identity on being blind: escaping everything difficult, numbing herself, wishing things away - and then trying to earn forgiveness for the things that she messed up because of it. After decades of living her life in that way, Sam thought she had finally grown out of it by the time she married Dave. It was discouraging - absolutely ridiculous, she thought - that she had fallen back so far. .

I was doing the exact same thing that Dave was. It had to look perfect.

The front door opened, and he was there, and Sam felt her heart speed up like it always did when she saw him.

Max had given her some interesting advice, just before they got into their cars and drove away from Jack's house. Sam was wondering how to approach Dave, because they'd never had a fight like that, not once. They rarely even argued.

"What do I say to him?" she'd asked.

"Know what, Sammy? You have a smokin' hot husband at home who worships you. So stop *talking*. Don't say anything. Just grab him, lock him in the bedroom, and find other ways to communicate." She laughed. "If you have any energy left after a few hours, you can talk then."

Dave was still standing in the doorway, searching for something to say, and Sam thought that Max could be right. They talked way too much, at least about things that didn't matter.

He met her on the walkway just off the front porch, and she put her hand over his mouth as he started to speak, shaking her head. Inside the house, she took his hand and led him up the stairs to their room.

As she locked the bedroom door, he said, "I'm sorry, Sammy."

"Me too." With her hands on his chest, she gently pushed him toward the bed until he reclined onto it, looking at her with amused curiosity.

She fell on top of him and whispered, "Enough said."

※ ※ ※

Will came into the bedroom from the shower, smiling lovingly at his sleeping fiancée. Max had curled up on the bed as soon as they walked in the door, and by the time Will returned with a cup of coffee, she was out.

He checked his schedule for the next day, pleased that he had nothing going on until late morning, when he needed to stop by the courthouse to pick up some documents - which meant he would have time for a leisurely lunch with her.

Then he remembered that he had scheduled an informal meeting with Jeff Marshall for around noon, and he wondered briefly why he had agreed to it. It was an exercise in futility, because Marshall wasn't about to give up any ground, and Will wasn't going to, either.

At least it'll make the judge happy. But I'll be phoning that one in.

He made a note to follow up with the associates he had assigned the new cases to, and make sure they were set up and ready to go; then, he decided that calling a meeting would work better. At the end of that day, Will had wondered if perhaps he could stay on after all, bringing in new clients, running the finances, and building the firm. Simple management. He and Dave had often discussed their need to run the firm differently, but neither one of them had wanted to be office-bound; now, it sounded good to him. It would give him time with Maxine, and the space to look into options such as teaching.

And buying a home with her. Making it our own.

Exhausted, he rubbed his eyes and looked toward the bed.

Like she did every night, Max had kicked the covers onto the floor. He smiled again as he gathered them up, careful not to wake her as he spread them over her, wondering how often the woman fell asleep in the clothes she'd worn all day.

He gently smoothed her hair from her face, thinking about how magnificent she was with Sammy earlier that night. It couldn't have been easy, confronting what had happened and taking Sammy down like that, and he thought that she dealt with it perfectly.

When he laid beside her, she rolled over immediately to lay her head on his chest. Will turned off the light, wrapped her in his arms, and his last thought before he fell asleep was that he was easily the luckiest man on earth.

✳ ✳ ✳

Simon drained the last bit of vodka from the bottle. He gazed blearily at the .357 in his hand, bouncing it lightly, then trying out the feel of it as he aimed it at the fireplace.

This'll do it.

He had no intention of putting a bullet in his own head, the way that so many other men did. In prison, Simon read online about a guy who got to visit with his kid even after he said - in *writing* - that he would kill him, and then the idiot blew himself away after he did it. Simon thought about the press he got afterwards, with all the people who talked about what a nice, peaceful man and terrific father he was, and he decided that the poor guy must have had a real piece of work for a wife.

At least he saved the kid from its mother. Taught her a lesson, too.

Simon knew another inmate, some guy they called "Jarhead", who got manslaughter for doing the same thing. He was being released in another year, a fact which thoroughly pissed off Alfred, a guy who was doing twice the time for the kiddie porn they'd found on his computer. Simon grinned as he thought that Alfred was literally pissed off: he made it a habit to relieve himself on Jarhead's feet whenever he got the chance.

And Simon knew about yet another guy who stabbed his girlfriend to death right in front of their daughter, and they couldn't even get him to trial. There wasn't even one scheduled.

No reason to take myself out. None at all.

Still holding the gun, he got a beer from the refrigerator and returned to the recliner, bringing back the memory of the brunette that Remmond had walked out of his offices with that afternoon. Simon found it gratifying that he had managed to stand within a hundred feet of him, and the hero never knew. He laughed aloud as he reflected on the fact that there was something else that Remmond didn't know: the hero was a walking dead man.

He figured the hot brunette was probably Remmond's wife, from the way they acted together, and he'd keep her in mind.

He had my kid smiling at him. Had his hand on her head. My wife looking up at him like he was God or something.

Simon cried out at the hollow, snapping click of the trigger, then silently congratulated himself for remembering to unload the gun.

He bounced it in his hand again. It was heavier than he was used to, but he had asked his father for something that would stop a big man dead in his tracks. He had his father believing that Brandi's family was gunning for him, and he chuckled softly as he thought about how gullible his old man really was.

"This will blow a hole through anyone," his dad had said. "Even a big man's going down fast if he's hit with this."

His father thought that Simon was talking about Brandi's dad.

chapter 18

"Mr. Remmond."

Will muffled a groan when he heard the tinny voice of Jefferson Marshall just behind him. The tone of it reminded him of a cat his mom had when he was a kid, the one that always meowed like it had a thumbtack stuck in its foot.

Will turned reluctantly to face him.

"Hey there, Jeff." Seeing his dour, studied expression, Will resisted the urge to add, "How they hangin', son?"

"We should talk," Marshall announced.

"Yes, Jeff." Will nodded solemnly, making minimal effort to hide the sarcasm that seemed totally lost on Marshall. "Yes, we certainly should." He motioned to the conference room down the hallway of the courthouse, indicating that he should go ahead of him.

In the conference room, Marshall set his briefcase on a chair and took the seat at the head of the table. Will stood casually by the door with his hands in his pockets, thinking that the guy really needed to hit the gym.

"Have a seat, Mr. Remmond."

Will leaned against the door frame. "What's on your mind, Jeff?"

"I'd like to try to reach an agreement on custody of Alexa Reynolds. There's no reason to take this into a hearing. My client is willing to be reasonable."

Will nodded. "I'm glad to hear it, Jeff."

Custody. I don't think so.

"He's willing to share custody." Marshall was getting edgy: Will seemed completely indifferent. "The basics, to start. Every Wednesday night, and every other weekend. Unrestricted phone, et cetera."

Will checked his watch. "Yeah, that is pretty basic."

"Anything from your side?" He was scratching at his ear, and it reminded Will again of his mom's cat.

"Tell you what, Jeff. You let me know if that's your red line, and I'll talk to my client. That work?" Will thought the guy was going to scrape his left ear off of his head.

"Well, yes - it is our bottom line," he said. He wasn't accustomed to an attitude like Will's. It was unnerving. "It's the very least we'll settle for, and you should know that we're considering our options for *full* custody."

He paused for effect, and Will had to make a conscious effort to avoid rolling his eyes.

"And additionally, I don't see the need for, or the benefit of your animosity, Mr. Remmond."

"Is that an reprimand, or are you just sharing?" Will asked.

Marshall was finally exasperated. "Are you taking me seriously?"

"Absolutely."

If that's all it takes to knock you around, your guy's walking away with one hour supervised.

Will checked his watch again as he opened the door to leave. "See you Friday, Jeff."

He was a few steps down the hallway when he heard Marshall calling from behind him.

"Mr. Remmond, a moment?"

"Crap," he muttered, then turned around.

"What's up, Jeff?"

Marshall was walking slowly towards him. Will watched the sea of gray and black suits that filled the area behind him, wondering if Max was going to be late.

"You know," Marshall began, "I'm aware that you're probably pretty nervous about the hearing. I'll just attribute your behavior to that."

Pretentious little peanut, aren't you?

"Yeah," Will sighed dramatically. "It can get pretty stressful."

"But just an FYI. You may want to keep in mind that you already have a reputation up here." He leaned in a bit, and Will thought he smelled like bacon. "May I call you Will?"

"Why, sure."

Porky.

"See, it's like this, Will..."

He forced an expression of sincere interest. "It's like what, Jeff?"

"From what I hear, you're an excellent attorney."

Eminent, actually.

Will wondered what Marshall was looking at. The guy was fixated on something behind him.

"My apologies. I'm a bit distracted." He nodded, indicating that Will should look.

Will turned around to check what was so interesting that it interrupted the mind-numbing tedium that was Jefferson Marshall.

He smiled as he watched Max winding her way toward them. She wore a pale pink business suit, with a tightly-fitting pencil skirt and matching heels. Her hair was swept to the side, straight, and cascaded most of the way down her back. In the crush of dark suits, Will thought she stood out like a rose in a gravel bed.

She stopped to greet a woman who called her name, stooping to pick up a folder that the woman dropped, and Will - like most of the men there, including Marshall - took a moment to appreciate the way her skirt molded to her body.

Marshall blinked nervously as she got closer to them. "Anyway," his smile was icy while his eyes were on Max, "do you really want to spend your entire career being known as the quintessential 'mama's boy'? Because that's already what they're calling you up here."

Max was close enough to hear it; and although she pretended she hadn't, her eyes flashed with anger.

She offered the men what Sam called her "Hollywood" smile, and in her best sultry tone, said, "Hi, Will." The kiss she gave him lingered well beyond what was appropriate for the moment. "Am I interrupting something important here?"

"Not at all," Will said. Her voice had him plenty distracted already; and after the kiss, it took him a moment to remember to introduce them. He could only imagine what she was doing to Marshall.

"Max Allen, Jefferson Marshall."

"Ms. Allen," he mumbled.

"Nice to meet you, Mr. Marshall." She extended her hand. "I thought I knew all of Will's colleagues. Are you a lawyer?"

Will looked away quickly, faking a cough to hide his grin. She knew exactly who Marshall was. He had never seen a man actually turn what he would call 'crestfallen', and he was having a difficult time not bursting into laughter.

"Yes, I am." He turned to Will. "Your wife?"

"From your lips to God's ear, Mr. Marshall," Max said, slipping her arm through Will's and kissing his cheek.

"My fiancée," Will answered, wishing he could plant one on her right there.

Pressing herself against his arm, she smiled demurely. "Take me to lunch, darlin'? You left so early this morning. I missed having breakfast with you." She continued to gaze at Will as she asked, "You'll excuse us, Mr. Marshall?"

"Certainly. Good to meet you," he muttered, but Max was already leading Will away. A few steps down the hallway, she started giggling.

Will spotted an exit, and he pulled her into the stairwell, backing her against the wall. The look on his face stopped her laughter, and she thought they had never before been that deep inside each other's eyes.

"I will never," he brushed his lips against hers, "be able..."

She slid her hands inside his jacket and pressed against him, watching him, unable to look away.

"... to tell you."

Several minutes later, a clerk came hurrying through the stairwell door. He stopped as he saw them, then grunted and rolled his eyes.

"Get a room," he muttered as he headed down the stairs.

"It's beautiful outside. Let's go for a walk after this."

They were finishing lunch, and Will was signing for the check.

"Sure you don't want dessert?" he teased. "I'm available."

"Not anymore, you aren't." She held her hand up, wiggling her ring finger.

"You got that right." He slid the folder to the edge of the table. "Neither are you."

Max wore a smile that seemed more wistful than happy, and Will asked, "What's on your mind?"

"You look so content. I've never seen you like this."

"It's all your fault."

"I know." She winked. "I'm absolutely irresistible."

"Pretty much. Especially when you take a moron apart in four words." He was laughing about it again. "'Are you a lawyer?' Poor guy looked like he wanted to dig a hole."

"C'mon, Remmond. You don't care what he thinks of you."

"Of course I don't."

"So why the dance in the stairwell?" She kissed his cheek, then smoothed the trace of her lipstick from his face. "Not that I mind, but you were pretty intense there."

"I know." He was surprised at himself, at how uninhibited he was becoming. At times, he felt reckless around her, and even more out of control because he didn't care anymore about being reckless.

In his quiet moments, the few that he had allowed himself before he met Max, he would think about the life that waited for him - how it seemed to be approaching more rapidly as the years passed. He didn't mind being alone back then. Not as long as he kept busy, which he always did. But he would occasionally wear down under the stress of the career that kept him so occupied, or he would start withdrawing from his latest relationship with a woman who wanted more than he did, and it was at those times that he felt the emptiness.

"It was you having my back," he said softly.

Max heard something come through in his voice, a loneliness that she never suspected, not with his usual bravado.

"I guess it was a reaction to not being alone anymore." Looking at their joined hands, Will could feel her eyes on him, and he wasn't sure he wanted to appear quite so vulnerable.

He quickly cleared his throat before he looked up. "And so I expressed it the way that a typical guy would."

"Yes, you did." He obviously needed her to drop it, so she took her purse from where it hung on the back of her chair as she rose to leave. "Funny, how accustomed I'm becoming to a typical guy."

They found a small park a short distance away, with a row of benches overlooking a pond, and they took one that was under a shade tree.

After several minutes of sitting quietly together, Max said, "It's one year tomorrow."

Will took his suit jacket off and laid it over the back of the bench. "I have to go in for a few hours in the morning, but I took the afternoon off."

"Thanks." She leaned against him and pulled his arm around her shoulders. "You know what? I don't want to do anything tomorrow but *live*."

"Good plan," Will said. "I think she would like that."

"So what's going on at work tomorrow?"

"Meeting with the associates, and we're looking to hire a few more, so I'll be talking with a couple of prospects. Then I'm going to go have a talk with Dave."

"What about?"

"I'm going to tell him I want to go strictly administrative."

"Really?" She leaned forward and turned to face him. "You *want* to be office-bound?"

"Yeah. I really do."

"Why?"

Will thought about how to respond. All of the introspection he was doing lately was beginning to wear him down.

It was simple: he wanted to build his life with her.

"It's time," he said. "My priorities have changed."

As though a reminder of his current priorities, his phone was alerting him to a call from the answering service.

"Sorry, doll. I'll be just a minute," he mumbled as he reluctantly answered.

"No problem."

"Will Remmond... Yeah. What's the message?"

Max watched his expression go from mildly interested to concerned.

"Thanks," he said. He disconnected as he stood up. "Be right back. Wait here." He walked a few feet away as he made another call, and she heard him say, "Brandi, what's going on?"

The rest of the conversation was muffled. Will stood with his back to her, several feet away; then, when he turned around, his face was lined with stress as he made yet another call.

"Sammy," he said. "Can you meet me at the office a little early?" He checked his watch. "Half an hour."

Max stood up and smoothed her skirt. "Work?"

"Yeah." Will shrugged as he returned to her. He allowed the resentment to come through in his voice as he said, "And that's it. Gotta go."

"I know."

"I'm sorry, darlin'," he muttered. "I'll make it up to you."

"Yup. You sure will." Max was determined that he was going to feel better, and that she'd make it happen before he went back to the office. "I'm *very* disappointed in you, Remmond."

He was starting to smile as he grabbed his coat. "You should be."

"And I'm not at all happy right now." She exaggerated a sigh. "I'm feeling very let down here."

"Channeling your inner dominatrix, Maxine?"

"You hope."

"You're right."

She busily fluffed her hair out, then turned to walk away. "Well, that's okay. I'll get even. I'm going to go spend oodles of money buying things I don't need."

"How does your going broke 'get even' with me?"

She turned around to face him, walking backwards as she held up his wallet. "You left it in your jacket pocket."

He looked mildly stunned for a moment, then patted his back pocket, groaning.

"Give me my wallet, Maxine."

She grinned, shaking her head. "Now, what percentage of the law is possession?"

"I think Clean Hands applies." He slipped his coat on, straightening his tie as he watched her warily. "At least it's not my clothes this time."

"We'll see about that." She was still backing away, picking up speed. "See ya, Remmond."

"Oh no you don't…"

She took off then, shrieking with laughter as he caught her.

Sam knocked softly on the door to Will's office before she opened it.

"Hi." She poked her head in. "Can I come in, or am I fired?"

"Get in here." Will got up from his chair and opened his arms to her. "Hey, you look wonderful, kiddo. Things going better?"

"*Yes.*" She kissed his cheek. "I guess I lost it for a while last night. Sorry."

"Happens to all of us." He motioned to a chair. "So you guys are okay?"

"Don't talk about it, Will. I'll cry." She took in his alarmed expression, and hurried to explain. "No, no - I mean I'll cry with *happiness*."

"Good. Don't scare me like that."

"So what's going on?"

He sat on the corner of his desk as he handed her a folder. "Look this over. We have an issue with Simon Reynolds. He's been calling Brandi, ostensibly to check on Alexa and to pester her for visitation..."

"And he made a few thinly-veiled threats," Sam finished for him, disgusted.

"Yup. Nothing we can get him on, but she's pretty distraught."

"Trash-talking her for the hearing." She looked up from the documents she was reading. "She doesn't have an O.P.?"

"Nope."

"Why not?" She returned to reading. Her mouth fell open as she said, "I can't believe the deal Reynolds got. What was up with the D.A.?" She paused, aghast as she read the notes. "And the *judge?*"

"Her first lawyer dropped the ball in the divorce, and the D.A. was..." He sighed loudly. "Actually, I have no idea what he was doing. As for the judge, he's known for leniency towards men. Doesn't matter anyway. We're screwed on several fronts at the moment."

"So Reynolds is gaslighting her."

"And it's working. She's going to be difficult to keep centered at the hearing, so be ready. And instead of having you behind her, I want you at the table. Right beside her."

Sam was frowning as she pulled a notebook from her bag. "Is there enough time to get that okayed?"

"It's different up here." He handed her a pen. "You're part of this firm. I'll just introduce you as such, and it'll be fine."

"Nice. So fill me in on what we're up against on Friday."

Will moved to his chair as he explained. "Reynolds went from mentioning how nice it'll be to have full custody of Alexa, to how glad he was that back when he shot Brandi, he wasn't as adept with a gun as he is now. Although why he thinks she would believe that, when he's been locked up for all this time, is beyond me."

Sam stared at him blankly. "Oh."

She was rapidly tapping her pen on her notebook, and Will asked, "You're thinking...?"

"That isn't enough cause to get her an O.P.?"

He shook his head. "We can't risk it. Not now. She has no proof, he was very clever in what he said - and besides, you know what opposing counsel will claim."

"That she's making it up to strengthen her case."

"That's right. And then we risk introducing the alienation issue." He sighed again, rubbing his forehead. "Which then goes to the custody issue."

"They do that up here, too?"

"Some do. And until I personally know more about Judge Franklin, we have to play the game like we're still in Mass."

"She needs something to protect her, Will."

"I know. I'm going to see if I can screw with Simon enough that he messes up in front of the judge. Can you meet with Brandi for an hour right before the hearing?"

Sam was writing notes, and she held up her hand. "Wait a minute."

Will checked his watch, thinking that if he got out of there soon, he'd be home in time for a leisurely evening with Max. Maybe take her to a movie, get her out of the apartment.

"So what were you saying?" Sam asked. Taking in his expression, she leaned forward. "Or maybe I'd rather hear what you were thinking, because you just looked *really* distracted."

He laughed. "Caught. It's a whole different life I'm living these days, Sammy. Anyway, I was asking you if you can meet with Brandi immediately before the hearing, instead of tomorrow."

"Sure. So that would be ten o'clock?"

He nodded. "I'll let her know."

"No, I'll do that. I want to swing by her house tomorrow anyway and check up on her." She winked. "I'll use the 'I need to check your court clothes' excuse." She took another look at the contents of the folder, then closed it and tossed it onto his desk. "Now go home, Will."

"You're all set with this?"

"Absolutely. Go home. Tell Max I'll call her tomorrow."

"Okay." He paused, debating whether or not he wanted to raise the issue, but he wanted to know what she'd be doing on the anniversary of Jo's death. "What are your plans for tomorrow?"

"You know Dave took the day off."

"Yeah."

"We decided to just spend most of the day at home with our kids, enjoying life. Besides," her smile was weak, but genuine, "we have to paint the living room."

"That sounds good." Will leaned across the desk to take her hand. "You're doing better with it now?"

"I am. Thanks again for last night."

He placed a quick kiss on her hand. "Long time coming, sweetheart. I'm glad you're okay."

As Sam rose to leave, she said, "If you and Max get bored, come on over. We'll grill hot dogs and drink beer."

"You're on."

Will opened the door for her, and she stopped halfway through it, looking up at him thoughtfully.

"Will, do you have a particularly bad feeling about this Reynolds guy?"

He shrugged. "No, not really. No more than the usual caution. Why?"

"I don't know... Something here is giving me a major case of the creeps."

He laughed. "You saw his picture, Sammy. This guy's literally rage on 'roids. You'd have to be pretty damned naïve not to get frosted out by that face."

Sam was unconvinced, but she said, "You're right." She stood on her tiptoes to kiss his cheek. "See you tomorrow."

On her way to her car, Sam struggled to dispose of the nervous energy that she felt over the hearing on Friday. She knew she couldn't allow herself to be distracted, especially not with Brandi Reynolds turning shell-shocked on her now.

All hail Simon. Another self-entitled moron. It never ends.

She thought that Will needed to take another look at Reynolds' attitude, because there was something there that went beyond the usual retaliatory rage that came out of men like him. She couldn't make a case for it, because she didn't know him personally - but what she'd read in the records had her on high alert.

As she got into her car, Sam decided that just to be safe, she would start carrying her handgun on her everywhere she could.

chapter 19

I'm not down with that. Sick. Don't want to know any more. Bye.

"Jackass," Simon muttered.

He moved to delete the email, then grew concerned: if his former boss - who was once his good friend - was that disgusted by what Simon had written, it was possible that he could let the email be known.

Simon hit "Reply" instead.

Just a joke, Jas. Bad one. Sorry.

As he sent it, he decided to keep his mouth shut from then on. He would mention to no one his thoughts about Brandi, let alone her future. Or her lack of one, which was what he wrote about to Jason. He smirked as he remembered that the next day was Friday. Didn't matter what Jason thought anyway, because the hearing would be tomorrow.

It was bizarre, he thought, that Jason was suddenly offended, because he'd done time for a stalking thing with his old girlfriend. Simon reread his first email to him, wondering what the problem was and not finding it. There was nothing there, nothing he'd written that he hadn't heard from Jason himself in the past, when the guy thought his girlfriend was screwing someone else.

He shrugged it off and brought up his Favorites list, scrolling down to the one he'd labeled "TRUTH." It was the website with the guys who talked about how the government was intruding on their families. Brainwashing the women, encouraging them to live without men - even to live with other women - and keeping kids away from decent, loving fathers.

There were several new posts, and Simon scanned them quickly, looking for the guy who seemed to know an awful lot about what he called "the state of tyranny against fathers." It was rumored that he was a lawyer out of Salem, one who had almost lost his wife and kids to the insanity of a feminist judge, and that he was a major player.

Simon read one of the ads at the right of the screen, about fathers retaining their rights, about how it was possible to stop her from divorcing you if you wanted to keep her.

Yeah, where was all this stuff three years ago?

Simon stopped on the lawyer's last post:

*Another loving father, driven insane with the grief of having his children taken away from him, goes over the cliff and kills his child and himself - and we blame **him**? He was essentially executed by the courts, and we all know it.*

We're being slaughtered, men.

It's far past the time that we kill the Feminist agenda, the influence these... WOMEN?... are having over our wives and children. For every wife who takes her husband's children and runs, there's a Feminist... WOMAN?... right behind her, filling her head with immorality, with all the ways she's 'mistreated' at home, when we all know the truth is, men are abused in far greater numbers than women are. And some of the greatest abuses are happening in the courts.

Now with the family courts being overrun with these Feminist... WOMEN?... and their anti-male, pro-lesbian agenda, good fathers are at a distinct disadvantage. Don't stand for it. Make your voice heard. We need to make an example of these... WOMEN?

Simon chuckled. The guy was brilliant.

His post continued with a rant about a Feminist lawyer in Rhode Island, one that he said "some brilliant attorney" had "beat bloody" in a hearing the week before. Turned out that by the time it was over, the woman client was asking about calling off the divorce. Some guys were responding with asking him for the name and address of the "Femiwhacked" lawyer, and Simon grinned, thinking it would be great to see the bitch get hers.

He wondered again why he had known nothing about these guys back when he'd needed them most.

He decided to search for one of the sites he'd heard about on the forum. The other men there said it did the trick a lot better than magazines, or even cable, because you could build your own fantasy woman - or women - and make them do anything you wanted.

I want to live inside this computer.

He thought about the brunette, the one he saw walking out with the hero, as he found the site.

❋ ❋ ❋

Alexa was sleeping against her grandfather's chest, exhausted from an entire day in the pool. He glanced down at her face as he sat on one of the chaises, smiling at the perfect circle of her open mouth, listening to her steady breathing.

Russ Lambert was a towering, imposing, lumberjack-type of a man, but carried the nickname of "Softie" within his family because of his easygoing, gentle nature. He stroked Alexa's hair, humming a lullaby.

"Dad." Brandi appeared behind him, wrapping her arms around his neck. "I should put her to bed. Long day tomorrow."

"In a bit." He hummed for another minute, then said, "She had a good time today. Brave kid. First time without water wings, and she just splashes and kicks her way straight to me."

Brandi kissed the top of his head and hugged him before she straightened up. Taking the chair across from him, she said, "I really think it's going to be okay."

A shadow passed across his face as he said, "This Remmond guy - what's he saying?"

"He's on it. And he's the best at what he does."

Russ snorted. "Says him." He tightened his arms around Alexa.

"No, says everyone else. He doesn't talk much about himself."

"Who's 'everyone else'?" he asked. What had happened to his daughter had destroyed his faith in the courts, and he was automatically suspicious of anyone connected to the system.

"Seriously, Dad - we need to teach you how to use the 'net," she laughed. "Check him out. Women like me, we sing his praises - and the people who try to mess with us tend to want him dead. That should tell you everything you need to know."

"I think you're exaggerating, Brandi. 'Dead'?"

"No, there are some pretty scary comments about him out there."

Russ appeared to be considering it. Alexa stirred then, and he put his finger to his lips.

Brandi asked softly, "Ready to let her go to bed?"

"Almost. That girl who showed up here this morning..."

"Sam Delaney. My advocate."

He frowned. "Why was she here again?"

"She's kind of like my hired best buddy for now. Works with Will. She wanted to make sure I wear the right clothes tomorrow..."

"*Clothes?*" Alexa stirred again, and he lowered his voice. "They're telling you what to wear, too?"

She nodded. "It matters. And we talked for a while. She's pretty confident about tomorrow, and I really don't think she would fake that."

"We'll see." His daughter did seem much calmer, and he was glad for that. He often heard her pacing in her room during the night, and he worried that she was starting to crack under the pressure of dealing with all of the craziness. Russ couldn't comprehend how the man who shot her, and then threatened Alexa, might be left alone with her - given full access to Russ' granddaughter, his only grandchild. Russ knew that if he had the chance, he would happily kill Simon himself; but whenever he talked that way, his wife started to cry. So if this Sam Delaney could help, then she was a welcome diversion.

He lifted himself from the chaise as gently as possible. "I'll take her up. Where's your mother?"

"In the kitchen. She's making coffee."

"I'll ask her to bring it out here. Be nice to sit out here and have it."

He walked slowly away, humming to Alexa again, and Brandi dropped her head into her hands, trembling, letting it go through her head like a mantra:

I can't do this. I can't. I can't.

※ ※ ※

Max wandered away from the patio, where Will and Dave were arguing about which Red Sox team was the best one ever.

She stood at the edge of the field behind their house, happy to be back in New Hampshire, wondering if there was something about the atmosphere in Hudson that made for more vivid, colorful sunsets. The horizon was a semi-circle of red and orange, and she breathed deeply as she watched it blend and fade.

Something moved in the distance, and her breath caught as she watched a deer meandering across the field. It stopped, lifting its head, looking in her direction for a moment before it wandered away.

I believe you can find God out here, Max. I really do.

She closed her eyes, remembering the summer before - the day that she and Jo sat gazing out over the field, sitting on the tailgate of the truck, eating ice cream and talking about life.

She thought about the moment when she scattered Jo's ashes there, watching helplessly as the summer breezes carried away what remained of her friend. Max recalled how she then felt the same kind of powerless, desperate melancholy that she'd experienced in the weeks of watching Jo slip away from life.

Max, did it ever occur to you that sometimes, the only power we have is the power to quit?

She blinked back the tears. "Not until you said it, no."
I don't ever want to get there, Jo. There has to be another way.

It occurred to Max that her life still seemed caught someplace between the past and the future, the living and the dead - like the people who had so deeply affected her, and who were now gone, were still entirely present; yet there were times that they were so distant a memory, it was difficult to bring them to mind.

She gazed into the sky.

I hope you're at peace, my friend. I hope God was right where you expected Him to be.

Then Sam was there, putting her arm around her, and they stood together quietly for a while.

Max broke the silence. "Know what I miss the most?"

"What?"

"How much she hated morons. What she could do to them..."

"She was brutal," Sam agreed. "I don't know which was funnier - when she told them off, or when she pretended to be crazy."

"Remember that guy at the restaurant who was hitting on her, and she started lecturing him about how 'man makes the light bulb, but only God can make the fire'?"

"Oh my gosh. He thought she was nuts. She sounded like a total lunatic."

"But at least he left her alone after that." Max was grinning as she said, "And the time she got mad at the cooks for messing up her orders... What did she put on that sign? The one she put on the cooks' window where they couldn't see it?"

"'Berry Crate Research: Turning Stupid Into an Art Form.'"

They broke into laughter as Max added, "And then she put the store microphone on them, and the whole restaurant heard them talking about how bad their jobs sucked."

"Their jobs, the customers - and then who was sleeping with who..."

Max said, "Wasn't smart, crossing her."

"No kidding."

Their laughter faded as they reflected on how true that was.

Eventually, Max said, "It gets easier. Bit by bit, it gets better."

"Yeah. It does. Did you talk to Matt and Johnny today?"

"Around ten o'clock. They said you and Dave already called."

Sam nodded. "They're coming to see the house next weekend. Johnny's bringing Bethany over - I think he's getting serious about her. Want to come?"

"Wouldn't miss it."

They continued to look out at the field, until the sunset had faded to thin strips of muted color and the breeze turned chilly.

Sam murmured, "We'll never forget."

"That's right." Max wrapped her in a hug. "Love you, Sammy."

"Love you more." She took a last look at the sunset and said, "Let's head back." They turned toward the house with their arms still around each other.

Dave was watching them, indicating to Will that he should turn around and look. "Think they're okay?" he asked.

"Yeah. They're fine."

He was starting to laugh, and Dave said, "What?"

"Max, actually, may still be a bit frazzled. She tried to do the homemaker thing today. Total disaster."

"Aw, no." He sat back in the deck chair, ready to be entertained. "What happened?"

"Let's just say, she's no domestic goddess. By the time I got home, she was ready to…"

The women were approaching, and Dave gave him a cautionary look.

"… wait it out until the Pats start the preseason," Will finished. He turned around to Max, offering his hand. "Seat right here for you," he said, pulling her onto his lap.

"We should head out soon." She laid her head on his shoulder. "I'm really tired. And you have court in the morning."

"Yeah, Will, by the way - can I ride in with you tomorrow?" Sam asked. "Dave's leaving me carless."

"Starter's shot in my car," Dave explained. "I need to be in Boston at eight-thirty."

"Sammy, you're such a pain," Will sighed.

She swatted him on the arm. "Be here at nine or so. And can you take me to the crisis center in Nashua after? Around two o'clock? I'm meeting for a few minutes with the Director there, and then I want to look around, check everything out."

He stared at her dully. "Anything else?"

"Is it okay with you, Max?" she asked.

"Fine with me," she yawned. Her eyes were closed. She drew her legs up and curled into a ball. "Whatever."

"Hey," Will laughed, "you gonna ask if it's okay with me?"

"Welcome to married life," Dave said.

Sam plopped onto his lap. "You love it."

"You're right."

Will watched them with a twinge of envy, and he held Max a little tighter. He looked down at her face, then smiled as he kissed her forehead.

"She's asleep?" Sam asked.

"Not yet," Max mumbled.

"Let's get you home." He stood up, and she slid off of his lap, leaning against him with her eyes still shut. "Delaney, what time will you be back from Boston? Max and I are heading to Maine tomorrow night."

"Not sure. No later than... Four?"

"That'll work," Will said. "See you in the morning, Sammy."

Dave walked with them to the driveway. As Max climbed wearily into the truck, he said, "Bust a few tomorrow, Remmond."

It was their version of "good luck," one that they hadn't used since the old days, and Will laughed. At their meeting earlier that day, Dave had agreed that they needed a managing partner, and he was very glad - and very relieved - that Will wasn't leaving the firm altogether.

"Thanks," Will said. "I fully plan on winning my last case."

"So what's up with Maine? You guys eloping yet?"

Max was settled into her seat, already dozing off, and Will shut the door as gently as possible. The thought crossed his mind that it wasn't any of his friend's business, and he bit it back, deciding there was no reason to take his frustration out on him.

He faced Dave and said, "Not yet. We're still in negotiations."

"Need a lawyer?" he grinned.

"I may. She's tough. After the epic fail today, she let me know that certain things - like housework, cooking, and anything that puts her within twenty feet of a washer-dryer - are deal-breakers."

"You don't care about that stuff anyway."

"Nah. She decided I must care about it because I'm a typical guy. She said she wants to go to grad school, and I'd much rather she did that." He checked his watch. "Gotta go. See you tomorrow."

"Never thought I'd see the day, Remmond. Your last case. It's really over for you, huh?"

"Yup." He went around to the driver's side, raising his hand in a wave. "It's over tomorrow."

chapter 20

WILL AWAKENED EARLY, before the sun came up. He laid on his back with his hands locked behind his head, staring through the window, thinking about the wedding that for all he knew would never happen.

Guess we each have something we can't understand.

He recalled what Sammy had said about his propensity for going Alpha-male and being dominating. But some things, he decided, had nothing to do with being a man - or a woman, for that matter. Some things were about needs, not wants. Not personality traits or preferences, but essentials. There were facets of life - of living itself - that needed to grow naturally. And two people who loved each other, who couldn't tolerate life without each other, should be married.

He was sure that Sammy would say it was his ego that bothered him, that Maxine was denting his pride in not wanting to set a date. That in regarding marriage like some kind of life sentence, she was poking holes in his macho mindset, and he felt a twinge of conviction before he decided that was ridiculous.

Maybe not.

Will understood that it was all new to Max, completely unexpected - but what he couldn't understand was why she wouldn't take the chance on *him*.

He thought about the day at the lake, the expression on her face just before she jumped into his arms. He brooded over the fact that she trusted him with so many things, but not with her future; then, he tried to imagine what would have happened if he hadn't caught her.

But the point is, I did. Others didn't, but I always will.
But others didn't.

He shifted, suddenly uncomfortable.

That isn't my fault.
It isn't hers, either.

Being locked out of a future with her was starting to wear on him, and he knew he'd better work on his waning patience. There was no other option anyway, and he thought that perhaps it was his lack of power within the situation that bothered him the most.

He took his phone from the nightstand and checked the time. It was only twenty minutes until he had to get up, so he decided he may as well start the day.

As he slid to the edge of the bed, he felt her hand on his back.

"Hey," she breathed, "where are you going?"

He turned to look at her, and his mood lightened. Her hair was spread across the pillow, and she was looking up at him with her eyes lidded, still distant from sleep.

It wasn't that long ago that I couldn't even touch her. She's doing all she can.

"I'll make some coffee," he said, leaning over to kiss her.

"What time is it?"

"Four-forty."

She sat up as he pulled away from her, wrapping her arms around his neck. "Do you really have to get up now? Court's at eleven."

"I have some work to do before." He laughed as she laid down again, still hanging on to him.

"You have a few more minutes," she mumbled, her eyes closing again. "Don't you?"

"Yeah." He rolled onto his back with Max still attached to him. She laid her head on his chest, and he listened as her breathing became slow and steady again.

Her left hand rested on his shoulder, and he gently lifted it so he could see the ring. He knew that he was expecting too much, way too soon - that he had been regarding what they were going through as though he was the brave one, the one doing battle with her past. The truth was, Maxine was the one on the front line. And what separated them was his inability to empathize with her, because his had been a happy, safe upbringing, in a good home with sane people around him; more than that, he knew too well that a man's life was nowhere near as fraught with danger as a woman's was.

She's wearing your ring. Give her time. She's exorcising him.

Will laid her hand on his chest and tried to think of something other than her father. Five minutes later, he carefully slid out from under her, sitting on the edge of the bed until his heart resumed a normal rhythm.

Max padded into the kitchen two hours later, going directly to where Will sat at the table, jotting notes on the inside flap of a folder.

"Morning, doll." He slid his coffee across the table for her. "'Bout time."

"Hey, Remmond." She flipped closed the folder he had in front of him, then took his pen from his hand and tossed it over her shoulder as she climbed onto his lap.

He watched his pen land in the sink. "What..."

"Quiet," she said. "I want a good morning kiss that'll last me the day."

He nodded dutifully. "Yes, ma'am."

The passion in her kiss surprised him, because she was always more cuddly than she was sensual in the morning.

When she finally pulled away, he asked, "What's this about?" Max wasn't at all a morning person. He smiled to himself as it occurred to him that she was barely an afternoon person.

"I can't wait to head back to Maine tonight. You're... I really love you, Remmond."

But she seemed a little uneasy, and he asked, "Anything on your mind?"

"Nah. Not really. Just every now and then I get scared."

"Of what?"

"Losing people." She waved it off. "I've always been this way. It's nothing."

"Well, I'm not going anywhere." He reached behind her for the mug of coffee, taking another gulp and then handing it to her. "Except to the office. And then..." With a quick kiss, he lifted her to her feet as he stood up, "I'm gonna find myself a smokin' hot blonde, and I'm taking her to Maine. Okay?"

Max raised an eyebrow and sipped her coffee. "Okay."

"And I love you, too."

"I know."

He tossed the folders into his briefcase and said, "Hey, I have to take Sammy all over the place today. The hearing should be done sometime around noon, and we don't have to be in Nashua 'til two. You going out anywhere today?"

"Actually, I have some shopping to do."

"Come have lunch with us."

"*Yes*." She handed him his tie. "I'll do that. There's an Italian place about a block from the center that I want to try. She can head over from there."

"You know, if you want to throw our stuff into a couple of bags, we could take off as soon as we drop her off."

"You got it."

Will patted the pocket of his jacket, then grinned as he retrieved his pen from the sink. "Okay, I'm outta here." He bent to give her a kiss. "I'll call after the hearing."

"Beat him up, Remmond."

A smile played on his lips as he headed for the door, and Max got the impression that he was looking forward to confronting Simon Reynolds. She tossed his keys to him.

As he caught them, he said, "No problem. He's going down."

✳ ✳ ✳

"Mr. Remmond, welcome to New Hampshire."

"Thank you, Your Honor."

As Will introduced her, Sam decided that she liked Judge Janice Franklin. She seemed completely different from the judges in Massachusetts, in large part because she appeared to be listening. And Sam thought she sounded sincere as she welcomed her to her courtroom.

"She seems nice," Brandi whispered.

Sam placed her hand on Brandi's arm.

Brandi remembered that it meant she should be quiet. She sat up straight and folded her hands on the table, trying to listen carefully, but she was too distracted by the fact that Simon was sitting less than fifteen feet away. Sam had told her not to worry about it if she couldn't concentrate, because she'd be her ears, taking notes and making sure that Brandi missed nothing important.

She couldn't stop herself from giving Simon a furtive glance, and she noticed that he was staring intently at Sam. Brandi grabbed a pen.

He's staring at you, she wrote on Sam's legal pad.

I know. Ignore him. Sam grinned then and wrote, *You're missing the good stuff right now.*

Brandi decided to focus on Will, to keep her eyes on him and refuse to even look in Simon's direction.

Will and Jefferson Marshall were doing battle.

"Your Honor, Mr. Remmond made no attempt at all to settle this issue before we had to come in here and waste the court's valuable time."

"Well, Mr. Marshall," the judge interrupted, "I *am* here anyway. Every single day. If there's a dispute, this is where we settle it." She didn't care much for lawyers who sucked up to judges, and certainly not those who did so by indicating that her input wasn't necessary. And the attorneys she found most annoying were the ones who tried to make an issue out of their personal dislike for opposing counsel, which Marshall did as a matter of course.

"Mr. Remmond, just for my own information - did you attempt to come to an agreement on this matter before we all met here today?" she asked.

"I did, Your Honor. My client found Mr. Marshall's bottom line to be completely unacceptable."

"I see." Judge Franklin returned to Marshall then. "You wouldn't fib, would you, Mr. Marshall?"

Will looked down at the table to hide the grin on his face. Jeff Marshall was getting too loud as he complained about Will's attitude in the conference room two days earlier.

"He arrived, Judge, with no intention of entertaining anything I had to say. I'm a highly respected attorney..."

"Wouldn't mind hearing a little foundation on that one, Jeff," Will muttered.

Outraged by the comment, Marshall made a strange, squealing sound.

"Mr. Remmond," the judge sighed, already exasperated with both of them, "would you like to share your comments with the rest of us?"

"I apologize, Your Honor."

"And Mr. Marshall." She turned her attention to him. "First, you will use your indoor voice. Second, your personal animosity toward Mr. Remmond is something that falls under the category of 'your problem'. And finally, with that being the case, you will now move on to the issue at hand."

Will resisted the impulse to check the color of Marshall's face.

Sam sat back in her chair as they finished, waiting for Simon to take the hot seat so she could stare back at him. She was surprised when Will asked for permission to approach the bench; and as he and Marshall stood in front of the judge, the line of sight between Sam and Simon was completely unobstructed.

She gently touched Brandi's leg, and Brandi turned her head away from where Simon was sitting. Sam could feel his eyes on her, and she allowed herself a brief daydream about flashing him an obscene gesture.

Brandi had told her that while Simon was rough around the edges when she met him, the real problems began with his steroid usage - but to Sam, that meant that Simon was simply a batterer on 'roids. No one forced him to use them.

Will was coming back to them, giving her an inquisitive look. She shook her head as if to say, "Never mind," and when he was close enough, she asked, "What's going on?"

"Going into chambers."

"Cool."

He turned to Brandi. "This is probably going to be over with quickly. Just try to stay calm."

She began trembling as soon as Will mentioned leaving the room, and she asked, "Has something gone wrong?"

"No." He smiled reassuringly. "Things are going right."

"Relax," Sam said, taking her hand.

"What does that mean?" Brandi indicated their joined hands. She didn't recall hand-holding as being a signal of any kind.

Sam laughed quietly. "It means I'm being supportive."

Will grabbed a folder from the table. "Be right back."

"I don't get it. What's he doing?" Brandi asked, watching him disappear inside the back room with Marshall.

"Trying to wrap this up quickly. Like, right now."

Brandi looked unsure.

"We'll know soon." She positioned herself so that Simon wouldn't be able to see Brandi easily, and then returned to her daydream.

Jeff Marshall was livid.

"Hey, don't yell at me, Jeff," Will said. "It was *your* guy who sent the email."

"That was a private correspondence..."

"Yup. Sent to Jason Matteson. His property, which he then forwarded - unsolicited - to me."

"How did he even know how to *get* it to you?"

With an expression of exaggerated sympathy on his face, Will leaned forward in his chair with his forearms resting on his thighs. "See, it's like this, Jeff..."

"Cut the sarcasm, Counselor," the judge warned.

"I apologize, Your Honor" he said, but he couldn't help his enjoyment of Marshall's outrage.

"Really?" She sat examining the email she was holding. "Uh huh. That's twice now, Mr. Remmond."

"Well?" Marshall demanded.

"My client spent a few months in physical therapy. You know, after Alexa's daddy tried to kill her mommy?"

"Your *Honor*..." Marshall whined.

Judge Franklin studied Will over the top of her reading glasses. "It appears that you've earned your reputation, Mr. Remmond. Let's settle this matter now. Just answer him." She returned to the email.

"Yes, Your Honor. I apologize."

"That's three," she mumbled, still distracted by what she was reading.

Will spoke slowly and carefully, with a cadence to his voice that suggested he was addressing a child: "Jason works part-time at the hospital where Brandi received her therapy. She and Jason became friends. Jason didn't want to scare Brandi, so he called her father, and her father made sure it got to me today. You have any friends, Jeff?" Without waiting for a response, and catching the fleeting amusement in the judge's expression, Will said, "I would think you'd want your friend to know if some guy expressed his opinion that 'someone' should one day get her dead - constitutionally protected though it may be - and that her kid was every bit as burdensome as she was."

Will leaned back in his chair, regarding him with exaggerated curiosity as he added, "But then again, I don't know you well enough to know what *you* would do."

"That'll do, Mr. Remmond."

"Sorry, Your Honor."

"I'm losing count," she sighed.

Marshall glared at him, knowing that his was a lost cause for the moment. "So where do you stand? What's your position?"

"On visitation? Nothing."

Judge Franklin looked up sharply.

"*Nothing?*" Marshall shouted.

Will turned serious then. He regarded Marshall with a quiet, seething contempt.

"Yeah. Nothing. He's threatened to murder Alexa before, right after he tried to make good on his threats to kill her mother. If it were up to me, your guy would be stripped of his parental rights and put away for good. But we all know that with the political clout of the kinds of men you represent, that's going to happen to Alexa's *mother* before it ever happens to him."

He paused, his contempt deepening as he continued. "I'm no collaborator when there's a five-year-old girl on the line. So here's my position, Marshall: if Alexa ever again winds up in the same room as her father, it won't be because *I* recommended it."

The room went silent for a minute, then Judge Franklin asked, "Do you have authentication on the email, Mr. Remmond?"

He slid some papers across her desk, then handed copies to Marshall.

She looked them over quickly, arranging them carefully in front of her as she said, "You know I have to give him something."

Will stared at her, quietly outraged. "I know you have full discretion."

"We will *not* tolerate a no-contact," Marshall snapped.

"Well, you'll be getting one when it comes to my client. Tell your guy to stop calling her."

Judge Franklin was tapping her pen on her desk. "Threats?"

"Obscure. Nothing we can prove," Will answered.

"And Mr. Marshall," the judge added, "I'm fully aware of the tactics used by certain groups in their attempts to intimidate judges."

Her eyes were directly on him as she said, "I'm a pragmatist, and I'll do what I have to do here, but make no mistake - what you will or won't tolerate is, again, your problem."

She turned to Will. "Reynolds completed a Batterer's Intervention Program in prison."

"Great. He learned how to pretend that he can manage an insane anger that he's not entitled to."

"Mr. Remmond..."

"What's next?" Will was getting loud. "Sex therapy for pedophiles?"

"*Hey!*" The judge was at her limit, and Will snapped his mouth shut.

She was silent for a few seconds, staring down at her desk and rolling the pen between her hands.

She looked up at Will and said, "One hour per week, supervised at a visitation center. And protection for your client."

"That's absolutely *absurd*," Marshall grumbled.

Will was staring out the window, drumming his fingers on the arm of his chair. "We finally agree on something, Jeff."

"That's the best either of you are going to do," the judge warned. "Keep in mind, Mr. Marshall, the rather daunting reasons that the Parenting Plan, support, et cetera have been difficult to resolve in this case." She was skimming the documents from the divorce. "It seems that prior counsel for Ms. Reynolds was a bit lax in her efforts. Are you attending to that, Mr. Remmond?"

He nodded. "Yes, Your Honor."

"If I go out there and tell my client he has one supervised hour a week, he'll..." Marshall's voice trailed off.

After another quiet moment, the judge asked, "He'll *what*, Mr. Marshall?"

"And there you are," Will muttered. He stared sullenly at her. "Let's send Alexa to visit with the guy whose own lawyer is afraid to talk to him."

"Go to hell," Marshall said under his breath.

Judge Franklin tossed her pen on the desk, fully annoyed now, and Will had the impression that she hated her job as much as he hated his.

"Okay, Mr. Remmond. Let's think about this. I deny visitation, and this guy," she inclined her head toward Marshall, "gets his Fathers Rights friends all riled up."

"I don't appreciate that, Judge."

"I don't care, Mr. Marshall. We're off the record here, so shut up."

He shifted restlessly, scratching at his ear.

She returned to Will. "They've already unearthed Redress of Grievances in this state, and they're finding ways to use it. They'll take it to the legislature - many of whom are in their camp - and the media, and don't even get me *started* on what they do on the Internet."

Will started to respond, and she said, "No. *You* shut up, too."

He closed his mouth and waited, still tapping on the arm of the chair.

"If I give Reynolds nothing, he'll be a martyred hero. And he may have options then, because I'll seem unreasonable. The focus will be entirely on my ruling, and whatever biases they can accuse me of having. But with giving him a supervised hour, he can't - with his history - be presented as a purely sympathetic victim of a Feminist judge."

She was right, and Will knew it, and he couldn't stand it.

"Okay," he said reluctantly.

"Mr. Marshall?"

He waited for a moment before he responded, "For now, yes."

She stared at him, unimpressed by the threatening undercurrent in his tone. "And that's my decision."

"My client would like to see his daughter today, Judge," Marshall said.

Will looked up at the ceiling and groaned.

Judge Franklin gave him a cautionary look as she said, "The Nashua Crisis Center has three visitation rooms, all fully equipped for supervision. We'll do it there, Fridays at one o'clock." She pulled several documents from her desk, avoiding Will's eyes. "Starting today."

Marshall opened his mouth to speak, and without looking up, she snapped, "*Out*. We're done."

Will knew it was the best they could have hoped for, and that it would be regarded as a victory. But it still felt like a deadening defeat to him, another exercise in abject futility, and he was glad he wouldn't have to do it again.

He forced a smile onto his face as he went back into the courtroom. The women were as he'd left them, except Brandi seemed a little more anxious, and Sam was sitting with her legs crossed and her arms folded. She was swinging her leg furiously and scowling.

"What?" Will asked quietly.

"Later," she mumbled. "I don't think it's appropriate for me to call what's-his-name over there," she jerked her head toward Simon, "a syphilitic son of a..."

"Hey." He shook his head at her. "C'mon, Sammy."

"Sorry, boss," she grinned.

Will stood in front of Brandi, leaning on his hands as he bent across the table to tell her the decision.

"It's the best we were going to do," he finished. He was taken aback by her response:

"Will, I just *love* you." She jumped from her chair, circling around the table and throwing her arms around him. "She won't be alone with him? I was so sure she'd wind up alone with him..."

"Okay. Settle down," he said, gently pulling himself from her grasp. It still bothered him that Simon had any access at all to Alexa, but Brandi's reaction lessened the sting of it.

Sam kicked his shin lightly under the table, and he turned his attention to her.

She inclined her head toward Simon again, and Will looked in their direction. Marshall was talking into Simon's ear, appearing to be almost as furious as his client was. Will couldn't hear what Marshall was saying, but the expression on Simon's face was one of undiluted rage.

Sam got up and stood between Brandi and Simon, blocking their view of each other.

"Let's go," she said. She took Brandi's arm and kept herself between them as they left the room.

They were almost to the building's exit when Will heard Marshall calling out to him.

"Mr. Remmond, a moment?"

Will stopped, thinking he should pretend he hadn't heard. Instead, he bent close to Brandi and said, "I'll be in touch. In the meantime, have Alexa at the visitation center at one, pick her up at two, and I'll make sure they know there's an Order of Protection on Simon. Stay away from him. Just do what they tell you to do."

"Okay." Brandi was watching apprehensively as Marshall rapidly approached them.

"I'll call you on Monday. If you need anything before then, let me know."

She nodded, then hurried out.

He turned to Sam. "Wait for me outside."

"I'll stay here."

"Sammy, I want..."

"Too bad," she said, and he could see it on her face. She wouldn't be giving in.

Marshall was in front of them then. "Conference room, Mr. Remmond."

Will had no intention of obeying, and no incentive to maintain a professional demeanor. He didn't need to collaborate with the Jefferson Marshalls of the world anymore. He didn't have to play nice, or exhibit proper decorum, or endure their posturing and their intimidation tactics for the good of a client, and his voice was filled with the years of his pent-up frustration.

"Forget it, loser. Not a chance. Say it here."

For the first time, Sam saw it: Dave was right. Will was done.

Marshall wasn't at all accustomed to being openly confronted, and certainly not in that manner. Everyone, including other attorneys, normally engaged him with an accommodating, even deferential approach. He made sure of it. Shaken now, he decided not to comment on Will's hostility, if for no other reason than the fact that being intimidated was a new experience to Jefferson Marshall.

He tried to stand taller, but the unusually high tone of his voice gave away his nervousness. "We're going to be requesting full custody at some point. It's only a matter of time before..."

"Yeah." Will cut him off. "Before your client grabs a gun again and kills her. Or Alexa. Or someone, *anyone* who tries to protect them from him." With his contempt on full display, Will added, "And you'll just move on to the next whack-job who - because of morons like you - feels fully entitled to blow away anyone who tries to hold him accountable."

Marshall tried to look indifferent, but his flushed face betrayed him. "What's *really* your problem, Remmond?" he smirked. "Hero complex?"

"Absolutely. What's yours? The fact that the price tag on your integrity says three hundred an hour?"

Marshall's mouth fell open. "You smug, sanctimonious bastard..." It seemed that he was about to take a swing at Will, but he took a step back and jammed his fist into his pocket. "Aren't you noble," he sneered. "Just the knight in shining armor, right?"

Sam put her hand on Will's arm, and he shook it off.

"Know what you do for a living, jackass?" He looked Marshall up and down. "You spend your life convincing sociopaths that they're actually victims, and then you turn them loose on innocent people."

Taking another step back, Marshall snapped, "You'll apologize for that, Remmond. I'll *see* to it."

"I'll tell you what, Jeff. You show me the hoards of men who are running screaming from their homes, living with their kids in shelters or on the streets. Introduce me to the all of the violent women who have the money to buy *you*, and I'll apologize." He put his hand on Sam's shoulder as he turned to leave. "Until then, you just keep chasing the money. And the revenge. *You* try to make it sound noble."

As they walked away, Marshall yelled, "You want to explain that?"

They turned to face him again.

"You said, 'revenge'?"

"Let's just go," Sam said quietly. "Please."

Will glared at him, chilled by his vacant expression, thinking that he was the prototype of the kind of attorney who had caused him to burn out. The kind who turned it all into a game.

"Yeah. I checked. Like you, I like to know what I'm up against. When was the last time your son had any contact with his mother, Marshall? Does he even remember what she looks like?"

"Will," Sam hissed. "Shut *up*."

The urgency in her tone got his attention, and he stopped.

"He's baiting you. And you're about to cross the line." She grabbed his hand, pulling him away. "Let's go."

It hit him all at once: she was right, and Will was shocked that he hadn't seen it. He nodded, and they turned for the door.

"See you soon, *Mr.* Remmond. Thanks so much for your time," Marshall shouted after them.

"Thanks, kiddo," Will muttered.

"No problem."

They walked silently to the parking lot. As Sam got into Will's truck, she took a brief look at his expression and said, "Go ahead."

He closed her door, then punched it hard enough to leave a dent.

✳ ✳ ✳

"You've had a dumb stare on your face for five minutes." Sam tapped Will's forehead. "And your fiancée just came in." She smiled affectionately as he immediately looked toward the door, rising as Max approached the table.

"Hey," he said, bending to kiss her. "You look wonderful."

Max laughed as she took her seat. "Jeans and a tee. I'm dressed like, you know - a beach bum?"

He took her hand, smiling, as Sam loudly cleared her throat.

"Oops." Max grinned at her apologetically. "'Lo, Sammy. Sorry about that. You guys ordered for me?"

"Yup."

"Good. I want to get going." She squeezed Will's hand and said, "I have one errand to run after this. You take Sammy over to the center, and I'll meet you there."

He nodded. "Don't be long, okay? We should try to beat the traffic."

"I won't. So, Sammy - Will said you two beat the crap out of the bad guys today."

She shook her head briefly. "Your man won the day, my love. I was just on sentry duty."

"You were a lot more than that," Will said.

She winked at him.

"Seriously, you were great." He gave her a playfully stern look. "Except for the comment about the syphilitic S.O.B."

Max paused with her water glass halfway to her lips. "Huh? What did you do, Sammy?"

"He's exaggerating. I didn't get the last word out, because he yelled at me." She stuck her bottom lip out.

"Let me guess," Max said. "Simon was being an ass?"

Sam opened her mouth to answer, and Will said, "Let's just leave it at 'yes.' I want to put this day behind me."

"You're no fun lately, Will," Sam teased. "Then again, maybe after I've worked in the system for as long as you have..."

"It gets old," Will agreed.

"One thing, though?" Sam asked.

"Sure."

"Watch out for Reynolds. He's gone over."

Max looked back and forth between the two of them, alarmed. "What happened?" she asked.

"The guy doesn't care anymore," Sam said softly. "He's over the edge. He was making some comments while you all were in chambers... Just watch your back, Will, okay?"

He was listening intently. "What did he say?"

"Just trashing. Trying to intimidate me. The usual pissing and moaning at first, but then he let me know that he's looking forward to the party he's gonna have with me sometime soon."

Will was staring at the wall behind Sam while she spoke. He focused on her then, and she thought that his expression would have scared her to death if he had been a stranger.

"Hey." She tapped his hand. "Settle down. He's not coming near me. I just want you to be aware."

Max was shaken. "Sammy, this guy's someone you shouldn't dismiss, you know?"

"I know. I'm not stupid."

"Anything you can document?" Will demanded. "Anything at all?"

"No." The intensity of his voice was unsettling. "I can take care of myself, guys. Okay?"

"You'll tell Dave?" Will asked.

His voice was raspy. Max could see his pulse racing in the veins in his neck.

"Yup," Sam answered, but it hit Max's ears wrong.

"Call him now, then," she said.

"I forgot my phone. It's at home." Seeing Max's expression, she opened her purse and showed it to her. "Look. I'm not hedging. I left it charging on the kitchen counter."

"Got your phone, Maxine?" Will asked. "Mine's in the truck. I forgot to grab it after the hearing."

She dug into her pocket and pulled it out. "Here ya go, Sammy. Call him."

Sam rolled her eyes. "Fine. Let's get him all upset."

She turned away as she talked to him, covering her free ear, and Max glanced over her shoulder at the phone to make sure she had actually called Dave.

"There." She set the phone down beside her purse. "I gave him the basics. And now he's cutting his day short and heading back up here."

"Good," Will said. "Because we aren't leaving until he's here." His head was starting to ache. He was weary of the cat-and-mouse games, and the guys who regarded themselves as masters of their own universes - who thought that the world owed them something. Anything they wanted. They seemed to be everywhere, and it sometimes felt like they were closing in on him. He couldn't handle the idea of one of them closing in on Sammy.

"He had another meeting, you know. He's cancelling it." Sam looked at them accusingly. "And there's no need."

Max shrugged. "You can be mad at us, Sammy, but it doesn't matter." Their meals arrived then, and she added, "So get over it. You have the kids to think about, if nothing else."

The tension was building among the three of them. After several minutes of sullen silence, Will said, "I think we all need a break from this stuff."

"Tell me about it," Sam sighed. "Maybe next year."

"You and Dave need to go away for a full weekend," Max said. "Set it up."

"Okay," she said, her tone sarcastically cheerful. "Sure. I'll just tell him to dump the thousand things he has to do, and then I'll tuck the kids into a closet and we'll head for the Bahamas."

Max and Will exchanged glances.

"We'll take over for you," Max offered.

"*Oh*, no," Sam laughed. "You have no idea what you're volunteering for."

"Come on. We spend so much time with you guys anyway, we should get our mail delivered to your house."

"We know what we're in for. Do it." Will reached across the table and touched her cheek. "We can handle it."

She was intrigued. "Really?"

"Yes," Max said. "Tell Dave tonight, and then start figuring out when and where you want to go."

"Wow." She was beaming. "Okay, I will."

"Good." Max patted her hand. "Let's finish up. We have to get going."

"Thanks, guys," Sam said. "Really." She looked uncertain then. "But are you sure? I mean, Hope's teething, and Ty's joining that baseball team next week…"

Max groaned. "Enough, Sammy. You're starting to sound like your husband."

Will was still brooding over Sam's comments about Simon Reynolds. He didn't like how indifferent she was toward the situation, because the guy was dangerous. Sam was fully aware of it - to the point where she was warning *him* - yet she wasn't taking it seriously enough for him to be comfortable. He decided he would talk to Dave as soon as possible.

Outside the restaurant, he gave Max a quick kiss and said, "Go run your errand. I'll wait at the center."

There was something playfully secretive in her smile. She kissed him again.

"I love you, Remmond."

As she turned to leave, Will grabbed her hand and pulled her back for one more.

"Love you, too, darlin'."

chapter 21

"I LIKE IT here," Sam said, taking in the view from the second-floor visitation room. She turned to Will and pointed to the four-by-six mirror on the opposite wall, on the other side of the conference table that sat in the middle of the room. "This is a two-way, an observation mirror," she said as they approached it. "You access it by going around the back of the room here, through the hallway. There's one of those in all three of the visitation rooms here. And this," she ran her hand along an indent in the paneling beside the mirror, "is actually a sliding door. An escape hatch, kind of. They're finally starting to update some of these places, at least here in New Hampshire - there's two exits in almost every room."

"How's security?" Will asked, examining the mirror. He thought it seemed poorly installed, noticing some bowing in the glass.

"No security guards. Not yet. And they don't use the wand on visitors too often, because apparently, no one here knows how to use it...?" She shrugged. "Strange."

"Yeah. It's not rocket science." He ran his hand across the mirror, thinking it was a hazard, too big for the opening it was mounted into. "So you like the Director, huh?"

"Yes, and you already asked me that."

He smiled sheepishly. "Sorry. Distracted."

"I know. Anyway, I start running the support group in two weeks, which means Dave and I had better hurry up and get that weekend away." She went toward the desk in the corner of the room, looking for the paperwork she needed to fill out.

Will checked his watch. "He should be here any minute." It occurred to him that they had probably just missed crossing paths with Simon. He glanced uncomfortably at Sam, then at the entry to the room.

"Something wrong?" she asked.

"Just worried. Wondering if Brandi picked up Alexa okay. I made sure everyone here knew that Simon can't be around her."

"We'd know by now if something went wrong."

"I guess. I think her father should either be with them, or do the exchange without Brandi there."

"Her father's pretty ticked off at the world right now, Will. That may not be the best idea."

Dave walked in then.

"Sammy?" He hurried over to her, opening his arms and holding on to her as he looked over to Will. "What happened today?"

"Nothing unusual. Reynolds is going to be a problem," Sam said.

Will nodded, his expression grave. "He is, D."

"How bad?"

"It's a concern. Want me to tell him, kiddo?"

"Sure." She looked up at Dave. "I need to fill out some papers before I go. And *you*," she hugged him, "keep your temper."

He watched her make her way to the desk at the far end of the room, thinking he was promising nothing.

Will motioned for Dave to come with him, and they started toward the corner near the two-way mirror.

"Hold on," Will said, looking across the room to the main entry. His senses were still on alert. "I want to shut that door."

Just as he reached it, the escape door at the opposite wall slid open. Alexa wandered in, her face white, devoid of any expression.

"Lexi?" Will was confused. "What...?"

Brandi followed her daughter through the door. Her head was tilted upward at a strange angle, and her eyes were focused to the side, wide with panic - and Will saw Simon behind her, hanging on to her hair, pulling her head back. He was holding something in his right hand.

Will knew exactly what was about to happen.

Dave was across the room to his right. Sam was at the desk in the left corner, several feet from Will. She and Dave looked up at the same time.

"*Sammy!*" Will shouted. "Get *out!*"

She hesitated, confused, her eyes darting from Will to Alexa, and then to Dave.

"*Sammy...*" Will spanned the distance between them in a few strides, grabbing her by the collar of her shirt. He threw her through the doorway and into the hall with enough force that her body slammed into the wall opposite the visitation room.

A shot rang out, and Will stopped in his tracks, closing his eyes. He lowered his head as he held his arms out to the side.

Sam heard Reynolds say, "Close the door. *Now.*"

Will looked up then, and their eyes met as he shut the door.

"Will..."

He could have made it out of there. He could have escaped.

Her head was bleeding from where it hit the wall, and she wiped the blood from the side of her neck as she ducked into one of the offices, grabbed a phone, and pressed *911*. She dropped the receiver on the desk, vaguely aware of the people on the first floor shouting and running for the exits. She thought of her children, and she knew that she should be running, as well.

She turned to look at the closed door of the room that held their father. Her husband, the love of her life. The only man her best friend had ever loved was in there, as well. And a battered mother and her terrified child were being held at gunpoint by a psychopath, and Sam understood that it was the moment in her life that would define her. If nothing else, she knew she wouldn't survive it if she let it happen.

He saved me instead.

She thought of the deadness in Max's eyes after Jo died, and she whispered, "Not again."

Not this time, Maxine. Not again. Not because of me.

As she made her way down the hall and around the exterior of the visitation room, she reached to the back of her trousers and pulled her gun from its holster. She took faint notice of the fact that she was completely calm. She felt numbed.

Not this time.

"Hey, this worked *out*. I thought I was gonna have to go find you, Counselor." Simon shoved Brandi toward the table. "Have a seat, honey."

She sat at the table with Alexa on her lap, staring with empty eyes at the child's shoes. Will thought that Alexa looked completely gone, lost in another world someplace.

He glanced at Dave, standing across the room in front of the mirror.

Dave appeared to be assessing the situation, weighing the chances of getting to Simon before he could fire; then, Simon leveled the gun at him.

"Sit down," he said evenly, and he shot him.

Dave went down hard, rolling onto his side and groaning. Will was vaguely aware of having shouted something, but he didn't know what. He moved quickly toward Simon, and the gun came up at him immediately.

"*Lace 'em*," Simon shouted.

Will stopped and laced his fingers on top of his head. He looked at Dave, on the floor directly underneath the mirror, with blood draining out of his upper thigh. He was conscious, staring at Will, and he was trying to get up.

Don't. Stay down. Will hoped Dave could read it in his eyes.

"So, Will Remmond. The hero. Get over here beside your buddy." Simon moved to stand behind Brandi, keeping the table between himself and Will.

Will noticed a large, bleeding bruise on her temple as he positioned himself in front of Dave.

"My wife just *loves* you."

"I'm not your wife anymore..."

He grabbed her hair from behind, yanking her head backwards so she was looking up at him, and she gasped with pain.

Will dug his nails into his scalp, picturing what he was going to do to Simon if he got the opportunity.

"*Why not?*" Simon yelled into her face. "Because some bitch of a Feminist judge *said* you aren't?"

Brandi tried to speak, but her neck was extended too far. She stared at him helplessly.

He let go of her, shoving her head forward again, and Will hoped she'd keep her mouth shut.

Simon returned to him then. "You need to learn a few things, hero. Want to learn?"

"Yeah," Will said quietly. He heard distant sirens.

"Why don't you say, 'Yes, *sir*.'"

"Yes, sir." He noticed the way Alexa's mouth was hanging open, and that she was drooling a little. She seemed catatonic.

"This," Simon waved the gun over Brandi and Alexa, "is my family, hero. *My* family. *My* daughter. *My* wife."

Will was suddenly, completely lost in the surrealism of the scene before him: it struck him as the essence of evil, as a vision of what it was that he'd spent his life fighting.

The shock of it drilled into him. The young mother, terrified, bruised, and bleeding, and the little girl

looks exactly like Maxine did

who was now emotionally dead, staring straight ahead in blank, uncomprehending horror, seeing nothing at all - they were the prisoners of the maniacal head of the household, standing behind them with his gun. Keeping his family with him at gunpoint.

His wife. His daughter.

Will's thoughts tumbled over each other as his mind retreated from itself.

This is the family portrait from Hell.

With that, Will felt his mind bending, tilting away from the reality of where he was standing, taking him someplace outside of himself. A cold, vacant sensation came over him as he detached from what was happening and from where he knew it was going.

Simon's voice was quietly menacing. "Don't interfere with a man's family," he said. "This is what you get when you interfere with a man's family. *Got it?*"

Will nodded slowly. "I sure do."

"Yeah?"

"Yeah. I get it."

"You know who the real heroes are, Will Remmond?"

"Tell me." Will was gauging the distance between himself and Simon.

"Fathers, husbands like me. Who stand up to the system. Who have the guts to take on the people who rip apart families."

Will nodded again. A thin stream of Dave's blood trickled past his shoe.

"Now," Simon casually waved the gun over Brandi's head, and she gasped as he suddenly leveled it at Will again. "Someone's gonna die here in the next minute."

On the other side of the mirror, Sam took aim.

That's exactly right.

Max was around the corner, locking Will's truck as the police cruisers and ambulances went screaming by.

"Wow," she muttered.

An elderly couple was walking past her, and the woman said, "There's a shooting at that place where they do those custody things. Some nut with a gun."

Max felt lightheaded. She put her hand on the door of the truck to steady herself.

Watch out for Reynolds. He's gone over.

"What..." she croaked. She tried again to ask, but there was no breath inside her.

She turned abruptly and started running toward the center.

Sam couldn't see where Dave was. She hoped that he was still over toward the corner, out of the line of fire.

But Will was standing directly between Simon and her gun, and she mumbled, "Get out of the way. Damn it, Will, *move.*"

She focused on keeping the gun trained beyond Will, on the spot she wanted to hit, and she thought about the people she loved the most.

Tyler, who adored his dad, thought he was the greatest man who ever lived, wanted to be everything that his father was. Hope, more likely to reach for Dave than for anyone else in the world, every bit a Daddy's girl. Will, finally settled, happy, so in love with Maxine - who, for the first time in her life, saw a purpose for all she had endured, and was starting to trust being loved by a good man.

Jo, murdered by the psychopath that Sam blamed herself for bringing into their lives. Jo had been destroyed by him, and by the kind of people who helped him - all carriers of the same kind of rage that now threatened to end them all.

"Dave..." she whispered, and a soft cry escaped her. She'd never felt so alone.

She bit hard on the inside of her cheek. Tears would blur her line of sight.

One is dead, two are in that room, and Max might as well be in there with them if Will doesn't come out alive.

Waves of sharp pain flooded her stomach as she thought about the murders at the center. Joanie Millerton had wanted to go to college. She wanted to be a teacher. Her acceptance letter arrived the same day that her husband stabbed her to death.

Jeremy hit the three-pointer that won the championship for his basketball team. Sam was there, sitting in the stands with his mom. She remembered the joy on his face as his teammates lifted him onto their shoulders. His father murdered him two days later.

No more.

Sam realized that she'd lost her mark, and she pushed the thoughts away.

It's got to stop.

Narrowing her eyes, she focused beyond Will to where Reynolds' neck would be, and she was calm again.

Simon was taunting Will.

"So who's dying, lawyer? You pick it."

Will looked up at the ceiling, straining against the impulse to try for the gun. The table was between them, and he knew he wouldn't make it.

Keeping his eyes on him, Simon brought his arm down toward Dave and fired again, and Will heard Dave make a low, gasping sound behind him.

Then he pushed the gun against the back of Brandi's head, and she cried out.

"*Who's dying?*" he screamed.

Will glanced down at the thin line of Dave's blood, tracking lazily along the grooves of the hardwood floor and forming a small puddle under the chair where Brandi held her daughter.

He knew that Reynolds was going to kill him anyway.

He thought about Max, about what would happen to her when she found out he was dead.

I love you. I'm so sorry.

"I am." Will's voice was steady, not betraying the mortal rage he felt at that moment.

"You are, huh? Okay." Simon nodded resolutely, as if they had just agreed on a business deal. Then he broke into a satisfied smile.

"On your knees, Counselor."

"Simon," Brandi sobbed, "don't."

"Hey! *Remmond!*" Simon aimed directly at Will's head, and Brandi shrieked. "On your *knees.*"

Will didn't move. A small, contemptuous grin was on his lips.

"I'm not going out on my knees, you son of a bitch."

"Oh, yeah - you are." Simon glanced down at Alexa. "Know why?"

He pressed the gun to Alexa's temple, and Brandi went limp. She had fainted.

"You'll do it because you're a *hero.*"

A surge of infuriated despair coursed through Will, so intense that his breath left him. He had a flash of a thought - that if not for Maxine, he wouldn't be all that anxious to live in a world where he could witness what he'd just seen.

He stared Simon down, going slowly to his knees. He heard Dave moan softly.

Then he laced his fingers tighter and closed his eyes, wanting her face to be the last thing he saw.

Images flashed before him: dancing with her at the wedding. Their first kiss. Watching her sleep. Catching her in the water. Her eyes - wide with laughter, flashing with anger, filled with tears, filled with passion. He recalled daydreaming about their first anniversary, and quickly pushed it away as the raging agony rose inside him.

Then his mind settled on the picture of the two of them, on their October day in Maine, and he waited for the gun to go off.

Simon moved the gun away from Alexa's head, relishing the victory.

"Here ya go, hero," he muttered.

Will felt the explosions as much as he heard them, two of them that were almost simultaneous, jarring his body as the sound traveled through him. He heard the shattering detonation that sounded like every window in the room had imploded. With his eyes closed, he lost his balance as a tearing pain coursed down his spine - and with it, the instantaneous impression that he'd been shot in the back, and he wondered how that could be.

A scorching pain flared in his arm, and his eyes flew open just in time to see Simon falling to the floor, his hands fluttering around his throat as the blood pumped rhythmically from his neck.

Will jumped to his feet and kicked Simon's gun away from where it had landed on the floor beside him. Simon was still alive, choking on his own blood and grabbing at his throat, his eyes rolling up and down in their sockets. Will had to force himself to resist the impulse to stomp on his neck.

He turned to see Sam shoving the escape door open, and then he saw the empty frame where the mirror had been. Shards of glass littered the floor. He realized that it had exploded behind him when she shot Reynolds.

They stared at each other as she calmly laid her gun on the table.

She gazed unemotionally at where Simon lay kicking. He rolled onto his side and drew his legs to his chest, still grabbing at his throat.

"Sammy," Will dropped to the floor beside Dave, "he's down."

She thought he meant Reynolds; then, she turned and saw him, bleeding from his head and his leg, unconscious. She crouched on the floor beside him to avoid falling, because the room suddenly started to spin. She hadn't been able to see him below the level of the mirror.

"*Dave...*" It had the force of a scream, but there was no breath behind it.

"I heard the sirens. There's help outside." Will ripped Dave's trousers open at the hole where the bullet had entered, checking how much blood was coming out of him while he tore off his tie and threaded it under Dave's leg.

Sam was staring paralyzed at where the blood was leaking from Dave's head.

"Sammy." Will quickly snapped his fingers in front of her face, but she didn't move.

He leaned toward her. "*Samantha!*" He shouted directly into her ear, and she cried out, finally looking at him.

"Paramedics can't come in here until it's safe." He nodded toward the window. "Go tell them it's okay to come in. Say the shooter's down, no one here is armed, and we need emergency assistance for a bystander." He pressed his hand to the wound in Dave's leg.

As she ran unsteadily to the window, Will looked down at his friend, quickly picking the bigger shards of glass off of his chest and assessing how much blood he'd lost. It was puddled around him, running across the wood floor and seeping into the cracks. He was clammy, his face ashen.

"Come on, D." He pressed his fingers to Dave's neck. His pulse was way too fast, and it was weak.

"Dave!" he yelled. "Open your eyes!"

Sam was beside him again. "What can I do?" She touched the area where the blood was leaking from his head.

"Give me your jacket," Will said, and she slipped out of it and handed it to him.

"Put your hand here." He jammed her hand against Dave's thigh, then wadded up the jacket of her suit, pressing it against his head. Simon's second bullet appeared to have taken a long swipe at the side of his head, not penetrated it, and Will was more concerned that the first bullet had nicked Dave's femoral artery.

He could hear the police coming up the stairs.

"*In here*," he called out as he sharply tapped Sam's cheek. "Sammy, are you listening to me?"

She nodded, staring at him wide-eyed.

"Say you're listening."

"I'm listening."

"Did you bring that gun here loaded?"

She nodded again.

"*No.* You did not. You had the gun in your holster, and the bullets in your pocket, and you loaded it after I threw you out of the room. What did I just say?"

She recited it back to him, and he said, "That's what you tell them about the gun. The rest, just tell the truth. Got it?"

"Okay."

Will flicked his finger against Dave's eyelids. "Dave! Wake up!"

As the police entered the room, Dave opened his eyes.

The police made Max - and the multitude of onlookers - stand behind the cruisers that blocked the street.

It's been way too long. Someone's dead.

She searched her pocket again for her cell, thinking perhaps she'd left it at the restaurant, and not knowing who she would call anyway. Everyone she loved was in that building.

She saw Alexa carried out on a gurney, and then Brandi, strapped down and thrashing about, screaming incoherently. But Max heard two of her words clearly:

"*He's dead!*"

Max choked back a sob.

Another gurney emerged from the building. She gasped, clutching at her stomach as she recognized Dave. He was coated with blood - the gurney was red with it. Sam was walking beside him, holding his hand. Max could see blood on her face and all over her clothes as she got into the back of the ambulance with him.

Then, Max heard a reporter somewhere behind her:

"... and early reports are that one of the attorneys in the room has been killed. We're verifying that right now. His identity will be withheld pending notification of next of kin..."

A body bag was being brought from the building.

Max looked at her feet.

Her mouth hung open, and she wondered vaguely why tears were pouring from her eyes when she wasn't even crying. She watched them dotting the ground; then, she raised her head and looked around for Will. He would show up, she knew
that he won't
that he would, because he promised.
"You promised me," she whispered.
He's dead.
Wait.
Dead weight? Clever stream of consciousness there, darlin'. Damn, he just loves that in you.

Max thought that she was laughing then, but people were touching her, concerned, asking her if she was okay.

She shoved them away, turning around and coming face to face with a woman holding an armful of perfectly-formed roses, asking her if she knew anyone in there. Max stared at the roses, unable to look away.

You were right, Will. This is what happens when they thaw out.

She fought it, horrified that she would think it as she felt a ripping, burning pain in her chest that left her nauseated, just before she felt her emotions turning to stone.

Police were exiting the building, and another ambulance was leaving.

Max slowly backed away, bumping into several people, desperate to leave. It seemed like the spectators were an audience, chattering and critiquing and enjoying the drama, and she felt claustrophobic - like all of life was on fire, consuming the oxygen around her and she couldn't find the exit.

Someone made a comment about the poor bastard who ate a bullet. Whoever the guy was talking to said actually, he got it in the back of the head, gangland-style.

"One less lawyer in the world, I guess."
No.

Max wasn't aware that she screamed it, only that the people around her scattered.

She needed to escape it. She wanted to avoid knowing anything more, because she thought that would work only to betray him. But at the same time her legs felt leaden, because she couldn't make herself take her first steps without him.

You would wait for me. You would wait to find out for sure.

"I *can't*," she cried out.

She was fully panicked, still watching the entry to the center, unable to move in any direction. Almost every part of her knew that he was dead, but there was still a fragment of hope inside of her - one that wouldn't have been there except for him, and she owed it to him to stay.

The officer was completing his report.

He looked up from his clipboard at Will, still concerned. "You really do need a doctor," he said.

"I'll go later." He wanted to find Max first, and make sure she was all right.

"Okay, then. We're done here, Mr. Remmond. Thanks."

"No problem." Will called across the room to the paramedic. "Brian, you called my fiancée, right?"

"Yeah. Left her a message."

"What - she didn't answer?"

"Nope."

Will frowned, adjusting the bandage around his upper arm where Simon's bullet had grazed him. He was in worse shape than he'd realized: he had several gashes on the back of his head and neck, several deep scratches and a decent couple of slices on his back, and the groove across his arm from the bullet that went astray when Sam shot Reynolds.

"You sure you called the right number?"

Brian nodded. "The voicemail message said 'Max Allen'. Are you sure you don't want to get checked out at the hospital? You need some attention. Definitely stitches. And I doubt we got all the glass from that mirror out."

"Yeah, I'm sure. Gotta go."

Will hurried from the building, trying to remember where he left his truck so he could get to his phone. He was momentarily stunned by the crush of people waiting outside, and he moved quickly through the crowd, ignoring the bewildered staring, the questions about who he was, what had happened, and if he needed help.

A woman shouted, "*Will?*"

He turned to see his associate, Melissa, gaping at him.

"Will?" she asked again, her expression a mixture of shock and relief.

"Melissa," he made his way to her, "have you seen Max?"

"I saw her on the other side of the barricades. Over there." She pointed across the expanse that was cordoned off by police cruisers. "I thought I heard her scream once, then I lost her in the crowd. Will, they said you were dead."

"What? Who decided I was dead?"

"I don't know. It was all over the place out here."

He was suddenly lightheaded. The combination of adrenaline and the blood he'd lost left him dizzy for a moment, and Melissa held on to his good arm until he steadied himself.

"I need to find her," he mumbled.

"Will, you need to get to the hospital."

"Give me your phone," he said, scanning the crowd for her.

Max's phone rang several times, then he heard a tentative, "Hello?"

Confused, he stammered, "Who is this? Sammy?"

"Will? Oh my gosh... I have Max's phone. Hey, they think Dave's gonna be okay. It didn't hit his femoral. He lost a lot of blood, but he's..."

"Yeah, good. Sammy, the story outside the center is that I'm dead. And she was out here."

"Max thinks..." Alarmed then, she asked, "Where is she now?"

"I don't know." He started to rub his neck, then winced from the pain. "I can't... I'm having trouble thinking." He turned to Melissa. "When was the last time you saw her?"

"Only a few minutes ago."

He disconnected without saying anything more, and handed the phone back to her.

She wouldn't leave.

"Okay. You're here someplace." He took off for the other side of the barricades, shoving past a reporter, working his way around the edges of the crowd and moving as quickly as he could.

Max sat wearily on the curb, thinking she should leave but not quite ready yet, and she thought about how quickly life had been fully drained of all meaning.

I get it now.

I understand why you had to leave, Jo.

Whatever else Jo might have become in life, had she not been so abused and betrayed, the truth was that she hated bullies a lot more than she loved anyone else. Much of her bravado came from her anger. And her anger came from a heart that had been broken beyond the point of any hope.

Max's chest still hurt, a dull, radiating ache, and she knew that her own heart had broken. Literally so. She'd read that it could happen, and it did, standing outside and watching her bloodied friends emerge - and then Will. In a body bag.

Not yet.

A panicked thought occurred to her. Desperate now, she tried to recall their last words to each other.

"It was 'I love you,'" she whispered.

She nodded, satisfied for the moment; but she vaguely wondered how many "lasts" she would panic over before she could finally die. Finally be with him again.

Because I won't go out the way Jo did.

Max knew that without him, her life was over. But Will hadn't fought for her just so she could regard whatever was left to her - however empty it would be - like it was something to toss away.

That wouldn't honor you, Remmond. You fought for me, and you won, and I owe you for that.

She gazed into the sky, mulling over the fact that sooner or later, it would hit her full force. For now, though, it could just play around the edges. She decided that staying sheltered inside her analytical mind would be the best plan, because she was weary of talking to dead people.

The question of what happened to him at his death was trying to work its way into her head, and she rose from the curb quickly, wrapping her arms around herself. She could feel the warmth of him, of his arms around her, his body beside hers. Then it left her, lifted away from her, and she felt nothing.

He's getting cold by now.

So am I.

A small, rasping sound escaped her. Max could feel something pushing its way into her head, a hopelessness that was both ugly and beautiful because of the hard, merciless finality of it, and she knew that she was about to accept it.

I never should have thawed out.

She dropped her head into her hands, hating herself for the thought, fighting the disjointed sensation of a force inside of her that was reaching to pull him back. Then she understood it: she was reaching for him because he was gone.

She dove back into her analytical mind. It would make for an interesting discussion, she decided - the searing anguish of the separation of two souls that formed one spirit.

Who will you discuss it with?

"I can still talk to you," she whispered. "You're still here, always around me."

Unaware that she was slipping into shock, she let her mind go dark, retreating far enough that she could hide from the fact that Will was dead.

Will spotted her as she stood up.

He opened his mouth to call to her; then he hesitated, because he suddenly had no idea how to approach her - no idea to what extent she would react, and he was concerned about how deeply his presence might shock her.

Her back was to him. She was looking toward the intersection that would take her out to the main road and back to her apartment.

His throat closed as he took in how alone she was.

Then he watched her head drop into her hands, and he moved faster. Several people stared at him as he made his way toward her. A woman gasped as she passed him, and a man touched his arm, his brows knit together in concern as he asked Will if he needed help. Will knew that his appearance was frightening, that he was still bloody and bandaged up, and he hoped it wouldn't be too hard for Max to take.

"I'm fine," he said to the man, brushing past him with his eyes on her. "Thanks."

He stood behind her, and he said the first thing that occurred to him.

"I'm here."

He watched her body stiffen. Her head lifted slightly, but she didn't turn around.

"I'm here," he said again, watching her carefully.

Max knew that if she turned and looked, he wouldn't be there, and she would lose the connection to him. She decided that she would stay right there for the rest of her life, if he would just stay there with her.

"Don't go." Her voice was an odd, dreamy monotone.

"I'm not a ghost, darlin'," he said quietly. "I'm right behind you."

She shook her head.

He stepped closer. "When you turn around, be ready, because I look bad."

Will barely heard her as she whispered, "Touch me."

As he put his hand on her back, he felt her flinch. Then she turned around.

She didn't recoil as he expected her to do, and she didn't burst into tears. She gently touched his face, pushed his hair from his forehead, ran her hand along the bandage on his arm. She was calm, assessing him, busily taking inventory. Will wanted to hold her, but he decided to let her maintain her own pace.

They were looking deep into each other's eyes, and it was then that Will saw how completely disoriented she was.

She cupped his cheek. "You're so cold," she said, and he saw the grief rising in her eyes.

He was cold because of the blood he'd lost, but he didn't think he should tell her that. He had no idea what to tell her. Although he had been picturing the many different ways that she might react, he hadn't expected that he would stand right in front of her, and her agile mind would convince her that she was hallucinating.

Unsure just how fragile she was at that moment, he decided to let her work through it for a few minutes.

Max thought that it must have been horrible for him. He was cut everywhere. His clothes were bloody, and the huge bandage on his arm was bright red.

She moved behind him. He stood perfectly still as she examined his ripped shirt and the cuts she could see on his back. His hair was matted with blood, clinging to the back of his neck.

"Oh no," she whimpered, reaching to touch the back of his head, but then quickly drawing her hand back. "Oh, Will..."

He knew it was time for him to help her along.

"Come here, Maxine."

She stood before him again, searching his eyes, and Will was at a loss. She was in some kind of emotional shock, and he had no clue how to deal with something like that. He knew only that he needed to win this one fast, and hugs and tears and "I love you's" would just enhance the drama of it all, so he tapped into her analytical side.

He took her hand, flattening her fingers out as he said, "Here." He pressed her palm to the center of his chest. "What's that?" he asked. "What do you feel?"

Her mouth slowly fell open. She stared at her hand, shaking her head again.

"Ghosts don't have a heartbeat, darlin'. I'm here."

She was frozen, drawing in shallow, gasping breaths.

"Look at me," he said, and when she did, her expression shifted. It was a barely discernable change, but it was there, and Will decided to take advantage of it.

He took her chin in his hand, lifting her head, and she moaned softly as he kissed her.

As he started to pull away, she clutched the front of his shirt to bring him back, to hang on to the kiss - and he grunted with the pain of the pressure on his shredded back.

Her eyes flew open. "That hurt you."

"Yeah. My back's a mess."

"Kiss me again."

He did. He felt her starting to tremble, her hands tentatively moving around his arms and his chest, searching for a place to touch him where it wouldn't hurt him. Her breathing was labored and ragged, and he drew back to find that her face was soaked with tears.

He looked into her eyes and said again, "I'm here."

The sound that came from her began as a quiet, broken whimpering, which grew slowly into a primitive wail as he wrapped her in his arms, stroking her hair and rocking back and forth, comforting her.

chapter 22

WILL WAS SITTING on the examination table, waiting for the emergency room doctor to return with a prescription, when Max entered the room. She stood before him with her hands resting on his thighs, her face pinched and exhausted.

"What did the doctor say?"

"I'm fine. They gave me an I.V., plucked some glass out of me, said I need rest and antibiotics. And she said it's a good thing I have long hair," he chuckled. "Then I got a lecture about how nothing could have been more important than how badly I needed a doctor." He pulled her to him for a quick kiss. "What do they know."

"Thanks for doing this. I was worried."

"I know. It was the right thing to do. And at least I'm cleaned up now."

"So, Mr. Remmond." The doctor was a young woman, pleasant looking, with curly red hair and hands that were shaking a little as she handed him two pieces of paper. "You were at that shooting today." She indicated the prescriptions she had just handed him. "Fill both of those before you leave. I gave you a pain killer, too. You're going to wake up tomorrow pretty bad off."

"Yeah," he grinned. "It's been kind of a long day."

Max sighed. "Only you could make light of it."

"It's all over the news," the doctor said. "What a mess. You're sure you want to go home?"

"I'm sure. It's..."

She interrupted him. "I want to strongly suggest, one more time, that you stay overnight for observation."

Alarmed, Max said, "You didn't tell me that, Will."

He folded the prescriptions and tucked them into his pocket as he slid off the table. "I can't. Sorry, Doc."

Skeptical, she asked, "You 'can't'?"

"Promises to keep." He reached for his torn, bloody shirt, and Max handed him the clean one she'd gotten from the bag she packed for him earlier that day.

"Will..." she began, and he shook his head.

"You won't win this one, Maxine. Let's go."

He sat carefully in the passenger's seat, protecting his back as Max started the truck.

"I just don't think this is a good idea," she muttered. "We should go back to the apartment. You need rest. And we need to check on Dave and Sammy."

"We'll do that on the road." He paused. "Maxine."

She turned to look at him.

"*I* need this."

Something in his eyes stopped her from arguing it any further. "Okay."

He nodded. "Thanks."

She pulled out of the lot, and they headed for Maine.

They made most of the trip in silence. Will dozed off a couple of times from the pain medication, while Max found it necessary to concentrate on driving. She was distracted, becoming more and more agitated as she tried to avoid thinking about what had almost happened - how tenuous all that they had really was.

Will jerked awake as the turn to the hotel was coming up, and Max said, "I'm going to get you settled in and then get you some food. And you need more fluids."

Her voice was tight and she was speaking so rapidly that she stuttered. Her knuckles were white on the steering wheel.

Groggy, Will reached for her hand. "Relax." His voice sounded strange to him, weak and straining. "You've been through something here. We need to take care of both of us."

She yanked her hand away. "*I've* been through something? *Me?*" She was going too fast as she turned into the driveway, and Will grabbed the frame of the window to steady himself. "It was almost over today. He was after *you*, right? He was going to kill you?" She tried to take a breath, but she couldn't get enough air, and she sounded like she was choking.

Will waited quietly for her to park the truck, trying to clear his head. She was spinning out of control, which he'd figured had to happen sooner or later, and he thought it wasn't such a bad thing that it came on so quickly. At least they could start getting back to life.

"I saw Dave come out, and Sammy, and the blood... It was all *over* them. And you should have seen these ridiculous people, standing around, talking about how awful it was and..." The breath she tried to draw in sounded like a muffled scream as she exhaled. "They brought out a *body bag*."

The truck was finally stopped. Will took her hand to bring her to him, but she jerked it away.

She pressed her hands over her ears, her eyes wide and staring straight ahead. "Do you know what he said? He said, '*One less lawyer in the world*,'" she cried out.

Will slid across the seat and grabbed her arms, pulling her to him.

"*No.*" Max struggled against him for a moment, then she reached for him. Not knowing where she could touch him, she pulled away again, swatting at his hands in her frustration.

He was talking to her, telling her everything was okay, that they just needed time - and she wondered if any amount of time would ever make things right again.

Finally, she wore herself out, and she let him hold her.

"They said you were *dead*." She knew she sounded angry at him for that, but she had no one else to yell at.

"I know." He kissed her forehead. "I know, darlin'. I'm sorry."

"I want you to tell me what happened. But I'm scared to hear it."

He nodded. "I'll tell you anything you want to know."

She moved to put her arms around him, then stopped herself. "I can't even touch you. Where I can touch you?"

"Don't worry about it."

Remembering that he needed food and water, she pulled away from him and said, "Come on. *Now.* You need to rest." She thought she could at least do that for him, because she wasn't being strong for him at all.

They were settled into their room a few minutes later. Max hovered over him, helping him get comfortable on the bed, persuading him to take more pain medication, ordering their meals and insisting that he drink water. Will thought she was being a little obsessive about it.

As she brought the third glass to him, he set it on the nightstand and said, "I'm good."

"You need fluids." She picked the glass up to hand it to him again.

"Stop. Sit down." He patted the bed. "Come on. Let's get this done so we can get back to living."

She moved to sit beside him, then quickly backed away, ambivalent.

"I can't... What if we can't get past this? What if things are never normal again?"

"What's 'normal' anyway?"

His expression was somber, but she could see the humor in his eyes, and it infuriated her.

"Damn you, Will... There is *nothing* here that's funny."

He was gratified that for the moment, she wasn't smothering him with maternal concern.

"Look," he sighed, "you can either come over here, or I'm getting out of this bed to come get you. And I just got comfortable, so you don't want me to do that."

She didn't move. She stood several feet away, picking at her nails.

"Three... two... one." He started to slide his legs off of the bed.

"No, don't. Don't do that." She hurried to sit beside him.

Will grabbed her hand to stop her from picking at her nails. "What do you need?" he asked. "Tell me."

"I don't... I'm not the one who was..."

"Look, at least I knew what was going on," Will said. "All things considered, I'd rather be where I was than where you were."

"That's just... that's absurd," she stammered. "That's *completely* insane."

He laughed, and noticed that her face brightened a little when he did. "It probably is. But I'm putting myself in your place, thinking about what would happen to me if I thought I lost you, and I think you got the bad end of this."

"I think... I need you to tell me what happened," she said. "I need for this to make sense."

"So do I." There was a knock at the door. "There's dinner. Go get it, and we'll talk."

They sat on the bed, with Max wedged tightly against him, reminding him to drink water after every few bites.

"You may as well start feeding me, doll. *No*," he said quickly as she reached for his plate. "It was a joke."

Max was jittery, detached; and even though she seemed to want to talk about what had happened, she kept shifting the discussion away from it. Will was growing more concerned by the minute.

When his cell vibrated on the nightstand, and she was startled to the point that she cried out, he decided he needed to do something. As she reached for his glass again, he grabbed her wrist.

"No," he said sternly. He waited for her to look at him. "Stop it."

Pulling her hand away, she asked, "What's wrong?"

"It's not going to get any easier until you ask me something," he said. She shook her head.

"Ask."

She was terrified of finding out, but she wanted it resolved within her own mind so she could quiet her imagination. At the same time, though, what she found within her imagination was something she could change on a whim. The truth wasn't something she could alter, and she was ambivalent about trying to deal with it with no escape hatch.

Then she decided that not knowing would separate them.

Timid, she asked, "How close did it come?"

"How close did what come?"

"How close did you get to dead?" Her voice cracked, but she kept her eyes on his and added, "And don't lie to me. I have to know."

"He pulled the trigger. Sammy shot him at the last moment, and it threw him off. That's why I have the crater in my arm."

She bit her lip and glanced at his arm. "What was it like? What was happening?"

"He decided that someone was going to die, and he let me choose who it would be."

"And you chose..."

"He was going to kill me anyway, Max." Her eyes were huge, and as her chin started to tremble, he asked, "Should I go on?"

"Yes." Her voice was hoarse as she asked, "What happened then?'

"He had me on my knees."

"What? How?" Picturing him on his knees with a gun pointed at him, she was beginning to think she was making a mistake - that she didn't really need to know.

He cleared his throat, grimacing at the pain in his head and neck. "He put the gun to Alexa's head. It was her or me."

"Oh..." she gasped. "Oh, no..."

"That was pretty bad, yeah. Then Sammy... I guess she waited until the gun was away from Alexa's head and not quite trained on me, and she blew him away through a two-way mirror in the room." He winced as he moved his arm, then tried to stretch it out. "Right through the throat. Severed his jugular."

Max felt suddenly, completely overwhelmed by a vengeful sense of satisfaction that she didn't want to think about.

Her mouth went dry as she asked, "How did he get in there? In that room with you guys?"

"From what we could figure out, he never left after he saw Alexa. And no one checked that he'd signed out. He just waited in the back hall, looking through the mirror until Brandi showed up. He took her back out there with him, and spent some time..." Catching the sudden change in her expression, he stopped.

"What was going through your head?"

"At which point?" He reached for his prescription.

"When you were on... When he was about to shoot." Max couldn't tolerate the idea of what Reynolds had done to him. She watched him toss a couple of pills into his mouth, and she asked, "You're in pain again?"

"I will be soon, and I want you right here." He opened his arms, and she cautiously, gratefully curled up against him. "I was actually thinking about a few things," he said. "The last thing I did was close my eyes and think of you."

She pressed closer to him.

"Before that, I was looking at him standing there..." His voice trailed off.

"What?"

"With a gun to the heads of what was supposed to be his family. I hope someday I can get past that."

Max closed her eyes, then opened them quickly as the picture came to her. "That's... Yeah. A hard one to get over."

"Maybe I need to hang on to it for a while," he shifted to look down at her, "because it gave me an understanding of you that I didn't have before."

"Of me?" It surprised her. "Tell me."

"It was as close as I could get to knowing you as a little girl. What life was for you. The fear you have of being married - it was all wrapped up inside that moment. I get it."

Max lifted her eyes to his.

He said, "After everything we've been through, a ceremony would be just a formality. I love you. This is permanent, and we both know it."

"Yeah, we do." She kissed his cheek.

Will thought that the strange, small smile on her face was from the relief of finally knowing.

"You look better," he said.

"I am."

"Anything else you want to know?"

She thought it over. "Later. You look like you're about to doze off."

"Wonder how Dave's doing."

"We'll check on him tomorrow. He was doing fine." She thought of something then. "Just one more thing?"

"Sure."

"Is Sammy in trouble?"

He shook his head. "Nothing's going to happen to her. First thing the cops asked me about it was who shot Reynolds, and then they asked if she was represented by counsel. More like suggested it." He laughed, then put his hand to his head. "That hurt. Anyway, I told them I'm her lawyer, so they had me sit there for what little they asked her while the medics worked on Dave. There's nothing they can prosecute on, but they really don't want to anyway."

"Good. Just one more…?"

"You bet."

"Can I kiss you, or will it hurt?"

He pretended to consider it for a while, and she nudged his ribs.

"Three… two… one…" she mumbled.

"What's the countdown to?"

She sat up, trying to look offended. "When I slug you."

"So what?" he grinned, enjoying the way her mood was lightening. "Go ahead. I'm on meds. I won't feel a thing."

"Oh. Okay." She rolled off the bed before he could grab her. "Then a kiss would just be a waste of my considerable talents."

"Uncle," he laughed. "This isn't a fair fight, doll. I'm injured."

"I *offered* to kiss you and make it better." She turned to face him, ready to deliver another playful comment, but her eyes caught his and she remembered where they were earlier that day. She knew that he was thinking the same thing.

"Get over here," he said softly.

Max knelt beside the bed, taking his hand and pressing it to her cheek, wishing they could stay up all night and just be together. Just live. But she knew that he needed to sleep, and she could wait, because there would be a tomorrow after all.

"Just one kiss," she said. "Then you rest."

"Not promising anything," he mumbled. He was getting sleepy.

"Yeah." She kissed him gently. "'Cause you would never break a promise."

chapter 23

WILL OPENED HIS eyes to the darkness, panicked by the claustrophobic feeling of the confines of his coffin, devastated that he would never see her again. He cried out, throwing his arms up against it, feeling nothing above him. Then the pain in his arm and his back went through his entire body.

"Will..." The light came on and she was there, hovering over him. She was stroking his forehead, talking to him softly, reaching behind her for the damp cloth she had used throughout the night to cool his face and chest.

As she gently touched it to his throat, she murmured, "You're dreaming again," and his panic returned as he wondered if the coffin was the dream or if she was.

"Are you hurting?" she asked, reaching across him for his medication.

"Yeah." He moved to sit up, grinding his teeth as bolts of pain went through him again, and he pushed her hands away as she tried to stop him.

"I need to... Don't do that." In raising himself to a sitting position, he felt the comfort of the physical world returning to him, and his heart was beginning to slow down again. "I need to be here. Where I am," he mumbled, and Max understood what he was saying.

"Okay." She handed him several pills. "It's time for these."

He tossed them into his mouth, then took the water she offered him. "What time is it?" His voice was gravelly, and he was still disoriented, but he knew where he was and he had no intention of going back to sleep.

"Four o'clock. Little after." She arranged the pillows behind him so he could sit more comfortably. "You've been out for a while now."

"Guess so."

She carefully put her hand on his back. "I should change these bandages. I tried to keep you off your back, but you were determined to sleep like you always do."

He swung his legs over the side of the bed, rising slowly, and Max wasn't sure whether or not to protest.

"Where are you going?" she asked, watching him intently. He was unsteady, so she followed him off of the bed, frustrated as she looked for a spot on his body where she could support him without hurting him.

"I need to see the sunrise. With you."

It occurred to her that the man had an uncanny ability to always know exactly what they needed.

Pulling the quilt from the bed, she said, "Let's go." She headed toward the balcony, then turned to see him shaking his head.

"No. I want to be out there with it."

Her initial reaction was to argue it, but she couldn't. This wasn't about a whim to see the sun come up: it was something more.

It took several minutes for them to make their way down the staircase and out to their rock. Max bunched up the extra blanket she'd grabbed from the bed, and they sat with the quilt wrapped around them as the sky began to lighten.

They were quiet for a while, then Will asked, "Did you get any sleep?"

"Some. You were dreaming a lot."

"I don't like these pain meds. I'm tired again."

She pulled the quilt tighter around them. "That's what they're supposed to do. You should be resting."

"I can't stand being so weak, you know?"

There was an odd tone to his voice, and Max checked his expression. He'd never looked so miserable.

She sighed, mildly amused that what was bothering him was the fact that he was human.

"You need me right now," he was saying, "and I'm down."

"You are not. If anything, you need to bring it down a notch and act like a mortal."

Will managed a wry smile. "Sammy called me an annoying Alpha-male."

She raised an eyebrow and didn't answer.

"What, you agree with her?"

"Well, I don't find you annoying. Not usually, anyway."

He laughed, and Max felt some of her tension falling away.

"Damn," he grumbled. "Between you and Sammy, I've lost my belief that I'm invincible."

"Good." She laid her head on his shoulder. "Because you're not. You need things, too."

Will remembered being on his knees, and the images of her that came to him at that moment.

"You're right," he said. "Like I need you."

Something about it touched her deeply, and she was surprised to feel tears in her eyes.

"When I thought I was going to die," he continued, "I thought about what would happen to you. I couldn't stand it."

She wiped at her eyes, nodding.

"I was thinking, I have a *life*. I have the most incredible woman I've ever known waiting out there, and I love her, and she loves me..."

Max realized that this was the reason he'd wanted to see the sun come up. There was something he needed to get out of himself. But listening to him, to the quiet fury in his voice, was shattering - it was a side of him that she'd never seen, and one which she suspected was foreign to him, as well. She pulled away, positioning herself so she could see his face.

"... and I wanted to kill him. I wanted to get to that gun and use it to beat him to death."

He was speaking softly, but with such a menacing tone that Max shivered. She wanted to try to calm him down; then she told herself again that he needed to say it, and she took his hands in hers, ducking her head so he would look at her as he spoke.

"Maxine, when I saw him breathing his own blood, I wanted to grab the gun and shoot him again. Stomp on his head. Ask him how it felt, knowing he was dying and everyone in that room was damn glad for it." He seemed conflicted then as he said, "I know I lean towards aggressive, that's just who I am - but I never knew I was capable of that."

"I don't get what you're saying." She thought he meant his refusal to do any more damage to Simon as the man died.

"I never knew I could go into that kind of a murderous rage. If Dave hadn't needed help, I don't know what I would have done. I went to a place inside myself that I've never seen before."

"Of course you did. Will, you were *in* a place that you'd never seen before. That was your reaction. It's survival."

"It was more than survival."

"It was how you reacted," she said again. "It's not like you went after *him*. Do you really think it's a problem?"

"I don't know. It's shaking me up pretty bad." He seemed calmer. "So you think it was normal."

"Yes. That bastard took complete control of you, and that's plenty bad enough..."

Something happened to him then. His face turned hard, and he quickly shifted his gaze away from her.

He was looking beyond her, staring out at the water. "It was. I don't know how to describe it. That moment - I think it's going to take me some time to get over it."

"But you will." She let go of his hands and cautiously wrapped her arms around him. "And by the way, if I'd been in that room, I seriously wouldn't have had your restraint at the end."

Will took her by the waist and lifted her onto his lap. She was still hanging on to him, tighter than she should have, but the pain killers blunted the effect.

"You'll be okay, Remmond." She laid her head against his neck. "I won't let you *not* be okay."

Will smiled at her determined tone. "I know that."

"I'm your best friend, after all," she whispered.

"Yeah." He tightened his arms around her. "You are."

The sky was turning a golden coral color, and he said, "Look at this, darlin'. It's beautiful."

As she turned to see it, their eyes met.

"Don't want to talk about it yet?" he asked.

"No." She shook her head. "I can't. Not yet."

"Okay."

She turned so that her back rested against his chest, pulling his arms around her, and they watched the new day dawn.

❋ ❋ ❋

I killed a man.

Dave was stirring, and Sam leaned forward in the chair, watching to see if he was waking up. He settled back into a restless sleep.

She moved to sit on the bed with him. He was still too pale, she thought, and his face seemed sunken in, like someone looked when they'd lost too much weight too quickly.

The monitor said his heart rate was exactly at 80, which the nurse said was okay, but Sam thought it was too high for Dave. His resting rate was a lot lower than that, because he took care of himself and he was healthy.

Until Simon Reynolds happened to him. Until he happened to everyone she cared about.

I wonder how long it took him to die. Probably a minute or two.

It wasn't bothering her much that she'd killed him. Not too much, anyway - after all, it was either him or Dave and the others, and that had been Simon's doing. But it haunted her, the curious, surprised expression on Reynolds' face when she hit her mark.

What bothered her the most was the calm, dispassionate way in which she pulled the trigger. It troubled her, that standing there on the other side of that mirror, she took the kill shot without a twinge of conscience - with the same pragmatic attitude that she would use to solve any problem. She thought about the fact that only a year ago, what she did would have put her under; yet the day before, she had actually ended a life with total impunity.

It was possible, she decided, that she needed to back away from the work she did. Just like Will was doing. It was so ugly, and so often futile: the victories were usually nothing more than delayed defeats, and the wins were so few and far between that the sheer weight of the insanity of it all tipped the scales to the side of continual despair.

Her gun hobby had been a good stress buster - until now, because she had actually killed someone. And Dave was recovering from coming within fifteen minutes of death, so of course she wasn't going to dump it on him. She couldn't take it to Max - she was dealing with her own fallout, as was Will - and Sam decided that she needed to try to get tough, suck it up, and take care of things.

She thought again that she needed to leave behind the work she was doing, because although it had been only a few months, she was already burned out. She was good at what she did, she knew that, and she had wanted to make a difference; however, her skill came from a desperate need to help women find a redemption that she knew she'd never receive.

Besides, she didn't think she was going to live well with the difference she'd made the day before.

The door to the room was slowly opening, and she looked up to see Max stepping inside.

"Can we come in?" she whispered.

"Oh... *Maxine*." Sam quickly slipped off of the bed and hurried over to hug her. She pointed to the hallway, taking a quick look at Dave to make sure he was still asleep as she left the room.

She closed the door quietly, and Will bent to kiss her cheek.

"How is he?" he asked.

"Holding his own. It's gonna be a while, but he'll recover." She touched his arm. "How are you?"

"Fine. No problems," he grinned. "Me big, strong Alpha-male, remember?"

She smiled weakly.

"Come here." He took her face in his hands and kissed her forehead. "Thanks for saving my life."

"I owed you one."

Max said, "My turn." She grabbed Sam and hugged her hard, holding on to her for a full minute. "How are you holding up?" she asked.

"I'm good."

Will touched the bandage on the side of her head. "Sorry about launching you into that wall, kiddo." As soon as he said it, he wanted to suck the words back into his mouth.

She let go of Max then, staring at him in disbelief. "You can't be serious. You could have - should have - walked right out of the room, and instead, you came all the way back *into* it to get to me."

He shifted uncomfortably, avoiding the way Max was suddenly staring at him.

"You did that?" she asked.

Sam was looking back and forth between them. "He didn't tell you?"

"No. He didn't."

"I was all the way on the other side of the room from the door."

"Sammy..." Will shook his head.

"No," Max said. "I want to know."

Sam told her about Will coming back into the room, grabbing her and throwing her out when he saw Simon with the gun - and how Simon had then made sure that Will stayed in the room.

"He got me out of there. He saved my life." She gave him a disapproving look as she said, "You shouldn't be embarrassed, Will."

He nodded, still avoiding Max's eyes.

"I'm going to check on Dave." Sam reached for the door. "I think you two need a couple of minutes. I'll be back."

After the door closed, Max asked, "Why you won't look at me?"

He did then, hurrying to explain it to her:

"She was standing over in the corner. There was no way she was getting out of that room in time, and we both know what his plans were for her, and I just... I reacted." Noticing that she didn't seem upset, that she was actually looking at him with something like pride in her eyes, he asked, "What are you thinking?"

"Well, I'm not thinking that you took some time to weigh who was more important, Sammy or me. And I'm not thinking you then decided that she was. I'm thinking that you had about a half a second to make a decision, and you did what you had to do."

Will thought it again, that he was just way too lucky in life.

Max cautiously leaned against him, balancing herself on her tiptoes as she reached up to kiss him.

"It's who you are, Remmond. It's part of why I adore you." She laid her hands gently on his shoulders. "But hurry up and get all better, because you're too banged up for me to hang all over you right now, and I haven't had a decent kiss in a day and a half."

"Here, I can fix that." He picked her up, bringing her face close to his, and she stiffened.

"Will, be careful..."

"I'm fine," he said. "I just love you. So much."

"I miss you saying 'marry me.'"

"Okay. I love you, Maxine. Marry me."

He waited for her to make a joke of it, but she gave him a lingering kiss, then pressed her lips against his ear and murmured, "I will."

As he set her on her feet, she wore the same mysterious smile that she'd had at the hotel. Sam opened the door just as he started to ask her about it.

"Hey guys, he's awake again. C'mon in."

She had raised the head of the hospital bed, and Dave was sitting up with his eyes half closed.

"Delaney," Will shook his head regretfully, "you look like hell, man."

He opened his eyes, smiling weakly. "If I can get out of this bed in the next day or two," he mumbled hoarsely, "maybe you can finally beat me at hoops."

Watching them, Max felt a lump in her throat, thinking about how different the day might have been. She gave Dave a quick kiss on the cheek and said, "I'm going to get us coffee. Can you have anything?"

"Later. You go ahead."

"I'm going with her. I need to walk around for a few minutes," Sam said. She felt his forehead and checked the monitor, frowning. "You're still..."

He pulled her hand from his head and kissed her palm. "Go. I'm fine."

As they left, Will pulled a chair over to the side of the bed, turning it around to sit with his arms resting on the back of it. "How are the kids doing?"

"Good." His voice was raspy. "Mom and Dad are at the house."

Will handed him the cup of water that was on the table beside him. "Do you need Max and me to take over, or are they there for the duration?"

"Duration. Thanks for saving my wife."

Will ducked his head, looking at the floor.

"No lie, Remmond. For the rest of my life, I'll remember the look on your face when you grabbed her. You were gonna save her or die trying."

"I didn't do anything that you wouldn't do for me." He looked up, grinning. "And nothing that Sammy didn't do for me."

"Yeah. She won't talk about it." After a few sips of water, he added, "All I know is that she killed the guy."

"She put a bullet right through his neck, Dave. One shot. And then she didn't come apart until she saw you on the floor." It struck him then, and he asked, "She won't talk about it, huh?"

"Help me make sure she's okay. I'm worried."

He nodded. "You got it."

"I have to give my statement. They'll be here for it any time now." He was getting tired again, finding it difficult to speak.

"I'll go work it. You need anything?"

"All set." He closed his eyes again. "Thanks."

"Back in a bit." Will took one more look at his friend as he left the room, thinking that Dave looked much worse than he'd expected. When he thought again about being forced to his knees while Dave was bleeding to death on the floor, the rush of raging adrenaline left him lightheaded, and he put a hand against the outside of the door to steady himself.

I'd kill you again if I could.

"Will?"

*I have a **life**.*

An aura flashed and rotated at the fringes of his vision, and he knew he was about to pass out.

"*Will.*"

Her voice sounded like it was coming through a tunnel. He felt her hands on his arm, and then his shoulders, and he could hear Reynolds mocking him again:

*Because you're a **hero**.*

"Come here." Max was there, guiding him to the bench outside Dave's room while Sam called for a nurse.

chapter 24

"I'M OKAY NOW." He started to sit up on the examination table.

"Just stay there a little longer, Mr. Remmond." The nurse removed the cuff from his arm, scowling at him in much the same way that Sam was. "Your blood pressure is good now, but when you get up, do so *very* slowly."

"How much longer should he stay put?" Max asked.

"Ten minutes or so. Let's make sure he's leveled out." She held her clipboard above Will's face and handed him a pen. "If you're really set on going home, I need you to sign this release."

Will scrawled his signature on the form, and she said, "I'll be back in a few minutes."

As soon as she was out of the room, Max handed him the bottle of juice he'd been drinking from, and he sat up.

"What are you doing?" Sam asked.

"Can't do this, kiddo. I need to get out of here." He took a long drink. "Who's with Dave?"

"The cops. He's giving them his statement. And what can't you do?"

Will didn't answer. He pivoted sideways on the table and reached for Max, almost yanking her into his arms. As they held each other, the expression on his face was one of raw, aching outrage, and Sam looked away, thinking she shouldn't be there to see it.

"Just give it time," Max whispered.

"I wish I could have killed him myself."

"I know."

Will looked up in time to catch the distress on Sam's face. He inclined his head toward her and said quietly to Max, "She needs some help."

She nodded and hopped up onto the table to sit beside him.

"You okay, Sammy?" she asked.

"Yeah."

"Are not."

She shrugged.

"You're having trouble with it," Will insisted.

"I am having some trouble with it." She turned around to face them. "I wasn't going to talk about it. I know you guys have a lot on your minds, but..."

Will put his hand up to stop her. "Sammy, I wouldn't be sitting here except for you. If you need someone to talk to, go for it."

Hesitant, wondering what they would think of her, she said, "I don't like the idea that I could be so cold about... I mean, I was standing behind that mirror, debating with myself where to put the bullet so that he'd go straight down without hitting you or Alexa." She swallowed hard. "I was aiming a gun at the guy's throat, and my hands weren't even shaking. I wasn't even *nervous*."

He was nodding like she wasn't saying anything unusual, and his reaction confused her.

"So what were you thinking about?" He tossed the empty bottle onto the counter. "Dave and the kids, right?"

"Yeah. And you. And Maxine. And all I cared about was making sure I got him with the first shot, and what does that say about me?"

"It says you love your family and your friends. Look," Max said, motioning for her to come over to them, "someday, you really need to forgive yourself. For whatever it is that you tell yourself you've done, you know? Stop looking for all the reasons that there's something *wrong* with you. I'll bet you have a laundry list of sins that goes back years."

"But I had a stronger emotional reaction to the bird that flew into my windshield last week. I *killed* someone..."

Max was shaking her head. "That's your way of defining at it. Truth is, you saved a whole bunch of lives. He chose to create the situation where someone was going to die, and it turned out to be him."

"Sammy," Will added, "police, the military - they can go through exactly the same thing. The moment comes and they go numb, because it has to be done. They need to take someone out. And after, a lot of them wonder the same things that you're thinking about."

"I didn't know that." She thought it reflected what she felt, but she was also thinking about the list of what she regarded as her unpardonable sins, wondering why she always ended up feeling like she was evil.

"If you'd been at all emotional, you would have been conflicted. You would have hesitated. And Dave and Will, Alexa and Brandi - they'd be dead." Max spoke in the same matter-of-fact tone as Will. "You did the only thing that could be done, in the only *way* it could be done, and now you're back into your catalyst-of-doom mode - looking for something awful about yourself because of the way you *felt* as you saved five lives?"

"Five?"

"Yeah. Because you saved mine, too."

The nurse returned then, and Sam didn't answer.

She watched them while the nurse gave Will instructions - the easy way that he and Max were continually in contact with each other, the connection between them so strong that it filled the room. She imagined Max living that day as her first one without Will, and she decided that any fallout was well beyond worth the cost.

As they walked back to Dave's room, Max put her arm around her.

"It's been a long time for us, you know. Too many years of too many things that brought us down."

Sam reached up and patted her hand. "To be honest, I'm kinda sick of it."

A gruff voice came from behind them.

"Ms. Delaney."

They turned to see Russ Lambert coming quickly toward them, his expression earnest, tinged with anxiety as he asked, "May I have a minute of your time?"

"Of course." She introduced Max, then said, "I don't know if you ever personally met Will Remmond?"

The men shook hands as Will asked, "How are they?"

"Not much change. They're keeping Brandi sedated, but Lexi is still unresponsive."

Will wasn't surprised by that. "What's the prognosis?"

"Brandi's tough. She's talking, asked about all of you. But Lexi... We're hopeful. Guarded, but hopeful. The doctors say there's no reason not to be. She just needs time." He regarded Will thoughtfully, with a brief, respectful nod. "Thank you for what you did. For what you do."

"No problem. And from what I've seen of her, Lexi's going to make it."

"She's like her mom," Sam said. "She's going to be okay."

Russ looked down at her, his voice shaking as he said, "They're alive, Ms. Delaney..."

"Samantha."

"Okay." He made an attempt at a smile. "Samantha." He cleared his throat, but it did nothing to cover the emotion in his voice. "They're everything to my wife and me, and they're alive, and we owe that to you."

She was studying her feet, embarrassed, painfully ambivalent about being the focus of praise.

Russ continued, "I don't know what this whole thing has been like for you, but I need to tell you something." He waited until Sam raised her head to look at him, and then he said, "The years will go by, and there will be birthdays and Christmases that we have together. And we'll have the everyday moments..." He rubbed the bridge of his nose, but the tears leaked out anyway.

He put his hand up to stop her as she began to speak. "This has to be tough for you. At least, I suspect that it would be. And if it is - if you ever, you know, wonder about what you did - we all want you to remember something."

He paused, regaining some composure, and then he gave her the words that finally changed her perspective. The words she carried with her, that she would recall whenever she felt herself falling - taking up where the abusers in her life had left off.

He said, "Every person who touches our lives in the future, every good thing that happens - it will all have your mark on it, Samantha."

She stood motionless for a few seconds, then looked at her friends. Max was nodding slowly, hopefully, and Sam could read her thoughts:

There you go, Sammy. See?

Will said, "She's an incredible woman, Russ."

"I know."

Looking at the love in her friends' eyes, Sam wondered if redemption wasn't about paying a debt, or perfect performance, or trying to prove anything at all - maybe it wasn't even something that could be earned.

Maybe it was something that came with being loved, which meant that she'd had it all along. And the only thing she needed to do was to let it in.

❋ ❋ ❋

Max turned into the lot at the apartment complex.

"You know," she sighed contentedly, "I really like getting to drive the truck all the time."

"Don't get used to it," Will warned her. "I love my truck."

She opened her mouth to respond, then seemed to change her mind.

"What were you about to say?" he asked.

"I was about to ask, 'More than me?' But seriously, Remmond, I hate women who ask those kinds of questions."

"That's why we'll be together forever," he laughed. "Tell you what. We'll compromise. I'll put you on the title."

"Nah. This is yours."

"And to think I used to believe there was no such thing as the perfect woman." As she opened her door, he said, "Wait there."

"Will..."

He was already coming around to her. "What? I'm tough."

"Remmond, you are just *so* arrogant."

He set her on the ground. "Remember what happened the last time you said that, darlin'."

"Mmm. I remember." She thought he seemed tired again. She kissed him quickly and said, "Let's get you settled in. You look like you're starting to hurt."

"Yeah. It's not bad, though." He started back around the truck. "Hold on while I grab my charger. My phone's dead."

"Okay."

Finally.

With a reserved smile, she took his hand and followed him to the passenger's side, then waited expectantly while he searched the glove compartment.

Will let go of her hand as he pulled out the small box.

"What's this?"

"It's something for you."

Intrigued, he gave her a hesitant, curious glance as he flipped it open.

"What the..." He took the ring from its velvet base, turning it over in his hands. "This is for me?"

"Yup."

It was white gold, with an emerald nestled on each side of a large diamond - a masculine version of the engagement ring he'd given her, and he looked at her again, puzzled.

"What for?"

"It's your engagement ring."

He started to laugh, then saw that she was serious. "You bought me an engagement ring?"

"I finally figured it out. What my problem was with marrying you."

Taking notice that she'd said the word "was", he realized that it still mattered to him. Not in the same way as before, but it mattered. He wanted it to be official.

"And...?" he asked.

"I need you to promise that you'll marry me back."

Her expression was one of calm resolve, and Will thought - like he had so many times before - that the woman had an innate ability to render him speechless.

He pictured her going through her days silently thinking about it, analyzing it, going over every aspect and nuance, and he searched for something adequate to say. He decided that as was always the case, there wasn't anything he could offer that would match her.

"Okay." He nodded. "I promise."

She took the ring from him, then gently took his left hand and slipped it onto his finger.

"It looks good there," she said. "It suits you."

"It does. And of course, I needed to find it in the truck, right?"

"I thought it appropriate." She grinned up at him. "But don't expect me to seal the deal by falling into a lake."

"How long has it been in there?" He lifted her back onto the seat, and she sat facing him, resting her hands lightly on his shoulders.

"It was the errand I had to run yesterday. I went to pick it up." Her smile faded slightly as she added, "I'd just put it in there when the cruisers and ambulances went by." She hurried to continue, wanting to stem his response. He was turning sad and serious, and it wasn't what she wanted for that moment.

In a playfully businesslike tone, she said, "In the spirit of full disclosure, Remmond, if you haven't figured it out already... I'm really bad at remembering important dates."

He remembered how she'd signed up for an all-day seminar on Descartes than ran on his birthday, and her distress when he reminded her. She felt awful, he thought it was adorable, and he'd decided back then that if it was her worst trait, he was lucky.

"You're like that," he said, and the affection in his tone relaxed her again. "Doesn't bother me."

"But October fifth... I don't go a single day without remembering it," she said. Her eyes began to fill, and she blinked hard a few times.

"Is that right?" She was talking about their first trip to Maine, the day that they moved beyond being best friends. The day that they started out on the journey that eventually became the moment they were now sharing. "You never told me that."

"Something else I never told you - I mean, you know I'm not any good at the gooey stuff, either - but I think I fell in love with you that day." She was distant, remembering how it all changed that afternoon. "Sitting on that park bench, it scared the hell out of me, realizing all of a sudden that life without you was to be avoided. At *all* costs. And then, later, that kiss..."

Her fingers went to her lips, and he smiled. "You fell in love with me because of a kiss?"

"No, I wanted you to kiss me because I was in love." She took his hand and said, "October fifth. I want that to be our anniversary. Agreed?"

He looked down at where their rings were touching.

"Agreed."

"At least you can count on me remembering it," she laughed. "And I know we need to get you inside. But first..."

Looking into her eyes, Will remembered the first time he got lost there, wondering where she had been all his life.

"... I want to kiss my fiancé."

A minute later, with her lips still against his, she whispered, "I love you, Will Remmond."

Will wanted the moment to last a little longer. He wrapped her in his arms, and she laid her head against him, and he remembered staring out the window of Sammy's kitchen on the day that he went to find her - thinking about the miracle of things coming back to life.

He said, "I love you too, darlin'."

Epilogue

"Wake up, Remmond. You need to feed me in the manner to which I've become accustomed." Her hair was spread out across his chest, and she grabbed a few strands, dragging them down his arm to tickle him and then tossing a handful of her hair over his face.

Will opened his eyes and blew her hair away, and she giggled as she crawled on top of him, laying flat against him.

"I can't believe you fell asleep again," she teased.

"Your fault, doll."

"I guess I just have more stamina." She kissed his nose.

"You also have lousy aim."

"Oh yeah?" She traced his mouth with her fingertip, then kissed his chin. "Getting closer?"

"Try again."

She skimmed her lips across his cheek. "Better?"

"Like this." He wrapped his hands around the back of her neck and pulled her in for a long kiss.

"So *that's* how you do it," she sighed. "Thanks."

"No problem."

"We need to get going." She pressed against him, laying her head against his neck. "Everyone will be here in a few hours, and we haven't even gone to the store yet."

He locked his arms around her. "You're kidding, right?"

"About what?"

"There's a hot blonde lying naked on top of me, and you want me to get out of bed?"

"Nah. Not yet." She wound her legs around his. "But we do need to get busy soon. So if you have any ideas, save them for tonight."

"Then this is about to be one long day," he said. "So tell me again - why are we having our reception at our own house?"

"So I can show off my house and my husband at the same time, and then get everyone the hell out of here."

He nodded. "That'll work. But they're gonna have to sidestep a lot of building materials."

"We shouldn't have done the kitchen first. We never cook."

"Yeah, but at least it's nicer for morning coffee now."

She laid against him for a while, listening to his heart.

Stroking her hair, he asked, "So you're liking being married?" They had eloped two weeks earlier, and were married in a ten-minute ceremony, standing on the oceanfront rock at the estate in Maine.

"I'm liking it better every day, Remmond." She held him tighter. "I really am."

"I still can't believe you took my name," he said, quietly awed.

Rolling her eyes, she said, "Sammy said that, too. So did my mother. I *want* your name. Why wouldn't I?"

"I just didn't expect it. But I'm such a typical guy that I start puffing my chest out when I think about it."

"Good." She kissed his neck. "I want you to. And we have to get to the store."

"You sure?"

"Yup."

"Damn." He reached for the pair of sweats he'd left on the floor beside the bed. "Meet you back here tonight."

Will sat up as she rolled away, and her eyes went to the scars on his back. He still had pain in his arm from time to time, but it was minor, and it was improving every day.

She reached for him one more time, wrapping her arms around his waist and kissing his scars, then smiled up at him as he turned to look at her.

He stood and held out his hand. "C'mon. Let's go have coffee."

It was a warm day for mid-October, and they took their mugs out to the deck, looking out over their land. The house had been the perfect find: an antique Federalist, in horrible condition, but on seven acres of beautiful, usable land. When Max discovered that there was an orchard already on the back end of the property, she refused to look at other houses.

Will had warned her about the amount of work the house needed. She didn't care, and they'd closed on it at the end of August.

Gazing at the autumn foliage while she sipped her coffee, she was stunned by the beauty of it. She thought that every single hue of every imaginable color was there in front of her.

"I still say there's something different about Londonderry," she said. "The colors are just more vivid here."

Will took a deep breath, enjoying the crisp air. "You may be right." He squinted out at the field then, thinking.

"What?" Max asked.

"I'm figuring out the options for clearing a couple more acres. It'll give us a clear path to your orchard."

"I really love it when you call it that."

He put his arm around her. "That's what it is." Pointing to the area in front of a cluster of white lilac bushes, he said, "Your roses will go right there."

She sighed happily. "I can't *wait* for that." They turned to go inside as she said, "And Sammy's jealous of my orchard, you know. She said Dave has to put one in for her now."

"Poor guy," he laughed. "I hope he's up for that."

"By spring, he should be a hundred percent again. Don't you think?"

"Yeah." He sat at the counter and slid his empty cup toward her. "I think he's almost there now."

Dave had faced a difficult challenge, initially spending over two weeks in the hospital, and then it was another two months before he was anywhere near fully healed. Even then, he'd walked with a limp for a few weeks. His parents stayed on to help until mid-July, while Will hired three new associates and ran the firm.

Dave finally returned to full-time work at the end of August, just in time for Will to plan for a couple of weeks off for the wedding - and some extra, much-needed time afterward to be with Max.

They'd spent the time working together on their house. Max had insisted that it was the perfect honeymoon, and Will agreed - and he found that rebuilding their home, with her, was even more meaningful than he'd expected it to be.

"Hey," Max refilled their mugs as she asked, "did Sammy tell you the good news?"

He shook his head. "What happened?"

"Looks like she'll be *matriculating* this January."

He smiled broadly. "She got in? Nice."

"Yup. She found out yesterday, just before we left Hope's party."

"Good for her. Did they give her a decision about the Pre-Law program?"

"Not yet, but I'm not worried about it. Hey, maybe Sammy and I will just start our own firm and create a whole new Delaney-Remmond. Put you guys out of business."

"And you probably would," he laughed.

"I'll get my J.D., take advantage of you and Dave for a while, and then she and I will rule the world."

"No doubt." Will had been pleasantly surprised when Max decided that she would be going to law school the next fall, but everyone was shocked by Sam's announcement that she wanted to go down the same career path. She had apparently been thinking about it for some time, but said nothing until she'd actually applied to the university.

"Hey, Remmond," Max took a quick look at the clock, "look at the time. I'm gonna hit the shower." She grabbed her coffee, then kissed his cheek before she hurried out of the kitchen. A minute later, Will could hear her hard rock music blasting from the master bath.

He decided to measure their bedroom again, and get the new carpeting ordered while they were out. He grabbed the tape measure from the counter and headed up the stairs, pausing to take in the pictures that lined the wall there. Max had insisted on putting them up on the day they moved in, first thing, even though they would have to take them down temporarily when it came time to renovate the entry.

"This is going to be the Family Wall," she said, hanging the largest picture in the center. It was the two of them with Dave and Sammy, taken at the restaurant they went to on Dave's first night out after the shooting.

As he studied their faces, Will thought that Max was right that day, when she was hanging the picture and she commented on how they all seemed to smile differently now - they all seemed to be more real. And that was when she finally told him what she had gone through that afternoon as she waited for him to come out of the building. She sat with him on the staircase of their home and poured it out of herself, every detail, alternating between tears and outrage.

The last thing she said about it, before she insisted that she wanted to let it finally fade away, was, "I saw the woman holding those roses, and I was thinking about what you told me, about that day you went to Michelle's grave. And I felt like I did that day when I was twelve - when that hard frost came so early, you know? But it was a thousand times worse, because this time it wasn't me. It was *us*. Our life together was over before it ever began."

He remembered her intense, tearful expression, and the determination in her voice as she said, "I'm going to forgive that now, Remmond. I need to."

Will decided at that moment that if she could forgive it, so could he.

He climbed the rest of the stairs and went into their bedroom. On the table by the door was a small picture of just their left hands, hers resting on top of his, showing the rings that they wore. Max hadn't wanted traditional wedding bands: she wanted to wear the rings they already had.

He laughed softly as he thought about his sudden nervousness in the moments just before they joined hands, standing on their rock while the preacher recited the basics of a wedding ceremony. All at once, Will had wondered if he would make for a good husband, and he blurted it out at the point in their vows where he was supposed to say something profoundly romantic.

She answered him that it really didn't matter, because she probably would suck as a wife, so they were a terrific match. And they wound up laughing their way through the rest of their wedding - until the moment that the preacher asked them if they promised to love, honor, and cherish each other. Until death.

Will's nervousness fell away. In his entire life, he was never as sure about anything as he was about that, and he nodded once and said, "Yes."

Max took his face in her hands, holding his eyes on hers as she said, "Yes. And beyond."

He gazed at the picture that sat on the dresser across the room, next to the photo of their first October fifth. It was their wedding portrait.

Her hair was windblown, and her emerald earrings caught the last of the light from the sun as it went below the horizon. She wore a long ivory dress that billowed out behind her, and he wore a dark blue suit, the one she liked best on him. It was their first kiss as husband and wife.

She held no bouquet, because she wanted her wedding flowers to be the rose bushes that he would plant for her in the back yard of the home they'd just bought. That way, she said, she could keep them forever.

And even if a hard frost got them, they would come back to life.

The End

Made in the USA
Lexington, KY
11 November 2015